FULL
CIRCLE

Also by A. O'Connor

This Model Life

Exclusive

Property

Ambition

FULL CIRCLE

A. O'CONNOR

POOLBEG

Published 2010
by Poolbeg Press Ltd.
123 Grange Hill, Baldoyle,
Dublin 13, Ireland
Email: poolbeg@poolbeg.com

A catalogue record for this book is available from the British Library.

ISBN 978-1-84223-392-4

Typeset by Patricia Hope in Sabon 10.6/14.5

Printed by
CPI Cox & Wyman, UK

www.poolbeg.com

About the Author

A. O'Connor is the author of four other novels published by Poolbeg – *This Model Life, Exclusive, Property* and *Ambition* – and is a graduate of NUI, Maynooth and Trinity College Dublin.

Acknowledgements

A big thanks to the team at Poolbeg – Paula Campbell, Kieran Devlin, Sarah Ormston, Niamh Fitzgerald, David Prendergast, and my editor Gaye Shortland.

For Deirdre Heavey

PART 1

CHAPTER 1

2010

Blanche Launcelot looked down at Dublin stretched below her as the plane continued to circle around the city. She glanced away from the view and down at her Cartier and was alarmed to see the flight was now forty minutes delayed for landing. Reaching forward, she took her glass of champagne from the small table and sipped at it while she looked around for a flight attendant.

She saw one making her way down the Business Class section and beckoned her over.

Smiling broadly, the attendant approached Blanche.

"Yes, Mrs Launcelot, can I get you something?"

"What time are we actually going to land this plane?" Blanche asked in exasperation.

The attendant's face became worried even though her smile was rigorously maintained.

She was saved from answering by the pilot suddenly announcing: "Ladies and gentlemen, I apologise for the delay. There's been a problem on the ground which has now been resolved, and I'm pleased to say we are now beginning our descent to Dublin Airport."

"At last!" said Blanche.

"Shall I just take this glass?" suggested the attendant, reaching forward and taking away the champagne glass, fixing up the table at the same time.

Blanche sat back in her seat and fastened her seatbelt, looking around the half-empty business section. As the plane continued to make its descent, she spotted the Launcelot plane hangar on the outskirts of Dublin Airport and sighed, reminding herself that her days of flying by private plane might be well and truly over.

Blanche made her way through Dublin Airport, several shopping bags in each hand. Her luggage was being pushed in a trolley beside her by an airport attendant.

Blanche was fifty and cut a glamorous figure. Dressed in an elegant silver-grey business suit, her figure was that of a woman twenty years younger. Her jet-black hair swept past her shoulders. Her beautiful features were often the topic of gossip as people speculated if she'd had any work done. She hadn't. As she came out of the airport she glanced around and spotted the black Mercedes waiting for her.

"Just over here," she instructed the attendant with the trolley.

On seeing her, the driver of the Mercedes got out smartly and opened the boot of the car, took the luggage and put it in. Blanche tipped the attendant, put some of her shopping into the boot and then got into the back of the car with the rest of it. There, waiting for her, was her lawyer William.

He smiled warmly at her.

"Sorry I'm so late," she said, closing the car door. "The pilot felt he needed to give us a tour of the Dublin skies."

"Good flight otherwise?" asked William.

She shrugged. "Fine."

As the car whooshed away from the airport, she reached forward to the shopping bags on the floor and handed William one.

"A little present from Fifth Avenue," she said.

He was surprised. "You shouldn't have." He reached into the bag and took out a brown-leather attaché case. "You really shouldn't have bothered!" He was embarrassed.

"Nonsense. You've been putting in a lot of hours recently."

"You get billed for them," he said.

She shrugged.

"Any luck in New York?" he asked, getting down to business.

She smiled sadly and shook her head. "No . . . when you're down, you're down. Have you had any luck here?"

"I found a few things in company law that might unfreeze funds, but it would take far too long to start court proceedings. I'm afraid the company would go bust before we'd even have our day in court."

She shook her head. "This is unbelievable. There must be something we can do. I have an awful lot of people to pay at the end of the month. If we can't release funds by then there will be a riot."

"I know." He wasn't used to seeing Blanche look desperate. It was a look that didn't suit her and he wanted to reach out and hug her and tell her it would be alright. But he would be lying.

He looked down at the rest of her shopping and spotted some bags from FAO Swartz, brimming with toys.

"Blanche?"

"What?"

"How is your grandson?"

3

"Fine. I can't wait to see him."

He spotted the first glimpse of happiness on her face.

"Blanche . . . I want to speak to you . . . not as your lawyer, but as a friend." Maybe the only friend you have left, he added silently.

"Go on," she shrugged.

"Blanche, I know how much you love the child, but hasn't this gone on long enough? Don't you think the rightful place for any child is with its parent?"

"It depends on what kind of parent it has!"

"I know, but –"

"But nothing, William. You know what situation I rescued him from."

"Look, Blanche." He reached over and forcibly grabbed her hand. "What they are doing to you is a scandal. Trying to take away everything you've worked for, everything you own, is cruel. But the child is something else. I don't want you to get confused about what's right and wrong with everything else that's happening."

Blanche quickly pulled her hand back. "It's not up for discussion, William. He is my grandchild and his safety and happiness are my first priority . . . I'm all he's got!"

And is he all you've got? William asked silently.

CHAPTER 2

Blanche was grateful to get away from William by the time the car reached the Launcelot building in the IFSC. He kept trying to bring the conversation back to her grandson.

The Launcelot building was a fine glass tower, the headquarters of the business, situated in the heart of the Docklands amongst all the other glass towers that had been built at the height of the Celtic Tiger, each competing symbols to showcase their company's strength and wealth.

The security man opened the door for her.

"Welcome back, Mrs Launcelot."

She nodded at him, wondering if his kind smile would quickly be removed when he discovered his wage wouldn't be paid into his bank account at the end of the month. She went to the end elevator and pressed the top-floor button. The lift doors swung open and she walked out into her reception, bracing herself for the amount of work that would have piled up in her week's absence.

A young woman and man sat behind desks there. They looked up from their work and smiled brightly at her. She was just about to get straight down to business with them and get them to start making the hundred phone calls that needed to be made when she became aware of another presence. She turned around and saw a fair-haired man of around thirty-six sitting there staring at her. She studied him for a few seconds before turning to her PA.

"Eh, Stella, in my office, please."

Stella got up and quickly followed Blanche into her office, closing the door behind her. Blanche walked across the porcelain tiles to her desk.

"Who is that waiting out there?" she asked, sitting down behind it.

"It's Lee Dwyer," said Stella. "He says he has an appointment that he made with you while you were in New York."

Blanche immediately recognised the name. Lee Dwyer was one of the most ferocious lawyers in the country. A man renowned for his thoroughness and ruthlessness. And she had made no appointment to see him.

"Show Mr Dwyer in."

Lee Dwyer halted inside the door and took in the scene before him. The office was gigantic with very high ceilings and at the end of it was a series of arched windows overlooking the city. It had cream porcelain tiles throughout and a huge glass-topped desk. A trail of red carpet ran from the door to the desk, a dash of vivid colour in all this contemporary design. There were two brown-leather couches facing each other and a glass coffee table in between.

And there she was. Blanche Launcelot sat behind the desk, resting back in her tall swivel-chair, her legs crossed.

"Thank you for meeting me, Mrs Launcelot," he said on reaching the desk. He offered her his hand.

She stared at it for a second and then reached forward and shook it lightly.

He sat down on a leather chair facing her. He studied the woman and was impressed. She was so chic and elegant and yet he could sense a powerful mind working behind sensual features. He felt she was sizing him up far more effectively than he was her.

"How can I help you, Mr Dwyer?"

"Mrs Launcelot, I'm a solicitor who –"

"I know exactly who you are, Mr Dwyer."

"Who has been engaged to win back custody of your grandchild for my client."

"That's a hard case for you to take on – considering the reasons why I was granted custody in the first place."

"Those reasons have now changed completely. My client was under severe pressure at the time which resulted in that situation . . . I want to appeal to you to sit down with my client now and sort this out before it goes to an ugly court battle."

"What you're asking me, in effect, is to concede custody," said Blanche. "And I won't do that. I can't risk my grandson's wellbeing again."

"I would have thought the last thing you would have wanted was a bitter court case, after all the turmoil you've been through recently – and your recent tragedy."

"I think we're through here, Mr Dwyer."

"In that case, we'll see you in court." Lee stood up and nodded at Blanche. "Just so you know – I will leave no stone unturned to prove that you are an unfit guardian and the child belongs back with the parent. You're one of the richest people in the country. Your fame and power goes far beyond these shores. You're a classic rags-to-riches story. Your life over the past thirty years is a story of building something out of nothing – emigration, returning home, riding the crest of huge success, and now finally at a crossroads for the future. Do you really want to risk your reputation in a tawdry custody battle?"

"Good day, Mr Dwyer." Blanche sat forward and began to look through paperwork.

Lee turned and walked out of the office.

Blanche quickly signed off the last of the papers sitting on her desk and, seeing it was nearly eight, cursed to herself. She hadn't wanted to be in the office so late. She had wanted to get back to her grandson early, but there had been just so much work piled up for her since she was away. She pushed her chair back and made her way out of her office. Everybody else had gone home except security as she made her way through the building.

"Goodnight, Mrs Launcelot," said the security man as he unlocked the front glass doors to let her out.

"Good night," she smiled at him as she stepped out onto the pavement and made her way across to her waiting car.

She closed her eyes as she nestled back into the cream leather. The flight was beginning to catch up with her and she looked forward to catching up on her sleep later.

Estelle Dwyer walked into the study of their home and found Lee at his desk searching the internet.

"I've just put Jennifer down to bed – she wants you to go up and read her a bedtime story," said Estelle, smiling as she moved around the desk.

"I'll go up to her in a minute," promised Lee.

On the computer screen there was a photo of two women. It looked very dated, from the early eighties. It was obviously a fashion photo and the women were models.

"Should I be jealous?" Estelle asked with a smile. "Of you looking at women on the internet? Or should I just be annoyed at your taste? At finding out you have a secret fetish for big hair and eighties' tat?"

Lee glanced up at her and smiled. "Nothing to worry about. I'm just doing a bit of research."

"On eighties' fashion?" she laughed.

"No. Remember I said I was meeting Blanche Launcelot today?"

"Yeah, how did it go?"

"It didn't. She showed me the door quick sharp."

"Well, she was hardly going to hand the kid over to you there and then."

"Look at this." He pointed to the computer screen. "This is her as a model in 1980."

"She was stunning."

"This is the only photo I could find of her from back then and this took some searching. Strange, isn't it?"

"Well, she was never exactly in Christie Brinkley's league, was she? It makes sense there aren't photos of her everywhere."

"I know but she's a legendary businesswoman. I'm surprised there aren't more of her modelling days circulating around, if just to cause her embarrassment if nothing else."

"So, I guess you're going after her with this court case then? Going right back to find anything you can on her. In true Lee Dwyer fashion?"

"That's how I win my cases."

"Look, Lee, Blanche Launcelot has a very ruthless reputation. I don't want you getting on the wrong side of somebody like that."

He got up and kissed her. "I'd better go up and read Jennifer her story."

Estelle sighed and threw her arms in the air. "I don't

know why I bother. You've already made up your mind, haven't you? From now on our lives are going to be breathing, eating and sleeping Blanche Launcelot, isn't that right?"

Lee shrugged and gave her half a smile as he left the room.

Estelle looked at the computer screen and the photo of Blanche.

"I hate you already!" she said to the screen.

Blanche's chauffeur drove up the long avenue to her home and pulled to a halt.

"I'll see you in the morning." Blanche gathered her shopping bags, walked up and down the steps to the front door and let herself in. The hallway was wide with marble throughout, leading to an imposing staircase.

"Orla!" Blanche called.

Orla appeared from the lounge on the left.

"Welcome home. You must be exhausted," she said.

"A little tired. I meant to get home earlier, but you know how it is." She handed over a shopping bag from Bloomingdale's. "Thanks for staying with him for the past week, Orla."

"But it's my job, Mrs Launcelot. There was no need to bring anything." She took the bag gratefully.

"Where is he?" Blanche asked, her eyes lively with expectation.

"Asleep."

"Oh!" Blanche didn't try to hide her disappointment. "Well, listen, you head home before your husband files for divorce."

"See you in the morning," Orla smiled as she left.

Climbing the stairs, Blanche walked down the wide

corridor to the nursery and found the door into the corridor open as usual. She tiptoed over to the cot, reached down and touched his cheek. He was fast asleep and didn't move.

"I'll see you in the morning," she said softly, and left the room.

Downstairs again, she walked into the lounge. She poured herself a glass of brandy and went and stood in front of one of the windows that looked out onto the gardens. The gardens were so beautifully manicured and tended.

She sat on the couch and nursed her brandy. She had been incredibly strong all her life. She had always done everything her way, and although she had plenty of scrapes and disasters she always knew she would get through, that she would survive. But she wasn't sure if she could survive if they took everything from her this time. She couldn't rebuild everything at this age. How could she – how could she even begin? You're only brave when you've nothing to lose. It's hard to be brave when you have so much to lose. Her mind drifted to Lee Dwyer. She thought of his expression for her – *rags to riches*. That showed how much he knew about her. She laughed lightly. She wasn't a rags-to-riches story. Not rags – more like slightly worn but elegant clothes.

CHAPTER 3

1980

Nineteen-year-old Blanche Fitzclarence turned over in her bed, yawned and stretched her arms into the air. She blinked a few times as the early-morning sun streamed through her white linen curtains. She had been out late the night before at a party and still felt tired and so turned over on her side ready to nod off to sleep again.

"Blanche?" snapped her mother Harriet as she walked into the room and crossed over to pull back the curtains. "It's nearly ten – aren't you going to get up?"

"I'm so tired," said Blanche with a yawn.

"No doubt out partying with those – *friends* – till all hours of the morning again."

Harriet was a tall elegant woman, her black hair tied up in a bun. Her face had a refined beauty.

"What are you going to do today?" she asked.

"I don't know . . . Maybe go down and do a bit of shopping this morning and I'm meeting some friends at the riding stables this afternoon."

"Have you given any more thought to repeating your exams?"

"Given it thought! The very idea gives me nightmares!"

"Well, you're going to have to think about repeating them . . . you can't spend the rest of your life being directionless."

Blanche sighed and closed her eyes.

"How was the Harrington party last night?" questioned Harriet.

"A bit dull, to be honest."

"Was Oscar Harrington there?"

"Of course."

"And how was he?"

"As dull as dishwater."

"You found him great fun at last year's Christmas party here, remember?"

"No."

"Well, don't forget he's coming over to dinner tonight. You make sure you're home early."

"I can't bear seeing him two nights in a row. I'll be in danger of dying of boredom!"

"Dinner will be served at eight. Make sure you're home by seven." Harriet looked pointedly at her daughter before walking out.

Blanche had a long leisurely bath and then dressed and went downstairs.

The Fitzclarence home was an old period house in Dalkey. There was a long gravel driveway leading from the road to the long rectangular house. The Fitzclarences had a lot of standing in the locality. Blanche's father was a businessman, always investing or selling. Money was always tight. Blanche supposed they lived beyond their means and her parents were big into show. They seemed to be on permanent overdraft. They were friends with all the much bigger, much richer families in the area.

She grabbed some breakfast and then went out to the front of the house to find her father. Dan was talking to a business friend in the driveway.

"Dad, can I borrow your car keys?"

Dan was dressed in his trademark green Husky coat and peaked cap.

"Where are you off to?" he asked.

"Just into the village," she said.

He reached into his pocket and threw her his Jaguar keys. Then he took out £20 and handed it to her. "Get yourself something nice."

"Thanks, Dad." She reached over and kissed him.

She walked over to the Jaguar and opened the door.

"Don't forget young Harrington is coming for dinner tonight," Dan called after her.

"Mum's already reminded me."

"I think he's quite taken with you," Dan chuckled.

"Oh please!" Blanche threw her eyes to heaven and got into the car.

She drove down the hilly road past all the grand houses towards Dalkey village. Blanche loved growing up in Dalkey, a beautiful seaside village close to Dublin.

She knew what her mother was trying to do. She was trying to set her up with Oscar Harrington. She couldn't imagine anything worse. Blanche craved excitement and glamour and Oscar Harrington could provide her with neither.

Everyone was at her all the time to try and sort out what she was going to do with the rest of her life. She was as disappointed as anyone she had done so badly in the Leaving Cert. Disappointed but not surprised. She couldn't concentrate in her final year in school as she had started going out with lots of local guys and put her social life before school. And at the same time started day-dreaming about leading a glamorous life in London or New York. She toyed with the idea of sending some photos to some model agencies, but didn't have the courage.

Blanche didn't know what to do with her life. But she knew she wanted excitement. And she was getting it through hanging out with her new friends. She supposed they were from the wrong side of the tracks and her other friends would be horrified with her association with them. But she didn't care, she was enjoying them.

"Hey, Blanche!" said the familiar voice as she was walking down Dalkey main street. It was Mike McGovern, a guy she had been seeing for the past three weeks. He worked as a mechanic in the local garage and was wearing his overalls as he came up to her. He went to kiss her.

"You're covered in grease, you'll ruin me!" she squealed.

But he didn't care and grabbed her and kissed her anyway.

"Not in public!" she insisted, pushing him away.

"Ashamed to be seen with me?"

She shrugged her shoulders and walked away. He walked alongside her.

"Guess what?" he said. "I'm finished work at three and then me and Tom and a few of the others are going drinking. Wanna join us?"

"I can't. I have to go to a dinner party tonight."

"I'm not talking about tonight. I'm talking about this afternoon – you can be back in time for dinner."

"I know what you're like. I'll end up not making it back in time."

"Ah, come on! We'll have a great time!"

She spotted another guy called Tony giving her dagger looks from across the street. She had gone out with him for a month before Mike and he had been very nasty when she dumped him, calling her every name under the sun.

Blanche stopped in the street and kissed Mike passionately, one eye on Tony as she did it, seeing his growing irritation.

"Okay! I'll see you up at the castle at three," said Blanche.

After Blanche dropped Dan's Jaguar home, she made her way up to where Mike said they were meeting, a field looking over Dalkey and down to the sea. Mike and his friends were already there, lying out on the grass, enjoying the sunshine and the views. They greeted her warmly and she started to drink with them.

It was an afternoon of bliss in the warm sunshine. She lay back looking at the sky, and didn't worry about her life and what direction she should take. She was just living for the moment.

That evening they made their way down to a takeaway and ate it at the beach. And then they went on to a pub for the rest of the night.

"Ah, come on, Blanche, just stay another ten minutes!" said Mike, kissing her passionately in the back of his car.

"I can't, Mike." She glanced at her watch as she continued to kiss him. "Fuck's sake!" she said loudly then, pushing him off her determinedly. "Look at the time!"

"It's only half eleven!" Mike said, trying to kiss her again.

She put up a hand to him. "It's time I was getting home, before my mother sends out the cavalry."

"Will I see you tomorrow night?" asked Mike.

"If you're lucky." She reached over and gave him a parting kiss, before getting out of the car.

"Call me at work," he said, getting out of the car and resting against it as he watched her waltz off.

They were parked just down the road from her home. She walked up the driveway, smiling to herself. She felt she was having the time of her life. She saw the lights were still on and sighed at the anticipated look of displeasure on her mother's face. Her parents had sent her off to an expensive school that they could not afford in the hope of turning her into a young lady with wonderful options in life. What they got was a young woman more interested in fun than career, bad boys than good boys. It didn't help that she was an only child so all her parents' attention was focused on her. If the truth were known, their house had been passed through generations of her mother's family and her mother held onto all the airs and graces that were also passed through the generations.

Blanche turned her key in the front door and walked into the hall.

"Blanche!" she immediately heard from the drawing room.

She raised her eyes to heaven. On entering the drawing room she saw her father standing by the fireplace, looking upset, her mother seated in an armchair looking angry, and Oscar Harrington sitting on a couch looking distinctly uncomfortable with a glass of sherry perched on his knee. She was astonished to see Oscar there.

"Where have you been?" demanded Harriet.

"Eh . . . just out," Blanche said lamely.

"You *knew* dinner was being served for eight. You *knew* Oscar was our guest and you decided not to bother your arse to come home!"

"I – I . . . forgot!" Blanche shrugged her shoulders. She was quite surprised to see the level of anger in her mother's face.

"You forgot? How could you forget when your days and nights are filled with nothing? You chose to forget."

17

"I think I'll head off to bed," said Blanche.

"Oh no, you don't," said Harriet, who looked in danger of exploding.

Oscar Harrington quickly stood up. "I think I'd better go home." He put his sherry on a side table.

"Oh, yes, Oscar . . . and I apologise again for my daughter's rudeness," Harriet said.

"Not at all," said Oscar as he quickly moved across the room. "Mr Fitzclarence . . . Blanche," he said, nodding to them and leaving the house.

Blanche rounded on her parents.

"Well, thank you very much!" she snapped. "Embarrassing me in front of him like that. It'll be all around my friends tomorrow."

"Embarrassing you!" exclaimed Harriet. "How could anyone manage to embarrass you if you haven't embarrassed yourself with your antics over the past few months?"

"What are you talking about?" said Blanche, her cheeks becoming red.

"You've shown no shame and no regard for me or your father. Hanging around with that awful crowd as you do, going to all those trashy nightclubs and generally getting yourself the name of the town slut!"

Blanche stared at her mother and felt tears burn her eyes. "I'm going to bed." she said and turned to go.

"No, you're not!" Harriet got up, marched across the room and grabbed Blanche's arm.

"Mum! You're hurting me!" Blanche tried to wriggle free.

"Good! I want to hurt you! I want to slap some sense into you! You've been spoiled all your life and what have we got in return but a reckless tramp! This is where it stops, young lady. So this is when you grow up. You stop drifting around all the day like Lady Muck, you stop hanging around with that crowd of yours in the town and you stop sleeping around!"

"Mother!"

"Now, Oscar Harrington, poor deluded creature that he is, has expressed an interest in you and he would make very good marriage material for you."

"Oscar Harrington! You must be mad, I wouldn't go near him!"

"No, judging by your taste he's probably too clean and decent for you. But you are going to meet him tomorrow and apologise profusely for your rudeness this evening and ask him out to lunch."

Blanche started to laugh but the tears were streaming down her face. "Not a chance!"

Her mother started to shake her. "I'm not asking you, I'm telling you!"

"Mum!"

Harriet let her daughter go and fell into her husband's arms.

"After all we've been through trying to keep this place, trying to keep the show on the road and now she's dragging us down!"

"I know, I know," Dan soothed his wife.

"Dad?" Blanche said, her eyes searching his face for some sympathy.

Dan looked at Blanche directly. "Call on Oscar tomorrow and invite him for lunch," he said firmly.

Blanche bit her lip. "Thanks a lot."

"It's time to grow up, Blanche," her father said.

Blanche turned quickly and walked out of the room. She ran up the stairs, flew into her bedroom, slammed the door and let the tears flow quietly.

Her mother's words had cut deep and she was very hurt by both her parents' reactions to her. The destiny they wanted for her would slowly kill her and she supposed that was why she was rebelling against it by going out with the likes of Mike and being wild. She wasn't a bad girl and she would show them that, but she just needed to live life on her terms. She did want to change. She wanted her life to change and this had given her the spur to move on. She wanted excitement and fun and she was going to get it.

CHAPTER 4

2010

Lee Dwyer could find hundreds of old articles about different business ventures of Blanche's, but information and photos from her long-distant modelling days were a rarity. Almost as if they had been airbrushed from her past. In the ones he did find, Blanche was modelling in fashion layouts with another model, a big-haired blonde called Darla O'Brien. And since they modelled together a bit, Lee wondered if she would know anything of Blanche from this time.

Samantha Armstrong was the social editor of one of Ireland's leading newspapers and long regarded as the high priestess of Ireland's social scene. Lee also knew that Samantha was a close acquaintance of Blanche's and that she had run the model agency that Blanche had worked for back in the early eighties. He knew Samantha would reveal nothing if he questioned her, but she might lead him to a source that could be informative.

Lee arranged to meet Samantha at her office in the newspaper building.

He found her to be true to her image – glamorous, shrewd and no nonsense. She was in her mid-fifties and Lee imagined she was a botox addict.

"Thanks for meeting me. I'm a lawyer –"

"I know who you are – you represented Heidi Kenny when she sued her husband for divorce earlier this year. Poor old Tom lost everything he had, including his yacht."

"I'm trying to locate somebody that I think you might be able to help me find," said Lee.

Samantha shrugged. "If I can help."

Lee handed over the photo he had printed off the internet of Darla O'Brien.

Samantha squinted at the photo. "Oh, that was Darla. Darla O'Brien. She did a lot of work back then . . . but the drink!"

"Drink?"

"She had a drink problem and was always turning up late for shoots, if she bothered turning up at all."

"I wonder where she is now?"

"I haven't seen her in years. She was fired by the agency in the end. Last seen disappearing into a sea of vodka somewhere, I'm afraid."

Lee leaned forward. "I bet you could find out where she is now if you really put your mind to it."

Darla looked at him curiously. "I'm sure I could. But why would I want to?"

"I represent a lot of important people, Samantha, and subsequently know a lot of important people. I'm a good contact for you – and I'd owe you a big favour."

Blanche sat at the top of the table in her boardroom, looking down at her chiefs of staff. William sat to her right at the top of the table.

"I can barely believe these figures," she snapped as she slapped her hand on the paperwork in front of her. Her department heads all squirmed.

"Peter – these figures for the hotel group. I don't know how you can present them to me and not offer your resignation at the same time."

Peter went bright red. "There's very little I can do in today's market to get people flocking in the way they did three years ago. We live in different times now."

"Different times call for different attitudes. Different work ethics, different marketing campaigns, different staff, different customer service . . . and different management if all else fails! It's survival of the fittest –"

There was a knock on the door and Stella came in.

"What is it, Stella?" snapped Blanche.

"Sorry, Mrs Launcelot, but this just came for you – and it's a legal document marked private." Stella handed the envelope to Blanche and left.

One of the other managers started to talk about cost-cutting in his department as Blanche opened the envelope and quickly read through it.

"I'm sorry," she interrupted the speaker. "I'm going to have to ask you to postpone the rest of this meeting until later in the week. You may all leave now."

There was a series of nods around the room, then the managers gathered their paperwork and rapidly exited the room.

William stayed stationed beside her.

Blanche looked at him. "I thought I said everyone was to leave."

William looked a mixture of surprise and hurt. "Sorry, I didn't realise that included me." He got up.

Seeing the look on his face, she regretted her sharpness. "Sorry, William – stay please."

He shrugged and sat down. She tossed the paper that had been delivered to her in front of him.

23

He unfolded the paper.

"It's a court summons – a hearing for custody," she said. "Can they do that? I won custody of my grandchild, didn't I?"

"Temporary custody."

"I can't believe I have to go through all this again." She got up and began to pace up and down the boardroom.

"Are you going to fight it?"

"Of course I'm going to fight it. As long as I've got breath in my body I'm going to fight it!"

"It's just things are different now from the time of the first hearing. They've cleaned up their act – and the courts do favour children being brought up by their natural parents in everything but extreme circumstances."

"This is an extreme case."

William sighed. "Right, well, you know I'll support you."

"Get me a meeting with the best family lawyers you can think of."

Seeing the fight and determination in her face, he got up and put his hands on her shoulders.

"Are you sure you want all this fight?"

"Yes, I want it and woe betide anyone who gets in my way."

"Just don't forget to look after yourself, Blanche. You're under a lot of pressure with the company and everything."

"I can cope, William. I've had my back against the wall in much worse situations before."

William took his hands off her shoulders with a sigh. "I know, but youth can cushion us sometimes, can't it?"

Blanche looked at him, trying to figure him out. When did you go so soft? she wondered.

As Lee sat in his car opposite the tatty terraced house in a back street of the north city centre, he pondered how people's destinies can turn out so different. It hadn't taken Samantha Armstrong long to track down Darla O'Brien. And as he looked across at her house, he thought how different her destiny was from that of Blanche Launcelot. Two women who started off at the same time in the same job.

He got out of his car and, locking it, walked across the cobbled street to her front door. He rang the doorbell and waited. He could hear a television on inside. Finally he heard the bolt unlock. A woman in her fifties answered. Despite the deterioration in her appearance, he recognised her immediately from her photos as Darla. Her hair was still blonde, but was now dyed too brightly from a home-dye kit, and her once-lustrous locks were dank and limp. Her face was etched with lines.

"Yeah?" she asked without a smile.

"Darla O'Brien?" asked Lee.

"What? TV Licence?" She reached to a sideboard behind her, grabbed the licence and threw it at him.

He smiled and handed her back the licence. "I'm not the licence inspector."

"Well, what do you want then?"

"You used to model, didn't you?"

She stood up straight, looking surprised. "Why?"

"Samantha Armstrong sent me in your direction."

"Did she indeed? The aul' bitch! What do you want?"

He smiled and laughed lightly. "Well, I've got a few questions. If you could give me some of your time I'd be grateful."

"What kind of questions?"

"I wonder could I come in for a chat? Samantha said you'd help me."

"She did in her hole! She never had any time for me. You've got two seconds to tell me why you're here."

"I'm trying to get some background information on Blanche Launcelot."

"Oh! I might have known!" Darla rolled her eyes and slammed the door shut.

Lee returned to the street where Darla lived in the evening. He parked down the road, keeping a careful watch on her house. At nine o'clock, her front door opened and she walked out. She was dressed up in a short dress and high-heeled shoes, a fake fur coat over her shoulders, her blonde hair tied up in a bun. Lee followed her at a discreet distance. He noticed she was wobbling a bit and realised that she'd already had a few drinks. He followed her into the next street and to the end of it where there was a pub with loud music and laughter spilling out of it.

She went through the front doors and he followed her in. The pub was packed and she was saying hello to lots of people as she made her way to the bar. At the bar, she laughed and joked with the barman as he poured her a large vodka.

Going to the other side of the bar, Lee ordered himself a pint and found a quiet corner where he could observe. The night wore on and he watched her get steadily drunker as she chatted away to different people, even doing a turn on the karaoke, belting out 'Anyone Who Had a Heart'. He was waiting for his moment and found it when she went over to sit at a corner table on her own. He watched her as she glared into her drink, a different person from the woman who had been singing earlier. He ordered a vodka for her. He went and placed the drink in front of her. She looked at the drink and then up at him.

"You again!" she said.

"Hi, there – do you mind if I sit down?"

"Fuck off!" She downed her own drink and then took the glass of vodka he had placed before her.

"Don't be like that," Lee said, sitting down opposite her.

"What do you want?" she demanded.

"I told you, I just want to hear about Blanche Launcelot – back then, when you used to model with her."

"I don't speak about her – ever."

"You must have been close friends, to show such loyalty to her all these years later."

"Whatever closeness we had was false. Blanche only cares about herself."

"So why are you being so protective of her?"

"I'm not being protective. She's just from a time in my life that I don't want to remember. Are you the press or something?"

"No," he said, shaking his head. "I just thought you might be able to tell me some interesting things about Blanche – for my own information."

He held open his blazer and leaning forward she could see an envelope of money in the inside pocket.

Her eyes lit up. "I'd be able to tell you things about Blanche that you would kill for." Her words were slurred. "Envelope first!" she demanded, putting out her hand.

He discreetly passed it to her, and she stashed it in her handbag.

"We were friends. At the beginning she was actually a nice girl. Didn't take herself too seriously, out for a laugh. More out to have a good time than being obsessed with power and money like she became later. She was looking for fun in those days, and love, like any young girl, I suppose."

27

CHAPTER 5

1980

Blanche got the bus from Dalkey into the city centre and made her way up through Grafton Street to the genteel streets around St Stephen's Green. She followed the address to Fashion Girls, which was one of Ireland's top agencies. It was situated in an old Georgian building. She stood outside, looking up at the building, clutching an envelope with some photos she'd had taken at a local photographic agency at home.

She managed to hide her nerves as she sat in the reception area of the agency.

A couple of other girls were waiting, clutching envelopes also. They gave each other a sneaky once-over every so often. There was a lot of activity in the agency with models coming in and out. They all looked so incredibly groomed and beautiful, Blanche thought, envying them. She spotted a couple of famous names, and she was sure one of the girls hurrying past was Michelle Rocca.

"Right. Blanche Fitzclarence, Samantha Armstrong will see you now," said the woman on reception.

Blanche got up and walked down the corridor. She paused at the door at the bottom, held herself up straight and knocked.

"Come in!" said the voice on the other side.

Blanche opened the door and walked in, smiling broadly.

There was an old Chesterfield desk in the office, in front of large Georgian windows and behind the desk sat a woman aged around thirty. The woman was dressed in a jade-green trouser suit, with her brown hair bobbed. She exuded presence.

"Hello – thanks for meeting me," said Blanche, putting out her hand to shake.

Samantha Armstrong ignored the hand and said, "Turn around," doing a twirling action with her fingers.

"Eh, okay!" Blanche said, hesitating for a second and then doing what she was bid.

"Take a seat. And hand me over your photos."

Blanche sat there expectantly as the woman scrutinised the shots.

"These are shit," Samantha said, tossing the photos to one side and stubbing out her cigarette. She suddenly got up and came to inspect Blanche's face. Then she took up Blanche's hands and inspected them also.

"What's your name?" she demanded.

"Blanche Fitzclarence."

Samantha returned to the other side of her desk and started to scribble something on a piece of paper which she handed over to Blanche as a doctor would a prescription.

"Go over to this address and ask for Shay. Tell him I sent you and get some proper photos taken."

"Okay . . . and thank you," said Blanche.

She allowed herself to breathe properly again once she got out. She felt crushed and was half-tempted to tear up the slip of paper but she didn't. She had to see this thing through and, if she had no future in this world, she needed to be told so she could think of something else to do with the rest of her life.

The photographic studio was in Ranelagh. It was a

small elegant terraced house with a nicely kept front garden.

The door was opened by a man with a camera slung around his neck.

"Yeah?" he asked.

"Shay?"

"Who wants to know?"

"I . . . eh . . . Samantha Armstrong in Fashion Girls sent me over to you. She said for you to take my picture."

"Ay," Shay yawned. "Follow me through."

Blanche recognised he had a strong Northern Ireland accent.

She followed him into the hall and then downstairs which was all open-plan and looked like a large photo-studio-cum-living area. She was surprised to see a blonde girl sitting on a stool in front of a screen.

"I'm just finishing up here," Shay said. "You can go on in and make yourself some tea in the kitchen if you want, and there's Custard Creams in the press."

"Oh thanks!" said Blanche, and she walked into the small kitchen.

"And make me a cup while you're at it!" he shouted after her. "Two sugars and plenty of milk."

Blanche found her way around the kitchen and made the tea.

"Right, that's us finished, thanks, love," Shay was saying to the model as Blanche came out of the kitchen with the two cups of tea and a packet of biscuits which she placed on a coffee table.

"Sorry, did you want tea?" she asked the model as she tidied away her things into her bag.

"No, thanks," the model said, dashing out the door. "Got to rush – on my way to my next job!"

Blanche was filled with envy. The other girl seemed so confident and established.

"So Samantha sent you over?" said Shay, taking up his cup of tea.

"Yes," said Blanche, wishing she could stop blushing.

Shay made a face and put down the cup. "Well, let's hope you can take a better picture than make a cup of tea. That's fucking awful!"

"Oh, I'm sorry!" said Blanche, going bright red.

"Come on over here," said Shay and she followed him. "Where did you get that dress?"

"Eh – Switzers. Why?"

"It's fucking awful! Does nothing for you." He began taking photos. "What's your name, love?"

"Blanche Fitzclarence."

They spent the next couple of hours taking photographs and slowly she became more confident with Shay's direction. She found him strangely compelling, with his strong accent and his good looks. He had coal-black hair, contrasting with fair skin and piercing blue eyes.

He eventually said, "I'll get a print off these and send them over to the agency."

She was dying to ask if they were any good, as she went to put on her coat.

"I'm fucking starving!" he said, making his way to the kitchen. "Are you hungry?"

She could hear him starting to work in the kitchen. It was tempting to stay rather than go straight back to her parents' displeasure.

"Eh – yes," she said, taking off her coat again.

He walked in from the kitchen holding an opened bottle of wine and two tumbler glasses.

"Drink?" he asked.

"Just a small one," she answered.

He poured two large glasses, put them on the coffee table and then returned to the kitchen. She sat down on the sofa.

It didn't take him long to rustle up an omelette. He put two plates and forks on the coffee table, then sat down on a big cushion and started to eat.

She picked up her fork. "This looks sumptuous," she complimented him.

He looked up and smirked at her. "Really – sumptuous?" He started to laugh.

"What's so funny?" she said.

"Just your choice of words – and your posh accent – you're a proper little princess, aren't you?"

She felt herself go red again. "No."

"Away and shite! I bet you were sent to some posh private school as well, weren't you?"

"What if I was? I'm sure my mother would be very pleased to hear your verdict of me – she just mightn't agree with you."

"Would she not?" He laughed again. "So what do your mommy and daddy think of you becoming a model?"

"I wouldn't say they'd be too pleased, if they knew . . . where are you from?"

"Belfast."

"You've been down here for long?"

"Yeah, a while. There's not too many opportunities for fashion photographers in Belfast at the moment – the modelling scene isn't exactly thriving – they've other things on their minds."

"I can imagine." Blanche settled back in the sofa and took a mouthful of wine.

Shay brought a plate of different cheeses from the kitchen and they tucked in. She found him funny and attentive. He was full of stories about the industry in Dublin and she was enthralled. They drank and talked to past midnight.

"Do you get on with your parents?" Shay pushed.

"They want me to settle down, get a career . . . maybe they're right . . . I haven't been signed by an agency yet."

"You'll be signed. Those photos will be fantastic – and besides, Samantha Armstrong wouldn't have bothered sending you over here if she hadn't already made up her mind."

"Really?" Her eyes lit up.

"Sure thing. Your look is very refined, and posh birds are in at the moment – it's the whole Lady Diana thing going on."

Blanche got a taxi home that night, and was grateful the lights were all off when she arrived. She crept up the stairs to bed.

Next morning she was coming down the stairs when the phone rang in the hall.

She had a headache from the wine the previous night and she lazily reached out and picked up the phone.

"Yes?"

"Blanche? Samantha Armstrong here from Fashion Girls. Get over to my office for ten, will you?"

Blanche had to rush to get ready. She jumped into a taxi and got to Fashion Girls just in time for ten, her heart pounding with fear and excitement.

Samantha sat behind her desk studying the photos Shay had taken.

"They're good," Samantha eventually said. "And I'd like to represent you, if you're willing."

"Of course!"

"Fine. I run a tight ship. I don't take any shit from my models. Understand?"

Blanche nodded enthusiastically.

"Good." Samantha handed her a slip of paper. "Get over to this address for twelve."

"Right. Is this my first casting?"

"No – yesterday was your first casting – with Shay. He liked you and wanted you for today's job."

"Oh!" Blanche was surprised and looking down at the sheet of paper saw it was Shay's address in Ranelagh.

"You never told me you were considering me for a job yesterday!" accused Blanche when she arrived at Shay's.

She saw there was a range of clothes laid out and two women in the studio.

Shay ignored her as he continued to set up his cameras.

"You were leaving it very late to select a model for today," she said. Then the penny dropped. "You replaced somebody else with me?"

"Guilty!" he said, continuing to toy with the camera.

"But what did the poor girl say?" asked Blanche.

Shay saw she looked stressed and came and put his hands on her shoulders.

"Listen, love. I had somebody else booked, but then I met you and realised the other girl would be all wrong for this shoot. If I had gone ahead with her the whole shoot would have been a disaster, which would make Fashion Girls look bad and make me look bad, and might cost me my reputation and I might never work again in this town. Now, you wouldn't have that on your conscience, would you?"

"No – but it's a bit ruthless, isn't it?"

"It's a ruthless business and a ruthless world and the quicker you wise up to that the better you'll survive this business, yeah?"

Blanche enjoyed the photo shoot immensely. And as the day progressed, she realised she was attracted to Shay and impressed by him. But he was very different from the guys she had gone out with at home and she didn't know quite how to handle him. She realised she felt insecure around him. Here was a man surrounded by beautiful women every day – what interest would he have in her?

"Okay . . . and I think we'll call it a day," said Shay, removing his camera from around his neck and heading off to the darkroom.

Blanche changed into her own clothes and the stylists tidied all their items into the suitcases they had brought.

"We're off, Shay," they shouted.

"Okay, see you later," said Shay.

Blanche stood there awkwardly, not sure if she should go. Time ebbed by and there was still no sign of him. He probably thought she had left with the stylists, she reasoned, and feeling embarrassed she quickly got her coat and started to creep out.

Suddenly the door of the darkroom opened and out came Shay.

"Where do you think you're going?"

"I . . . eh, thought we were finished, so I was just getting out of your way."

"No – there's a party on tonight, and you're going with me," he said, opening a bottle of wine.

"Oh – okay!" she said taking a glass of wine from him with a smile.

CHAPTER 6

"What is *this*?" demanded Harriet one evening storming into the kitchen waving a copy of the *Evening Press* in the air.

Blanche looked at the paper and there was a photo of her modelling a fur coat in an advertisement.

"Oh – I meant to tell you – I've signed up with a model agency," she explained and waited for the fallout.

"*You've done what?*" screamed Harriet.

"Look – you wanted me to have a career – and now I have one!"

"I wanted you to have a profession, something that will use your education and yours brains, where you can mix with nice people and meet somebody nice."

"I want this career – and I think I can be good at it."

"You're a little fool! You could have everything if you did things my way. You could make a good match and have standing, position and protection."

"Mother, you might not have had options when you were growing up, but I have. I can be in control of my own destiny and life, without having to answer to a man. I'm part of the feminist movement."

"Don't fall for any of this feminist bullshit, Blanche. It's men who still rule the world, and women can only play by their rules. You think you're so modern and in control . . . can't you see I'm only trying to save you from yourself? You will *never* have control over your own destiny. The only way you'll have it is by marrying the right man, a nice man, who will provide it for you. You try and do it your way, the modern way, and you'll just be a joke passed from man to man and nothing to show for it. You'll end up without a husband, without a home, without anything."

Blanche's cheeks were blazing. "We'll see."

"Yes, we will see . . . There's no use talking to you." Harriet looked down at the photo. "Funny how your idea of feminism is being dolled up looking provocative in a magazine."

Shay had a green convertible MG, and he would spin her around to shoots in it.

"I love this car!" she said as they drove through the leafy streets, the top down.

He reached into the car pocket and threw her a set of keys.

"What's this?" she asked, looking at the keys.

"A set for the car. You can borrow it any time you want."

Work seemed to flood in for Blanche. Most of it came through Shay, who seemed to want to block-book her for all the work.

Blanche didn't mind in the least. She loved working with Shay. And he seemed to enjoy showing her the delights of the city. He began to take her to eat at the Shelbourne and to the clubs in Leeson Street afterwards. Shay was quite a drinker and she had to pace herself to keep up with him. They would start at one end of Leeson Street and literally go down to all the basement clubs, one after another. Shay seemed to know everybody and he seemed to delight in showing off this pretty young thing and everyone was curious as to who she was.

One night, they got a taxi back to his house. She had drunk more than she had intended to. He opened a bottle of wine and poured them two glasses. He sat down on the couch beside her and chinked his glass against hers.

"To your future – you're going to be big."

"I hope so," she said, staring into his eyes.

He stared back into hers.

"You're very young, Blanche," he said eventually.

"Not that young," she shrugged and then she leaned forward and kissed him.

His hands moved over her body and she lay back on the sofa as he lay on top of her.

"I think I could fall for someone like you," he whispered into her ear as she held him tighter.

Blanche nestled into Shay as they lay upstairs under the fur duvet in his bedroom.

"Happy?" he asked, his arm around her.

"Very," she whispered in the night. "You know, I never met anyone like you before. I've always been attracted to guys who were wild and dangerous, but I found them unambitious and small-minded. And then there were the guys my parents wanted for me, and I found them just boring. But you're wild and interesting, you know so much about life."

Blanche awoke the next morning, blinked a few times and moved around under the fur duvet.

"Shay?" she said, reaching out and discovering the bed was empty.

"In the shower!" he called from the bathroom.

She saw it was ten o'clock.

Shay came out, drying himself with a towel. She went to him and kissed him.

"I have a shoot this morning, starting in exactly twenty minutes downstairs. And you, if my memory serves me correctly, have a casting in one hour. So you better get your act together and get ready," he advised, smiling.

She hugged him tightly. "Oh, I just want to spend the day with you in bed."

"And believe me, there's nothing I'd like better, but duty calls, okay?"

She nodded happily. "Okay."

Blanche made the casting on time and then headed into the agency. As she walked into the building a young man with brown hair came out of the neighbouring building. She figured he must work there as she had seen him a few times coming in and out. He smiled at her and she nodded back.

She had a brief meeting with a couple of the bookers who advised her what was coming up. Blanche loved the camaraderie of the agency. All the girls were very welcoming and supportive and there was no bitchiness or jealousy.

She bumped into the blonde girl who had been on a shoot at Shay's studio the first time she went there. She had spoken to her a few times in the agency in passing.

"Hey, we're working on a shoot together next week," said the blonde girl, Darla. "Listen, me and a couple of girls are heading over to the coffee shop across the road for a drink and a natter. Want to join us?"

"Yeah, thanks!" said Blanche, delighted to be included.

They got a corner seat and launched into talking about modelling jobs they had been on that week. Blanche sat in awe at their glamour and sophistication, particularly Darla.

Soon the conversation moved on to their boyfriends.

Darla took out a small mirror and started to fix her lipstick. "Don't even get me started about him. He's been so tied up in work recently I've barely seen him."

"Well, you know what Shay is like – work comes first!" said one of the other girls.

Shay? Blanche sat listening intently.

"I know, but give me a break! Anyway, we're going to the cinema tonight and then we're heading for dinner afterwards. I'm going to let him spoil me."

"Well, don't keep him up too late – he's photographing me tomorrow at nine!"

"Shay?" Blanche suddenly mumbled out and everyone looked at her.

"Sorry?" said Darla.

"Shay from Belfast, you're seeing him?"

Darla looked at her curiously "Well, of course!"

Blanche went bright red and tried not to look upset as her mind flew out in a hundred directions.

Blanche marched down Ranelagh on a mission to Shay's house. She nearly took the little iron gate off its hinges as she stormed up the garden path and rang the doorbell over and over again.

Shay answered the door, a camera around his neck.

"What's all the commotion?" he demanded.

"You bastard!" she spat as she stepped inside and slammed the door shut.

"What the fuck is wrong with you?" he demanded.

"I just had lunch with your girlfriend, Darla, only I didn't know she was your girlfriend when we were fucking last night, did I? Why didn't you tell me you were seeing Darla?"

"Because I thought you knew."

"How would I know? You never said anything."

"Ach, I thought you'd have heard from the other girls in the agency."

"No, I didn't. And do you honestly think I would just hop into bed with you if I knew you were seeing someone?"

"Well, I don't know – would you?"

"Of course I wouldn't!" She stared at him angrily. "How serious are the two of you?"

"We're . . . serious."

"Well, you can't be that serious about her if you jumped into bed with me . . . and don't try and tell me I was special and you haven't done this before with any of the other models!"

"Well, you are special, very special, but no . . . you're certainly not the only other model I've slept with."

"You've used me!" She threw her hands into the air with exasperation.

"Away and shite! Nobody used anybody."

"Am I missing something here? Shouldn't you be apologising to me, or making some excuse or something, instead admitting to everything!"

He started laughing.

"What is wrong with you?" she demanded.

"Here I was, thinking I was dealing with a proper grown-up! This is the 1980s, love, there's no using going on . . . we're two people who like each other very much and ended up showing our liking in a physical way."

"But what about Darla?"

"What happened between us isn't interfering with Darla and me. That's the way the scene is up here, love, in this business, and if you don't like it, then you'd better head back to Dalkey and marry one of those safe lads your family knows."

Blanche ran her hands through her hair. "I just thought I meant more to you than that."

"Ahh, love, I adore you, I really do, and maybe I should have explained the rules before – but do you understand them now?"

"Clear as crystal." Blanche didn't try to hide the bitterness in her voice. She turned and stormed out, slamming the door behind her.

Blanche did a lot of crying and thinking that night. She thought about what he had said. He was a breath of fresh air, compared to all she was used to. She was wrong to accuse him of using her. They were both adults who didn't have to answer to anybody.

Next morning found her pressing the doorbell on Shay's door. He answered it after a short while. He looked at her cautiously.

"Can I come in?" she asked sheepishly.

He nodded and beckoned her in.

"I'm sorry I got so angry yesterday," she said. "I just felt used, but now I realise I might have been coming across as a bit of a prude. I'm just not used to the way things are done around here."

"I would never use you."

"You've been a big help to me since I arrived."

"And are we still friends?"

She studied his face. "Friends," she confirmed. "Although I can assure you – we will never, ever sleep together again."

CHAPTER 7

Blanche spent the next few weeks working hard. Luckily for her, Samantha liked her and worked tirelessly at promoting her to clients all the time. Blanche in turn worked tirelessly on the shoots and became a favourite with the PR agencies, magazines and photographers. That's when Shay gave her a chance to work with other photographers – he guarded her protectively and got jealous if other photographers worked with her too much. She kept her heart well guarded around him, never forgetting the impact he'd had on her before. She moved him firmly into the friend category and he seemed happy to be there as well, taking on the role of big brother with her almost, vetting any men who asked her out. She went on a few dates, but nobody lit her fire.

She had become friends with Darla as well. And they went out to lunch a bit. When she was sober, Darla was the best model around, but if she started to drink she quickly became a complete mess. They were working on a shoot once advertising gin. It was an unfortunate product for Darla to be employed to work on, as she kept helping herself to the prop every time the photographer wasn't looking. Soon she was legless and the very angry photographer had to cancel the shoot. Blanche poured Darla into a taxi and brought her back to Shay's. She directed the drunken Darla up the garden path and started to ring the doorbell.

To Blanche's surprise, Shay roared with laughter when he saw the state Darla was in. He picked her up, carried her up the stairs and put her to bed. He came down the stairs still laughing.

"Poor cow, she can hardly stand!" he said.

"I know! I had to carry her here. The photographer on the shoot was furious."

Shay laughed even louder. "Good! Can't stand that fucking div anyway. Anyway I tucked her up in bed and she can sleep it off. She'll be right as rain in the morning."

Blanche imagined her warm under the fur duvet, waiting for Shay, and felt envious of their relationship.

He poured them both a glass of wine and sat down opposite her.

"Thanks for looking after the old girl anyway," he said, raising his glass.

"No problem . . . Shay, why do you put up with her?"

"What do you mean?"

"Oh I know she's beautiful, and charming – when she's sober. But she's a nightmare when she's drunk. And that seems to be every other day."

Shay laughed. "The days in between are worth it."

"Just looking on, it seems a bit bizarre. With her drink and your affairs . . ."

There was a twinkle in his eyes. "Well, maybe we deserve each other then?" He stretched back in his seat. "I don't know, maybe I'm just attracted to vulnerable women. When you come from where I do, you get a feeling for the underdog."

"Oh, you mean the Troubles," said Blanche.

"No, I mean Disneyland! For God's sake, what else would I mean?" He looked annoyed. "When you see people in a bad place, you reach out to help them. I always have and I guess I still do."

"There's a big difference between a model with a drink problem and people being the victims of political violence," said Blanche.

"I fucking know that . . . I'm just saying Darla probably has reasons why she drinks. You from your protected background can never understand what other people have gone through growing up."

Blanche raised her eyes to heaven as she sipped from her drink.

Her nonchalant attitude irritated him. "You know, if you grew up where I grew up you'd be completely different . . . You'd have wanted to be an activist."

"But I didn't . . . and where I grew up I just wanted to be the blonde one in Abba!"

"You can joke about this? You make me sick." He poured the drink back his mouth and slammed the glass on the coffee table. "You're like everyone else down here. Look away, pretend it's not happening. Let's pretend it's not just a couple of hundred miles away. As long as it doesn't affect our cosy little lives, right?"

She studied his angry face. "Look, what's happening in the North is terrible, Shay, horrible. I can only imagine what you and your family have gone through." She sighed and tried to smile at him. "I don't know how we even got on to this conversation. All I was doing was being nosy about your relationship with Darla."

He sat back and began to relax. "They say never discuss politics or religion, hey?" he said smiling.

"You're wasting your time talking about them with me anyway, Shay. I'm not that opinionated."

He raised his glass to her. "If only everyone could be like that."

CHAPTER 8

As Blanche began to earn more money for her work, she really started enjoying her independence. Going to nightclubs every other night, and to restaurants. She had a readymade network through the agency and through Shay, who seemed to know everybody.

Blanche admired Shay's car so much that he organised for her to buy her own second-hand MG, in green with a black convertible roof, same as his. She felt quite the socialite spinning around the city, going to functions and having her photo appear in the social pages. Her name was getting known and she loved it. One night herself and Shay had been at a function in The Berkeley Court and they ended up in a nightclub in Leeson Street. They sat at a table with a bottle of red wine in front of them and two glasses.

"How's the car going?" asked Shay.

"I love it . . . when it goes!"

"What do you mean?"

"It just has a little trouble starting occasionally."

"Away and shite, that's a classic car you've got there –

a little engine trouble is a small price to pay," he said, smirking at her.

She became aware of a man of around forty looking over at her. He was sitting at the bar with a group of five men around him.

"Who's that guy over there?" she asked, nodding over to the bar.

Shay followed her nod and then laughed lightly. "That's Eamonn McNamara," he said in a tone that indicated she should know immediately who that was.

Blanche shrugged.

"As in McNamara Supermarkets," Shay urged.

"Ohh!" Realisation dawned on Blanche. McNamara supermarkets were on every high street in the country. "Well, he's staring over at me."

Eamonn waved over to Shay who waved back.

"Do you know him?" asked Blanche.

"Yeah. I shot some commercials for their supermarkets."

"Is there anybody you don't know?"

Suddenly Eamonn was walking over to them, two of his friends in quick pursuit.

"Eamonn, how's it going?" asked Shay, shaking Eamonn's proffered hand.

"I'm good, and you?"

"Getting by, you know how it is," said Shay. He saw Eamonn looking at Blanche expectantly. "Eh, Eamonn, this is a friend of mine, Blanche Fitzclarence."

Eamonn offered his hand again and Blanche shook it.

"Very pleased to meet you," he said, smiling at her.

Blanche nodded back and smiled. She felt attracted to his handsome features.

Eamonn was going to say something further when one of his friends put a hand on his shoulder.

"We need to be heading – you've a very early start, remember?" said the friend.

"Ohh, yeah, better get going," Eamonn said and nodded to Blanche. "Nice meeting you – another time?"

She smiled at him again.

Suddenly all of Eamonn's friends were around him and they all exited the club.

Blanche looked on in confusion. "What was all that about? What's the story with his friends?"

"I doubt they're real friends, more like bodyguards," explained Shay.

"Bodyguards?" Blanche's eyes widened.

"As one of the wealthiest men in the country, Eamonn McNamara is a number-one target for the terrorist groups for kidnapping. In fact, I think he's already been targeted once and they failed to get him. After that his father employed a team of bodyguards for the whole family. They don't go anywhere unaccompanied now."

"What a horrible way to live!" said Blanche.

"Did you like him?" Shay asked.

"Maybe. That's the last we'll see of him now though."

"Somehow I doubt that," said Shay.

Suddenly a waitress arrived over with a bottle of champagne and a couple of glasses.

"We didn't order this," objected Blanche.

"Compliments of Mr Eamonn McNamara," explained the waitress.

Shay looked at Blanche and winked.

"Eamonn McNamara was just on to me looking for your phone number," said Shay.

"And did you give it to him?" Blanche was startled.

"Of course. You said you liked him, didn't you?"

"Yes – but –"

"But nothing. He likes you, you like him, what's the problem?"

"The fact that he can't go to the bathroom without five men watching his every move. It's not going to make for a romantic evening, is it?"

"Listen, he'll lose them for the night, don't worry about that. You just be your most charming best when he phones you, alright?"

"Alright," she agreed and she replaced the receiver.

No sooner had she done so than the phone rang again.

"Hi, Blanche? Eamonn McNamara here. We met the other night in Leeson Street, if you remember?"

Blanche met Shay for coffee in the Burlington.

"Well?" demanded Shay.

"We're meeting tomorrow night at eight in a restaurant called O'Mara's – it's in Ballsbridge – have you heard of it?"

"Sure have. Great place, you'll enjoy it."

"It's a bit weird. He said not to ask for him when I get to the restaurant and that he put the reservation in my name."

"I've heard he does that – he doesn't want to draw attention to himself."

"Understandable, I suppose."

Blanche got a taxi to O'Mara's. It was a discreet location on a quiet street. She was wearing a long shimmering silver gown that showed off her figure. Inside at reception the manager greeted her.

"And the name is?" he asked.

"Blanche Fitzclarence."

"Ahh, yes, Miss Fitzclarence, if you could follow me."

He led her through to the restaurant. She surveyed the plush interior filled with diners, trying to spot Eamonn.

She followed him to the back of the restaurant where he reached a door. He turned and smiled at her, then opened the door without looking in.

"Your room as you reserved it, ma'am."

Confused and nervous, Blanche walked into the room and the door was closed behind her.

She took in the large grand room, with portraits on the walls and a thick carpet underfoot. In the centre of the room was a large table laden with food. And sitting at the table was Eamonn McNamara.

"Hi there!" he said, coming to meet her.

"Hi!"

He reached for her coat and she let him remove it and hang it up on a coat-stand.

"You've gone to a lot of trouble!" she said, approaching the table and looking down at all the food.

"My pleasure," he said, opening a bottle of champagne.

"I have to say this is very impressive, booking a private room and everything," she said, accepting a glass of champagne.

"Well, I thought this would be more discreet, don't you?"

"You couldn't get more discreet than this!"

He went to a chair and pulled it out for her. She sat down and as he pushed her chair in, he bent down and kissed her neck. She shivered slightly and was surprised by his forwardness. He went and sat opposite her.

"Please, help yourself. The oysters are amazing," he urged.

She reached out and took some paté.

"And don't worry – I've left instructions that we are not

to be disturbed for the night. I don't think we require anything else, do you?"

"No, I think this is quite . . . satisfactory." She felt uneasy. She had thought this would be a normal dinner date, but all this was over the top. Impressive, but also a little scary.

"So, I believe you're doing very well in the modelling world?"

"Yes, I've been very lucky."

"There's no such thing as luck. We get what we deserve in this life."

She shrugged. "Maybe. A bit of luck helps along the way though, doesn't it?"

He laughed heartily. "I love you! Beautiful and witty!"

She smiled at him. "You didn't bring your friends along tonight?"

"No, I managed to lose them. I wanted us to be alone."

The conversation went along smoothly, but Blanche couldn't relax in his company. She thought initially it was the grandeur and privacy of their surroundings. But after a while, she realised it was him. He had a commanding presence about him and she felt he wasn't really interested in anything but himself. He reached over and took her hands regularly and rubbed them. When he had gone to such effort for her, she felt it would be rude not to show an interest in him, but she found the whole thing a turn-off. Suddenly there was a knock on the door.

It opened slightly and she heard the manager's voice say: "Miss Fitzclarence, a phone call for you, they say it's urgent." The door closed again.

Blanche was startled and Eamonn looked annoyed.

"Who is that phoning you?" he asked in irritation.

"How would I know until I go and see?" she snapped, rising from her chair.

"Get rid of them quickly," he ordered.

She looked at him, annoyed with his arrogance, and didn't reply.

She walked to reception where she took the call.

"Hello?"

"Blanche, Shay here – look, I'm really sorry to disturb your dinner and all."

"You're okay – what's the matter?"

"I'm after finding out something about Eamonn McNamara. He's married, Blanche, with a couple of kids up in Wicklow. I only found out tonight."

"I thought you said you knew him!"

"Only on a professional basis. Those McNamaras are so fucking private, nobody knows anything about them. Sure you saw those gorillas around him that night in Leeson Street. Are any of them there tonight?"

"The bodyguards? No, he came alone."

"I'm really sorry, Blanche, but I thought I'd better tell ya."

"You did the right thing. Thanks, Shay. To be honest he's a crashing bore. You've just given me the excuse to finish the night early. Talk to you tomorrow." She hung up the phone and thought for a couple of minutes before returning to the private room.

She sat down at the table, joined her hands together and looked at Eamonn pointedly.

"I don't think you've been completely honest with me, have you, Eamonn?"

"I don't get you."

"You're married, are you not?"

He looked at her, confused. "Yeah. So what?"

"So what?" She laughed in disbelief. "I think you might have let me know."

"But you knew that already."

"No, I didn't!"

"Everybody knows I'm married. Shay knew."

"No, he didn't, for your information. The night is beginning to make sense to me now. Booking the restaurant in my name, the private room, nobody allowed to come into the room. You were obviously frightened of being seen out with another woman. Not to mention your familiarity with me – kissing my neck within a few seconds of meeting me, telling me not to worry – you obviously thought that we both knew the set-up and I was up for it. Sorry for the confusion." She stood up and went to get her coat.

"But you can't just go!" he said, leaping to his feet. "Not when I've gone to all this trouble!"

"I'm sure you'll find any number of girls willing to take my place for the night," she said, putting on her coat.

"But I can't just go around picking up girls, not in my position. I have to be discreet, to go through contacts. That's why you're here!"

She looked at him and felt angry at what he thought of her. That she was just somebody who could be ordered in for the night.

"Good night, Eamonn."

She turned to leave but he grabbed her arm.

"You're not going anywhere. I've gone to a lot of trouble organising tonight, organising you."

He grabbed her by the back of her head and forced his lips on hers. She kicked him as hard as she could on his shin.

"You fucking little bitch!" he shouted at her and went to hit her.

"You lay one hand on me and I'll scream this place down!" she shouted at him.

He stood there, his hand hovering in the air. He let her go. She pulled her coat around herself and left the room.

CHAPTER 9

Blanche found it hard to sleep that night. She kept thinking of McNamara and what a creep he was. What annoyed her most was that he had absolutely no respect for her. He thought that he could just order her in the same way he ordered everything in life. The whole thing made her feel seedy, and powerless and unimportant. She was wising up quickly.

She had a job at eleven the next day. She made her way into town and stopped off in a newsagent's to buy some cigarettes, another habit Shay had introduced her to recently. She stopped abruptly. There were big photos of Eamonn McNamara on the front of all the papers under headlines like 'Supermarket Tycoon Kidnapped'. She could hardly catch her breath as she read quickly through an article.

Blanche was both ringing the doorbell and hammering on Shay's door at the same time. Eventually he opened up, still in his dressing gown.

"Whoa! What's the big emergency?"

"This!" she shouted, waving the newspaper and rushing inside, closing the door behind her.

She paced up and down the studio while Shay read through the newspaper.

"Fucking unreal!" said Shay. "He was kidnapped last night on his way back to his home in Wicklow. His car was ambushed."

Blanche was shaking. "Is it the IRA?" she asked.

"Nah! The paper says it's one of the smaller paramilitary organisations. They're demanding one million pounds."

"Fuck, Shay! What'll we do?"

"What is there for us to do?" He shrugged his shoulders.

"Well, I have to go to the police!"

"Why?"

"Well, I need to let them know he was having dinner with me beforehand."

"First of all, the police knowing you had dinner with him beforehand is not going to help them find him. Secondly, if you do tell them, then tomorrow it will be *your* photo on the front page as the woman having an affair with McNamara."

"But I wasn't!"

"It won't look like that. Everyone will think you were shagging him. And your career will be over before it starts. Imagine what your parents and everyone at home will think of you!"

Blanche started to shake uncontrollably.

"And thirdly, I wouldn't be telling his wife, as she might be mightily pissed off and decide just not to pay the ransom in revenge, which would mean if anything happens to him it will be on *your* conscience."

"But Shay! It will get out! The police will find out and wonder why I said nothing!"

"Look, nobody knows except for me and you. You said

the booking was in your name, yeah? No doubt he took you to that infamous back room where all the husbands take their mistresses, right?"

"Yes, but how did you know about it?"

"I know all the secrets in this town and that room is an open secret. The husbands enter by the back door and the mistresses by the front. Generally, not even the restaurant knows who the man is."

"Nobody saw us, he made sure of it."

"Right. So even if the restaurant suspected he was there, they aren't going to say anything – they aren't going to risk losing half their business." He got up, put his hands on her shoulders and looked her straight in the eyes.

"This isn't going to get out as long as you keep your trap shut. The last thing he would want is for you to go public saying he was out with you, no?"

"I guess it makes sense."

"Sit still, go about your business as usual, and it'll all be over in a week."

Blanche was glued to every news report and every newspaper each day devouring all the information about the case, hoping and praying Eamonn would be released soon and this mess would be over. Thank God Shay had warned her – otherwise, who was to say she might not have been with him when the kidnappers struck.

She huddled up on her couch looking at the nine o'clock news. Eamonn's wife, Susan, had decided to appeal directly to the kidnappers for her husband's release. Elegant, blonde and articulate, she sat between two high-ranking Gardaí and addressed the camera, pleading for her husband's life. The media made a huge hooray about how it was the first time a member of the McNamara family had spoken to the media, but then these were exceptional circumstances. Blanche wondered what kind of a marriage they had. Was he a loving and caring husband and father in the home, and then hit on every young thing when he was out?

On the Friday morning, Blanche came into the kitchen and immediately put on the radio. As she filled the kettle she heard:

"Gardaí have confirmed that kidnapped supermarket boss Eamonn McNamara was found unharmed in the early hours of this morning. In a message sent to the RTÉ newsroom, the dissident terrorist group, the National Freedom Army, gave an isolated location in County Tipperary where Mr McNamara could be found. Gardaí were immediately informed . . ."

"See, I told you it would all be blown over in a week," said Shay as he and Blanche watched news reports of the kidnap.

"I never want to go through a week like that again. I kept expecting the police to call at my door any minute – or worse, the media."

On the TV, a crowd of media people had gathered at the gateway of the McNamaras' house. Eamonn and his wife Susan were walking down the winding driveway to give an impromptu interview to the press as had become the norm for freed kidnap victims. Susan had her arm linked through her husband's and they looked relieved and very happy.

"May that be a lesson to him not to have secret rendezvous in the future," said Blanche. She suddenly became alarmed. "He won't tell the guards he was with me, will he?"

"You joking me? That's the last thing he'll be admitting

to in case that lovely wife of his finds out. He'll just say he was late out of a meeting, I'd put money on it."

"But what if they hadn't freed him, what if the family hadn't paid?"

"Of course they'd pay. What's a million quid to them? Tell you what though – he might have thought he was being kept under heavy security before. He won't even be allowed out of the house from now on."

CHAPTER 10

"Do you like it?" Darla asked as she stretched out her hand and showed off the sparkling gems on the bracelet that adorned her wrist.

"Fairly impressive!" remarked Blanche. The two were walking down Grafton Street on a shopping spree as they had just been on a job together.

"It's a gift from Shay," said Darla as they went through the doors of Brown Thomas.

"He's very generous," said Blanche, trying to fight off a feeling of jealousy.

"He is, actually – he bought me this coat as well!" She tugged the long mink coat closer to her.

"He obviously cares about you very much," said Blanche, wondering if Darla knew of his dalliances, and if she did, did she care?

Darla picked up a fur coat. "This would look gorgeous on you. Why not buy it?"

"I don't think I can afford that," said Blanche.

"I thought you were doing great. You bought that little sports car, didn't you?"

"Yes, I bought it on the HP. And it's years old and getting harder to start every morning."

Blanche desperately tried to ignite her car's engine again. It spluttered and spat for a few seconds and then went dead. She cursed loudly and for the thirtieth time viciously turned the key again, but to no avail. Damn Shay for persuading her to buy this heap of junk! It had given her nothing but trouble since she'd bought it.

It was the afternoon and she was parked in the street outside the agency. She was about to abandon the car and go back into the agency when the young man she had noticed before came down the steps of the neighbouring building. He spotted her and heard the engine die again. He paused for a few moments and then headed over to her.

"Sounds like your battery's dead," he commented.

She looked up at him. "I know. I'm just about to ring a mechanic. I've about had it with this car."

"Shouldn't be a need to do that. I've a pair of jump leads in mine. Give me a second." He walked over to a nearby car, got in and drove it up to the bonnet of hers, then got out. "Open your bonnet," he said.

She pulled the lever and her bonnet popped open.

He opened his own and then she saw him messing with leads, attaching them to the two engines.

"Now, when I tell you start your engine, start revving really hard, okay?"

She shrugged. "Okay!"

"Right, start it!" he commanded.

Her engine began purring perfectly.

"I don't know how to thank you!" she said.

He smiled at her and put out his hand. "Billy Forrestal."

She took his hand and smiled. "Blanche Fitzclarence."

She felt herself drawn to him. It wasn't just his looks – there was a kindness in his handsome face and a sincerity in his eyes. He stood there awkwardly for a few seconds.

"You're with the model agency?" he asked eventually.

"Yes, I am."

"I work in the building next door," he said. "Do you want to grab a coffee?"

She nodded. "Yes, sure."

They strolled down to the Westbury Hotel where they sat in the front area by the fire and ordered a pot of coffee.

"So – what do you do – in the building next door?" she asked, pouring the coffee.

"I'm a state solicitor."

"I see," she said, becoming more intrigued. She judged him to be no older than twenty-five and yet his manner came across as older.

The coffee developed to them ordering lunch and the afternoon passed by quickly. She felt she could listen to him forever as he talked about his work and his life. He had come top of his year in law at Trinity. His father had been a prominent barrister before him and in a way Billy's whole life had been mapped out for him. But he had a burning desire to fight the criminals in society and make it a better place and that's why he went to work for the government. Money wasn't his motivator, he explained to her. She discovered both his parents had passed away – they had him late in life. But he seemed to have a wonderful close network of relatives and friends. He was unlike any other man she had met before and completely different from the men she had met recently like Eamonn McNamara and even Shay. She imagined they would have nothing in common with him.

As the afternoon ran into the evening, they found

themselves moving into the bar and still they didn't run out of things to say.

That night he walked her to the taxi rank. By the time they awkwardly said goodbye, Blanche realised she had feelings for him that she had never experienced before.

Blanche saw Billy every day for the next week. She found it impossible to get him out of her mind. And he seemed as interested in her. They went out to dinner every night. He brought her around to the family home that his parents had left him. It was a large Edwardian two-storey-over-basement semi-detached house overlooking the park in Dartmouth Square. It had high ceilings and was filled with antique furniture.

"I wonder whether money is not a motivator for you because you were left this big house?" asked Blanche as she accepted a glass of wine. She was lying out on a couch looking at the ornate ceiling.

He sat on the floor beside her, stroking her hair. "The house was just about the lot of it. There was no money left. My father spent most of his life working on causes for next to nothing. I'll be the same. I earn just enough to maintain this house, pay a woman who comes in to clean and cook, and have a nice life. Do I want any more than that?"

She shrugged. "No." She found his unspoilt nature refreshing, his lack of greed enchanting.

He reached forward, took her glass and put it beside his on the coffee table.

As he gently lay down on her, she reached up and put her arms around his neck.

"Do you feel how I feel?" he asked tentatively.

"I think I do – if you feel crazy about me, then that's how I feel about you."

"Why don't you move in with me here?"

She pulled back and looked at him. "Are you serious?"

"Never been more so. You know life passes by very quickly. You have to grab what you can when you can. If you don't, you might miss your opportunity and it won't come round again. I know my parents waited far too long to settle down and have a child. I don't want to be getting married older, and being an old father." He held her close.

Blanche realised that, despite the fact that Billy was well set up in life and had a tremendous network of friends and colleagues, he wanted the security of family life.

And she was just delighted he wanted her.

CHAPTER 11

Blanche glanced at her watch and wished Shay would hurry up with the shoot. She had arranged to meet Billy for lunch and she was in danger of running late.

"Blanche!" cried Shay. "Smile! Please!"

"Oh, sorry, Shay!" She knew she wasn't concentrating and tried her best to be attentive to his demands.

"Right! We'll call it a day," said Shay as he moved away from the camera. Blanche jumped off her stool and headed over to get her coat.

"Fancy a bit of lunch?" suggested Shay.

"Oh, Shay, I'd love to! But I've something on. Maybe tomorrow?" She put on her coat.

"Also, I've got somebody for a blind date for you. Nice guy and not married!"

"Oh, I don't think so, Shay . . ."

"What do you mean, you don't think so?"

She smiled at him. "Look, Shay, I really do appreciate you playing matchmaker . . . but I've met somebody. Somebody wonderful!"

The smile fell from Shay's face. "Who is he?"

"Oh, you don't know him, Shay. He's not in the business. He's a solicitor. I'm mad about him."

"I see!"

"I know . . . in actual fact, you *were* kind of playing matchmaker. The car you organised for me broke down, and he came to fix it, and it just went on from there."

"You know, Blanche, you need to calm down a bit here. You're a young beautiful girl and a guy will think nothing of telling you he loves you when he doesn't really mean it."

Her face soured. "I know that, Shay. Nearly all the men you've introduced me to have been of that type." Including you, she added mentally. "But he's asked me to move in with him," she added triumphantly.

"He what? Are you crazy? Why the fuck should you leave all that to settle down with some fucking idiot?"

His anger surprised her. "I thought you wanted me to settle down? Why else do you keep setting me up with eligible men?" Or not so eligible, she again added mentally.

"Because you're precious to me and I want to see you with someone nice."

"Oh, come *on*, Shay. There was nothing *nice* about Eamonn McNamara. Billy is different. He's lovely and kind."

"Billy!" Shay repeated the word as if it was a curse. "You're too young to settle down with Billy, or Barry, or a Timmy or Tommy for that matter!"

"I don't know why you're so upset. You're in a happy relationship with Darla. I just want to be happy too. I know I'm young, but I know that Billy is the love of my life. And I feel really privileged to have met him early in my life. I could have spent years trying to find somebody I really loved, going through the likes of Eamonn McNamara looking for Mr Right." She was upset by this time. She turned and walked over to the window, tears in her eyes.

He came and placed his hands on her shoulders. "I'm sorry, sweetheart. I just worry for you, and I want the best for you, you know."

She turned and faced him. "I know. And he is the best, Shay, he really is."

"Expect the worst," warned Blanche as Billy drove them into the driveway of the Fitzclarence home. Blanche had already informed them of her intentions of moving in with Billy and they had gone mad.

"It'll be fine." He leaned over and kissed her, and they made their way into the house.

"Billy . . . my parents, Harriet and Daniel," said Blanche when they entered the lounge.

"So nice to meet you." Harriet crossed the floor with hand outstretched.

Smiling, Billy took her hand and shook it.

"Em . . . can I get you anything?" asked Harriet. "Maybe a ring on my daughter's finger, for starters?"

Billy crossed over to Blanche and stood behind her, putting an arm around her.

"I mean. If she's good enough to live with, then she's good enough to marry, no?" quizzed Harriet.

"Mother!" Blanche nearly shouted.

"We are very much against the two of you moving in together," stated Daniel.

"And I'm sure if your parents were still alive they would disapprove of you living together as much as we do," added Harriet.

"They were actually quite liberal," said Billy.

"It's amazing how the most liberal of people can become conservative when it comes to their own children," said Harriet.

"Mum, you are embarrassing me beyond belief," said Blanche.

"And you are embarrassing me beyond my wildest imaginings!" said Harriet.

"This is 1980!" insisted Blanche. "People live together all the time. There's nothing wrong with it!"

"This is Ireland, Blanche! Not one of those glossy mags you read."

"This is all about power, Mum, isn't it? This is me being independent, and not leading the life you had mapped out for me."

"You can say that again. You're continually underselling yourself."

"Now, you seem a nice enough young man," said Dan. "But you have to see it from our point of view."

"We're committed to each other," said Blanche, "and we don't need a ceremony to prove that." She squeezed Billy's hand tight.

"You're also twenty, Blanche. You don't know what you want in life and you're making decisions that could ruin the rest of your life."

"I'll live it the way I choose, following the rules that I want, not any that are imposed by other people."

"Well, I guess there's nothing left to be said then, is there?" said Harriet.

Blanche made her way upstairs to pack and Billy followed her.

"They're just worried about you, I can understand that," Billy soothed her.

"They're not worried. They just want to control me and wear me down and do what they want. And they'll never do it, Billy. I'm so happy and I'm not changing anything."

Blanche was over at Shay's, having dropped in for a cup of coffee.

"So, how's Love's Young Dream?" he asked, a hint of sarcasm in his voice.

She couldn't help from smiling. "He's just so good and kind. And I could listen to him talk about his work forever. The cases he's working on, trying to fight corruption, trying to make this country a better place."

"Listening to legal shit all night? Who gives a fuck?"

She didn't disguise her hurt. "Well, I do actually. I think it's amazing to have such a social conscience. We had a group of his friends over last night."

"Ah, come on, Blanche, when are you going to get real? You don't want to be mixing with all those boring legal eagles. You want to be kicking your shoes off and dancing on a table in a nightclub. That's the real you."

She raised her eyes to heaven. "Well, why don't you and Darla come over for dinner. Meet him. Say, how about Thursday?"

"Do I have to wear a tuxedo and watch my language?"

"No . . . you just have to be yourself."

"I guess it would be my privilege to meet this giant amongst men."

Just then Blanche noticed something on the news and turned up the volume on the TV. It was a report about the kidnapping of a German industrialist in Dublin called Wilbur Von Dieter.

"Another kidnapping," she sighed and turned off the

television. Since her own brush with kidnapping, she felt an extra degree of sympathy with such cases.

Blanche checked herself in the mirror in the drawing room in Billy's house and pushed a stray strand of dark hair back. Billy came behind her and gently held her arms as he leant forward to kiss her cheek.

"You look beautiful," he whispered.

She turned and smiled and kissed him. They walked together across the hall into the dining room where Billy's cook had set the table.

Blanche felt nervous about Billy meeting Shay and Darla. Although she had met all Billy's friends, she hadn't really introduced him to hers. And she was nervous they would have nothing in common.

The doorbell chimed.

"Here they are!" said Billy, his arm still around Blanche as they headed to greet their guests.

Billy opened the front door and there stood Shay and Darla on the steps.

"Hi there!" they both sang in unison.

Blanche kissed them both on the cheek as they entered the house.

"Billy, this is Shay and Darla," said Blanche.

They greeted each other with hearty hellos and handshakes.

Shay then handed Blanche a box of Milk Tray and Billy a bottle of Blue Nun. Billy tried not to wince at the bottle as he had spent an hour carefully selecting a French wine to accompany the pheasant that was to be served.

"Come on through to the drawing room," said Blanche as Billy took their coats.

They followed her in.

"What do you want to drink?" asked Billy as he headed over to the drinks table.

"Just a Harp for me, if you have it," suggested Shay.

"And I'm a G&T girl," said Darla as she and Shay sat down on the couch. "You know, gin is supposed to be a depressant. I should really stay clear of it. You know, one night I drank nothing but gin and the next morning I felt so depressed! I was reading a newspaper and suddenly I was crying reading about what was happening in Rhodesia! I mean, I wouldn't usually give a shit what was happening in Rhodesia!"

Blanche and Shay laughed, and Billy managed a smile as he handed them their drinks. He then went to Blanche by the fireplace and gave her one of the two balloon glasses of red wine he had poured for them. He placed his arm around her waist. Shay looked on in growing irritation.

By the time dinner was served, Darla had had her sixth gin and tonic.

"Well, I believe congratulations are in order!" she said.

"Congratulations?" asked Blanche.

"I believe you got the modelling contract for Soul Soap."

"Oh, yes, thanks," said Blanche. She knew that Darla had gone for the job as well.

"Look at you!" said Darla. "The face of Soul Soap and living on Dartmouth Square – haven't you done well for yourself, my dear!"

"I don't care where I live as long as Billy is there," said Blanche and she reached out and held Billy's hand.

"Touching!" said Darla.

"Aye, money goes to money," said Shay.

"I haven't a bean!" declared Blanche.

"And neither do I!" said Billy.

"Just enough to pay your cook?" There was venom in Shay's voice as he continued. "Away and shite! You two might want to play at being poor, but you really don't know anything about it. Blanche tells me all about the great work you do as a barrister, working for little or nothing representing the poor who can't afford their own legal advice. You're just trying to ease your conscience that you were born into all this when they have nothing. But you're still drinking this fucking French fancy wine when you get home, aren't ya?"

"Shay!" Blanche snapped.

"So you can get on with your perfect lives. I can see it now – Billy Forrestal, barrister extraordinaire, and his beautiful model wife Blanche. You'll be the toast of the town!"

"All salute the new society couple!" Darla raised her full glass of gin, but unfortunately dropped it all over the table.

Later Shay helped Blanche bring the plates downstairs into the basement kitchen.

"You don't have to be so rude!" she snapped.

"I'm not being rude – he just makes me sick – living in this house and playing the saint doing loads of good works."

Realisation suddenly dawned on her. "You're jealous! You're jealous of Billy!"

"Ah fuck off!"

"You are! You're jealous of his upbringing, and his education and his manners."

"You fucking bitch!" He grabbed her shoulders.

"Let go of me, Shay!" she hissed at him. "The more I see of men like you and your friend McNamara, the more I realise what a gem Billy is."

Calm came over Shay's face. "I'm sorry, Blanche." He

let her go. "And the way I've been speaking tonight is unforgivable."

"Yes, it is!" She saw he was getting upset. "Look, I know we're the best of friends and it might be hard for you to see me with somebody coming into what you consider your zone. But you have to allow me to have my own life."

He nodded and she went to him and hugged him. "Look, I'll never forget the kindness you've shown me. You've been the best friend I could ever have had. And we're going to remain best friends, okay?"

He nodded. "Okay."

"Now, come on and help me make the coffee." She took out the coffee pot.

Shay started to set out the coffee cups, then stopped and looked at her.

"Just one thing – does Billy know we fucked?"

Darla was well sozzled by the time they arrived back with the coffees.

"The only coffee I want is an Irish one," stated Darla, rejecting the cup Blanche was offering.

Blanche glanced at her watch, then went and turned on the television.

"Sorry, everyone, I just want to catch the late news. I want to check if there's any update on that Von Dieter kidnapping."

"Yeah, how's about that? Poor fucker!" said Shay.

The male newsreader announced: *"Gardaí today stated that they suspect the ear that was posted to a Dublin newspaper this morning belongs to kidnapped German industrialist Wilbur Von Dieter. In a letter that accompanied the package, the group calling themselves the National Freedom Army claimed that they had severed the ear from Mr Von Dieter, and also threatened a further physical injury*

*on Mr Von Dieter if the ransom of one million pounds is not
paid within five days."*

"What a barbaric thing to do. Poor man!" Blanche cried
out.

"They're showing they mean business," said Shay,
sighing.

"What'll they do if the ransom isn't paid in five days?"
asked Blanche.

"Probably cut off his other ear," said Billy.

"Bloody bastards! Why doesn't the family just pay the
damned ransom and get him back?" said Blanche, turning
off the TV.

"I know a couple off the guys working on the case, and
they've told me that the family just can't raise the money,"
said Billy.

"Don't be stupid," said Shay. "The Von Dieter family
are worth millions."

"The trouble is they actually are not. The company has
been in freefall for years – they're just hanging in there."

Blanche and Billy saw their guests to the front door.

"Thanks for having us," said Shay, as he supported
Darla from falling.

"Our pleasure," said Billy.

"I'll give you a shout tomorrow," said Shay with a quick
wink to Blanche.

"Okay, and thanks, Shay," she said, shutting the door.

She rested against the door a while looking at Billy.

"I'm sorry!" she eventually said.

"Sorry for what?" He looked confused.

"Sorry for tonight! Sorry for Shay getting all obnoxious
and Darla falling down drunk and . . ."

Smiling, he approached her and enveloped her in a hug.

"They're fine, don't worry about it. They're your friends and they're welcome here any time."

She stared at him, loving him more with every word.

On Friday morning Samantha called Blanche into her office. Then she sat silently scrutinising her, making Blanche feel increasingly nervous.

"Is anything the matter?" she finally asked, breaking the silence.

"No, nothing's the matter," said Samantha. "In fact, everything's very good. I'm hearing some very good reports back about you, Blanche."

"Really?" Blanche's eyes widened with excitement.

"Yes. In fact, everyone's singing your praises. The photographers love working with you, the advertisers love the results . . . and . . ." Samantha glanced down at a photo of Blanche and Billy at an opening on the social pages of the *Herald*, "you're building quite the reputation in the social pages as a socialite, with your lawyer boyfriend."

"Me and Billy? We don't go looking for it." She felt the need to excuse herself.

"In fact, I'm thinking of putting you forward as the new face for Fortune Face Cream."

Blanche beamed a smile but then her smile turned sour. "But that's Darla's gig – she's the Face of Fortune."

"Don't I know it! Unfortunately Darla is becoming less and less reliable. The people at Fortune are pretty pissed off with her, and so am I for that matter. If she doesn't straighten out and sober up, not only is she going to be fired, but I'm going to lose Fortune as one of my main clients. I need to act before I lose them."

"But Samantha! Darla's a friend of mine. I can't –"

"She's a time bomb waiting to explode, the way she's going. Shall I put you forward for a casting?"

"Look, it's not that I don't appreciate the offer, and your belief in me, but I'm going to have to say no. I'm sorry. I can't do that to a friend."

Samantha shrugged. "I guess I admire your loyalty, if not your stupidity."

Later, as Blanche was coming back from a casting for a new brand of mascara, she stopped at a newsagent's to buy the *Evening Press*. On the front page was a big photo of Wilbur Von Dieter under the headline: *"Kidnap Victim Released."* She read on as she slowly walked down the street.

Blanche folded over the newspaper, relieved that the industrialist was released and wondering who had paid the ransom if what Billy had said was true – the newspaper hadn't mentioned any payment.

Who would want to be rich, she thought as she walked home. Or even *thought* to be rich, as Billy had said.

On the Saturday night at a drinks party at the house, Blanche was going around making sure everyone's glass was full.

As she filled Samantha's glass, she asked, "Is everything all right? Do you want more food, something else to drink?"

"No, Blanche, I'm fine thanks. But if I can have a word?" She pulled Blanche a little closer, so there would be no danger of the roomful of people hearing what she had to say. "You know that casting I sent you on yesterday?"

Blanche nodded. "The one for mascara?"

"It wasn't actually for mascara at all. It was for Fortune

Face Cream. I didn't tell you the truth, because I knew you wouldn't go."

"Oh, Samantha, I told you I wasn't interested!" Blanche didn't hide her anger.

"They want to sign you," said Samantha.

"Well, I'm not taking it," Blanche insisted stubbornly.

"You are taking it. I'm insisting."

"I . . . I . . ."

"Don't even bother fretting about it, Blanche, because I've already done the deal. You're going to be the new Face of Fortune. Just keep it under wraps for now, until we make the announcement." Samantha glanced over at Darla who was knocking back the gin and slurring her speech as she talked to some solicitor. "And until I tell Darla."

CHAPTER 12

It was the first of December and the first of the Christmas cards were displayed on top of the mantelpiece.

Blanche and Billy were on the sofa, tucking into chocolates and drinking red wine, while they half-watched *Dallas* on television in the background.

"I just feel so bad, Billy. I don't want to take Darla's job from her."

"You don't have to take it."

"Samantha might blacklist me. She'll be furious. This could affect my whole career."

"Samantha shouldn't be putting you in this situation anyway. Pitting you against a friend like this!" He got up. "It's getting cold. I'll throw some logs on the fire." He stoked up the blazing fire, throwing some logs on at the same time.

Blanche met Shay in the Shelbourne the next afternoon. The hotel was busy with Christmas shoppers and crowds from offices out to enjoy pre-Christmas drinks.

"Shay . . . how's Darla?" asked Blanche.

"She's cool. Why?"

"I'm a bit worried about her."

"Why?"

"Well, the drink of course!"

"Don't be daft. She's fine."

"I don't know if she is, Shay. Look, I'm going to spell it out for you: people are talking about her. They're not saying it to your face because she's your girlfriend but she's getting a real bad reputation for being a sloppy model."

Shay lit a cigarette, put it in his mouth and laughed.

"What's so funny?"

"I'm just thinking how you arrived up here green as a cabbage – and here you are having the best parties in town and lecturing me about my girlfriend, who is a far superior model to you incidentally."

Blanche's face clouded with hurt. "I wasn't being patronising. I'm only trying to help."

"Yeah, well, when me or Darla needs help then we'll ask for it, okay?"

She was startled by his aggression. "Okay . . . I'm sorry if I spoke out of turn."

"Blanche?" came a voice beside her. She looked up and saw it was an English friend of Billy's called Antony Barclay. She was grateful for the interruption.

"Oh, hi, Antony!" She got up and kissed him on the cheek.

"Billy's not here?"

"No, he's at work."

Antony smiled, his eyes lingering on her. She felt herself blush.

"Let's meet for lunch some day," he said as he scribbled down his number on a piece of paper and handed it to her. "Call me . . . any time." With a smile at her, he left.

Shay was looking out the window watching Antony

Barclay exiting the hotel and getting into a chauffeur-driven car.

"Antony Barclay? How does Billy know him?" he asked.

"Oh, I haven't a clue. He works at the British embassy and he's dealt with Billy over some legal proceedings. That's all I know."

"He works at the British embassy alright. He's a very senior diplomat there."

"Is he?" Blanche shrugged.

"A top man. And he seems to have a thing for you."

"Don't be daft!"

"I'm not. Don't tell me you didn't see the way he was looking at you. Billy has a bit of competition if you ask me."

"You are being ridiculous. Anyway, I'd better be going. Oh, and Shay, me and Billy are thinking of having a New Year's Eve party, if yourself and Darla could make it?"

Shay put out his cigarette. "Sure. Wouldn't want to miss one of the hottest parties in town." He smiled at her sarcastically.

Billy had got her a huge Christmas tree and they spent hours laughing as they put it up and decorated it and the house.

She agonised for days about what to get him for Christmas and in the end settled for a Mont Blanc pen inscribed with his name and an attaché case that she also had inscribed.

"Do you think we should invite your parents for Christmas dinner?" suggested Billy as they walked around Stephen's Green laden down with shopping bags on their way back to Dartmouth Square. A light snow was falling down around them.

"All they'll do is nag me and irritate me. I want this

Christmas to be about us. We'll call over to them at some stage."

In a way she was a little more concerned with the continuing coolness in her friendship with Shay. No matter how she tried, he seemed to have put up a wall against her that she couldn't break through. Samantha hadn't been back into work since a bout of flu and had now taken herself off to her house in the South of France until the New Year to recuperate. Blanche would have to wait until then to discuss the Fortune job with her and tell her she was rejecting it.

On Christmas Eve they met with some of Billy's friends for drinks in the Westbury and then got a taxi back home. They laughed and joked as they made the stuffing and put the turkey into the oven. Then Blanche made mulled wine and they went into the lounge and lay out in front of the roaring fire as Christmas carols were being played on the television.

Billy gave a little laugh.

"What's so funny?" she asked gently.

"I'm just thinking about how last year I was on my own in the house and I guess I was lonely without realising it. And then you came along and here we are." He chinked his glass of mulled wine against hers. "Lucky me!"

"Lucky me!" she replied.

He got up and searched among the array of beautifully wrapped presents under the tree and brought her back a small one.

"What's this?" she asked, throwing her unfinished cigarette into the fire so she could give it her full attention. "It isn't Christmas morning yet!"

"I know, but I want you to open this present now."

She unwrapped it and there was a small velvet-covered

box inside. She opened it and a diamond ring sparkled out at her.

"Is this . . .?"

He nodded. "I want us to get married."

She continued to stare at the ring. "I don't know what to say."

"Try 'yes'."

She took out the ring, slipped it on her finger and whispered, "Yes!"

CHAPTER 13

Blanche and Billy spent the whole of New Year's Eve day preparing the house for the party.

"We've got vodka, gin, whiskey, martini, cognac, beer, wine, Baileys, rum, Guinness, and of course champagne for midnight," said Billy as he surveyed the huge array of drinks set out in the dining room.

"Yes, that should keep Darla going, at least," said Blanche, giggling.

"I guess I'm on bar duty for the night," said Billy.

"And I'll be hostess with the mostest." She hugged him. She had taken off her engagement ring. They had decided they would make an announcement in the New Year, once they had told her parents. Blanche had her hair tied up, and was dressed in a long black sequinned gown.

The doorbell rang.

"That's the first of them arriving," said Billy.

"I'll get it," she said, going into the hall.

She opened the door and Antony Barclay stood there.

"Blanche!" He came in and gave her a kiss on the cheek. She felt his hand on her back, holding her a little too tightly and slipping a little too low.

"Antony, delighted you could come," she said.

After meeting Antony in the Shelbourne that afternoon, she had questioned Billy about him. True for Shay, he was a top-ranking British diplomat, based at the embassy. According to Billy, Antony was working on a very delicate peace negotiation for the North that had made him hated by extremists. As she closed the door she spotted two men waiting in his car whom she assumed to be security.

"Come on in and I'll get you a drink. Billy's in the dining room." She beckoned him to follow her.

The house soon filled up with guests and Blanche was kept busy circulating while Billy ensured everybody's glass was full. The music blared loudly through the house – everything from Human League's 'Don't You Want Me?' to David Bowie's 'China Girl'.

Shay and Darla stood in a corner, looking distinctly unhappy.

Blanche was slightly irked by Antony Barclay who was being a little too friendly with her during the night and kept trying to corner her. It was very obvious he had a thing for her. And she didn't know if it irritated her more that he had no regard for Billy, or that he didn't care how indiscreet he was being.

She made her way over to Shay and Darla.

"Hi, you two, I haven't had a chance to speak to you all night," she said.

"Yeah, too busy with your new hob-nob friends," snapped Darla.

"*He* seems to be your biggest fan," said Shay, nodding over at Antony.

"No man can resist our Blanche!" snapped Darla.

"If you're both going to be like that, I'll leave you to it," said Blanche. "It's New Year's Eve and I'm going to enjoy myself and you two can stand in the corner with chips on your shoulders if you want."

She walked off, glancing at her watch. It was a quarter to midnight and she decided to pop upstairs to the bathroom while she had a chance. She went up the stairs and down the corridor to their bedroom. The bedroom had cream carpet throughout and the furniture was all gold and cream. She took up another box of streamers and paper horns which she wanted to hand out to the guests before midnight.

She heard a sound behind her and swung around. Darla had come into the bedroom. Taking a swig from her Martini she said, "I was speaking to Samantha over the holidays."

Blanche looked at her. "Yeah?"

"I rang her in Cannes to wish her a happy Christmas and she told me that you were to replace me as the Face of Fortune." Darla didn't disguise her anger.

"Darla –"

"Don't Darla me! You manipulative little bitch. Pretending to be everyone's friend and working behind the scenes to get me sacked and get my job!"

"Darla, it's nothing like that. Darla, I promise you, I'm not taking the job with Fortune."

"Well, that's not what Samantha said."

"Samantha has been away. I haven't been able to talk to her to tell her I'm not taking that job. I wouldn't do that to a friend."

"We're not friends, Blanche. I wouldn't be friends with somebody who has been trying to undermine my job – and my relationship."

"What are you talking about?"

"Shay told me how you're always insinuating that I'm a drunk and have a bad reputation, and asking him what's he doing with me."

85

Blanche rubbed her face. "I wasn't trying to undermine your relationship, Darla. I was trying to point out to Shay that you might need some help."

"Yeah, right, your concern is touching. You just wanted to have Shay to yourself again. I know you fucked him."

Blanche's heart started beating faster. "That was before I knew he was seeing you."

"I don't believe you!"

"Look, Darla, you've had a few too many to drink. Let's go downstairs and join the party and talk about this tomorrow."

"Don't you dare try to condescend to me!" Darla's voice was venomous. "You take my job, you fuck my boyfriend, you play socialite and happy families with your perfect new man and you are just a silly, stupid little bitch who knows nothing!"

"Darla!"

"If you even knew how stupid you actually are! It makes me laugh how stupid you are! How you've been used and you don't even know it."

"Let's go downstairs, Darla –"

"Why do you think you were set up on that date with Eamonn McNamara?"

"What are you talking about?"

"Do you really think that Shay was just trying to play matchmaker?"

"I don't understand."

"No, you don't, you never do. Shay used you to get McNamara away from that security blanket he lives his life under."

"But why would he do that?" Blanche was bewildered.

"You still don't understand? Shay is one of them, you idiot. McNamara has been on their hit list for months, and you provided the opportunity to get him on his own, away from his security, away from his life. Away from where he should be and ought to be, so he would be an easy target for them to kidnap."

"What are you saying? That Shay is with the National Freedom Army? That's he's a terrorist? I don't believe you, Darla!"

"No? You were to be used with Wilbur Von Dieter as well. Shay tried to organise a date between you and Von Dieter the week before he was kidnapped. But you'd found Billy Boy by then, so he had to think of another plan to get Von Dieter where he wanted him to be so they could get him. You're a honey pot, Blanche, plain and simple. You've been used to lure men to their fates."

Blanche felt like throwing up.

She turned and left the room quickly, needing to get away from that woman and her obscene talk. She made her way downstairs to the crowd who were beginning to count in the New Year.

"*Ten . . . nine . . . eight . . .*" chanted the crowd as Blanche came quickly into the drawing room.

"There you are!" said Billy, grabbing her and holding her.

She held him back tight, trying to erase what she had just been told.

"*Five . . . four . . . three . . .*"

She looked over at the corner and saw Darla arriving back to Shay and whispering in his ear. A look of concern spread over his face.

"*Two . . . one . . . Happy New Year!*" shouted the crowd and the streamers started to shoot around the room and the paper horns were blown as they sang 'Auld Lang Syne'."

"I love you, Blanche," Billy whispered into her ear.

She continued to stare at Shay who was staring at her.

"Blanche?" said Billy.

"Yes, I love you too, Billy."

People were kissing and shaking hands.

"This is going to be *our* year," Billy whispered.

Shay came up to Blanche and stood before her, his eyes piercing.

"Happy New Year, Blanche," he said coolly. He leaned forward and enveloped her in a hug and she couldn't stop shivering.

The New Year's Eve party had gone on until the early hours. Blanche was unable to relax for the rest of the night as she thought about Darla's revelation. She tried to dismiss it as a drunken fool talking rubbish. But it kept coming back to her and ringing true. But Shay couldn't be capable of doing such a thing. Not her Shay. He couldn't have been using her all along. She was relieved when the crowd started to go home, more relieved when she saw Shay and Darla leave. Billy had had plenty to drink and went off to bed. She had sat amongst the leftovers of the party, trying to make sense of what Darla had said about Shay and about the role she had played in it, with a Roxy Music LP playing over and over on the record player. She kept putting the needle back on the track for 'The Party's Over' as she chain-smoked.

CHAPTER 14

New Year's Day was passed quietly enough. They cleaned up the house, went out for a stroll, had dinner and watched *Dr Zhivago* on television that night.

"You alright?" Billy whispered at her. "You seem a bit quiet today."

"I'm fine. Just tired after the party."

"Hmmm, back to work tomorrow," he sighed. "I've had the best Christmas for so long, Blanche. I'm so looking forward to our life together. Living here in this house, having children, bringing them up. I can't wait."

She smiled up at him and concentrated on the television.

The next morning Billy headed off to the office early. Blanche was glad of the time to herself so she could think about what to do. She sat at the kitchen table in her long satin dressing gown smoking a cigarette while she drank a coffee. Then the doorbell rang. She got up, made her way upstairs and through the hall to the front door. She got a start to see Shay standing there.

"Hi, Blanche," he said, smiling broadly.

"Shay! It's a bit early for you to call, isn't it?" She stared at him.

He eventually gave a little laugh. "Well, aren't you going to invite me in? It's fucking cold out here!"

"Sure, sorry, come on in."

He walked past her and she closed the door. She followed him into the drawing room. She tried to look relaxed but she knew she was failing.

"Great party the other night. Me and Darla really enjoyed it," he said.

"Did you? Good."

"I'm just here to discuss what Darla told you at the party."

She tightened her dressing gown around her and coughed.

"Told me?" she asked, trying to look confused.

"Don't try and bullshit me. She said she told you everything . . . She's a great girl, but you might be a little right about her. She's a fucking liability with drink on her."

"Well then, is it true?"

"What do you think?"

She studied his unsmiling face. "I think it is. There are too many coincidences otherwise. How could you use me like that, Shay?"

"It's nothing personal. It's about our cause."

"And what kind of a monster are you? Putting those men through that terror, and their families?"

"That's fairly tame – don't you read the newspapers?"

Blanche shivered.

"Anyway, now you know. The thing is, where do we go from here?"

"What do you mean?"

"Well, you're not one of us, and you happen to be living with a state solicitor. That puts us in a vulnerable position."

90

She forced herself to stop shivering.

"Having said that, you're not going to tell anybody what you know, because it would blow your life apart, wouldn't it?"

"How do you know I haven't already?"

"Because you're not stupid. You would be an accessory. You took McNamara out for dinner that night to entrap him."

"Don't be ridiculous, nobody would believe that."

"Why wouldn't they? The scandal alone would destroy you, and your family, and your boyfriend."

"You're a cold bastard."

"I can never expect somebody like you to understand what we're fighting for, so I'm not even going to try. But believe me, if you expose me, it's you who'll end up in prison, not me. And maybe Billy will too."

"What do you mean?"

"We'll finger him as an accessory as well. He was the one that told us that the Von Dieter family couldn't afford the million-pound ransom, and that's why we accepted the half million. In fact, Billy saved Von Dieter's other ear with giving us that information."

"This would never stand up."

"Do you want to risk it? That's all the worse-case scenarios. But there's another option. You keep your mouth shut, and nobody will ever find out about this and you can go on living your perfect life with Billy Boy."

"I never want to see you again, or speak to you, or have you in my home!"

"The feeling's mutual. But we just need to do another little bit of business with each other before we can part company."

"And what's that?"

"Your friend Antony Barclay. I want you to deliver him to us."

Blanche managed to laugh. "You're fucking insane if you think I'm going to do anything like that."

"The British government will pay good money to have Antony Barclay returned to them. If we can't get him, we'll get Billy Forrestal, not quite as important to the Irish government but worth a ransom all the same."

Blanche burst out crying. "Why are you doing this?"

"I told you, it's nothing personal. It's just a way for us to raise money to fund our cause."

"I hate you."

"I'm sure you do. I've seen the way Antony looks at you. I saw him hand you his phone number. I think he'll be delighted when you ring him and ask him to meet for a drink this week."

Blanche wiped the tears away from her face. "I'm not going to do this."

"Well, then we'll target Billy. And you know, you try and keep personal feelings out of this, but I don't particularly like Billy . . ." Shay lifted the receiver of the phone. "Come on, phone him. You're going to meet him in Danny Byrne's at two on Thursday. And now you need to listen carefully because you're going to follow my instructions to the book."

Blanche didn't change out of her dressing gown all day. How did she get herself into this situation? And, more importantly, how could she get out of it? She thought about just picking up the phone and calling the police and trying to explain everything. But she knew that what Shay was saying was correct. It would look like she was an accessory, it would destroy them all. But even beyond that, she mostly feared for Billy. She knew what they were capable of as she remembered all the news reports of the acts they had committed over the years. She really didn't have to do much. Shay had been very precise in his instructions.

She had phoned Antony and he had been surprised to hear from her.

"Antony . . . it's Blanche Fitzclarence here." She had forced her voice to remain calm – not easy with Shay standing beside her.

"Blanche! What a lovely surprise! How are you?" Antony had almost sung down the phone.

"Oh, you know, good – busy – you know how it is."

"Only too well!"

"I just . . . em . . . wondered if you'd like to meet up for that drink sometime?"

"I'd love to! What evening suits?"

"Em . . . it's a little difficult. I was hoping to meet in the afternoon?"

Antony paused for a second, realising that Blanche was hinting at more than just a social drink. Antony Barclay had had enough affairs with married women to understand the signs of when a wife or girlfriend was interested in him.

"Sure, Blanche, whatever suits you." His voice adopted a slightly more serious tone.

"Shall we say two o'clock, somewhere discreet, maybe that pub Davy Byrnes, do you know it?"

"I look forward to it," said Antony.

In reality Blanche had to do very little, Shay had assured her. Meet him for a couple of drinks, flirt with him, act all coy. Explain to him she was interested but had to be very careful and discreet. And then organise to meet him at a rendezvous at a discreet hotel on the Saturday night. That was where her part stopped. She really didn't have to do much at all. Just set up Antony Barclay away from his normal routine and security so Shay and his gang could easily grab him. McNamara and Von Dieter had been released in a few days. And this time the British government would pay up straight away. And then she could get on with her wonderful life with Billy, away from these awful people, and knowing that Billy was safe.

The front door opened.

"Hello!" Billy called.

She stubbed out her cigarette and went running into the hall. She threw her arms around him, holding him tightly.

"Hey! That's some welcome!" He hugged her back.

She pulled back and looked him in the face, her heart tearing at the thought of anything ever happening to him.

"Are you alright? You look pale," he said.

"No, I'm fine. Just tired, you know."

They walked into the drawing room, their arms around each other's waists.

CHAPTER 15

Blanche made sure to be in early to Davy Byrne's on the Thursday afternoon, so she could get a discreet corner. She ordered herself a glass of wine and went and sat down. Shay had met her that morning to go through all the details again, and also impart the same threat to her. He made her skin crawl. How could she not have seen through him before? How stupid and naïve she was!

Antony came in, looked around the pub and spotted her. He came over and smiled charmingly at her, then bent to kiss her cheek, lingering a bit longer than he had to.

"You look lovely," he said.

"Thank you," she smiled.

"Drink?"

"No. I have one." She pointed to the glass in front of her.

"So you have." He went to the bar and got himself a whiskey and, returning, sat near her.

She opened her cigarette box and took one. She offered him one, he declined, but took out his lighter and lit hers. She put her hand over his as he lit it, and in the most subtle way gently gave his hand a rub.

"I was very surprised to hear from you," he said, sitting back and observing her.

"I think I was a little surprised myself as well." She looked at him meaningfully.

"Surprised, but delighted," he said.

"How's work?" she asked casually.

"Tense. I'm just in the middle of these negotiations at the moment in Belfast. So we're kind of reaching make or break time."

"It must be very stressful for you."

"I'm used to it. I was stationed in Tel Aviv before this. I was always trying to broker a deal between the Israelis and the Arabs."

"It probably doesn't give you time for a wife or family?"

"Not really. Maybe one day." His eyes pierced through hers. "But the kind of life I have has taught me to take happiness where I can find it . . . with whom I can find it."

"I'm very happy with Billy," she whispered.

They continued to stare at each other for a long while, before he reached over and took her hand gently and held it. She put out her cigarette with her free hand.

"I need to be very discreet," she said. "We need to be very discreet – I can't let Billy even suspect."

"I understand." He nodded at her. "It wouldn't look good for me to be seen with the partner of one of our Irish colleagues either. What do you suggest?"

"There's a hotel called Kelly's – it's a bit out of the way in Stillorgan. Have you heard of it?"

"I'll find it. When?"

"Saturday night."

"Time?"

"Nine . . . just ask for me in reception."

Afterwards, she walked home through Stephen's Green. Shay appeared and was suddenly walking beside her.

"Well?" he asked.

"It's all arranged. As you said . . . nine o'clock Saturday at Kelly's Hotel."

"Good girl. It's been nice knowing you, Blanche. See you around."

She stared at him as he walked off.

Blanche was consumed with guilt over the next couple of days. On the Saturday she was tense all day.

Herself and Billy went out shopping, but she couldn't concentrate and they ended up going home with her complaining of a headache. He kept asking her if she was alright. She had barely eaten for the past couple of days and that evening Billy forced her to sit down and eat. She managed to eat some but mainly pushed the food around her plate as she looked out at the snow falling against the Georgian window as the sky darkened. She imagined Antony making his way to this sleazy hotel for a night of romance, when in fact he would be accosted and bundled into the back of a car in the car park and taken to some hideout for a few days. She wondered what condition he would be kept in.

"I bumped into Antony Barclay the other day in town," she suddenly blurted out.

"Yeah? How was he?"

"Good, asking for you . . . we ended up going for a drink together."

"Did you?" Billy glanced up from his food and smiled knowingly. "That would be Antony Barclay alright."

"What do you mean?"

"He has a reputation for being a real ladies' man. I bet he tried to flirt with you?"

"I – I didn't notice if he did."

Billy looked sceptical. "He was based out in the British Embassy in Tel Aviv for a long while."

"So he was saying. He said he was working on Arab-Israeli relations."

"Oh, he was doing that alright, and doing some great work there. Unfortunately he had to be transferred in the end because he was damaging Anglo-Israeli relations."

"I don't understand."

"He bedded far too many Israeli politicians' wives and caused far too many ructions."

"I see."

"He's a brilliant diplomat, if only he could just keep his trousers on! Still, he's about to deliver a major advancement in the North's peace process."

"Good for him."

"Good for everybody. I just hope he can pull it off."

"Well, why wouldn't he?"

"A lot of extremists want him out of the way."

Blanche put down her fork and looked at Billy. "Billy, I'm really worried about your safety."

"Huh?"

"That you might be a target for kidnappers or something."

He started laughing. "Who'd kidnap me? They only go after business tycoons. I haven't a penny."

"No, but with your job. They might target you because of your job."

"Why would they? Darling, I'm on the bottom rung of the ladder. I'm very junior. Working on things like social cases, nothing political. Nobody would be interested in me."

"But you're still working for the government. If they kidnapped you, they could demand a ransom from the government."

Billy sat back and roared with laughter. "Darling, you're letting all this media stuff about the kidnappings carry you away. The government wouldn't pay a penny if I was kidnapped. Why would they? I'm a junior state solicitor. I'm of no interest to anybody. Besides, western governments do not negotiate with terrorists. They do not pay ransoms, from a practical point of view. If they were stupid enough to pay one ransom, they would be targeted over and over again."

"Even the British government?"

"Especially the British and American governments. If they paid a ransom, or gave in to the demands for one civil servant or diplomat to be released, it would open the floodgates around the world for their personnel to be targeted."

Blanche stared at Billy in horror, a hundred thoughts running through her head. If Shay knew the British government wouldn't pay for Antony's release, then why target him?

She thought of what Billy had just said about Antony: *"A lot of extremists want him out of the way."*

Blanche suddenly jumped up.

"I've just remembered something!" she said.

"What?" Billy looked at her in confusion.

"Samantha! I was supposed to meet Samantha!"

"What – tonight?"

"I'd better run." She went into the hall, threw a coat around her, and grabbed her car keys.

"Blanche?" Billy came out after her, confused.

She opened the front door and raced down the steps to her car.

"*Blanche!*" Billy shouted after her, as she started the engine and drove the car out of the drive as the snow continued to fall.

Blanche sped towards Stillorgan.

"Please don't let me be too late! Please!" she said aloud over and over again. In Stillorgan, she stopped to ask a passer-by for directions to the hotel.

A red neon sign emerged in the distance and she realised as the hotel came into view that it really was out of the way and must be a spot for lovers to meet. She drove into the large mostly empty car park, except for three cars parked in a far corner. She looked around, trying to see Antony. Looking at her watch it had just turned nine. A Granada drove into the car park and she spotted Antony as the driver. Feeling relieved and terrified all at once, she quickly drove over to him and pulled up beside him. She opened her car window as he did the same.

"Well, hello – looks like we're both right on time," he said, smiling.

She stared at him for a few seconds and then said quickly, "Go home, Antony!"

He looked quizzical. "Sorry?"

"I said go home, Antony!" she said much louder.

The snow blew between their two cars.

"Blanche!" he said and he opened his car door and started to step out of the Granada.

"Don't!" she almost shouted. "Don't take another step out of that car. Go home if you know what's good for you!"

He stopped and studied her face. He wasn't sure what was going on, but he saw fear across her face and he had been in enough dangerous situations to realise when something wasn't right. And, as he took a quick look around at the deserted car park and the rundown hotel, this felt very wrong.

He slammed his door shut, turned the car around and sped off.

Blanche watched the car disappear from view, filled with relief.

She drove home as quickly as she could, but the snow was now falling heavily which made driving conditions hazardous. She couldn't even think of the consequences of her actions. But she knew she would now have to tell Billy everything and let him decide what to do. She dreaded telling him. She looked at her watch and saw it was nearly ten.

"Billy!" she called, taking off her coat.

She walked into the drawing room and put her coat on the couch. The lights were still on and so Billy couldn't have gone to bed. She was so tired she just wanted to go to sleep.

"Billy?" she called down the corridor to the kitchen.

She walked up the stairs. Maybe he had fallen asleep on the bed. She made her way down the landing to their bedroom. The light was on as she walked in. Billy was lying on the ground in a pool of blood. The blood had seeped and spread out over the thick-pile cream carpet. His face was a mess of cuts and bruises.

Blanche paced up and down the hospital corridor.

"If we can just go through this one more time, Miss Fitzclarence?" asked the Guard.

"I've already told you – I just arrived home and found him like that on the bedroom floor and rang the ambulance and the police." She ran her hands through her hair.

A detective came over to them. "It looks like the back-door lock was forced and they came in that way. It looks like a burglary that went wrong. When your boyfriend regains consciousness, hopefully he can explain what happened."

Blanche saw the doctor who was attending Billy walk down the corridor and she ran over to him. "Please, is there any news? Is he going to be okay?"

The doctor glanced over at the Guards before speaking. "He suffered a very severe beating. I imagine from the head injury he has sustained that he was hit from behind first. He's in a stable condition. It's going to take a long time for him to recover, but there's nothing life-threatening about his injuries."

Blanche felt herself go weak with relief. "Can I see him – please?"

"Only for a very short while."

Blanche sat on the chair beside Billy's bed, holding his hand tightly. He was conscious, every so often stirring.

"I'm sorry, Billy . . . I'm really sorry for this," she said and bit her lower lip hard. "I'm going to make it up to you, I promise."

His eyes opened slightly. "Blanche, I don't know what happened. Suddenly these thugs were in the house and started attacking me. It's so lucky you weren't there."

Blanche started crying. "Billy – it's all my fault."

"What are you talking about?"

And suddenly she was blurting out the whole story, everything about Shay and the date she went on with Eamonn McNamara and the blackmail.

"Why didn't you tell me?" he demanded, a look of disbelief and disgust on his face.

"I didn't want to get you mixed up in it all."

"So you went along with them instead?" His face twisted with contempt. "Get out, Blanche!"

"Billy!"

"*I said get out – I don't want to see you again!*" he shouted.

The detective drove her home and brought her into the house.

"I don't know if it's such a good idea you staying on your own in the house tonight. Can't I call your family or friends?"

How could she call her parents? What would they think of it and how could she put them through the worry? And she didn't want any friend's company. Friends. She had thought Shay was her best friend in the world, and look what that monster was capable of.

"No. I'm fine. I want to be on my own."

He looked at her curiously. "Well, the lock has been changed on the back door and just put on the burglar alarm straight away, okay? And phone me any time of the night if you're scared or anything, okay?"

"Thank you."

"You look exhausted, try and get some sleep."

"Thank you for everything." She smiled at his kindly comforting face.

After he left, she went into the sitting room, poured herself a strong whiskey and lit a cigarette. She was lost in thought for ages, wondering what was to become of her now. Billy looked so angry. They were finished, she knew that. And would he now report everything to the Guards? And what about Billy? How would he be affected, mentally and physically?

The phone blared through the house's silence.

"Hello?"

"You stupid bitch . . . you don't know what you're messing with," said Darla's voice down the phone.

"Look what you've done! Billy's in hospital because of you lot."

"I'm not one of them, Blanche, but I know what they're capable of and you have pissed them off big-time with your stupid stunt turning up and warning the diplomat like that."

"I'm not going to stand by and watch somebody be hurt." Blanche wasn't sure if her voice was quivering because of anger or fear. "They're just sick bastards to take revenge by doing that to Billy."

"Blanche, that's only the start of it . . . they expected you to be in the house tonight when they broke in, and it wouldn't have just been hospital you'd have ended up in. You have no idea how angry they are with you, and frightened that you're going to expose them . . . They're not willing to take that chance, Blanche. Listen to me, nobody would be able to protect you, not the police nor anybody. You need to get out of there – you need to run."

"Run where?"

"I don't know, I don't want to know in case they ever found out I knew."

"I'm not going anywhere. This is my life, I can't just leave it."

"You won't have a life if you don't run and you better go quick, Blanche, for your sake and Billy's. He might not be so lucky next time either . . . Now I have to go. We never had this conversation."

It was as if Blanche was operating on auto-pilot. Whether it was from lack of sleep or fear, she didn't know, but she didn't even have to think as she went upstairs, took out a suitcase and started packing clothes. As she packed, she ignored the smart selection of cocktail dresses and gowns in her wardrobe and opted for practical clothes instead. She sat at the kitchen table, nervously looking out the patio window as the morning light slowly started to filter through on the long back garden.

She wrapped her thick camel-coloured winter coat around her, carried her luggage outside and locked the door behind her.

She nervously glanced around as she hurried to her car.

At the hospital, she went and sat beside Billy's bed. He lay there staring at the ceiling, refusing to acknowledge her.

"Billy – I've just come to say goodbye. I'm leaving. I think it's best for us all."

He continued to concentrate on the ceiling.

"Billy?"

She nodded and got up and left.

She made her way to a garage where she sold the car, realising that Shay had ripped her off big-time with what he had said the car was worth. Then she went to her bank and took out most of the money. She was shocked how little there was there. She realised she had spent without thinking over the past few months. Money had never been an issue for her, so she never gave it much thought. She got a taxi to the port and went to the B&I terminal where she bought a ticket on the next ferry going to Liverpool.

She steadied herself as she picked up the phone again and dialled her parents' home.

"Yes?" Harriet answered.

"Mum, it's me."

"Blanche!"

"I'm just giving you a quick call to let you know that I'm off abroad for a while."

"And what about the love story of the century?"

"Me and Billy have split up."

"I knew that was only a matter of time!" Harriet's voice was laden with smugness. "But would you listen? You never do!"

"Anyway, I'm going to try the modelling scene abroad."

"What do you mean – abroad?"

"I don't know yet. London, Paris, New York. I haven't decided."

"Oh, save us, please! More twitty ideas to distract you from real life. I would have thought you would have learned your lesson with the whole Billy thing. Isn't it time you stopped living in the clouds and came back down to earth? London, Paris, New York – I've never heard anything so stupid. You'll never settle down, will you?"

"I have to go, Mum. My plane is boarding. I'll give you a call in a couple of weeks." Blanche hung up the phone.

Everybody started boarding the boat and she joined the queue. As she walked across the glass tunnel into the ferry, she felt as if her heart was breaking leaving Billy behind. And having screwed up her life. She put her suitcase into the luggage department and went to one of the lounges on the upper deck that had rows of leather seats. She found a seat by the window and from there she watched Dublin disappear from view. She managed to ignore the screaming children and loud chatter around her and drifted off to sleep for a long while. She awoke with a start, not recognising where she was, then rose from her seat and walked through the wide corridors of the boat, passing the bars and restaurants filled with people, the slot machines in the corridors where children were playing.

She slid one of the doors open and stepped out onto the deck. Most people were staying indoors due to the cold weather. Only a few hardy people strolled up and down the decks. There was a group of students gathered around one of the benches and they were playing the guitar and singing 'You're A Bad Dog, Baby'. She stopped and looked at them in their jeans and their long hair. They didn't seem that much younger than her and she envied them how carefree they seemed and how much older she felt than them. She went to the end of the boat and looked out at the expansive sea wondering what would happen next.

CHAPTER 16

2010

William walked into Blanche's office with a smartly dressed woman by his side. The woman was in her late thirties, wearing a sharp business suit and a smile that didn't carry to her eyes. She was slim and had short-cropped peroxide-blonde hair. Blanche stood up as they approached her desk.

"Blanche, this is Francine Hamer, the family-law lawyer who I'm recommending to take on the custody case for you."

Francine stretched out her hand and her smile became wider, but still did not carry to her eyes.

Blanche shook her hand and nodded at her before they all sat down.

"Thank you for meeting me, Mrs Launcelot. I've always been a big fan of yours," said Francine, who had a faint European accent.

Blanche nodded while continuing to scrutinise her.

"William has given me all the details of the case, Mrs Launcelot, and I would like to represent you, but I must warn you we are involved in an uphill battle."

"I can't see why. You've seen the grounds that I won

custody on – would you trust children to a parent like that?"

Francine glanced at William before answering. "No judge would grant children to a parent as that parent then was. However, the original judge did leave grounds for this case to be appealed and I believe he did that because he was aware the situation was temporary. He was aware at the time there were exceptional circumstances that had driven the parent over the edge . . . or at least to the edge. And they will be arguing this."

"That's very easy to say." There was a growing irritation in Blanche's voice.

Francine glanced again at William. "Now they have Lee Dwyer on the case, I imagine they'll put up a ferocious fight. They'll use doctors' reports, counsellors' reports, references –"

"Bah! That lot will say anything they are paid to!" Blanche waved her hand dismissively in the air.

"The court won't look at it that way, Mrs Launcelot. These are highly paid professionals whose opinion will be respected."

"And *you* are a highly paid professional who is being paid to make sure my grandchild stays safe with me!"

"Mrs Launcelot –" began Francine.

"*I am talking*!" Blanche all but shouted.

There was silence for a while as Francine went red.

"Blanche –" objected William.

"Shut up, William!"

William looked down at the floor and they all sat in silence for a while.

Blanche's voice was calmer when she resumed speaking. "Ms Hamer, I would like to employ you to represent me in this custody case . . . your credentials are excellent . . . But I'm in this to win. My grandchild's welfare is my main concern and I will do anything to make sure that continues as it is."

Francine stood up and stretched out her hand. "I'm looking forward to working with you, Mrs Launcelot."

Blanche shook her hand.

"Leave me a day or two with the file. I need to dissect every detail of it to examine our weaknesses and more importantly our strengths," Francine said and smiled at both of them before leaving the office.

Blanche lit up a cigarette and she and William sat in silence for a long while.

Eventually Blanche broke the silence. "Don't sulk, William, it doesn't suit you."

William looked at her angrily. "I don't appreciate being spoken to like that in front of people. Telling me to shut up. Don't take your troubles out on me."

"I apologise if I offended your sensibilities."

"And shouting at Francine Hamer like that. She is one of the top legal minds in this country and deserves a little more respect."

"Oh, pooh, William! Francine Hamer is out to make a quick buck like everyone else. She's a hardnosed bitch whose mettle will be tested much more by the end of this court case than just by me raising my voice. And she'll rise to the occasion."

"She's incredibly expensive."

"Good, that means she's incredibly good."

"As long as you can still afford to pay her when the bills start arriving in."

For a moment Blanche's face lost its confidence. "She'll be paid."

"Out of the family silver? Because if this company problem is not resolved soon, all capital will be frozen and you'll have no money to pay your secretaries let alone Francine Hamer."

"Everything will be resolved soon."

"How? How bloody how? Think about it, Blanche. No money to pay for anything. Everything compounded. This building, your staff, your luxury cars, those expense accounts. All because you won't compromise –"

"Do you really think that's what I live for?" she asked loudly. "Do you really think I couldn't survive if all this went tomorrow?"

He sat back and folded his arms. "No, I don't think you could. You are this empire you've built. What would you be without it?"

She got up and started pacing up and down in front of the wall of windows, dragging on her cigarette.

"I'd survive, William, I always have . . . You think you know me. You think the clothes, and the diamonds and limousines and country estates are all there's to me. There's so much more. I've had nothing before and I survived very well. I could do it again."

"You've never been poor." William was dismissive.

"Yes, I have. You see the model turned businesswoman. The papers leave out what happened in between. They leave it out because they don't know. Nobody does."

William looked at her for a long while. "Well, tell me then."

She leaned against the glass wall and studied him as the smoke snaked up into the air from her cigarette. "Do you really want to know?"

"Yes."

"Okay then," she said.

CHAPTER 17

1981

As they disembarked from the ferryboat in Liverpool, the snow had stopped falling but it was still bitterly cold. Blanche pulled her coat tighter around her and gripped her suitcase as she made her way through the crowd to a ticket office. There were rows of buses parked in the car park and all had different destinations on them.

She joined the queue at the ticket office and bought a one-way ticket for London. On the bus, people were grabbing seats as she made her way down the aisle. Finally she managed to find two seats unoccupied and sat in beside the window. A minute later an older woman sat beside her, making her feel claustrophobic. It was now evening and they would be travelling through the night to get to London. That was easier, she thought. Better to arrive in London in the morning; it would be easier to find accommodation. Finally the bus pulled out.

The landscape looked bleakly industrial under the darkening sky as the bus made its way along the motorway to London. She stared out at the passing giant electricity pylons and the tower blocks of distant cities.

She woke with a jolt as the bus came to a halt and there was an announcement over the intercom.

"We're stopping here for an hour," said the bus driver. "There a café here for refreshments."

It was three in the morning. She looked out the window and saw they were parked in a huge service station off the motorway with a Little Chef restaurant. She got off the bus with everybody else. She joined the queue at the long food counter and ordered a fry. After paying at the till, she took her tray and found a quiet corner of the café. She was starving and ate quickly. She then went to the bathroom and washed her face. Looking in the mirror, she spotted the dark circles under her eyes. Then she went for a walk in the cold night air in the car park. She stood looking out at the cars whizzing past on the motorway and the tears started to trickle down her face.

The early morning sun was shining by the time they hit London. Finally they reached Victoria Station and Blanche left the bus, collected her suitcase from the luggage compartment and headed into the giant station. The sheer volume of people struck her immediately as they all rushed about their daily business. She stood there, clutching her suitcase, feeling as if she wasn't really there, she felt so removed.

"Looking for a place to stay?" a voice said beside her.

She turned to see the speaker was a middle-aged Asian man.

"I have a place for you to stay," he said as he went to take her suitcase.

"No!" she said, filled with alarm, stepping back from him.

"You need a place to stay. Come with me." The man edged towards her.

"No, thank you!" she snapped again.

He went to reach for her suitcase again.

"I said no!" She raised her voice to a shout and walked away from him quickly.

She felt herself shivering and, when she was safely away, she turned and looked around to where she had been approached. She saw the same man now talking to a young girl who looked Scandinavian. The girl seemed naïve enough to talk to him and now he had possession of her suitcase. She was walking alongside him as he made his way from the station.

As Blanche looked around the bus depot, there seemed to be lots of young people who looked as lost and vulnerable as she probably did. They were easily spotted amongst the bustling crowds of people. She turned and hurried from the area.

She went to where the public telephones were and looked through a copy of the Yellow Pages. She was searching for hostels. She nearly laughed as she thought of how she frittered away money in Dublin. Now she knew the value of money, and was fully aware of how little she had. There seemed to be quite a few in Earls Court and she jotted down the addresses and telephone numbers, and then headed to the tube. She managed to negotiate the tube out to Earls Court and track one of the hostels down. It was in a large terraced building. On closer inspection, the white paint on the building was peeling and a lot of the net curtains on the windows looked dirty. She walked up the steps of The Happy Valley Hostel and up the stairs. Inside, the place was basic but comfortable. A small reception was down the corridor. Inside a lounge to the right, which had threadbare carpets and armchairs that had seen better days, a group of Spanish students were chattering away. A couple of young guys came down a winding staircase talking in strong Australian accents. And the brown-skinned middle-aged woman on reception had an unusual accent. The rooms were cheap and she had to pay each night in advance.

"Room 34, third floor, end of the landing," said the woman, handing over a door key.

Blanche took the key and made her way up the stairs. The whole place had a feel of the 1950s about it, and Blanche reckoned that was because that was the last time it had been done up. She got to the room and, putting the key into the lock, let herself in and closed the door behind her. The room was long and narrow with a single bed in the corner, an armchair and a free-standing wardrobe. There was a sink in the other corner. She unpacked her suitcase, hung up her clothes and sat down on the side of the bed, looking up at the ceiling that was stained from cigarette smoke. How had she gone from doing a job she loved, living with a man she loved, to this? She was sorely tempted to just go running home. But how could she? She was a fugitive. If she went back she was risking her life and everyone she loved. And if she tried to explain things to the police she would be arrested as an accomplice. She had no choice but to keep going.

Blanche remembered coming to London with her mother for an occasional shopping trip. She remembered visiting the beautiful stores and having teas at Fortnums. For the first few days in London she was drawn back to those areas as they were the only part of London she knew. But as she walked around them, and as she noticed the dwindling money in her purse, it only served to accentuate the difference between her and everyone else in those places. True for her mother, she was qualified to do absolutely nothing. Where could she look to get a job, when she had nothing to offer? By the seventh day, she realised she'd better get something soon and went into Selfridges. She asked for the personnel department and made her way there. She was told there were no vacancies, and to try again during the summer.

Another week went by and Blanche still hadn't managed to find work. She felt she had walked every street in London, from companies to see if she could get a job as a receptionist to restaurants asking for waiting jobs. All to no avail. Wearily one evening she climbed the steps up to The Happy Valley Hostel with a copy of the *Evening Standard* under her arm to spend the night looking for jobs.

The manageress with the unusual accent was behind the reception and she coughed loudly to get Blanche's attention.

"Are you staying here again tonight, dear?" she asked.

"Oh yes! Sorry, I meant to pay you this morning," Blanche apologised and went to the reception, taking out her purse and handing over the money. She then closed her purse quickly, not even wanting to look inside to see how much was left. She walked into the lounge area and sat in one of the old armchairs to search through the jobs pages.

After a while the manageress came in.

"Job-hunting?" she asked.

"Yep. Unfortunately there doesn't seem to be much out there at the moment."

"This recession is beginning to bite hard. So many out of work." The manageress shook her head in despair.

"I know."

The woman sat down beside her and opened her packet of cigarettes. Taking one, she offered Blanche one as well.

"Thank you." Blanche gratefully accepted the cigarette and lit it. Smoking was one luxury that had been cast aside since arriving in London. "Where are you from?" asked Blanche.

"Kenya . . . I always say as long as a girl can type or cook, she can get work."

"Unfortunately I can do neither," Blanche sighed.

"And you're running out of money quickly?"

Blanche smiled but said nothing.

"You know . . . I might be able to help you. You seem a nice girl – I'd like to."

"Really? Is there a job going here?"

"Not exactly . . . but I can put you in contact with somebody who can get you work . . . guaranteed work."

Blanche sat forward eagerly. "If you could I would be so grateful!"

"There's a lot of money to be made if you're not too fussy . . . a lot of girls find themselves in positions like you are, running short. They just do it for a short time . . . earn some extra money to get them by."

Blanche looked at her in confusion.

"You can even use your room here to start off with . . . I'd turn a blind eye . . . for a certain fee . . . And if my friends like you when they meet you, you can earn a lot more . . . meet them in nice hotels, make a lot of money."

Blanche stared at the woman as realisation dawned. Then she stubbed the cigarette out in the ashtray on the stained coffee table. She stood up and marched out. Upstairs, she locked the door behind her and put a chair against the door handle.

Next morning she came down the stairs and the

manageress was waiting at reception, a cold look on her face.

"Are you staying here tonight?" she demanded.

"Yes," said Blanche coldly, taking out her purse and offering the usual amount.

"That's not enough. My rates have gone up."

"Well, how much more?"

"Three times that amount."

"But that's ridiculous!"

"Pay up or get out!"

"But you can't just demand three times the usual rate."

The manageress leaned forward and said quietly, "Did you consider my offer?"

"Never," Blanche said.

"Then get out! And you'll find all the rates around here have just gone up – for you!"

CHAPTER 18

Blanche seemed to spend the day drifting through streets that all looked like each other, carrying her suitcase. She was so lost in her thoughts she didn't even know where she was heading. She felt degraded by that whole experience with the manageress. Had her life come to that? She would get out of this hole and never allow herself to be talked down to again. She would have money and respect and not have to stay in disgusting hovels like that. She would be safe and not frightened of people like Shay again. And she would never be stupid enough to get herself into a situation like this again.

As the day wore into the evening she realised she had better find a place to stay quickly if she didn't want to end up on the streets. She bought a newspaper and moved on wearily, looking for a café or pub where she could sit and search the paper for a place to stay.

She found herself in a rough area. There was a pub on the corner and she made her way into it. Inside, the pub was fairly packed and from the accents it was obviously an Irish pub. She went to the bar where a pretty barmaid seemed to be run off her feet.

"Yes?" she snapped.

"A gin and tonic, please," said Blanche.

The drink was nearly thrown at her.

She made her way to a quiet corner at the side of the bar where she managed to find a seat. It was wonderful to rest her tired feet and she surreptitiously kicked off her shoes under the table. With a sigh of relief, she picked up her glass and took a long drink.

A blonde middle-aged woman came down the stairs behind the bar with a huge glass of rosé wine in her hand.

"Katy, there's a customer wants serving down the end of the bar," she snapped at the barmaid in an Irish accent.

"Okay, I've only one pair of hands, Dolores!" the girl cried in desperation.

"Well, learn to use them a bit quicker then!" Dolores snapped back.

The crowd seemed very rough and were giving the girl a hard time, Blanche observed. Suddenly a fight started up and two men began to struggle with each other.

"Oy! Stop that!" yelled Dolores at the top of her voice.

The men ignored her and continued to fight. One threw the other over the bar and the barmaid screamed.

"Timmy!" Dolores shouted up the stairs and a big burly man came down.

In a matter of minutes he had caught the two men by the scruff of their necks and thrown them out. The other customers didn't seem too concerned.

"Right! That's it!" said the barmaid as she looked at all the broken glasses on the floor behind the bar. "I'm out of here!"

"You're not going anywhere, my girl! There's people need serving here," said Dolores.

"Well, you'll have to serve them your bloody self!" yelled

the girl and, grabbing her coat and handbag, stormed out of the pub.

"Fuck's sake!" Dolores snapped, abandoning her glass of rosé. "Right, who's next?"

Blanche thought hard for a few seconds and then she was on her feet and up at the bar.

"Excuse me, if there's a barmaid's job going, I'd like to apply," she said.

"Who the fuck are you?" demanded Dolores as she continued to pull a pint.

"My name's Blanche Fitzclarence and I need a job and you look as if you need help."

Dolores handed over the pint, then came back and stared at Blanche. "You don't look like you could handle this crowd one little bit!" she said, looking her up and down.

"Try me. Just for tonight."

"Well, what experience have you got?"

"Just get her behind the bar and get her serving us our drinks!" demanded a customer.

Dolores looked around her at the crowd. "Right, come on, and quick sharp."

Blanche quickly came behind the bar with her suitcase.

"What's this?" demanded Dolores, looking at the suitcase.

Blanche hesitated, not sure how she should reply.

"Oh, just chuck it back there and get to work."

Blanche had only ever worked behind a bar once before and that was at her father's golf club for an afternoon and for a laugh. However, she was a dab hand at mixing drinks at all the parties.

"Ahhh!" screamed Dolores when she saw her pulling a pint disastrously. "Leave the pints to me and you stick with serving the shorts!"

"Give me a fucking whiskey now!" demanded a customer.

"Okay!" Blanche was startled by his aggression and hurried to get his drink.

"I was here first!" objected another.

Blanche spotted Dolores observing her.

"I'm sorry, you're right," she said to the second man. "What can I get you?"

"A bottle of Harp."

"Don't you fucking dare serve him before me!" yelled customer number one.

Dolores's beady eyes were watching.

"I'm sorry, you'll have to wait your turn," said Blanche.

"Don't you fucking –" started the man.

"I said *wait your fucking turn*!" Blanche yelled at him.

The man, shocked, backed off and Blanche noticed Dolores smiling.

The evening passed in a relentless series of demands but at last the pub was empty and the doors barred.

"Clean up that shit, will you?" Dolores said to Blanche, indicating the broken glass on the floor from the fight earlier.

Blanche ran to get a brush and dustpan and got to work while Dolores cashed up the till.

"Fuck! This till is fucking miles out. I don't know how you've been operating it all night. But according to this print-out we took in £500,000!"

"Sorry! I'm not that experienced with that type of till."

"That's for sure!" Dolores grabbed her glass of rosé, walked over to a table and sat down. "Come over and join me."

Blanche put down the brush and nervously approached the table.

"Sit down, you're making me nervous!" Dolores snapped.

Blanche sat down quickly.

"There's your wages for the night!" Dolores tossed over some cash to Blanche.

"Thank you!" Blanche face was full of relief as she put the money into her purse. She had never appreciated money so much.

"So, where are you from and when did you arrive?"

"I'm from Dublin. I arrived about a week ago."

"I'm from Tipperary and I arrived about a hundred years ago," said Dolores.

Blanche smiled.

"So what do you want a job in a shithole like this for?" asked Dolores.

"Honestly? Because there's nothing else out there. I've tried everywhere and I can't get anything."

"And this is your last resort, is it? And here I was, thinking you were naturally drawn by our down-to-earth charm, I'm sure! You don't fit in here, one little bit. You'd be better off walking out that door and keeping on walking."

"I've nowhere to walk to."

Dolores studied her hard. "The job is yours. I'll give you proper training on the till tomorrow – and how to pull a decent pint. Our customers are bitter and desperate and I'm a bitch to work for, that's the negatives. Can't think of any positives." She took a gulp from her rosé. "And only I'm allowed to drink on the job."

"Thank you. I really appreciate this."

"Right, report back here to me at two tomorrow." Dolores stood up.

Blanche glanced at her watch and saw it was midnight. Her eyes went to the darkness outside.

"What's wrong?"

"I haven't arranged anywhere to stay for tonight."

"For fuck's sake! Alright, there's a spare bedroom upstairs and you can stay there tonight. A friend of mine runs a block of bed-sits down the road. I'll send you down to him tomorrow and you can rent a flat off him."

"Thank you," Blanche whispered.

Somebody being kind to her brought tears to her eyes.

"Oh please! I don't do emotion. Your room's the second on the right upstairs." Dolores took her glass of rosé and headed off behind the bar.

CHAPTER 19

Weeks seemed to drift by. Blanche rented a flat from Dolores' friend. It was basic enough, a little sitting room with a kitchenette off it, and a small bedroom. The landlord had recently done up the flats and had decked them out nicely. Unfortunately it still looked a bit cheap. But Blanche didn't care. She was just relieved to have a safe haven.

Dolores was right: she was a bitch to work for. But Blanche never forgot how she had literally saved her from the streets. And the customers *were* bitter. She took none of their nonsense, and would end up shouting at least a few times a night to keep control. In a funny kind of way she liked it there. Everyone there was lost and even though she didn't look or sound like them, she felt she fitted in because of that.

"Fucking bastard!" screamed Dolores, hanging up the phone one afternoon and coming out to the front of the bar.

"Problems?" asked Blanche.

"The fucking owner is on giving out shit that profits are down," explained Dolores.

"Owner? I kind of thought you owned the bar," said Blanche.

"No, I just run the fucking hole. The pub is owned by an Irish guy. He's a millionaire, owns about twenty pubs around North London, in all the Irish areas."

"He never comes in?"

"He lives on a big farm in Ireland. He used to come over all the time but now he's getting on a bit he sends his sons. Right little gobshites they are too! Well, actually the oldest one, Jack, is a bit of *craic*, but the younger lad, Troy, wants to be here less than we want him here. And he's sending him over next week on a reconnaissance mission to check up on all of us."

"That's bad news?"

"Well, I'd be more concerned if Jack was coming, he's fairly sharp. But Troy will just show up to keep his daddy happy. Still we'd better put on a good show for the little bastard."

Troy Launcelot arrived one afternoon in the following week.

Blanche was serving some young people who were all dressed up in frilly shirts, with their hair wildly combed. Both the girls and the guys wore make-up. They were part of the New Romantic movement – a crowd of them had started coming into the pub, attracted to the area because of the cheap rents.

"Freaks!" spat one of the old timers at them after Blanche had served them.

"You watch your manners and keep your opinions to yourself!" she warned him.

She turned around to see a man in his mid-twenties with sandy hair standing at the bar, dressed casually in jeans and an open-necked shirt and blazer. He smiled broadly at her.

"Hi," he said.

"Hello," she smiled back. "What can I get you?"

"Is Dolores about?"

"Sure is. Who will I say is looking for her?"

"I'm Troy Launcelot."

Blanche went to the back of the bar and called for Dolores. A minute later Dolores came tottering out in her high heels, glass of rosé in her hand. On seeing Troy she quickly put down the glass.

"Troy! How are you?" Dolores beamed a smile that looked obviously fake.

"I'm good. You?"

"Can't complain, and who'd care if I did?" said Dolores in a sing-song voice. "Come on through to the back, I've got the books out and we can take a look through the figures."

As Troy came behind the bar and headed out the back, Dolores whispered at Blanche, "Why didn't you tell me who it was, you stupid cow! Me tottering around with a glass of wine in the afternoon – he'll think I'm an alkie!"

"Sorry," said Blanche.

"Give me ten minutes and then go into the kitchen, make a plate of sandwiches and tea and bring it in."

Dolores headed into the office.

"Who's the doll?" asked Troy.

"Doll? Oh, you mean Blanche? I don't know, she arrived in here one night looking for a job and so I gave her a go. I didn't think she'd last the distance, not with our clientele. But they don't seem to bother her in the least. She's well able for them and works hard so she's still here. Still can't get to the bottom of her though. How's your father?"

"He's good. Sends his regards. Anyway, let's take a look at these books."

"I wish he'd fuck off!" Dolores whispered to Blanche behind the bar. "He's got another nineteen pubs to check on, so I don't know why he's been in and out of here all week."

"Uumm," Blanche casually agreed.

It was now Friday and Troy had been into the pub every day and a lot of the evenings. He'd sit at a table in the bar, looking through paperwork, or even come behind the bar and start helping out. Blanche found him very polite and amiable. He was driving Dolores mad.

"I can't relax with the little bastard around," explained Dolores, taking a long drink from the contents of a teacup she was holding.

Blanche saw that the teacup was filled with rosé wine.

"Anyway, I've put you on an early tomorrow, alright?" said Dolores.

"Eh, no, Dolores. You said I could have Saturday off if I worked Wednesday, remember? I've made plans."

"Well, cancel them," snapped Dolores.

"But this means I'll have worked ten days in a row!"

"Big fucking deal! I've worked thirty years on the trot!"

Dolores turned and walked off. Blanche started cleaning up the bar, almost throwing things around in her fury at being fooled by Dolores into giving up her day off.

"Everything alright?" Troy was leaning across the bar, looking concerned.

"Everything's fine!" Blanche snapped.

"I couldn't help but overhear . . . do you want me to have a word with Dolores for you? She's being unreasonable."

Blanche stopped throwing towels around and looked up at Troy angrily. "No! What do you want to do, get me the sack?"

"Well, you won't get sacked. Not if I have a word with her."

Blanche looked at him and alarm bells rang as she tried

to figure him out and the trouble he could cause for her with Dolores. "No! I really don't want you to get involved."

He put his hands up in the air. "Okay . . . sorry!" he said, before returning to his paperwork.

The next week came and Troy was still around most days.

"I'm going to end up in a psychiatric hospital if he doesn't fuck off back to Ireland soon!" muttered Dolores as she watched him serve a customer. "He's not even any good with the customers! His brother Jack would have them splitting their sides with laughter, but Troy . . . forget it!" Dolores raised her eyes to heaven, and headed up the stairs.

Blanche smiled to herself and went to serve a customer.

"Eh, Blanche . . . I wonder if you could do me a favour?" Troy asked.

"I'll try my best!"

"It's just that we're getting a few of them students in all dressed up like I don't know what."

"The New Romantics?"

"They're spending quite a bit of money, more than our usual lot. And I was going to put some music on the juke box that they'd like."

Blanche shrugged. "That's a good idea."

"It's just . . . I'm not that great on that kind of music and wondered could you give me some pointers on what to put on?"

"Oh! Yeah, I'd love to help," Blanche said as she spotted Dolores coming back into the bar and giving them a beady look. "Actually, on second thoughts, maybe that's not such a good idea. This is very much Dolores' patch and I don't want to be seen to do anything that might annoy her."

"Well, she wouldn't need to know! I wouldn't tell her you'd helped me. Please, you'd be doing me a big favour."

He broke out into a smile. "And saving me watching *Top of the Pops* to see what music is in!"

Blanche laughed. "Okay, as long as Dolores doesn't find out. I'll make a list and give it to you tomorrow."

"I'm meeting the juke-box people in the morning. Any chance I could get it from you tonight?"

"I'd have to look through my record collection to see what I'd recommend," said Blanche.

"I'll make you a nice cup of tea while you're doing it," Troy offered with a grin.

Blanche was on her knees in her flat looking through her records. She was surprised she had bought as many as she had.

"Definitely some Bowie."

"What about The Rolling Stones?" said Troy, who was sitting watching her.

"No, that's rock. Spandau Ballet maybe. Dexys Midnight Runners."

She sat down on the couch to write out a list. When she glanced up, he was looking at her. He smiled and looked away quickly.

"It's a nice flat," he commented.

"It's a bit of a shithole but I'm happy I have it!" she laughed.

"Dolores set it up for you?"

"Yeah, she was very good."

"She also gets a commission from your landlord for referrals."

"Why am I not surprised? That's the way of the world, isn't it?"

Troy shrugged. "I guess . . . What are you doing working there, living here?"

"What do you mean?"

"You stick out like a sore thumb. You're far too classy to be working in a place like that."

Blanche laughed cynically. "Being classy doesn't pay your rent. Working long shifts does."

"You're very intriguing," he said, smiling at her.

"Your list!" She smiled thinly as she handed it to him.

"Thanks," he said, glancing at the list. "I haven't heard of most of these!"

"Well, I'm sure your juke-box supplier will have," she said, looking at her watch and seeing it was nearly midnight. "Well, it's getting a bit late. I need to get to sleep."

"Oh, yeah. Sorry for keeping you up." He put down his cup and got up.

She got up to see him out. At the door he stood nervously for a while, prompting Blanche to say, "Well, see you tomorrow, no doubt."

"Eh, yeah . . . eh, Blanche, would you like to go out with me . . . for a drink, or dinner, or cinema or something? On your night off?"

She stared at him in surprise. "Eh, no thanks, Troy," she said decisively.

He looked mortified at the rejection and, opening the door, stepped out quickly.

"Well, see you tomorrow!" she said, closing the door.

CHAPTER 20

"May all the saints in heaven save us and protect us!" said Dolores loudly as she heard OMD's 'All I Needed' roaring from the juke box. "What kind of shite is that bellowing around my pub?"

"I think Troy was updating the juke box this morning," explained Blanche.

"With that shite? What's he trying to do – frighten my customers away?"

"Well, *they* seem to be enjoying it." Blanche nodded over at a bunch of students.

"Them fly-by-nights? They have as much loyalty to this place as a tinker! They'll be off to somewhere else next week and I'll have lost my regulars in the meantime. If that little bastard keeps on going on like this, I'm going to ring his daddy and tell him to get him out of here before he bankrupts us all! I need to go and have a lie down!" She stormed off. She gave Troy a dirty look as she passed him.

"Well, what do you think?" asked Troy.

Blanche laughed. "I love it, but I think Dolores is having a breakdown."

After all the customers had left that night, Blanche was clearing up the bar.

"Blanche, can I ask you something?" asked Troy who was lending a hand.

"Fire ahead."

"Why didn't you want to go out on a date with me? Is it just that you don't fancy me?"

She stopped putting chairs up on the tables. "Troy, to be honest, I never even gave you a passing thought in that way . . . but, the real reason is that I just don't want the hassle, thanks very much."

"But why would it be hassle?"

"Because, believe it or not, this is my life here. I find it hard to believe it myself but . . . You're just on holiday, and once you've had your fun with me you'll head back to that big estate you live on in Ireland and I'll be left with having my life disrupted over nothing."

"But I'm not like that."

"Maybe you're not, but I'm not willing to take that chance. Besides, you're my boss, and I don't want to complicate things here. I know where I am, and that's what I want. I work, I earn and I'm not beholden to anyone. And I want to keep it that way."

"You might be missing a great chance," he said, smiling. "We might be really good together." He paused. "Dolores thinks you're running away from something."

"Really?" Blanche looked at him, annoyed, and put her hands on her hips. "And Dolores says you're a spoilt daddy's boy, who's not a patch on your older brother."

Troy's face dropped with shock and hurt.

"Troy . . . I didn't mean to say that . . . I'm sorry!" Blanche was angry with herself.

But not as angry as Troy looked as he grabbed his coat and stormed out of the pub.

"Troy!" she called after him.

"Looks like Troy isn't going to show up today. Thankfully! If I had to see his sorry face moping around here for one more day, I'd have vomited! His one contribution was leaving us with that crap he's put on the juke box."

"Don't be so dismissive of him, Dolores!" snapped Blanche. "He was always eager to help out around here."

"Fuck him! Good riddance to bad shit, that's what I say."

"You know, you can be a real bitch sometimes," Blanche accused.

"No! You're kidding me? I never knew . . . I'm sure!" Dolores sauntered off, poured herself a large glass of rosé and went chatting to a customer.

Troy didn't show up the next day, or the day after that, or all the rest of that week. Blanche tried to put him out of her mind. She knew she must have hit a raw nerve with him and she could tell by his reaction that he was deeply insulted. But so what? By the Saturday though, she felt she needed to apologise and sort it out. She crept into the office and looked Troy up under L in Dolores' address book.

There were two addresses for Launcelot, a house in Kensington and a place called Winterfield in Ireland. She jotted down the Kensington address and tucked it into her pocket.

That evening as she walked through the Kensington

streets, she knew she might be making a wasted journey. He might be working in one of the other pubs. As she walked up the elegant street of white stucco townhouses, she realised that the Launcelots might make their money in poor areas, but their own lifestyle was very removed from that of their clients. She noticed the classy young couples of the area who had been nicknamed Sloane Rangers by the press.

She stopped at the address, walked up the four steps to the front door and rang the doorbell. A few seconds later Troy answered.

"Hi . . . you're a surprise!" he said, looking confused.

"I sneaked into Dolores's address book to find where you live," she explained.

"Oh? Well, come on in!"

She walked into the entrance hall.

"Can I take your coat?"

She handed it to him and he hung it on a coat-stand. She followed him through to the lounge on the right and sat down on one of the big plush couches. The furniture was modern and expensive.

"It's a lovely house," she complimented.

"Isn't it? Dad bought it years ago for his base in London. He used to spend a lot of time here . . . now it just gets used if any of us are over here. Drink?"

"I'll have a glass of red wine . . . if you've got any?"

"Of course." He went over to the well-stocked drinks cabinet and fixed them both a drink.

"Thanks," said Blanche as she accepted her drink. "It makes a nice change to be served a drink for a change."

He sat down opposite her and looked at her expectantly. She took a deep breath. "Troy, I really just came by to apologise for that ignorant remark I made the other night. I didn't mean to offend."

He sighed. "That's alright . . . it's not like I've never heard it before. Just a bit annoying when even somebody like Dolores who barely knows me is saying it."

"Don't mind Dolores. She's fine and everything, but she says the first thing that comes into her mind. You've been great around the pub. The music is going down a treat with the clientele."

"Not with the old war soldiers sitting at the bar all day?"

"Well, besides them, I grant you."

They both laughed.

She looked around the room again. "You're lucky to be staying in such a beautiful place."

"Do you think so? I hate it. Well, not the house, but I hate London. It's so big and impersonal, and I don't know anyone here, except for the bar managers who are all suspicious of me with their guards up."

"Well, you are their boss."

"Don't you hate it?"

"London? No. You're right, it's big and impersonal, but I guess I need that right now. But why come near the place if you dislike it so much?"

"Because I have to. My father makes me come over, to show an interest in the business."

"Well, why don't you just say no?"

"Because my mother would kill me if I gave up on the business."

"I suppose I can sympathise with you. My mother has tried to – direct – my life as well." She started laughing. "But I've always just ignored her and pleased myself!"

"Well, I think I'm going to start doing that from now

on. The idea of coming back here again . . . I'm happy at home – not over here – with those grubby pubs."

Blanche started laughing. "From what I hear those grubby pubs have made your family a fortune!"

"You know what I mean."

"Well, I've always thought people should please themselves, as long as they're not hurting anybody else."

He looked at her. "Have you eaten? There's an Italian down the road if you're interested?"

"No . . . I don't think so. I just wanted to apologise and be on my way."

"Look, it's not a date, it's just dinner!"

"Look, you're good company and I like you, but I think I'd better not. I don't want to blur those lines."

"Is it something about me?"

"No! Whoever asked me out at the moment, I'd just say no. Look, a year ago I'd have said yes to anyone. But I've learned a lot since then. I just need some time to myself, so I'll take a rain check."

"It just seems a bit silly. There's you spending all your time in that pub, and here's me spending all my time in this house, when we could be keeping each other company."

She studied him for a while. "Alright then. But I'm paying."

"Don't be stupid!"

"Either I'm paying or I don't go."

"Why are you insisting on paying?" questioned Troy as he chomped into a slice of pizza.

"Because money has never been important to me. I never bothered even thinking about it. It came, it went. I didn't mind borrowing money off strangers for deposits for cars.

But you're beholden to people then, aren't you? But it's only when you run out of money that you realise that you're not just beholden to people, you're at their mercy."

"So am I now beholden to you, because you're buying dinner?"

She laughed. "Maybe."

After, he walked her to South Kensington tube station.

"Well, thanks for coming out to dinner with me," said Troy.

"You're welcome."

"Hopefully see you soon?"

"See you." She turned and walked into the tube station.

CHAPTER 21

The students had put Visage's 'Fade To Grey' on the juke box and it was now blaring around the pub.

"Whatever about fading to grey, my hair is going to turn pure grey if those fucking students put that song on one more time!" said Dolores as she sipped her glass of rosé.

"Oh, come on, Dolores!" said Blanche. "It's livening the place up."

"Oh and that's all I need! Bloody Huckleberry Finn back to torment me!" She threw her full glass of wine down the sink as Troy came in and walked up to the bar.

"Troy! I thought you'd gone back to Ireland," said Dolores with a huge big false smile.

"No. I'm going to be here for another while yet."

"Wonderful . . . I'm sure!" Her smile faltered and she tottered off to the back office.

Blanche couldn't help laughing. "She's going demented over the music you've put on the box."

Troy laughed with her. "You need any help back there?"

"Could always do with another pair of hands."

"I was hoping you'd say that," he said, coming behind the bar.

"I'll walk you home," he suggested as they left the pub after close-up that night.

"There's really no need," she objected.

"This is a very rough area. I think there's every need. You've no choice. I'll just follow you if you won't let me walk alongside you," he threatened.

"I manage to walk quite safely on my own every night, thank you."

He looked disappointed and then she said, "Oh, alright then. Come on."

"How long more are you going to be over here anyway?" she asked as they set out.

"We're in April now. I don't know, another couple of months should satisfy the family."

"And then you can get back to the estate?"

"The farm, yeah."

They got to the front of her building and he hovered there. She pictured him going back to his lonely beautiful house.

"Come on up for a drink," she said with a sigh and he followed her smiling.

She opened a bottle of wine and poured it into two mugs.

She sat down on the sofa and he on the armchair opposite her.

"You know, you really need to make more of your time in London. With your money you could really enjoy the city and make friends."

"I'll leave that to my brother Jack. When he's over here he tears the arse out of the place. He thinks he's James

Bond heading off to casinos and having parties back at the house."

Blanche felt that Jack cast a long shadow over Troy's life. He seemed a larger-than-life character who Troy seemed in awe of.

"How much older is Jack than you?"

"I'm twenty-five and he's twenty-nine. He's actually only my half-brother."

"Oh?" Blanche was curious and surprised.

"My father was married before."

"I see . . . now you're the one that's being intriguing."

"It's quite straightforward actually. My father's first wife died when Jack was barely a year old. My father then went on to marry my mother Lauren . . . then I came along. But my mum raised Jack as her own and we're all treated the same."

"And what about Winterfield, this estate? What's that like?"

Troy's face lit up. "It's the most beautiful place, Blanche. It's stunning. On the coast. My father grew up near there. He came to London to make his money after the war through the pubs and the dance halls. Winterfield was an old Protestant estate that had fallen into complete disrepair. My dad bought it and restored it."

When at last he was leaving, he turned and hesitated.

"Look, I'm feeling a bit compromised," he said.

"Really? How?"

"It's just what you were saying before about being beholden to people . . . well, I feel very beholden to you, because I haven't bought you dinner back."

She laughed. "You're not beholden to me in the least! Forget about it."

"No, I really insist. Next Saturday. I'm taking you out

to dinner. A nice little spot on the King's Road. I'm not taking no for an answer."

Blanche was glad she'd bought a new dress as she sat in the restaurant looking around at the grandeur of the place.

"What's wrong?" Troy asked.

"Nothing," she said, looking down at her menu and trying to concentrate. The waiter came and took their order.

"You look as if you fit in here," Troy said. "You fit in here much more than at the pub. What were you thinking about just then, staring dreamily around the place?"

"Nothing much."

"I wish you'd open up to me a bit."

"This was the kind of place I was used to back home. But I took them for granted. I took my life for granted."

"So why don't you just go back to it?"

"I'm not in the same situation as you. You can just happily go back and take up where you left off. I can't."

Troy stared at her. "Why can't you?" His expression clouded over. "It's a man, isn't it?"

She nodded. "In a way, yes . . . Did you ever meet the person you thought you'd spend the rest of your life with? Thought that everything was planned for the rest of your life, and then it all just fell apart? It's just taking me a while to get over it. I used to be a model back in Ireland and when my relationship ended, I just needed to get away — that's how I ended up working in your pub."

He stared at her. "I'm jealous of him . . . that you think so much of him . . . I wish I'd met you before you met him."

She studied him. "You seem a very straightforward nice guy, Troy . . . and you're just lonely in London and think you have feelings for me. Trust me, as soon as you get back to Ireland, you won't give me a second thought."

"I wish you'd give us a chance . . . What's the worse that could happen?"

"I just don't think you'd find happiness with me, Troy. I'm in love with somebody else and I'll never have those feelings for you."

"Is there a chance you'll get back with him?"

"No."

"So what are you going to do? Wait around like Mrs Haversham for the rest of your life?"

"I like how uncomplicated things are right now."

"But what about your future? You can't live in that flat forever, work in a pub forever?"

"Why not? Dolores has done it, and she looks very happy to me."

"Dolores knows no better. You do."

"And you're the answer to all my dreams, are you?" She lit up a cigarette and smirked at him.

He looked down at the tablecloth. "Don't mock me."

"I'm sorry. I'm not. I just want you to be aware of what you're getting involved in."

"And are we getting involved?"

She didn't answer.

CHAPTER 22

Blanche enjoyed being with Troy. He was easygoing, funny, and nice to a fault.

But she never really let her guard down fully with him. She was sure nothing would come of it. He would go back to Ireland and forget her. And those feelings she had for Billy just would not go away. And once she had experienced those feelings, what she felt for Troy was pale in comparison.

Much to Dolores' frustration, he still spent a good bit of time at the pub.

"I think you better go and check on your other pubs," suggested Blanche. "I've got Dolores's sanity to think of. She doesn't like you hanging around!"

"Shucks, how will I ever recover?" laughed Troy.

"Out!" Blanche snapped with a smile.

"Troy! Phone call! It's your father!" Dolores hollered from the back.

"Better take this before I go," he said.

Blanche shook her head, put empty bottles into a crate and then carried it out the back. As she stacked the crate with the others, she heard Troy speaking on the phone.

144

"Okay, Dad, will do . . . I'm not sure, I'll check it out for you. Okay, I'll talk to you later . . . Hi, Mum, yes, everything's fine . . . No, I haven't had chance to phone her . . . Well, I'm sorry but I've been pretty busy here keeping an eye on everything . . . Okay, apologise for Rosalind for me and give her my love and tell her I'll call her over the next couple of days. Okay, love you too, talk later, bye."

Troy put down the receiver and looked up to see Blanche there leaning against the door smoking a cigarette.

"My folks! They drive me mad! Have you done this and have you done that . . . They treat me like a five-year-old."

"People act as you allow them to," said Blanche. "Who's Rosalind?"

"Rosalind?"

"Yeah, the woman you're sending your love to?"

"Rosalind is our neighbour. She lives in the next farm to us. She's been like a sister to us. She grew up with us, always over in our house, so she's like one of us . . . one of the family."

"Cosy."

"Um, I guess!"

"Call her."

"Sorry?"

"She's obviously giving out that you haven't called her, so call her now."

"But she's probably at work, she works at a local newspaper."

"Well, you can try calling her, can't you?" Blanche smiled at him.

"If that's what you want." He took out his phone book and looked through the numbers and dialled.

"Oh, Rosalind? Hi, it's Troy . . . Yes, I know . . . Yes, I'm sorry . . . How've you been? . . . Been over to Winterfield much? . . . Nothing new there then!" Troy looked up at Blanche and smiled.

She quickly returned his smile, and left the room.

Just checking, thought Blanche. She would never be made a fool of again.

The weeks seemed to go by quickly. She knew Troy was falling in love with her. She also knew he would get a call from home one day to say his stint in London was up and he'd head back to this magical place called Winterfield that he never shut up about, and that was the last she would see of him. She didn't love him, but she was very fond of him.

They went out to dinner in the West End and headed on to a club afterwards. It was now the beginning of June. She sat at a table listening to him going on about Winterfield. She felt she knew the place intimately, he described it so well.

Blanche's mind drifted off while Roxy Music's 'Jealous Guy' was playing.

"Blanche? Blanche?"

"Sorry, Troy, what's that?"

"You weren't listening to a word I was saying, were you?"

"I'm sorry."

"I wish I could force *him* out of your mind!" Troy looked angry. "What's so special about him that you can't forget him? That everything I do doesn't impress you. If you love him so much then why don't you just go fucking back to him?" Troy got up from the table and marched away.

Blanche got up quickly and raced through the dance floor to catch him, grabbed his arm and swung him around.

"I'm sorry I'm like this, Troy! I can't help it! I can't switch my emotions off and on, much as I'd love to. If I can't reciprocate what you're feeling, then maybe we shouldn't see each other any more."

He grabbed her, pulled her close and kissed her.

They walked back to the house in Kensington.

"I'd better get a taxi home," she said.

"Don't go back there, Blanche. There's supposed to be a riot around there tonight."

It was true there had been a lot of social unrest in the area. And it was just one area of many that were flaring up around Britain from Toxteth to Brixton, protesting against social deprivation and Thatcher's Britain. It was strange because these riots seemed to be in direct contrast to the royal wedding that was fast approaching. As she looked around Troy's street, she saw this was the other side of Britain, the wealthy secure side that seemed a million miles away from those riots.

"I heard a lot of taxi drivers won't even go there this weekend."

She looked at him and smiled crookedly. "Is this your way of asking me to stay?"

"Er . . ." He looked guilty and uncomfortable.

"Come on." She reached up and kissed him and they went into the house.

CHAPTER 23

"Those fucking bastards!" screamed Dolores. She was inside the pub with a brush in her hand sweeping up the broken glass. The whole area had erupted in a riot the previous night and all the windows of the pubs had been smashed.

"Are you alright?" asked Blanche, full of concern.

"Well, I am now. But you should have seen me last night at around three in the morning! I was hiding under the bed with my bottle of rosé praying that I'd see the morning light. The screaming and shouting and noise! What about you? Did you hear much down your way?"

"I . . . eh . . ." Blanche had spent much of the weekend over at Troy's.

Dolores studied her. She had been guessing what had been going on.

"I'd be careful of them, Blanche. The Launcelots. They're not exactly the nicest family you could meet, get my meaning? They're rough and coarse and ruthless. I don't think you'd like their ways. Troy's about the best of them. In fact, girl, they'd eat you up and spit you out."

"Dolores, I'll never meet that family, I can assure you. Troy's due to go home soon and that's the end of that."

Dolores shut the pub early that night as there was a police warning that there would be a very big riot.

At midnight Blanche was sitting on her couch with her legs pulled up and her arms tightly around her knees as she listened to the rioting going on outside. She could hear screaming and shouting. She got up and glanced out the window. People had constructed barricades and were throwing things at the police. Further down the street there was a fire burning and police were fighting with rioters. The whole neighbourhood seemed to have erupted in violence. She dashed back to the couch and huddled on it again.

There was a sudden buzz from the intercom. She ignored it. But it kept buzzing.

"Blanche . . . Blanche!" she suddenly heard from the street.

In confusion she jumped up and went to the window. Troy was down at the front door. She quickly buzzed him in and opened her door.

Troy came racing up the stairs.

"What the fuck are you doing out in that, you maniac?" she shouted at him as he came in. She slammed the door and locked it.

He held her tightly. "I was worried about you – the riot is all in the news."

"Such a stupid thing to do, coming through that war – anything could have happened to you!"

"I just wanted to make sure you're alright."

"Oh Troy! Don't ever do something so stupid again!"

He led her over to the couch and sat down, holding her hands tightly.

"Blanche. . . I'm going back to Ireland . . . on Friday. I

149

really must go – I've been away too long. They need me on the farm for the summer."

"Oh!" She felt sad at hearing the news she had been waiting for. "Well, keep in touch."

"Come with me, Blanche," he said quickly.

"What?" She started laughing.

"Come back to Winterfield with me. Away from this kip and this life. You weren't meant for here, you were meant for much better things."

"And what would I do in Winterfield?" she laughed again.

"Don't you understand? I'm asking you to marry me."

"Don't be daft, Troy . . . I can't marry you."

"But why not?"

"Because I don't love you. You know that my feelings for you aren't right."

"But my feelings for you are right. And we'd have a great life together."

"This is ridiculous, Troy. I'm not going to marry you."

"And what are you going to do for the rest of your life then? Live here?"

"I'll move on eventually. I'm just getting my bearings, that's all."

"I'm offering you a great life, Blanche. Marry me. I'm just asking that you give me a chance. Give us a chance."

She stared at the honesty in his face.

"I can't imagine my life without you!"

"I'm sorry, Troy, I can't marry you. The feelings just aren't right."

They stared at each other for a while and then he fell into her arms and she comforted him as she smoothed his hair.

Troy left the flat the next morning asking her one last time to reconsider, but she gave him the same answer.

She thought about Troy for the whole morning. How nice and wonderful life would be with him. She seemed to make him happy and he would do everything to make her happy. They could have a lovely life together. But her feelings for him didn't come near to how she felt about Billy. And that made her realise she needed to speak to Billy, to see him again.

Outside, she was shocked to see the condition of the streets. There was debris all over the place. Windows broken, shops looted. The telephone box on her street had been vandalised, and the one in the next street and the one after that. Finally she found one that was working. Her heart was beating as she picked up the phone and her hand was shaking. She would just phone Billy and say hello and let the conversation be natural after that. She steadied herself, put some coins into the phone and dialled. She waited and finally it was picked up.

"Hello?" said a woman's voice on the other end.

Blanche was surprised and said nothing.

"Hello?" said the woman again.

"Oh hello, is Billy there, please?" asked Blanche.

"Billy? Oh you mean Billy Forrestal? He's not, I'm afraid. We've applied for a new phone line, but you know how it is, it can take months, so he kindly let us keep his phone line."

"He's not living there any more? Has he sold the house?"

"No. We're renting it from him. He's moved out."

"I see. Do you know where's he's living now?"

"I believe he's gone to Australia."

"I see!" Blanche was stunned. "For how long?"

"Quite a while, I imagine. We've signed a two-year lease for the house. Himself and his girlfriend headed off together."

151

"His girlfriend?"

"Yes . . . Are you a friend of his?"

"Yes, a friend."

Blanche hovered for a second and then hung up. She came out of the phone box and walked slowly down the street, feeling numb. Who was the girl? Why had they gone to Australia? Had he been able to get over her so quickly? He must really hate her. She could hardly think straight as she crossed the road. A car beeped at her and she quickly avoided it. She looked around, trying to concentrate on where she was going. And suddenly there was a face she recognised staring at her from across the street. She stood still, staring at Shay. He was staring back at her and looked as shocked to see her as she felt. Once she got over the shock, she felt terrified and started to shake. Shay suddenly moved and started to walk across the street. Frantically she looked up and down. A taxi was approaching and she nearly threw herself in front of it.

"Oy!" shouted the taxi driver.

She jumped in the back. "Kensington, quickly, please hurry!"

"Where in Kensington?" began the taxi driver.

"*Just go!*" she shouted, seeing Shay reaching out to open the door nearest to her. She quickly snapped the lock, stopping him from opening it. She saw his determined face through the window as he tried to open the door. The taxi pulled off, leaving him there.

The black cab made its way quickly through the London streets. Blanche sat in the back, willing her heart to stop beating so fast. She rubbed her face and ran her fingers through her hair. Billy was gone; she couldn't waste any more time thinking about him. And she was in danger. She couldn't go back to that area now that Shay had seen her there. She needed to get out. She wanted a nice life with a nice person. She was sick of poverty and long hours in grubby pubs, and crime and riots. She wanted to be safe and she wanted to be loved.

She climbed out of the taxi, paid the driver and ran to Troy's door and knocked on it loudly. Troy opened a minute later, surprise written all over his face.

She rushed in and he closed the door behind him. She saw his packed cases in the hall.

"Blanche?"

She turned to him. "I want to go with you, Troy, if you still want me?"

"What?" His face twisted in confusion.

"Go to Winterfield with you. Leave with you tomorrow on that flight . . . if you want me to go, I'll go."

"Blanche!" He stumbled towards her, smiling. "Are you sure?"

"I've never been surer of anything in my life!"

He enveloped her in a hug and squeezed her tight. "And get married and stuff?"

"Yes, if you still want to?"

"Of course I do!"

She relaxed into his arms and hugged him back.

Part 2

CHAPTER 24

2010

The tall well-groomed man bounded up the steps of the Shelbourne Hotel and made his way through the swivel doors.

"Good afternoon, Mr Launcelot," said the concierge with a big smile.

"Nice one too, isn't it?" The man returned a smile and made his way into the luxurious lounge area on the right.

Lee Dwyer was sitting in the far corner of the lounge. He had purposely selected a discreet corner with no other table too close so he could speak to Launcelot in private. Lee spotted him as soon as he entered the lounge. A tall good-looking man, in his mid-fifties, with a fine head of hair that was turning grey. He was casually dressed in jeans, a white shirt and a blazer. As he made his way through the lounge, people at different tables were greeting him and calling him over. Launcelot seemed to have an easy charm and had a smile and a few words for each of them.

Launcelot then looked around, scanning the lounge.

Lee stood up and waved at him, and he came bounding over to him.

"Lee?"

"Yes, Mr Launcelot, thank you for meeting me. I do appreciate it." Lee shook his hand firmly.

Both men sat down.

"Well, to be honest, I wasn't that sure whether to meet you or not. This is a pretty tricky situation you're dealing with."

"I know that. And that's why I thought it was so important to meet you."

"Whiskey and Coke, your usual?" asked a waitress.

"Atta girl!" He smiled at her.

"Well, I guess you know why I wanted to meet you. The forthcoming custody case concerning your grandson." He observed that Launcelot looked immediately uncomfortable. "You didn't get involved in the first custody battle?" He already knew the answer.

"No, I didn't. And to be honest, I don't think I'm going to get involved in this one either."

"Can I ask why?"

"Where do you want me to start?" The waitress placed the whiskey and Coke in front of him and he picked it up and took a drink. "Firstly, I don't know who's right or who's wrong on this. I mean, in the first case, the child's safety is the most important issue."

"We're not disputing that." Lee reached into his briefcase and laid a file on the table. "As you will see from this file, we're accepting that there were problems in the past. But things have changed since then. Blanche knows that and is refusing to accept it. She just doesn't know when to stop."

"Yep, that sounds like Blanche alright. She never did know when to stop!"

"She won't compromise, she won't negotiate."

157

"Well, you know, Blanche has got many faults, I should know. But her judgement is always proven to be right."

"Well, not in this case . . . If we could get you on our side, it could really help us to win this."

"Me and Blanche have been through enough wars over the years and, to be honest, I don't want to enter any further battles with her. This family doesn't need any more battles."

Lee observed him. "Are you afraid of her?"

He sighed loudly. "I'm not afraid of her. I'm frightened of what this court case will do to her, to us all . . . You know, in spite of everything, I owe a lot to Blanche. We all do."

"So you won't get involved and help my client?"

"I'm not saying that at all."

Lee sighed. "I'm going to leave you this file to read . . . There's a personal letter inside it appealing for your help from my client . . . Thank you for meeting me, Mr Launcelot."

Lee got up, reached for his briefcase, nodded and walked away.

The waitress appeared. "Another drink, Mr Launcelot?" she asked, smiling.

"Eh, no thanks, darling. I'm okay for now." He stared down at the file.

She turned and went away, leaving him lost in his thoughts that were drifting back through the years.

CHAPTER 25

1981

It was a blazing hot day as the sun shone down on Winterfield House. The estate's main house was a Georgian mansion built in a location that was considered the most beautiful part of the farm – near the small cliffs above the seashore, the back of the house offering spectacular views out to the sea. A long tarred driveway led to the front of the house.

That afternoon Troy's father, Niall, was sitting with Rosalind Dawson on sun loungers near the swimming pool at the back of the house. The back garden was beautifully landscaped with a large patio overlooking it. At the end of the garden a wall had been built along the cliffs' edge and below that was the sea crashing against the rocks at their base.

Niall was sixty-seven, a powerfully built man in his youth who still had a strong frame. Rosalind was an incredibly pretty girl of twenty-four. She had long blonde hair, a curvaceous figure and mischievous blue eyes that matched an equally mischievous smile that seemed to be permanently on her lips.

Niall's eyes were fixed firmly on the sun's rays twinkling off the blue sea beyond the garden wall. Rosalind was working on her tan.

"I think you're very mean sending poor Troy off to London these past few months. You know he doesn't enjoy being over there," said Rosalind.

"Pity about him. Hard life, living in a beautiful house, London at his feet, and all he has to do is check in on the pubs and pretend to be busy. Which I hear he hasn't even been doing."

"Poor Troy! You shouldn't make him go."

"Sure, and then I'd have to listen to his mother nagging me saying how I don't give Troy a chance at running the business. I'm damned if I do and I'm damned if I don't."

"And leaving me here with nobody to play with all this time!" Rosalind pulled a petulant face.

"You still have Jack to have fun with."

Rosalind tutted. "Jack, he's *too* much fun."

Niall started laughing. He loved Rosalind as if she was his own. She was from the neighbouring farm. He had known her father all his life – he had been his best friend. Rosalind was family. He loved her vivaciousness and her humour. But she had been spoilt and indulged all her life.

"Jack never complains when he goes to London to look after things," said Niall.

"That's because he's out enjoying himself in casinos and nightclubs all the time!"

"So? He keeps those managers on their toes. Unlike Troy – profits manage to go down when *he's* over, for some reason."

"Leave poor Troy alone!" snapped Rosalind, giving Niall a dirty look that caused him to laugh out loud.

They sat in silence for a while enjoying the sun, eyes closed.

"I hear Tom Gannon's daughter's getting married this weekend," commented Niall.

"I know, I'm invited."

"How old is she?"

"Twenty-three."

"And she's been engaged this past two years, I believe."

"So I believe."

"You wouldn't want to leave it too long yourself," said Niall.

Rosalind sat up abruptly. "Leave what too long?"

"Getting married. Time goes by quickly, you know."

She looked at him knowingly. "I would get married, if there was anybody around here worth marrying."

"There's my two boys there – either of them would be glad to have you, and vice versa, I'm sure." He didn't open his eyes as he spoke.

"Hmmm," Rosalind sat back and, picking up a magazine, began to fan herself. "If either of them would pick up the courage to ask me."

"Oh, is that the delay?" said Niall with a smirk.

Rosalind didn't answer.

"Out of my sons, Jack is the one who's got it, you know what I mean?"

"Got what exactly?"

"*It*! He's the brightest, cleverest, full of charm. He could charm the birds out of the trees, Jack."

"That he could."

"Wonderful husband material." Niall opened his eyes and looked at her pointedly.

"Yeah, if you could keep up with his antics and wandering eye."

"Jack just needs a nice girl to settle down with, that's all."

"That's some task, if you ask me," said Rosalind.

The patio door opened and Niall's wife, Lauren, stepped out onto the patio.

"Town was busy," she announced as she put down a load of shopping bags and walked over to them.

Niall observed the shopping bags. "Well, somebody has been busy anyway."

Lauren cut a glamorous figure at fifty-six. She was slim and tall, her face had a striking bone structure and her ash-blonde hair was thick down to her shoulders.

"Hi, Rosalind." Lauren bent down and kissed her cheek. "Great news. Troy is coming home tomorrow!"

"I thought he was supposed to be in London for another week," said Niall.

"Well, he says he's finished all his business there and can come home a bit earlier."

"*I* tell him when he has finished his business!" said Niall.

"You know, he's been really bad keeping in contact this time. He's hardly phoned me at all!" said Rosalind.

"He's been so busy running all those pubs – keeping on top of the job," Lauren said, giving Niall a triumphant look. "He takes that business very seriously."

Niall scoffed.

"Is that a new pendant?" asked Rosalind, looking at the diamond around Lauren's neck.

"Yes." Lauren began to toy with it as Niall's eyes fixed on it with an unhappy look.

"It's beautiful," complimented Rosalind.

"It's your anniversary present to me, Niall," Lauren informed him. "It was our wedding anniversary yesterday."

"I must try and remember our anniversaries in the future. It would probably work out much cheaper for me if I did."

162

"Our love is priceless, darling," said Lauren.

"By the look of that necklace, you're certainly trying your best to put a price on it," said Niall.

"*And* you're throwing me a surprise anniversary party on Saturday night here at the house," Lauren informed her husband.

"Am I?"

"Everything's arranged. Rosalind, can you phone the usual crew and tell them the party starts at eight?"

"Of course I can," Rosalind smiled.

"And make sure you warn them all not to let it slip to me beforehand. I don't want my surprise ruined!"

Niall raised his eyes to heaven and sighed heavily.

At that moment a large man in his early thirties came around the corner of the house onto the patio. He was wearing blue jeans and a check shirt. He had a lazy slow way of walking. He was strong-looking, with a face that still had signs of being handsome even though it had been weathered.

"What is it, Seán?" said Niall with a sigh, expecting to hear trouble.

Seán Ford worked on the farm. He had been there for years.

Seán spoke in a lazy, almost bored way. "Two cows broke out of a field on the coast road and they fell down that hole that has been excavated."

"Ah for fuck's sake!" snapped Niall. "Aren't I supposed to be semi-retired? Ask Jack to deal with it."

"Can't find him," Seán said and yawned.

He's probably still sleeping off a hangover at some married woman's house, thought Rosalind.

"So it's left to me, as per fucking usual!" snapped Niall, getting up off his lounger. "Come on!" he said to Seán and the two of them headed off.

Lauren waited until they had gone and then she quickly went and sat on Niall's lounger. Leaning forward to Rosalind, she said, "Go on! What's he been saying?"

"The usual! Singing Jack's praises and giving out about poor Troy!"

"Fuck him anyway! This is looking bad, Rosalind. I really think he's going to give the farm and business to Jack. I mean, I love Jack and everything like my own, but he's not my own, do you know what I mean?"

"I do, Lauren. But he's always been Niall's favourite. And Troy doesn't seem to be able to impress him with the business . . . Niall was hinting to me again about marrying Jack."

Lauren sighed heavily. "That's his dream, you know."

Rosalind gave a dismissive laugh. "Well, that just isn't going to happen. I've tried going out with Jack in the past. He's just unreliable. He loves his freedom too much. There's no room for a wife in his life. A girl might go out with a guy like that, but she doesn't want to settle down with him, get my meaning?"

"Of course I do. You would never know where he was any night."

"Or whose bed he was in," added Rosalind. "No, it's just not there between me and Jack."

"Well, then, as I said to you before, we're on the same team. We have to get behind Troy, the two of us, and show Niall that it's Troy that needs to be taking over here. But time is running out. I think he sent Troy to London to get him out of the way, to give you and Jack a chance."

"There's no chance!" said Rosalind.

"Sooner or later, Niall is going to realise just how unreliable Jack is. And with you married to Troy, I think that's the best way of showing him that you two are the future. But we can't waste any more time, love. Troy has a habit of dilly-dallying, so you need to be announcing an engagement by summer's end. Understood?"

"Understood," Rosalind nodded. "What time will Troy be home tomorrow?"

"He didn't say. I'll phone you as soon as he's home. Oh, he said he's bringing a friend home with him as well."

"Oh? Who, I wonder? You know my friend Tammy? She's just broken up with her boyfriend, so I might play matchmaker and try and fix her up with Troy's friend. I hope he's good-looking."

Niall spent the rest of the afternoon with Seán and some other farmhands getting the cows free. Afterwards he drove through the estate. He drove up to one of the cliffs and parked his car. Getting out he looked out at the sea and breathed in the air. He loved this place, it gave him strength. His eyes looked along the beaches that meandered along the coast until he recognised where Winterfield stopped and where the neighbouring farm started. That was the Dawsons' farm. He could see the fine period home of the Dawsons. Their farm was only small compared to Winterfield, but was still a wonderful farm. The best of land, better than any of the pastures at Winterfield. And it was in a pivotal location on the road to Castleford. When Niall was growing up in this area, his own family had very little money and he had a tough upbringing as his parents struggled to make ends meet. The Dawsons were rich compared to them. But Rosalind's father John had still become his best friend. He spent a lot of time over at the Dawson home, and they were like another family to him. When he grew up, Niall headed over to London to make his fortune. It was tough the first few years. He did everything from construction work to working in bars to try and put some money together. Finally he managed to get a lease on a pub. He worked every hour he could to make it a success. It was an Irish pub in a rundown area. But suddenly he turned the pub around and started making a profit. It wasn't long until he took a lease on another pub and then another. Suddenly he found himself running a flourishing business and needed an accountant and a solicitor. That was how he met Jack's mother, Elizabeth. His solicitors were an old established firm based in central London. They had been recommended to him by a group of successful Irish businessmen who had befriended him. Despite his growing pub empire, he still felt intimidated every time he had to visit his solicitors. They just seemed to be from another planet from the life he knew. One day he was waiting nervously in the reception area of the legal firm for an appointment.

One of the office doors opened and he could hear a woman say, "Alright, Father, that's fine. I'm out with Geoffrey this evening, so I'll be home late."

The speaker then came out into the reception area and closed the door behind her. He still remembered the impact she had on him. The young woman oozed all the glamour of a Hollywood star. The black, slightly curled hair, the tight light-green dress, and the swathe of fur around her shoulders. She looked at him and smiled, then sashayed over to the receptionist and said, "Sally, is Geoffrey finished yet?"

"He's with a client, Miss Templeton."

"Thank you, I'll wait," said the young woman and turned and smiled at Niall again.

She stood for a little while and then walked over to one of the free seats beside Niall and sat down. Niall was piecing together everything in his mind. Miss Templeton. She was obviously Jonathon Templeton's daughter; he was a senior barrister at the practice. And she must be waiting for Geoffrey Ashdown, a young and dashing solicitor who sometimes handled Niall's account. He felt nervous sitting near her, the strong smell of her perfume enveloping him. She opened her small handbag and took out a cigarette.

"Do you have a light?" she asked him, treating him to a dazzling smile, her green eyes focused on him.

"Eh, yes," he said, fumbling in his pocket for his lighter. She leaned forward as he lit it for her.

"Cheers!" she said, and smiled at him again.

He nodded and looked straight ahead, trying to concentrate on the meeting he had before him.

"Do you have the time?" she asked.

He looked at her and she was dazzling him with a smile again.

He glanced down at the beautiful diamond-encrusted watch on her wrist.

"Eh, yes, it's nearly five."

Their eyes locked for a few moments and her face went serious.

Suddenly Geoffrey Ashdown was bounding down the circular staircase, dressed in an immaculate tailored suit and wool coat.

"Darling, I'm so sorry I was held up," said Geoffrey as he walked across the marble-floored reception.

"It's alright. I was just in with Daddy," she said, standing up and offering her cheek for him to kiss.

"Oh, hello, Niall, are you alright there?" asked Geoffrey.

"Y-yes. I'm waiting to see Timothy."

"He should be free in a few minutes." He put his arm

around the girl. "Come on, darling, I've booked dinner for six at my club."

She nodded at Niall and smiled, and he watched them walk off together.

There was a huge dissatisfaction burning away within him when he left the offices that evening and made his way back to his main pub for an evening's work. He couldn't get the Templeton girl out of his mind. And as he pictured her and Geoffrey dining at his club, he was burning with jealousy. She would never even look at somebody like him.

That evening the pub was packed and he was kept really busy behind the bar. He nearly fainted with shock when he looked up and saw Geoffrey walk in with Miss Templeton. Geoffrey looked very uncomfortable as they made their way through the crowd. But she didn't. Her eyes were fixed on Niall as she smiled.

"Hi there!" said Geoffrey, obviously forcing himself to sound cheerful.

"We just happened to be in the neighbourhood," she said.

"Hardly!" Geoffrey muttered.

"Elizabeth Templeton," she introduced herself, stretching her white-gloved hand across the bar.

Niall tentatively shook it.

"And what can I get you to drink?"

"Champagne please," said Elizabeth.

Niall went red in the face. "I don't stock any."

"Well, whatever you have then." Her gaze never left him.

"How about some Babycham?" he asked with a laugh.

"That will do nicely for me, thank you."

Geoffrey and Elizabeth spent the night at the bar. And she continued to gaze at Niall as he worked away. It was obvious Geoffrey was growing more and more irritated with the situation. When the pub closed, she still sat there at the bar and asked Niall to join them for a drink. As the three of them sat alone in the pub, to Geoffrey's anger it was like as if he didn't exist.

"Come on, Elizabeth, let's get you home," he insisted at last.

"No, I want to stay another while," she said.

"Okay, I know when I'm not bloody wanted," said Geoffrey, standing up in anger. "Have you lost leave of your senses, Liz? Look at him! He's nothing! A Mick on the make! Your father will go mad!" Geoffrey stormed off.

Niall looked on in amazement.

"I thought he'd never go," said Elizabeth, smiling at him.

And they were inseparable after that. For four wonderful happy years. Sure there was opposition from her horrified family and friends. She didn't care and defied them all and married Niall. They did everything together and he felt he could do anything with her by his side, as he opened pub after pub. She had a small trust fund and they used it to buy out the leaseholds to all the pubs. They bought the house in Kensington. They never had a cross word, as if it was that each had a life ambition to make the other one happy. He brought her home to Ireland and she fell in love with his home place. He took her up to the old Winterfield estate. It had been lying in ruins since it had been destroyed in the War of Independence.

She insisted they buy it and restore it to its former glory. They were the talk of the place. Niall Launcelot, a self-made millionaire, and his beautiful wife who was restoring the old Winterfield estate. As the business continued to thrive in post-war Britain, they divided their time between

Winterfield and London. And when Elizabeth became pregnant and Jack was born their happiness was complete.

Until the day Elizabeth went riding out alone along the coastline of Winterfield, and was thrown from her horse and killed. Left alone with a baby son, Niall was inconsolable for a very long time. He had lost his soulmate. He locked himself up in Winterfield and hardly came out. If it wasn't for Jack he felt he would have ended it all. But slowly he had to rebuild his life for the sake of his son.

Lauren sat down at her dressing table and began to remove her jewellery, while Niall started to run a bath. They had been out for dinner in Castleford, the large town that was a five-mile drive away.

"You know, I don't think that steak was as good as it was before," Niall complained, coming out of the bathroom and taking off his tie.

Lauren started brushing her hair. "I didn't think there was anything wrong with mine. Maybe it's your taste buds – aren't they supposed to get less keen as you get older?"

"I'm not *that* old, Lauren. The way you talk all the time about my age!"

"And the way you talk you'd swear you were a man of thirty."

"I feel like a man of thirty."

"Well, you're not a man of thirty!" Lauren snapped. "You need to slow down, Niall, and start entrusting your sons to take over."

"I let them take over enough. If I let them take over any more, I'd be bankrupt in no time."

"Don't talk bullshit, Niall! Troy has been doing a wonderful job running the pubs over in London. And nobody knows this farm better than him."

"Jack knows this farm better than him," quipped Niall.

"Jack!" Lauren scoffed. "Jack knows the inside of every bar in Castleford, you mean. And he knows the inside of every married woman's bedroom in Castleford as well!"

"Shut up, Lauren!" Niall snapped.

Lauren swung around and glared at Niall. "Well, maybe you want to turn a blind eye to Jack's antics, but people are only too happy to tell me of my stepson's behaviour when I'm in town!"

"They're just jealous of us, and of Jack. Jack is just spirited. He just needs a good girl to settle down with. Somebody like Rosalind."

Lauren jumped to her feet. "Rosalind! Oh, husband, you can wish for snow in July, because there's more chance of that than Rosalind marching up the aisle with Jack."

"She was talking about Jack to me today. I think she's mad about him."

"You're deluded! It's Troy she wants."

Niall raised his voice. "I know what you're at! Plotting and planning and trying to push Jack out of the way. Well, I've news for you: Jack isn't being pushed anywhere. He's my eldest son, and he has first dibs on this place and first dibs on the business. And if Rosalind has any ambitions for the future then she better let Jack have first dibs on her as well!" He turned and went into the bathroom, slamming the door behind him.

"He might be your eldest son . . . but he's not my eldest son," Lauren said quietly.

CHAPTER 26

Blanche watched Troy as he signed the paperwork at Avis to hire a car at Dublin Airport. She wished he would hurry. She wanted to be away from the airport and into the country before she bumped into anyone she knew.

It felt strange being back in Ireland. She was obviously nervous about meeting the Launcelot family. But after what she had been through over the past few months, she imagined they would be easy to deal with.

"All sorted!" announced Troy, arriving back with a big smile on his face and dangling the car keys. He swooped down, picked up their two suitcases and the two of them made their way out to the front of the airport. They walked out into the sunshine to where a black open-topped Mercedes waited for them.

As they drove through the countryside Blanche felt increasingly nervous. They drove through Castleford and Blanche studied the country town and found it hard to believe that this would be her new home. It wasn't the destiny she had planned for herself.

They veered out of the town along the coast road until Troy turned the car into the large entrance of Winterfield and then up the driveway that seemed to go on forever through rich pasture land. The house came into clear view and Blanche was surprised at the size of it. She looked down at the sparkling engagement ring on her finger and, with a sigh, she slid it off and put in carefully in a zipped pocket in her handbag. They had agreed that they wouldn't reveal the engagement straight off as it might be a bit too much for the family to take in all at once.

Blanche stepped out of the car and looked up at the manor house. Troy came behind her and put an arm around her waist.

"Don't look so nervous, love. We don't bite!" he said.

She smiled at him and they made their way to the house. The front door opened and Lauren came rushing out and down the steps.

"Troy!" She flung her arms around her son and hugged him. "It's just so good to have you home!" She then quickly turned to Blanche and a look of surprise and confusion crept across her face.

Blanche nodded at her. "Hello."

Niall came out of the house and clapped a hand on his son's shoulder.

"And who's this you've brought with you?" he asked, looking curiously at Blanche.

"Mum, Dad, this is Blanche."

Lauren and Niall stared at Blanche in amazement.

"Nice to meet both of you," said Blanche, managing to smile.

"Likewise." Lauren's confused look switched from Blanche back to Troy.

Blanche quickly realised that Troy looked very similar to

Lauren and, apart from their height, bore no resemblance to his father. They all stood around awkwardly.

"Why, eh, don't we all go inside?" suggested Lauren with a forced smile.

"I had this room prepared for you," said Lauren as she entered a large bedroom upstairs, followed by Blanche.

Blanche looked around the spacious luxurious room with a view out the back over the gardens to the sea.

"It's lovely, thank you," she said, placing her case on the bed.

"Please, feel free to use anything in the house you wish," urged Lauren, holding her hands together, her eyes inspecting every inch of the girl before her.

"That's very generous of you."

"Well, any friend of Troy is always welcome at Winterfield," Lauren smiled again – an obviously forced smile. "Em . . . how long do you think you'll be staying with us . . . exactly?"

"I-I'm not sure," said Blanche in confusion and she could feel herself blushing.

"Well . . . I'll let you in peace to unpack."

Lauren walked slowly down the staircase, rubbing her hands slowly together as a thousand thoughts raced through her head. As she tried to understand who this beautiful girl her son had arrived back with was.

The phone rang. She crossed the hallway and picked up the receiver.

"Hi, it's Rosalind," said the excited voice on the other end of the phone.

"Oh, hello, Rosalind."

"Well – is he home yet?"

"Oh, yes, he is."

"Well, why didn't you phone me right away? I'll be straight over."

"Actually, Rosalind, don't. He's exhausted. Why don't you give it a couple of hours until you come over."

"Oh alright! I can't wait to see him. And what about his friend, has he arrived over too?"

"Yes, his friend is here as well."

"Oh good, I've been telling my friend Tammy that Troy's bringing home a surprise for her. Is the friend good-looking?"

Lauren sighed. "Yes – I think you could safely say the friend is definitely good-looking."

Blanche was unpacking her suitcase when there was a knock on the door and Troy entered.

"How are you finding it?" He came over to her and enveloped her in a hug.

"All a bit strange, to be honest," she said.

"You don't like it here?"

"How could I not? It's beautiful. It's just being in a house of people I don't know. It's a bit weird."

"A day or two here, and it will be like you were never anywhere else, darling."

"Your parents are staring at me with this look of complete puzzlement."

"Well, they won't for long. We'll tell everyone over dinner tonight that we are engaged. Okay?"

She nodded and kissed him. "Okay."

"We're in here!" called Lauren from the lounge as Blanche and Troy came down the stairs that evening.

Niall and Lauren were on the couch when they entered.

"What do you want to drink, Blanche?" said Lauren, getting up and going to the drinks cabinet.

"A red wine would be lovely, thank you."

"Troy?"

"Just a beer!"

"Here – catch!" Lauren took up a can, flung it through the air and Troy caught it. She poured a glass of wine and brought it over to Blanche.

"So how do you know each other?" asked Niall, deciding he needed to quickly get to the bottom of what was going on.

"Eh, Blanche was working in one of our bars in London. You know, Dolores' bar."

"Oh! You work for us?" said Lauren.

"I, eh, I've handed in my notice."

"I see," said Lauren. "And what job are you going to go back to when you return to London?"

"She's not going back to London," said Troy, smiling. "We're engaged." And he lifted up Blanche's left hand to show them the diamond glittering on her finger.

"Well! That is news!" said Niall, smiling broadly as he jumped to his feet. He went and clapped Troy's shoulder and shook his hand before kissing Blanche on the cheek.

"Thank you!" Blanche smiled at him.

"Mum?" Troy said and gave a little laugh as he looked at his mother who was standing still with a look of shock on her face.

"Oh, eh, congratulations." She forced herself to smile as she came over and gave her son a kiss on the cheek. She turned to Blanche and, even though she was smiling, she also managed to look deeply unhappy.

"This is all a bit sudden, isn't it?"

"I guess it is," Blanche agreed.

The front door slammed.

"Hi, everybody – it's just me!" said Rosalind loudly.

She appeared at the door of the lounge, clearly overjoyed at the sight of Troy.

"Oh welcome home!" Rosalind walked straight towards Troy, not even looking at anybody else, threw her arms around him and kissed him firmly on the lips. She pulled back and smiled warmly at him, then glanced around at everyone else. It was then that she noticed Blanche and her face creased in confusion.

"Eh, Rosalind, honey . . . this is Blanche," said Lauren. "Troy's fiancée."

They were seated around the dining table, Rosalind pale as she studied Blanche and Troy seated side by side.

"I'm actually from Dublin and I was over in London for just a short while, working in Dolores' bar, when I met Troy," said Blanche.

"Classy," said Rosalind as she reached over and took a sip of her wine.

"Em, where is Jack?" asked Lauren, fearful of what Rosalind might do or say.

"He's probably delayed with work," said Niall.

"Well, you'd think he'd make a little effort to be here for his brother's homecoming," said Lauren. "We can't wait any longer. Let's just start eating."

"If you don't mind me saying," said Niall to Blanche, "you don't look or sound as if you should be working in one of our bars."

"Well, I was grateful for the job, to be honest with you. They are thin on the ground in London at the moment."

"Same everywhere," said Lauren.

"Handy that a nice man came along and rescued you then, isn't it?" snapped Rosalind.

177

Blanche cleared her throat and looked down at her plate, embarrassed.

"Rosalind!" warned Lauren.

"Em, Blanche is actually a model," said Troy. "She was working as one in Dublin and then was just working in our bar till she got a break in London."

"A model, fancy that!" said Lauren, forcing a smile.

"Save us all!" said Rosalind under her breath.

Blanche looked around at them as they chatted and realised what a close-knit group they were. She reckoned the whole area was like that and she felt a complete outsider. Judging by the reception that Rosalind had given Troy, she was looking forward to quizzing him on exactly what was the nature of their relationship. She studied Rosalind – her candyfloss blonde hair, her pert prettiness, and her sugar-sweet voice – and realised she was very used to being number one around there.

Rosalind was eyeing Blanche's engagement ring from across the table.

"That looks like it cost a good bit," she commented, smiling sweetly. "I write for the local newspaper, so I'll have to do a nice big announcement in the next issue. *Son of Prominent Businessman Marries Bar Girl.* I just love a rags-to-riches story."

"You'll make no such announcement, Rosalind," ordered Lauren. "We're having a party here on Saturday for our anniversary and we can announce the engagement to all our friends there first."

The lamb on Blanche's plate looked delicious but Rosalind's open hostility was making her lose her appetite.

Niall raised his glass. "Well, I'd like to toast the happy couple, Troy and Blanche!"

Lauren and Rosalind raised their glasses, half-heartedly repeating: "To Troy and Blanche!"

It was clear that Rosalind was simmering with resentment. A few moments later she said: "You know, I'm reading those fashion magazines all the time, and never saw your face in one, Blanche."

"Well, I obviously wasn't a particularly successful model then, was I?" Blanche said coolly.

Niall cleared his throat. "And as a gift to my son and his new fiancée, I'm going to give him the area of the farm on the coast road."

"Ah, Dad, that's great," said Troy, looking joyful.

"Really *really* generous," said Lauren, almost spitting the words as she gave Niall dagger looks.

Blanche didn't know what was going on, but it was obvious there was a lot under the surface.

"You can put in planning permission to build your dream house there, son," said Niall.

"Great, Ken and Barbie can live happily ever after in their very own kingdom," said Rosalind.

Troy's temper snapped. "Rosalind, would you ever shut the fuck up? What's your fucking problem?"

"*Please!*" Lauren demanded.

"Maybe I should just go home," said Rosalind, sighing.

"Maybe you should!" snapped Troy.

"Now, you'll just have to forgive that little outburst, Blanche," said Lauren. "Your announcement is just a bit of a surprise and we're still getting used to the idea, that's all."

"It's fine. Don't worry about it," said Blanche.

After dinner they went into the lounge for drinks.

"I guess I'll go home," said Rosalind eventually.

"I'll walk you out to your car," said Lauren.

"No doubt we'll be seeing a lot more of you," said Rosalind to Blanche.

They walked out the front door and down to Rosalind's car.

"I can't believe this! Did you know anything about this?" demanded Rosalind, sounding like a sulky schoolgirl.

"Of course I didn't!" said Lauren.

"What's he thinking of? We don't know anything about her."

"We've got to work quickly, Rosalind."

"Well, what can we do to get rid of her?"

"Leave it to me and I'll see what I can come up with."
Rosalind smiled. "I'll drive her to the airport myself."

"Just you keep your mouth under control and make no more snippy comments like tonight again. All you're managing to do is anger Troy."

Blanche and Troy walked to the very end of the garden and rested against the wall, looking out at the ocean in the darkness.

"What's going on, Troy, with Rosalind?"

"What do you mean?"

"Don't bullshit me. She kissed you like you were lovers when she met you, and she is bristling with anger over our engagement."

"We . . . had a thing a while back."

"How long ago and how serious was it?"

"It's complicated."

"Well, try explaining it then!" Blanche was becoming exasperated.

"We never were officially boyfriend and girlfriend, but we've just had a fling every so often."

180

"How often?"

"We grew up together. We had a fling when we were teenagers. Once when we were twenty. I don't know . . . we went out for six weeks when we were twenty-two. And we had a fling last year. As I said, it's complicated."

"So why didn't it ever work out between you two?"

"Because I never really loved her. Not like I love you."

Lauren tried to digest the day's news as she removed her make-up that night. She looked at her watch and saw it was after one. Niall often went out walking at night.

The bedroom door opened and Niall came in, looking happy.

"Nice warm night out there," he said, closing the door after him. "Was just having a celebratory cigar."

"Celebratory?"

"Yes, my son's got engaged or hadn't you noticed?"

She turned and faced him. "Oh, you're celebrating alright. You've got just what you wanted."

"What are you talking about?"

"Troy arrives back with this girl he hardly knows and Rosalind is out of the picture. You'll have Rosalind and Jack married off by Christmas."

"So? What will be will be. With all your plotting and planning Troy has followed his heart and is marrying somebody he really loves. Good for him!"

"And that was so touching, giving him the land on the coast road for him to build a house. You might as well have announced there and then that he is out of the running for the main estate here and the business. Set poor Troy up on a measly little farm and give everything else to your precious Jack who couldn't even be bothered to turn up for dinner tonight, as per fucking usual!" Her voice was rising all the time.

"Yeah? Well, I don't blame him. He's right to do his own thing and stay out of your fucking way. You've really shown your colours recently over Jack. Playing the good mother to him all these years, while in fact trying to work behind the scenes to get him out of the way!"

"I wouldn't have to if you didn't favour him so much. He can never do any wrong in your eyes and yet he never does any good!"

"Listen to me: if Troy took over he would run the place into the ground. Did you see that ring he put on that girl's finger? How much did that cost? He hasn't a fucking clue when it comes to money or business – he's just like you."

"And I suppose Jack is just like his beautiful and vivacious mother – Elizabeth. The magnificent Elizabeth who never could do any wrong."

"Don't you dare speak ill of her!"

"No, we can never speak ill of her. I'm sick of her. She's been dead decades and you can't let go of her. Well, you're *going* to let go of her. And Jack is *not* getting everything here."

"It's not your choice, it's mine." He turned and stormed off, slamming the door behind him.

Blanche sat up in her bed. She had woken from her sleep to the sound of screaming and shouting. She immediately recognised the voices of Niall and Lauren as they tore each other to pieces. Finally, the shouting stopped, and she lay back down, but was unable to fall asleep.

Blanche and Troy drove out to the land that Niall was giving them, having arranged to meet Castleford's most prominent architect Tom O'Hara there.

The land had wonderful views over the countryside and ran along the coastline.

182

After some preliminary examination and discussion, they decided on a precise location for the house.

"So you're happy with this site?" said Tom at last.

"Yep. We'll be able to walk out the back of the house and onto the beach," said Troy.

"I'll get back to the office and start coming up with ideas. What kind of thing are you looking for?"

"Something very modern and avant garde," said Blanche.

"Lots of huge windows," said Troy.

"Okay, I'll try and have something for you by next week."

"Great. You're coming to the party on Saturday night?" asked Troy.

"Wouldn't dare not turn up. I'd be frightened of what Lauren would do to me!" Tom laughed as he got into his car.

"This is great, isn't it?" said Troy, as they watched Tom drive off. "Our own home."

"Yes, your father is very generous," said Blanche.

An Audi pulled up beside them, Lauren in the driving seat. She wound down her window. "Seán told me you had come out here," she said.

"We just met with Tom O'Hara to discuss the design for the house," said Troy.

"That's nice." Lauren didn't bother to sound too enthusiastic. "Troy, I need to have a word with you about something."

"Oh, okay, fire away," said Troy.

Lauren glanced over at Blanche and looked awkward.

"It's okay, you can talk in front of Blanche," said Troy.

Lauren looked even more awkward.

Blanche opted to be diplomatic. "I need to do some stuff back at the house, so I'll leave you two alone."

"Here, take the car." Troy offered her his car keys.

"You know, it's such a beautiful day I think I'll walk it. I'll see you later." She leaned forward, kissed Troy and headed off.

"That was very rude," Troy said to his mother.

"She needs to get used to rudeness if she's going to stay around here."

"What wrong anyway?" questioned Troy.

"It's *you* I want to talk about. I can't get you alone in the house." Lauren stepped out of her car and confronted her son. "What are you doing, Troy?"

"I don't get you?"

"Arriving back with this girl, being engaged after knowing each other for two minutes. The whole thing is insane."

"I love her. There's nothing insane about that."

"And what about Rosalind?"

"What about her?"

"She's heartbroken after you."

"No, she's not. There was never anything serious between us."

"That's not what she thought. She was talking about marrying you to me last week."

"Ah, bullshit! She's flitted between me and Jack so much she doesn't know whether she's coming or going."

"Exactly, and now she's going to flit over to Jack full stop."

"Good. I think they'll make a lovely couple."

"You are such an idiot. You're so happy with the gift of this land to you, aren't you? Don't you understand what Niall is saying with this 'gift'? It means that is *all* you're going to get. You're out of the running now for the main farm and the business. Let's face it, Jack was always ahead of you in the race, and the only thing that would have secured your future is marriage to Rosalind. Niall dotes on her. Now you've handed everything over to Jack on a plate."

"You're talking nonsense. And even if you aren't, who gives a shit? Let Dad do what he wants with his precious farm and business."

"Oh really?" Lauren pointed to Troy's gleaming new Mercedes. "Well, you can say goodbye to that then. And all the other nice things in life. Because these few acres around here aren't going to give you what you're used to, are they?"

"I love Blanche. I've never met anyone like her and I'm getting married to her and nothing you or anyone else says is going to put a stop to that."

Troy turned his back on his mother, jumped in his car and raced off.

As Blanche walked along the country road, she thought about how she had better phone her parents, tell them she was back in Ireland and announce her wedding plans to them. Goodness knows how they would react to that. They might actually be happy for her. After all, she was finally doing what her mother wanted her to do: marrying into a successful family. Having said that, she wasn't sure what her parents with all their airs and graces would make of the Launcelots. They seemed to be a 'take us as we are' lot.

Back at Winterfield Blanche stopped in the hallway and studied the huge portrait of a beautiful woman hanging on the wall. Troy had told her it was Elizabeth, Niall's first wife. As Blanche toyed with her own dark hair, she realised she was similar in type to Elizabeth.

She made her way over to the phone and picked it up. She steadied herself and dialled her home number.

"Hello," said Harriet's voice.

"Mum, it's me."

"Hello, Blanche. How are you?"

"I'm fine. In fact, I'm back in Ireland."

"Oh?"

"Yes, Mum. I'm down in Castleford."

"What on earth has you down there?"

"Mum, I'm engaged to be married."

"Oh Blanche!" There was exasperation in her voice. "But whatever happened to your international modelling career? Castleford doesn't exactly sit easy with Paris, New York, London, does it?"

"Well, life doesn't always work out the way you want it to, does it?"

"You can say that again!" sighed Harriet. "Well, who is he? Does he have money?"

CHAPTER 27

Rosalind walked down one of the main streets in Castleford the morning of the party.

"Hi, Rosalind," said a woman passing her.

"Hi there," replied Rosalind.

"Good morning, Rosalind," said a man as he passed her.

"Morning, Dermot!"

She was well known in the town. She loved Castleford. She loved her life. Her family were well respected, her looks made her well known, her vivacious personality made her popular, and her job at the paper made her well connected. Marriage to Troy was the next step to make her life complete. And now everything had been torn asunder. She opened the door of the local hairdresser, Lulu.

"Hi, Rosalind," said Lulu who was sitting on reception.

The salon was fairly packed and Rosalind recognised most of the women having their hair done as being the wives of local businessmen getting ready for the party at Winterfield that night.

"Come on over, I'm going to do you myself," said Lulu.

"Good," said Rosalind, following her.

"And you can tell me all the gossip from Winterfield at the same time," said Lulu as Rosalind took a seat. "Is it true that Troy Launcelot has arrived home with a stunning fiancée from London?"

"Well, it's true he's arrived home with a fiancée. Whether she could be described as stunning or not is a matter of taste."

"I hear Lauren isn't too happy about it?" said Lulu as she draped a cape around Rosalind's shoulders.

"Well, I expect she had hoped for something more than just a barmaid."

"I heard she was a model!"

"Word gets around this town very fast. I don't know what she was. She acts as if she's royalty, but I can assure you there's nothing royal about those pubs Niall owns that she was working in."

That evening Blanche checked her appearance in the full-length mirror in her room. She was dressed in a cream halter-neck gown that flowed straight to the floor with a matching stole.

A knock sounded on her door and Troy came in wearing a tuxedo.

"You look gorgeous," he complimented.

"You don't scrub up bad yourself," she smiled.

"There are people already arriving downstairs. Will we head down?" He offered her his arm and they left the room.

"And I still haven't met the mysterious Jack," said Blanche. "Will he be here tonight?"

"He should be, although you can never tell with Jack," Troy smirked.

"They make a handsome couple, don't they?" commented

Niall, watching Troy and Blanche as they circulated around the crowd.

"Stunning!" said Lauren sarcastically.

"I don't think I've ever seen him look so happy."

"Don't rub it in, Niall," snapped Lauren as she took a glass of champagne from the tray of a passing waiter.

Just then, in walked Rosalind.

"Hi, everybody!" she called out.

Blanche watched Rosalind vivaciously work the room. She looked lovely, in a black dress, her blonde hair gently curled out. Blanche was very wary of her. Rosalind was very much marking her territory and, as she engaged Troy in a close conversation, it looked like she was including him in that.

A band was playing out by the pool where couples were dancing, and the music drifted in through the open French windows. Blanche saw Niall interrupt Rosalind's exchange with Troy and lead her outside to join the dancing couples. Then Troy came and led Blanche outside too.

The band was playing The Beatles' 'Yesterday' as they emerged onto the patio, but before they could join the dancers a group of women approached Troy and asked to be introduced to Blanche.

"It's a good band," commented Niall to Rosalind as they swayed to the music.

"Uh huh," agreed Rosalind, her eyes fixed firmly on Blanche who was now surrounded by women admiring her engagement ring.

"Come on, Rosalind. You might be a little sore over losing Troy, but your miss might be your mercy. There's still Jack."

"It might just be a little surprising for you to hear, Niall, but there's more men for me to choose from than just your sons in this town!"

"Is that so? Well, then, why don't we ever see you near any of them? No, come on, Rosalind, you always said you were going to marry a Launcelot. Now, with Troy out of the picture, why not just settle for Jack?"

"I don't think I want to have this conversation," snapped Rosalind.

"I know Jack has his faults. But his pluses far outweigh his minuses."

"Jack is never going to settle down, Niall. Not with me, not with anybody, and even if he did I couldn't cope with him."

"I want to see Jack settled down, Rosalind. And the day he does is the day I turn everything over to him. The day I name him as my heir."

Rosalind blinked a few times. "Don't you think Lauren might have something to say about that?"

"She'll have nothing to say about it. It's nothing to do with her. Jack is the best man for the job."

"And why are you telling me all this?"

"Because I want you to see your right destiny. Being here, side by side with Jack. Do you understand me?"

Blanche had gone upstairs to the bathroom and was coming back to join the party. She was walking down the stairs when she saw him. He stood in the middle of the hall, with a group of people around him, mostly women. There was an aura about him that was palpable.

She was startled when he suddenly glanced up at her and smiled a big beaming smile.

She reached the hall as he left the group of people and walked across to her.

"Blanche?"

"Yes."

He reached forward, put his two hands on her shoulders and kissed both her cheeks. "Welcome to the family – sis!"

"And you must be Jack?"

"Got it in one!"

He offered her his arm. She took it, half-smiling and half-wary of him as they made their way into the lounge.

"So tell me, what is a girl like you doing with a brother like mine?"

"I would have thought that was obvious. I love him."

"Ah, but are you in love with him?" He stopped a waiter, took two glasses of champagne and handed one to her.

"Isn't it the same thing?" she asked.

"No!"

His eyes were lively and twinkling. The smile never left his face. He was very attractive and he knew it. He bore no resemblance to Troy.

"I want to know all about you. Everything. Start to finish. No detail left out. You're mine for the night. My brother might have you for the rest of your life – but tonight, you are mine!"

Blanche was beginning to feel uncomfortable. She was sitting on a stylish chaise longue in the lounge with Jack beside her. He stared into her face as he spoke and asked her questions, making sure her glass was continuously full.

"I wonder if this could really be happening?" he asked. "Is it possible that I could be falling in love with my brother's fiancée?"

"No, I don't think that could be possible." She looked at him sceptically and half-laughed. "I'd say there's a law against it, and if there isn't then there should be."

"Are you rejecting me?" he asked, laughing.

"Outright!" she confirmed. She was relieved to see Troy entering the room. She found Jack's flirting entertaining but outrageous.

"Blanche, there's loads of people dying to meet you!" said Troy as he approached them.

"Yes, and I want to meet them too," she said, standing up. "Your brother has been keeping me entertained."

"Yeah, he's good at that alright," said Troy.

"Welcome home, Troy. I didn't get a chance to meet you since you returned from London."

"Thanks."

"She's wonderful," said Jack, standing up and offering his hand. "Congratulations."

"Thank you, Jack." Troy took his hand and shook it.

Rosalind was choosing her moment carefully. All night long, she had heard people say how beautiful and charming Blanche was and what a happy couple they made. She wanted to puke. She waited until Blanche was with Troy and the rest of the family out by the pool before she made her move.

Rosalind marched up to Blanche and clicked her fingers in front of her face. "A red wine, please!"

Blanche looked at Rosalind, confused. "I'm sorry?"

"A red wine – well, you are the bar girl around here, aren't you?"

"Rosalind!" snapped Troy, moving towards her.

There was suddenly a shout from down the gardens. Everyone looked over to see Seán Ford come staggering across the lawn.

"Rosalind – oh Rosalind!" he called.

"Oh, for fuck's sake!" snapped Rosalind. "That's all I need."

"Rosalind! Rosalind!" shouted Seán as he came nearer.

"Will somebody get that fucking eejit away from here!" snapped Niall.

Rosalind stormed to the edge of the patio and shouted: "Go home, you drunken fool! Go home!"

Seán stumbled and fell and then managed to get up again. "Rosalind, sexy Rosalind, come to me!"

Jack and Troy quickly made their way across the lawn to Seán.

"Come on, Seán, let's get you home," said Jack, putting an arm around him.

"That bloody drunk!" said Rosalind as she watched Seán being led away.

Blanche went into the house to get away from the venomous Rosalind but some time afterwards Jack came flying in, Rosalind and Troy behind him.

"Okay, Blanche, time for a change of scene. Let's find another venue!"

"What did you have in mind?" said Troy. "Everywhere will be closed in town."

"Martin's will still be open," said Jack.

"Martin's?" Rosalind pulled a face. "Oh, please, Jack, that place is a dump."

"Yep, but it's a place that serves alcohol until five in the morning!" said Jack.

He put a hand out to Blanche. "Coming?"

Blanche looked at Troy for direction. Troy shrugged and Blanche put her hand into Jack's and stood up.

Martin's was a rundown bar on the outskirts of Castleford. It was a diner during the day and operated as a bar at night. It broke all the licensing rules and the Guards turned a blind eye to it. Jack drove them from Winterfield to the bar.

Troy was in the front. With Blanche and Rosalind sitting frostily in the back.

"We have to show you how we party down here, Blanche," Jack said, looking back at her.

"This is ridiculous, Jack," said Rosalind. "Martin's is a dump and we're walking in there dressed up to the nines."

"Well, you didn't need to come, honey," said Jack. "We would have managed just fine without you – isn't that right, Blanche?" He smiled back at her.

Blanche gave Rosalind a cool look. "That's right, Jack."

Rosalind rolled her eyes and then looked out at the countryside in the moonlight.

They drove through the town and into a rough area that looked slightly industrial to Blanche. They pulled up outside a long flat-roofed building with a red neon light over it that read '*Martin's – Diner, Grill & Bar*'.

Blanche stepped out of the car and looked up at the sign.

"Oh well, at least Blanche will feel at home here," said Rosalind, looking up at the rundown building.

Jack came up behind Blanche and placed his hand on her shoulder.

"They'll even serve you a steak with your vodka and tonic if you ask nicely," he said. He put a hand on the base of her back and gently led her to the front door following the others.

They walked into the bar and there were only a few tables occupied. 'Country Roads' was playing on an old juke box in the corner. They did cut an unusual sight, dressed up in tuxedos and gowns, as they sat down in a booth beside a net-curtained window.

"How do you find these places, Jack?" sighed Rosalind, sitting down.

"I just have an instinct for what's cheap, baby," answered Jack, winking at her.

"Ain't that a fact!"

A tired-looking blonde waitress came over.

"Okay, what's everyone having?"

"Whiskies all round, sweetheart," said Jack.

The waitress sighed. "Okay, but no trouble tonight, please, Jack?"

"Goes without saying, baby!"

Blanche found it hard to keep her eyes off Jack. He was living up to everything she had heard about him from Dolores on. He was larger than life and with an amazing way about him. She thought it interesting that Troy seemed to be completely overshadowed by him.

The whiskies arrived and Jack forced everyone to down them quickly, then he ordered another round, and another.

Blanche looked coolly over at Rosalind. "You didn't bring your fan along with you?" she asked her.

"My fan?" asked Rosalind.

"Seán, isn't that his name? He seemed to be looking for you." Blanche was enjoying making Rosalind uncomfortable.

"That old drunken fool, he needs to go and get a life." Rosalind turned and looked at the others. "You know he turned up at our house a couple of weeks ago, drunk as a skunk, and hollering my name. My daddy had to threaten the Guards on him."

"Maybe you should give him a chance, go out on a date with him," suggested Blanche, enjoying being mischievous.

"Would you ever piss off!" Rosalind snapped at her.

Blanche shrugged but couldn't help smiling. "I'm sorry."

"I'm sure!"

"Blanche, do you want to come up and help me put on some music?" suggested Jack.

"Okay," said Blanche.

Troy looked slightly irritated as the two made their way over to the music box.

Rosalind leaned over to Troy. "Well, I have to say that this is a nice way to treat me after all these years."

"Why are you being so awkward and mean to Blanche?"

"Oh, I wonder why? I wonder if it's anything to do with that fact that she arrives home engaged to my boyfriend."

"I wasn't your boyfriend, Rosalind."

"Well, then, you must forget what happened the night before you left for London."

"I remember," Troy said, feeling awkward.

"So all that meant nothing to you?"

"It meant something at the time. But I've fallen in love with someone else. Besides, you were never going to settle down with me."

"That's what you think. You're going to get tired of this infatuation, Troy, and when you do I'll be there to pick up the pieces."

"How about some Kenny Rogers?" suggested Jack to Blanche as they looked through the music selection.

"I don't think so. Gosh, all this music is so old!"

"It's country and western, baby."

She felt him standing a little too close to her.

"They don't seem to be getting on too well," Jack said, nodding over to Rosalind and Troy who seemed to be having an argument.

"Maybe we should go back and rescue them?"

"Nah, leave them to it. They've a few issues to resolve."

"Like what?"

"Ah, she's still in love with him."

Blanche chose to ignore the remark.

"Did you hear what I said?" pushed Jack.

"I heard." She continued to look through the music.

"Doesn't that worry you?"

"No. Now if you told me he was still in love with her, then I would be worried. She's just going to have to deal with it."

"You're a tough woman."

"Life has taught me you just have to be."

"Let's have a dance," he suggested, taking her by the hand and leading her out into the middle of the floor.

"Why don't you do us all a favour and you go out with Rosalind?" suggested Blanche. "That would keep her mind off my fiancé."

"Nah, it wouldn't work."

"How do you know it wouldn't?"

"Because we've already tried!"

Blanche stopped dancing and looked him in the face. "You're serious? You've been out with her as well as Troy? What is she – the family whore?"

"Now that's not nice!" he said, laughing, and forced her to start dancing again.

Suddenly there was a roar from the other side of the bar. "Launcelot! You fucking bastard!"

Jack turned around and looked. "Oh shit! Listen, darling, you get over to the others and get them all out to the car. *This* party is over now too!"

Jack pushed Blanche away.

Blanche made her way over to Troy as the man who had shouted at Jack came rushing across the bar to him.

"Now, David, you just calm down!" warned Jack.

"Calm down? I know you were over my place last night, you cheating bastard! She's admitted everything to me!"

"I don't know what you're talking about!" said Jack.

"My wife, Launcelot, my wife!" shouted the man.

"All lies!"

"I don't bloody think so!" The man took a swipe at Jack but missed him.

Troy rushed over to help his brother.

"Troy! Don't!" yelled Blanche.

"You're going to get what's coming to you!" shouted the man as he took another blow at Jack and again missed.

"Keep out of this, Troy!" shouted Jack. "Just get them out to the car and I'll be out in a couple of minutes!"

Troy hesitated.

"Get them out!" shouted Jack.

Troy did what he was told and ushered Blanche and Rosalind out.

"Troy, we've got to do something. Let's call the Guards!" insisted Blanche.

"Oh, relax, you silly cow!" snapped Rosalind, looking bored and resting against the car.

Troy put his arms around Blanche to calm her.

A minute later Jack came out, with a cut to his mouth but a big smile on his face.

"Are you alright?" demanded Blanche.

"You're such an asshole, Jack," said Rosalind, sighing.

"Okay, everybody, the party is over at Martin's. But guess what – we're going to continue it back at mine!"

Jack lived in an old hunting lodge on the estate. It was perched up in a hilly area overlooking an inlet from the sea.

The drink continued flowing until everyone was becoming sleepy. Rosalind got a taxi home at four. But Blanche and Jack were still partying at five, dancing to Roxy Music's 'There's a Band Playing', even after Troy had fallen asleep on the couch.

"Was it true what that man back at that bar was saying? That you were with his wife?"

"Nah! Well, if I was, I can't remember!"

"You're incorrigible! I'm sure if the walls of this place could talk, they would have a few tales to tell."

"Well, this is the party hot-spot of the Castleford area, I'll have you know."

"At least I'll know where to come for a good party then."

"Or anything else you can think of," he said, staring into her eyes as his hand crept to her lower back.

She stopped dancing and looked at him, and then over at her sleeping fiancé.

"We'd better get home," she said, pulling away from him.

"What's the rush?"

"It's very very late, that's the rush." She went to Troy and shook him awake.

"Darling, we'd better get home," she said.

Troy sat up, rubbed his eyes and stumbled to his feet.

"Will I call you a taxi?" asked Jack.

"No, we'll walk it quick enough," said Blanche.

Troy took off his blazer and put it around Blanche's shoulders.

"See you soon," said Jack as he let them out the front door.

He watched them walk off into the rising sun.

CHAPTER 28

Rosalind came into the large modern kitchen of her home. Her mother Peggy was sitting up at the island reading the newspaper while she drank a cup of coffee.

Rosalind went over to a large mirror on the wall and started brushing her luxuriant hair.

"Aren't you late for work?" asked her mother, not raising her eyes from the newspaper.

"I guess so," said Rosalind.

It was nearly midday.

"You don't want to take the piss out of them too much, Rosalind. They are friends of ours."

"I work plenty when I'm there," said Rosalind, admiring her hair. The proprietors of the newspaper were old friends of the Dawsons and had offered Rosalind a job when she left school. She had started off filing and answering the phone. Since she seemed to know everyone and everything that was happening in Castleford, her bosses decided to take advantage of her natural connections and she found herself covering local stories soon enough. The job suited her. She could pick her own hours to work most of the time. And she enjoyed local gossip, so it made sense she made a career out of it. She didn't take the job too seriously and had planned to give it up as soon as she had married Troy Launcelot.

Peggy got up and went over to the fridge, opened it, took out a bottle of white wine, poured herself a drink and looked at her daughter who was still admiring herself in the mirror.

"Of course, if you were a young woman planning on getting married soon then I could completely understand you not being too fussed about showing up on time. However, if you've decided you're not the marrying kind, then maybe you should show a little more interest in your work and try building a career."

"I don't know why everyone is so interested in my marital status all of a sudden."

"Quite simply, darling, your chance of marriage has just been halved with my boyo's engagement next door. Now you would want to nab Jack before the two of them are taken off the market altogether."

Rosalind sighed and turned and looked at her mother. "I'm going to work."

CHAPTER 29

Blanche walked through the Castleford streets. The whole place seemed so laid back and quiet after London and Dublin. Strangers smiled at her and said hello in the street and she could see people taking a second look at her.

Troy had given her some money and insisted she go and buy some clothes. Everything at Winterfield and Castleford was laid back. Nobody seemed to be interested in causes like Billy was or politics like Shay. They were extraordinarily self-absorbed and if something didn't involve themselves or their friends or their business, they really weren't interested. They intrigued her. And she felt safe here. And after all the trauma of being mixed up with the terrorists, and what happened to Billy and the horror of being alone and poor in London, this was what she wanted and what she craved for. Troy made her happy, it was as simple as that.

Often her thoughts went to Billy and she thought about what they had and how it could have been. She wondered what he was doing in Australia and who he was with. She still felt a terrible pang when she thought about him. But at least he was safe now.

A car pulled up beside her.

"Hi, been shopping?"

The speaker was Jack. Sunglasses on and wearing a big smile.

She looked down at the shopping bags she had got in the boutiques. "Yes, I have."

"You manage to find anything in this kip that actually looked good?" he asked, laughing.

"I found some very nice stuff, thanks all the same."

"Where are you off to now?"

"I was just going to get a taxi home."

"Hop in and I'll give you a lift. I was just heading up to the house anyway." He leaned over and opened the door.

"Well, if you're sure?"

"I'm sure!" he smiled at her.

They chatted amicably as he drove out of town towards Winterfield. He pulled over in a petrol station and got out to fill up the tank.

"I'm just going to pop in to get some cigarettes want anything?" asked Blanche.

"No, I'm good," he said, smiling.

Inside the petrol station, she chose a couple of magazines and as she got to the till she could hear shouting outside.

"Hi, twenty Benson and Hedges, please," she said to the girl behind the till who was occupied staring out the window.

Blanche glanced out and saw some woman shouting at Jack on the forecourt.

"The cigarettes?" she said to the girl again.

The girl reluctantly dragged herself away from the window and served Blanche before returning to her ring-side view.

Blanche hurried out to the forecourt.

"Would you just calm down!" demanded Jack as the woman continued to rant at him.

"You cold bastard!" she shouted at him. "I gave up my marriage for you!"

"You gave nothing up for me, Charlotte! You had no marriage to give up. It was over long before I ever came on the scene." He saw Blanche approach and quickly threw some money at the petrol attendant and sat in.

"How dare you! Dumping me and then flaunting your new floozy around town!" Charlotte shouted, pointing at Blanche.

"Get in, Blanche!" said Jack.

Blanche did as he asked.

"See you around, Charlotte!" said Jack as he quickly drove off.

"Not if I see you first!" Charlotte shouted after him

They drove in silence for a while.

"Well, there's never a dull moment with you around!" Blanche said eventually.

"It's not my fault – I'm a popular boy!" he said, flashing a smile at her.

"You can be too popular, you know."

He suddenly drove off the main road and down a dirt track.

"Hey, where are we going?" she asked, concerned.

"I want to give you a sightseeing tour."

"So all my suspicions are confirmed!" said Lauren.

Rosalind had gone into the newspaper offices for just an hour and then pretended she had to go out to do an interview. She headed over to the hotel bar to meet Lauren. She had more pressing things on her mind than writing about the social events in the town for the upcoming week.

"He told me straight," she said. "The day I get engaged to Jack is the day that Jack becomes his heir."

"You know, it's frightening how well I know my husband," sighed Lauren. "I've tried speaking to Troy and it's no use. I've said everything to him from the fact he barely knows Blanche to he'll lose everything, to no avail. He just doesn't seem to care. All he cares about is Blanche and building this fantastic new home for the two of them. Little does he know that every brick he builds is cementing Jack as the heir . . . The trouble is that Troy doesn't really know what it might feel like to lose everything and when he finally does it will be too late."

The waiter came over to them. "Do you want anything else, Mrs Launcelot?"

"Two more gin and tonics, Kevin, and make them large ones."

Jack had driven Blanche to a stunning beach that seemed to go on forever.

"Troy hasn't brought you here before?" he asked.

"No," she said, stepping out of the car and taking in the view.

They went down to the beach and started walking along the strand.

"I like to come here a lot," said Jack. "You can just walk on forever and often never see a soul, except for a few tourists in the summer."

"It's nice to be alone with your thoughts," agreed Blanche. "Who was that woman back at the petrol station? Charlotte – wasn't that her name?"

"Oh, she's nobody. I just had a drunken fling with her one night."

"That's the second married woman you've been

involved with, that I've witnessed. Are there many more?" She looked at him, smirking.

"I'm no saint, Blanche, and never pretended to be."

"Or ever tried to be, by the sound of it."

He studied her. "Something tells me you're not exactly whiter than white either."

She felt herself blush and stared off into the distance as they continued to walk.

"You know, I would never have put my brother with somebody like you."

"Well, who would you have put him with, then?"

"Rosalind, to be honest!" He laughed loudly.

"Sounds like everyone put him with Rosalind."

"Except for my father."

They came to a large boulder and he halted. Then he climbed up on it and sat cross-legged, looking down at her.

"My father wants me have Rosalind. He wants me to have everything. The estate, the business."

"I see!" said Blanche. "And why are you telling me this?"

"I don't know. I just think you should know. I don't want you to get any nasty surprises later on."

"And does Troy know all this?"

"I imagine Lauren has made him pretty sure of it . . . I imagine he knows deep down anyway."

"And what's so special about Rosalind that your father wants you to marry her?"

"Beats me! He adores her, and her family . . . I think it's a pride thing. When he was growing up he had nothing and they were the local big shots at the time. So he thinks it's a bit of an honour for me to marry Rosalind."

"But you don't think it's an honour?"

"Well, honour is one of many words I can think of to label such a union!"

206

She laughed. "I'd better be getting back." She turned and started to walk back. He jumped off the boulder and followed her.

"I hope I haven't said anything to put you off your engagement?" he said.

"Was that your purpose – to try and put me off Troy? Presenting him as a pauper in the making to me?"

"No . . . but I do love my brother, Blanche. I wouldn't like somebody marrying him for the wrong reasons."

"I'm with him because I want to be, Jack. But I won't let him just be side-stepped by anyone either, and that includes you."

Troy was at the land where they were to build the house, hammering in a pole for a planning notice at the front of the site, when Niall drove up beside him.

"Just finished those plans today for the new house," said Troy. "Architect is sending them into the council tomorrow."

"That's good," said Niall, stepping out of his car. "I'm going to get the solicitor draw up the deeds of this land as well next week and get it officially signed over to you."

"Thanks, Dad, I really appreciate it."

"Not at all, you deserve your own place . . . you'd want to get yourself a herd of cattle as well and start farming your own herd here on this farm. I'll set you up with a herd, if you like."

"That's really kind, Dad, thanks."

"And I want to pay for your wedding, no expenses spared!"

"Thanks again!"

"And I've ordered a new car for your wife. An engagement gift from me to her."

"You're being overly generous."

Troy stared at his father, his mother's warning coming more to mind the more generous Niall was being.

"And anything else you need, you just let me know."

"How about Winterfield?"

Niall looked at him curiously. "Sorry?"

"The whole of Winterfield. How about you give me that some day as well?"

Niall gave a nervous laugh. "Son, let's not get ahead of ourselves. I'm setting you up here, but don't ask for the shirt off my back at the same time!"

"I'm not asking for the shirt off your back, but I do want to know what your plans for the future are."

"I haven't decided yet."

Troy walked up close to him. "Can you just be honest with me? I would appreciate it if you could. There's a strong rumour going around that Jack is going to be in charge at Winterfield and the business and I am going to get the crumbs. True?"

"Your mother has got some big mouth as well as a wild imagination."

"True or false, Dad?"

"Do you know something? It's none of your business."

"I just want to know why you love Jack more than me, Dad?" Troy stared at him.

"You're talking nonsense, as per usual. I'll see you later."

Niall went to walk to his car. Troy stood in his way.

"You know, I never could understand why you loved Jack more than me. I always knew you did. And I thought maybe, because his mother was gone, you had to try and compensate. And as we got older, I just thought, well, maybe it was because Jack just worked so much harder than me and so he deserved your love more. And then I thought, maybe it was because he was better at everything than me. And I know all this is true, but still I can't understand why you love him so much more than me. Can you answer that, please, Dad?"

Niall stared at his son and his face clouded over. "Maybe you just think too much, Troy – maybe you should give your brain a rest."

With that, he jumped into his car and tore off.

Blanche sat at her window looking out at the view, thinking about her talk with Jack. He was flirting outrageously with her and she knew under different circumstances she would be very much drawn to him. He might have been trying to put her off Troy but all he had managed to do was make her think more highly of him.

She left her room, hoping he was home, and made her way down the corridor to his room where she found him lying on a couch.

"Troy?"

"Hi, Blanche," he said, sitting up.

She raced across the room and, sitting beside him, put her arms around him and pulled him near. He melted into her arms and it felt as if this was the first time she had really shown love for him.

"Hey, what's all this?" he asked as she hugged him.

"I just want you to know I really do love you. And I'm so looking forward to our life together."

She pulled back and smiled at him and only then realised he had been crying.

"Troy!" she said, her face filling with concern. "What's wrong?"

"Ah, nothing. I'm just being a bit daft, ignore me."

"I want to know, Troy."

"Nothing! I just had a stupid run-in with my father. You're marrying into a mad family here, just so you know!"

"Look, nobody else matters but the two of us, okay? We'll build our house and live our lives and the rest of them, the rest of the world, doesn't matter, okay?"

"Okay!" he kissed her.

CHAPTER 30

Rosalind could only look on with increased frustration as the early weeks of the summer passed by. Blanche seemed to get her feet under the table very quickly. Not only with Troy, but Jack and Niall as well. Only Lauren kept a sceptical distance from her. Jack as ever was the host with the most and was busy organising everyone's social life. The Launcelots and their friends were often out socialising around Castleford, and the parties that summer at Jack's were becoming legendary as they continued on until the early morning.

And there was a lot to celebrate. Planning permission came through for Troy and Blanche's house, quickly guaranteed by Niall's close friendship with all the town councillors. And then there was the announcement of Blanche and Troy's wedding. They had opted for a day in September.

"What's the hurry?" asked Lauren.

"Oh, no hurry! Otherwise we'd be having it in August!" answered Troy happily.

Rosalind looked on, bored, one night out at the pool at

Winterfield, as Blanche and Jack had a drinking competition that involved tequila. They had been out on the town at a disco earlier. Now Rosalind and Troy, who had both opted out of the competition early, looked on as Blanche managed to fire another drink down her throat.

"Okay!" shouted Jack. "One more shot! Winner takes all!"

Duran Duran's 'Girls on Film' was blaring from the record player.

"Don't you think we should try and be a bit quieter?" suggested Rosalind. "You'll wake your parents."

"Ah, relax," snapped Jack. "Their room is at the front of the house."

Nobody was listening to her as they did their final leg of the competition and were declared joint winners.

As they watched Jack and Blanche get up and dance together, Rosalind asked Troy, "Don't you think it's a bit funny that Blanche never discusses her modelling career?"

"No, why should she? It's over."

"Well, if I was an ex-model, I think I'd like to talk about it."

"I'm sure you would never shut up about it!" said Troy.

"She changes the topic pretty quickly whenever it's brought up."

Troy turned and looked at Rosalind. "What are you getting at, Rosalind?"

"Oh, nothing. Nothing at all."

Rosalind knew what she would do first thing on Monday.

Rosalind set off early to drive up to Dublin and found herself sitting in the reception at Fashion Girls Model agency by twelve thirty, waiting for an appointment with its boss Samantha Armstrong.

The receptionist smiled over at her and said, "You can go in now."

"Thank you," said Rosalind.

She made her way down the corridor to Samantha's office. As Rosalind entered, Samantha stood up and smiled. Rosalind took in the glamorous brunette.

"Thanks so much for meeting me," said Rosalind, shaking her hand and taking a seat.

"You're more than welcome. Always available to discuss new business ventures."

"Sure."

"So, what did you have exactly in mind?" said Samantha, getting down to business quickly. "A charity fashion show in Castleford, is it?"

"Yes. Raising funds for the local hospital. We were thinking of hiring some big-name models to ensure we get the crowds in."

"Yeah, those kinds of events are being run all around the country and are proving to be very successful."

"People always like a bit of glamour!"

"They sure do."

"So what date are you thinking of?" pushed Samantha, taking out her diary.

"Em, maybe August some time. Mid-August."

"Okay, so maybe you could let me know what models you would like to book and I could check their availability?"

"Em, I was thinking of Toni Loftus."

"Uh huh, she's always very popular at events."

"And Diana Moran. Clodagh O'Neill."

"Good choices. And they're available."

"And maybe Blanche Fitzclarence?"

"Oh, I'm afraid Blanche Fitzclarence is no longer with the agency."

Rosalind managed to look very disappointed. "Oh no! The women on the charity board specifically asked for her – she's so beautiful! Can you track her down and employ her for us. We'd be willing to pay top rates."

Samantha sat forward. "Impossible. I don't even know where she is. She was a huge disappointment to me, to be honest. I really had her earmarked for the top."

"What happened then?"

"She just walked out one day, not only on me but her fiancé as well."

"Her fiancé?" Rosalind's eyes widened

"Yes, a lawyer – Billy Forrestal."

"Were they engaged for long?"

"Well, they were together a while, they lived together."

"Really?" Rosalind's face lit up.

"There was some nasty business. A break-in at their house and Billy was badly attacked. She discovered him and then just walked out on him when he was still in hospital. I think she behaved abominably."

"For sure!"

"So, no, she's no longer in the running, I'm afraid. What about Cassandra Spencer? She's fast becoming one of my top girls."

Work started on their new house and Troy spent much of his time down on the site watching the builders' progress. Blanche had observed that Troy was very excited over the work but also seemed to be glad to have something to do during the day. Yes, he drove around the farm a bit and did some work around Winterfield, but he didn't seem to have an actual role. The running of the farm seemed to be in Jack's very capable hands. She saw that, when something had to be decided on the farm, Jack made a quick decision while Troy was still dithering. Niall had a huge office on the ground floor at Winterfield. Jack would disappear for hours into that office with Niall and there would be a steady stream of visitors there during the day. She recognised a lot of them as local bank managers, businessmen and politicians. A couple of times she had found the office door ajar and had crept over and listened. She heard them discussing profit margins and buy-outs. She heard them on the phone to the managers of the pubs in London, either berating them or praising them over the latest sales figures.

One afternoon, Blanche was sunbathing on a lounger by the pool. She suddenly felt a splash of cold water over her. She sat up quickly to see a grinning Jack there, having just scooped some water from the pool and thrown it over her.

"Thanks for that!" said Blanche, shaking the water off.

"Well, you're a sight for sore eyes sitting there in the sun!" he said.

She felt a bit self-conscious in her bikini and reached over for a towel and put it over her.

"What you up to?" she asked, putting her hand up over her eyes to shade them.

"Oh, just been in a meeting with Dad, heading on home now. Going out later if you're free?"

"I'll check with Troy."

"You do that."

That night Troy and Blanche drove to Castleford to meet Jack and his friends in a local nightclub called Silvers.

"Is Rosalind coming out tonight?" asked Blanche.

"Don't know. I guess she is – isn't she always?"

Blanche sighed. "Unfortunately."

Troy glanced over to her. "Does it bother you?"

"What? The fact that she despises me?"

"No, she doesn't."

"She would despise anybody coming into her precious domain."

"She's fine – she's just a bit spirited."

They drove on in silence.

"Troy?"

"Uh huh?"

"Why don't you sit in on more meetings in Niall's office?"

"I sit in on enough of them."

"Not compared to Jack. He's always there."

"Well, bully for Jack!"

She reached over and gently touched his leg. "It's not a criticism. I'm just wondering."

Troy sighed. "Because they don't want me there."

"I'm sure that's not true. Your father dotes on you."

"Yeah, in the way you'd dote on a pet! But he doesn't want me involved in serious issues or decisions. I guess he doesn't trust my judgement."

"And how's that going to pan out for the future?"

Troy shrugged and, seeing he was becoming more uncomfortable, she dropped the subject.

Blanche couldn't keep her eyes off Jack that night. She was intrigued at how sociable he was. He knew everyone and everyone knew him. He was sending drinks over to other people's tables and they were sending drinks back. Women flocked to him. And when he turned and spoke to Blanche, she actually felt special to have the attention he was giving her.

Surprisingly, Rosalind didn't turn up that night, which Blanche was glad of. After the nightclub closed, they went back to Jack's for a party. By four most of the guests had gone home. Troy had gone upstairs to one of the bedrooms to sleep, leaving Blanche and Jack out on the patio drinking whiskey. They sat at the table, both with their legs stretched out and resting up on other chairs. It was just starting to get light and Blanche looked down at the little cove beneath them. In the wood that stretched down to the banks of the cove the early-morning singing of hundreds of birds could be heard.

"You know, I've never met anybody who could last as long as I do except you," said Jack.

"Last?"

"Yeah, usually I'm the last one standing, everyone else has gone home. But not you, you can stay up with me to the end."

"I'm not sure if that's an accolade."

"There's worse!" He winked at her and took a drink. "Where did you get your stamina?"

"I was always hanging out with the wrong crowd growing up, much to my mother's chagrin. Then when I modelled, I guess we partied pretty hard then as well. I guess I don't need that much sleep. Which is just as well, living at Winterfield."

"Why?" He looked at her mischievously. "Is Troy keeping you up all night? I thought Lauren was insisting on separate bedrooms."

She leaned over and slapped his arm. "I'm not talking about that!"

"Oh, sorry!"

"I mean the shouting matches that seem to go on every night between Niall and Lauren."

"Oh those!" He looked out to the harbour, almost disinterested.

"It's a bit unsettling to listen to . . . did they always argue like that?"

"Not really. I remember them having a mostly happy marriage when I was growing up."

217

"Do you remember your own mother?"

"Yeah, just about . . . I remember her being beautiful and kind and lovely. And she and Dad were so happy and we were all so happy . . . and then suddenly she was gone."

"That's horrible."

"Yeah, it was. And I remember a change in Dad. He could hardly function for a long while. And all the safety and security and happiness were gone. And then he started getting better and Lauren arrived on the scene and he married her and life went on."

"And did you get on with her, as a stepmother?"

"Yeah, she was fine . . . she was great. Very nice and very loving actually. Good for Dad, good for everyone. Lauren's a strong woman."

"I gathered that. So why's there so much tension in the house now?"

"Everything was fine until Lauren realised that I was so much better than her own son. Better at business, better with people, cleverer."

"That's not nice and it's very big-headed of you," snapped Blanche.

"But it's fucking true, and I'm not making any apologies for it any more, baby." He looked at her pointedly. "She started getting funny when she realised that I'm a much better man. The mothering instinct kicked in and suddenly she was out to protect her own."

"That sounds very hard."

"But it's true. Whatever bond was between me and Lauren is gone now."

Blanche looked at him and didn't know whether to feel angry with him for his arrogance or sorry for him for losing two mothers.

"And do you really think that Lauren would just reject her stepson because he's 'better', your words not mine, than her own son?"

"Oh yeah, of course! There're big things at stake here, baby. We're talking control of the business and Winterfield. And Lauren is all very glamorous but she's from the poor side of town in Castleford. She knows what it's like not to have much. Do you know she was employed as my nanny? That's how she and Dad met."

"Well, as far I can see, this is all your father's fault. He should just divide everything squarely between the two of you."

"That wouldn't work. There has to be a clear heir. Besides, why should I use all my talent and brains and hard work to keep the rest of the family in the life they are accustomed to? I love them, but is it fair?"

"Oh, I don't know what's fair, Jack. It's a messy situation."

"You know, I was due to go to London this year to check on the pubs, not Troy. Only Lauren stepped in and insisted that Troy went instead. So off he went . . . and met you."

"I'd say she wishes she'd kept him home now, safe with Rosalind," Blanche said wryly.

Jack looked at her. "I wish she'd kept him at home too . . . then it would have been me who would have met you and not Troy."

She looked at him and shrugged. "So?"

"Well . . . it would have been us that ended up together."

Blanche's voice turned cynical. "Very doubtful, Jack. I doubt you would have even given me a second look pulling pints behind that bar."

"That's what you think. I would never have let somebody like you go."

Blanche sighed. "Jack, you're a born flirt."

"I'm not flirting, Blanche, I mean it . . . I've never met anybody like you." He looked at her meaningfully.

She looked into his eyes and felt something stir inside her.

"Don't, Jack," she warned.

"Why? I'm only speaking how I feel."

"Jack! I'm not one of your sluts in Castleford – I'm your brother's fiancée!"

"I know! I know! I'm not saying this lightly. I've struggled with myself since I first saw you to contain how I feel . . . and now . . . maybe it's the whiskey, but I can't hold it in any more."

"Let's just put it down to the whiskey and forget we had this conversation, shall we?"

"I can't, Blanche. I've fallen for you."

"You're being ridiculous, Jack. What are you suggesting? Are you really so immoral that you'd fuck your brother's fiancée? Another notch on the bedpost along with everyone else's wife in this shitty town?"

He reached out and grabbed her hand and his touch gave her a start. "No! It's not like that, I swear! I can't get you out of my head, Blanche. I can't bear to see you with Troy . . . I can't bear living my life without you."

"So what are you suggesting?" Her eyes widened with incredulity.

"Whatever you want, Blanche. I can give you anything you want."

"So are you suggesting I leave your brother and go with you and we all just go on with life as normal? That'll be very interesting over Christmas dinner, don't you think?"

"No, of course not. We'll leave here."

"You'd never leave Winterfield, Jack."

"Do you think? Do you know sometimes I think I'm going to go mad here! It's so fucking small and provincial. Sometimes I long to get the fuck away from here. That's why I party so much and fuck around trying to make life fucking interesting."

"And is that what you're doing now, making life interesting? I guess it would be an interesting situation – sleeping with your brother's wife!"

"No, Blanche!"

"Well, it wouldn't be the first time you shared a woman. Rosalind, remember?"

"This is nothing like that!" His grip on her hand tightened. "Let's leave here, Blanche. We can go anywhere. Let's give Lauren and Troy what they want – we'll leave them at Winterfield, and we can go and run the pubs in London."

"For fuck's sake, Jack! You've got it all worked out!"

"Or if you want no connection with Launcelots, we can go somewhere else – New York, Los Angeles. I'm not like Troy, I don't need to rely on my father's money, Blanche. I can make it on my own – with you by my side."

He reached forward and his lips were on hers. She struggled to get away, but suddenly she was responding and kissing him back.

The sound of somebody walking down the stairs inside the house jolted them away from each other.

"Blanche?" Troy called from inside.

Blanche and Jack stared at each other.

"I mean what I'm saying, Blanche. Think about it," whispered Jack.

She stared into his eyes and then called, "We're out here!"

Troy came out onto the patio, rubbing his eyes and face.

"What are you two like?" said Troy with a laugh, looking at the near-empty whiskey bottle. "You know, you're a bad influence on each other."

Blanche got up, forcing a smile.

"Are we staying here the night?" asked Troy.

"Eh, no, let's head home," said Blanche. "Come on."

As they left, she turned to look at Jack who was still staring at her.

CHAPTER 31

Rosalind was at her desk, working on an article about a local sports event. She picked up the phone and rang Winterfield.

"Hi, it's me," she said when Lauren answered.

"Oh, hi! What you up to?"

"Just writing a review of that shitty sports day I had to attend last week. Trying to make it sound like last year's Moscow Olympics instead of the dullest day I've endured for some time."

Lauren laughed her throaty laugh. "Well, you got to earn a buck somehow, darling."

"Hmm, I shouldn't complain. Where else could I work my own hours and hear all the local gossip first hand."

"Yeah – don't knock it, darling."

"I was going to invite myself over for dinner tonight."

"Great ."

"How's Troy?"

"I don't know what to say, Rosalind. He's going around as happy as I've ever seen him. Sleepwalking towards his own destruction. Down at that fucking building site all the

223

time, building this dream home of theirs. I'd swear he goes down there to avoid me trying to get him to see sense."

"And what's Bianca Jagger doing all day?"

"Blanche? Oh, if she's not down at the site with Troy, she's in Castleford shopping, or out by the pool sunbathing. You can just see that she was brought up as a spoilt bitch. Then she goes off walking for ages on her own, off down by the coast."

"Well, don't worry, after tonight I don't think she's going to be around for much longer."

"What do you mean, Rosalind?" demanded Lauren.

"I don't want to say anything else, because I don't want to ruin the surprise!"

Blanche walked along the beach on her own, staring out to sea as the waves came tumbling in. She breathed in the fresh air wishing it would clear her mind, but it didn't, her mind remained clouded. She had been deeply shocked by Jack's declaration, but even more shocked by how she had responded to it. She was filled with shame but also a sense of excitement. She had been suppressing how she felt about Jack since she met him. But he excited her, in a way that Troy didn't. She didn't feel that all-encompassing love that she felt for Billy, but she felt passion for him. It was impossible, she knew, but she couldn't walk away from it either and now she was deeply troubled. Could she really marry Troy, when she had these feelings for his brother? Sighing, she turned and began to walk back to the house.

Blanche could hear a lot of laughter and talk coming from the lounge as she came down to dinner. Rosalind was there. Her heart sank. Rosalind made her feel more and more uncomfortable, and she seemed to never be out of the house. As she came into the hall, she heard the office door open down the corridor and she could hear Jack say a few words to his father before closing the door and coming into the hall. They stared at each other and Blanche felt herself go red.

"Hi, Blanche," he said, smiling.

"Jack." She nodded at him.

He walked up close to her. "Have you been thinking about what I said?"

"Of course I have. I haven't been able to think of anything else."

"And?"

"For fuck's sake, Jack. You've put me in an impossible situation." Her eyes filled with tears.

He reached out and touched her arm and her body responded to him.

"Just tell me you feel the same way and we can start a new life together," he said, a look of pleading in his face.

"Ah there you are!" said Lauren coming into the lobby. "We're waiting on you and Niall for dinner, Blanche."

"Sorry, I didn't realise the time." Blanche smiled at Lauren and blinked away a few tears.

"You joining us for dinner, Jack?" Lauren asked, smiling at him while still managing to give him a steely look.

"No, thanks, Lauren, I've an appointment in town."

"What – at this time? What kind of an appointment is it? Somebody's wife?" She looked wryly at him.

He gave her a filthy look. "No, Lauren, with a cattle dealer we're selling some of our herd to."

"Oh, I'm sorry, darling. I didn't mean to offend. Mud sticks, you know how it is."

"I'll see you later." Jack glanced at Blanche and then walked past Lauren out of the house.

"That was a bit mean," commented Blanche.

"I only speak the truth. Now, I'm starving. Go on in while I call Niall."

Troy was regaling everybody with descriptions of the house he was building.

"And then in the lounge there's a really high ceiling, like a church ceiling, that goes right up to the roof of the house – and a huge wall of windows looking out over the sea. And the landing upstairs is like a balcony looking down on the lounge with –"

"Oh, for goodness sake, Troy, if I hear another word about that house, I'm going to vomit on my steak!" snapped Rosalind. "Pass the gravy."

"I'm sorry for boring you, Rosalind," said Troy, managing to look a mixture of hurt and angry.

Rosalind seized her moment.

"Having said that, it sounds like the house is going to be glamorous enough for a former model like you, Blanche, huh?"

Blanche ignored her.

"Are you going to invite all your model friends down to see the new house?" pushed Rosalind.

"I'm sure they're all too busy to make the long journey down here."

"Surely not. I was talking to an old friend of yours recently."

Blanche felt herself tense.

"Samantha Armstrong. She was your old boss, wasn't she?"

Blanche coughed slightly. "Yes."

"Well, the things she didn't say about you! She's pretty pissed off with you. You left her in the lurch and she had to cancel all your contracts. But she wasn't half as pissed off with you as your former fiancé seemingly was. Some fella called Billy Forrestal, ring any bells? The lawyer guy you were living with? The poor fella was beaten up and in hospital and Christie Brinkley here decides to fuck off and leave him there . . . Such good character. She's sullied goods, I'm afraid to tell you. Seemingly she shagged half of Dublin while she was at it."

Blanche felt everyone look at her. She got up from the table and walked quickly from the dining room. She raced up the stairs and down the corridor to her bedroom. Tears filled her eyes as she took out her suitcase and started packing it with her clothes.

Her bedroom door opened and Troy came in. She ignored him as she continued to pack.

"Blanche, what are you doing?" demanded Troy.

"What does it look like I'm doing, Troy? I'm leaving here."

"Don't be so stupid! Why?"

"Are you kidding me? You've just heard all that downstairs. I'm not going to hang around here any more. And Troy, if you have any idea what's good for you, you'll let me go."

Troy went to her. "Blanche, will you please stop packing and talk to me!"

She ignored him.

"Blanche!"

She stopped and looked at him. "I know what people of your parents' generation think about living together before marriage. I had to endure my own parents' reaction. And now with all those other little revelations they'll always see me as a whore. Lauren doesn't like me anyway. Believe me, you'll thank me in the long run."

She went to start her packing again but he gripped both her arms and held her tightly.

"Blanche, what's this about? You're hardly doing a runner just because you have a bit of a past and you ran out on a modelling career?"

"Don't you care that I lived with somebody before?"

"No. We all have a past. Mine's Rosalind, for fuck's sake!" He managed to laugh.

He loosened his grip on her arms and slipped his hands up to her shoulders.

"Come on, level with me. Tell me the real problem."

"I can't!" She started to cry.

"Come on," he encouraged. She looked into his kind face and suddenly it was all coming out. About Shay, the men she dated, about Billy, and then about the terrorists and the blackmail and finally Billy's attack and her running away. By the time she finished, she was crying as he held her in his arms.

"So you see I have to go. They might find me here and none of us would be safe."

"Shhh!" he soothed. He held her face firmly in his hands. "Nobody is going to come near you. You're safe here. Leave Rosalind to me, and I'll sort her out. You're not leaving me, Blanche."

"But I've been so stupid. I fucked up so much. I handled everything badly. If I had gone to the police in the first place . . ."

"Shhhh . . . then I would have never have met you. And I'd be living a half-life, married to Rosalind. I'm very glad you fucked up."

She felt so safe with him and so relieved to have told somebody about it all. She felt free from the burden of it.

Rosalind sat in her sitting room at home after pouring a glass of wine for herself. Her parents were at a function in town. She was still savouring the look of shock on everyone's face when she'd revealed Blanche's past. This area was very conservative. The Launcelots would be horrified that Blanche had set up home without a ring on her finger. And then running out on her poor fiancé as he lay half-dead! It showed lack of common decency.

She heard a car pull up aggressively out the front of the house. The front door opened and she heard Troy's voice shout her name.

Troy came storming into the sitting room. She took one look at his face and got a fright he looked so angry.

She stood up quickly and jumped behind the sofa.

"Now don't go and take it out on me just because your fiancée is a slut!" warned Rosalind.

"You shit-stirring bitch!" he shouted at her and came lurching across the room at her.

"*Ahhh!*" she screamed as she dodged him and went running to the other side of the sofa.

"What do you think you're doing poking around Blanche's past?"

"Well, if the dirt wasn't there then it wouldn't matter how much digging I'd do, would it? She's a tramp, Troy, pure and simple. She went out with married men, she was living with this guy —"

"Did you tell this Samantha Armstrong that Blanche was here?"

She was frightened by the anger in him.

"Did you?" he demanded.

"No! I just did some enquiring."

"Now, you listen to me. You're never going to contact this Samantha Armstrong again, understand? You're never going to go messing in my relationship again. Understand? And if you ever try to damage Blanche again, then I will get you. Do you understand me?"

"I understand," she gasped.

"And don't just come by Winterfield any more like it's your home. Your behaviour means you're not welcome any more."

He turned and stormed off.

"So?" Lauren asked, sitting on the bed where Niall was sitting up reading a book.

"So what?"

"So what are you going to do about your son's engagement now we know all about your future daughter-in-law?"

"Nothing," he said, looking down and starting to read his book again.

"Niall!" her voice rose. "We need to act on this. We can't let Troy make the biggest mistake of his life."

"You mean the biggest mistake of *your* life, Lauren. Rosalind and her idle tittle tattle, who cares?"

"I care! And you should care too!"

"Look, from the moment Blanche came here I have found her polite, well-mannered, intelligent and good-humoured. But most importantly, she makes the boy happy. Good luck to the two of them."

"Niall, she was living with some guy in Dublin. She's been out with married men. She just isn't respectable!"

"Big deal! You know, this town makes me sick. Everyone's so judgemental, and if the truth be known half of them are riding outside their marriages. Hypocrites!"

"If they are riding outside their marriages it's probably because Jack Launcelot is riding them!"

Blanche lay in her bed, wide awake. She could hear Lauren and Niall having a shouting match in their bedroom. Troy had come home and said he had sorted Rosalind out and she wouldn't go back to any of the people in Blanche's past again. Then they had held each other tightly and both cried.

Blanche looked at the clock and, seeing it was three in the morning, she slipped out of bed and put on a dress. Then she crept out of her room and down out of the house and into her car. She started the car up and drove off as quietly as she could.

She wasn't surprised to see the lights on in Jack's house when she drove up. The man never seemed to sleep. She got out of the car and knocked on the door.

A few seconds later she heard Jack's voice.

"Who is it?"

"It's me, Blanche."

He quickly unlocked the door and she saw a big smile across his face.

"Come on in!" he invited.

She quickly came in and he closed the door. He looked at her for a few seconds and then suddenly he had his arms around her and was trying to kiss her.

"Jack! Stop!"

"What? This is what you want. Why else have you come to me in the middle of the night?"

"No, Jack, it's not what I want. I've come here tonight to tell you that we will never be together. I think you were insane even to suggest it. I don't want it mentioned again."

"I don't accept that. Look, Blanche, there's this huge attraction between us –"

"Jack! I don't want to be with a man like you. I've been attracted to men like you all my life. Somebody who is fun and full of life and dangerous to know. Well, men like you *are* dangerous to know, and I've known enough of them to know when to stay away. I'd never be happy with you. It wouldn't be stable – you'd get bored with me one day and move on to somebody else."

"I wouldn't, Blanche, it would be different with you!"

"I've met men like you and you'll say and promise anything to get what you want, and then treat women like dirt."

"Not me!"

"That's what they all say. I know the warning signs, and for once in my life I'm listening to those signs. With Troy I've got somebody who loves and respects me. A wonderful life partner who I'm going to have a wonderful life with. Not somebody I can't trust, somebody with a wandering eye and selfish nature like you."

"Blanche, that's not me!"

"Now I'm going back to my fiancé who I love. And we're going to have a wonderful life together. And I don't think we should come around partying here any more. I don't think it's appropriate, under the circumstances." She walked to the door.

Jack's face showed all his hurt. "Troy will never satisfy you, Blanche, never."

"I've been offered happiness, Jack, and I'm taking it." She opened the door and left.

CHAPTER 32

Rosalind sat with her mother watching Lady Diana walking down the aisle to marry Prince Charles. She took out a handkerchief and dabbed at her eyes, then took a drink of her gin.

"Looks like we'll be having our own royal wedding next door soon," said Rosalind's mother. "Since you haven't managed to spilt up my boyo from his model."

"I just wanted my own prince and my own fairytale ending!" said Rosalind, as the tears came down her face.

"You believe in fairytales, Rosalind. Do you honestly think those two are really in love?" She nodded at the royal couple exchanging vows.

"Well, of course they are!"

"Bullshit! It's a show if you ask me. Now, if you really want a prince, you get up to Jack Launcelot's door and get the deal done before he slips away as well!"

Rosalind parked outside Jack's hunting lodge and looked up at the ivy-clad building nestled into the forested hill. It was late afternoon. She sighed and got out of the car.

The door was usually open at the lodge so she just pushed it in.

"Jack!" she called.

"Out here!" came a voice from the patio.

Jack was sitting on a sun lounger, a beer in his hand, looking out at the view. On the stereo player, Crystal Gale was singing 'Don't It Make My Brown Eyes Blue'.

Rosalind sauntered over to the empty chair on the other side of the patio table and sat down.

"I heard about your revelations at dinner the other night about Blanche," said Jack. "That was dirty trick, going hunting around in her past."

Rosalind shrugged. "Do I care?"

"You can be a nasty little bitch."

"If the cap fits."

She studied him. He seemed in a thoughtful and depressed mood.

"Anyway, from what I hear, you didn't manage to frighten her off," he said.

"Nope, I think she's here to stay."

"You must be heartbroken over Troy?"

"Oh pooh! Troy! I never even gave him a second thought."

"Who are you kidding?"

"He's history . . . I just wonder where this leaves us?"

"Us?"

"Well, if we don't do something, we'll be out in the cold. Troy and Blanche are very much taking centre stage. In fact, I've already been told not to arrive into Winterfield any more unexpectedly."

He looked at her, surprised. "Who said that?"

"Troy . . . they'll be saying it to you next."

"I'd like to see them try."

"They're already trying." She paused. "Our daddies want us to hitch up, you know."

"Tell me something new."

"Well, maybe it's not such a bad idea."

He looked over to her, startled. "What am I? Your second choice?"

"And what am I? Your tenth? There comes a time when you have to be practical. How many bars, or married women's beds can you continue to be thrown out of?"

"Are you being serious?"

"We've been out before. We didn't make each other totally unhappy."

"We didn't exactly make each other happy either, did we? I don't know if that's a good enough reason to get married."

She dropped her voice and spoke more intimately. "I always found the chemistry between us much stronger than between me and Troy . . . before you decided to be so unreliable. We could tell them all where to go, Jack. Me and you together, we could rule this place. Nobody would come near to us. Blanche and Troy, ha! They'd be an afterthought. Do you hear me?"

"I hear you."

"Sometimes if you can't have what you want . . . then you have to take what you can have."

He glared at her, wondering if she knew. Had she observed his feelings for Blanche?

Rosalind and Jack stood in the lounge at Winterfield surrounded by all the Launcelot family, Rosalind's parents and some close friends. The champagne bottle popped and there was a cry of celebration from everyone.

Rosalind stretched out a hand that was proudly

displaying a gigantic engagement ring. Jack stood beside her, arm around her waist, beaming a smile.

"It's going to be the biggest wedding Castleford has ever seen!" declared Rosalind.

Both Niall and Rosalind's father, James, stood near the happy couple. They were talking and laughing, clapping each other on the back. Their long-held dream finally had come true. Rosalind looked ecstatic. Jack looked very handsome and happy beside her.

Blanche sat on the couch, a glass of champagne in her hand. Jack glanced over at her and held her stare, suddenly serious.

Blanche felt a hand rest on her shoulder and she looked up to see Troy.

"What do you make of that?" whispered Troy to her.

"They make a lovely couple." She laughed. "I know Niall is delighted to be getting his hands on the Dawson farm . . . but, you know, Rosalind's father really doesn't need to give a dowry."

"Why not?"

"Because he's already giving one cow!"

Standing beside Niall, Lauren muttered: "I guess you're happy!"

"Very!" He smiled at her and raised his glass.

Blanche came out the back to have a quiet cigarette. As she walked along the pool, she spotted a figure at the bottom of the garden. It was Lauren. Blanche hesitated and then walked down the garden towards her.

"I didn't realise you smoked," she commented as she spotted the cigarette in Lauren's hand.

"I don't . . . but I just fancied one tonight." Lauren took a drag from her cigarette.

Blanche leaned on the wall and looked over it to the straight drop to the rocky beach with the waves crashing against it.

She looked back at Lauren. "That's good news about Jack and Rosalind," she said.

"I guess."

Blanche gazed at Lauren's stressed and unfriendly face. "You don't like me much, do you, Lauren?"

Lauren sighed loudly. "Don't take it personally, sweetheart. I'm sure you're a very nice girl. It's just you've stepped into a minefield here and you don't even realise it."

Blanche laughed cynically. "On the contrary, I think I realise it very much."

Lauren studied her. "You don't strike me as a girl who's played second fiddle much in her life, have you?"

Blanche shrugged. "I don't think so."

"Well, you might as well get used to it, because you're going to spend the rest of your life playing second fiddle to Rosalind and Jack. She'll take over here."

"I thought you and Rosalind were close," said Blanche, confused.

"We were, when we were on the same side . . . I know what it feels like to spend your life playing second fiddle, Blanche. That's why I was so determined that my son wouldn't as well."

"And who have you played second fiddle to?" asked Blanche incredulously, looking at the determined and indomitable frame of Lauren.

"Elizabeth. Jack's mother. Niall's first wife." Lauren flicked her half-finished cigarette over the wall and watched it fall down the cliff face to the rocky beach below.

"But she's been dead for years."

"She's still here, in Niall's mind. The great love of his life. Oh, he loves me, but he's still in love with Elizabeth. I know he thinks about her all the time, still, after all these years. He sees her in Jack. Every time Jack comes into the house, it's like her ghost is following him . . . and now she's won . . . her son will live here and not mine. Niall told me once that sometimes he still thinks he sees her. Out by that swimming pool that she had built, or walking down a corridor. Or riding across the fields on that horse that threw her and killed her . . . As I said, I know what it's like to play second fiddle, and you might as well get used to it as well."

"I'm not going to play second fiddle to anyone, Lauren, and I'm not going to let Troy either."

Lauren shrugged and smiled. "Darling, you're not even sitting at the table when it comes to this poker game . . . however, you have one advantage. It's easier to fight the living than the dead."

Blanche had been avoiding Jack all night and decided she couldn't put it off any further. She went up to him.

"Congratulations, Jack," she said, smiling warmly at him, and reached forward and kissed his cheek.

He looked at her coolly. "Thanks," he said coldly, and walked off.

Rosalind stretched out her hand in front of Blanche and Troy, admiring her ring. "I'm a bit embarrassed by the size of this engagement ring," she said, flashing the diamond. "It's *too* big if you ask me. I said it to Jack. I said I just can't arrive back to Winterfield wearing that thing – it would just embarrass poor Blanche too much with her little rock."

"Well, you were never too bothered about embarrassing me in the past," said Blanche acidly.

"You're just too sensitive, Blanche. And now we're going to be family and, well, we just *have* to get along. Isn't that right, Troy?"

Troy nodded.

"We're aiming for a winter wedding. I said to Jack, there's no point waiting around. Having said that, we didn't want to be too near your wedding, because we didn't want to overshadow you." Rosalind smiled and walked off.

Blanche stroked her fiancé's back as he stared after Rosalind.

"Don't mind her! She's just trying to stir it," said Blanche.

"She and him are going to be running this place," said Troy glumly.

Blanche looked at Rosalind as she threw her head back and laughed at something Niall had said. We'll see, thought Blanche, I've come up against a lot worse than her in the past.

CHAPTER 33

Blanche was driving back from Castleford when she spotted Jack's car by a field at the edge of the Winterfield estate. She pulled over and got out of the car. She walked past his car to the gate of the field and saw Jack there inspecting a horse.

"Hi there!" she called.

He looked up and, leaving the horse, strolled over to the gate.

"What you up to?" he asked.

"Oh, just coming back from shopping, and I spotted your car. Um, I didn't manage to have a proper chat with you the other evening at your engagement party."

He looked at her coolly, no sign of the former flirty warmth he always showed her. "So? What was there to chat about?"

"Don't be like that, Jack. We're going to be family, so we might as well try to get along . . . I don't want what happened between us to stop us being friends."

"What happened between us? Nothing happened between us, Blanche."

"I know that . . . but you know what I mean."

"No, I don't." He suddenly had a knowing look and laughed. "Oh, you mean *that*! Darling, you are sadly deluded if you believed for one second that I really was ever interested in you!"

She studied his mocking face, but his eyes were filled with hurt and anger.

"Okay, Jack. If that's how you want to play it – if that makes you feel better about the situation – then that's okay by me. Everyone has their pride."

"Yeah? Well, yours should be on the floor. Because when Rosalind and I get married, we'll be taking over, and you and Troy and Lauren can live by our rules or no rules. Understand?"

"I don't want us to be like this, Jack."

"Well, tough, because that's the way it's going to be."

"And they say that there's no fury like a woman scorned! A man is just as bad."

"Scorned? In your dreams! Now fuck off!"

Blanche spent the rest of the morning going through old photo albums. After going through tons of photos of Lauren through the years, she finally came across an album with photos of Elizabeth. Blanche stared at the photos of the beautiful woman. Dressed in ballgowns with Niall by her side. Photos of Elizabeth with a baby Jack. Photos of Elizabeth on horseback, wearing cream jodhpurs and a cream shirt. Blanche looked at her black hair, and going over to the mirror, began to brush her dark hair into the same fashion.

Blanche steadied herself outside Niall's office and then knocked on his door.

241

"Yeah?" shouted Niall from inside.

She opened the door and looked around it.

"Niall? Sorry for disturbing you!"

"That's alright." He was smiling at her but looked puzzled. "Can I help you with anything?"

"Yes, you can. It's just that I went down to the stables today to go riding and Seán said I needed your permission before I could take a horse out."

"Oh!" He sat up and looked uncomfortable. "Are you an experienced horsewoman?"

"Yes. I spent a lot of time on horses growing up. It's a big hobby of mine."

It was almost as if he was looking at her with new eyes.

"I would have thought you'd be more into cocktails and nightclubs than being an outdoors type."

"I love horse-riding."

Her hair had grown quite long and the sun coming in the window behind him made her dark hair shine. For a moment he was lost in thought and time as she reminded him of Elizabeth all those years ago.

"Niall? Is it alright if I take one of the horses?"

"Eh, yes, of course you can."

"You're sure Niall said you could take the horse out?" asked Seán as he helped Blanche mount outside the stables.

"Of course I'm sure. I'd hardly lie." Blanche leaned forward and patted the horse on the neck.

"It's just he doesn't like women out on horses as a rule. Ever since the accident. You heard about the accident?" Seán was looking up at her with that permanent leering smile he seemed to have.

"Yes. I heard all about it."

Seán was holding the reins of the horse tightly.

"If you could let go, I'd like to get on," said Blanche, and he let go.

She began to trot the horse out of the courtyard. She had chosen cream jodhpurs and a matching cream top.

Niall was outside Winterfield talking to Troy.

"The house should be finished in a couple of weeks, Dad. If you want to come and take a look as we put on the finishing touches?"

"Yeah, I'll try and get time to take a look next week," said Niall.

Suddenly his attention was caught by the sight of a woman riding through the fields. Her long dark hair was flowing behind her and she was dressed in cream.

"Dad? Are you alright?" asked Troy, seeing his face.

Niall's eyes followed the woman on horseback as she rode on.

"It's Blanche!" said Niall, staring.

"Of course it's Blanche. Who else would it be?" said Troy smiling.

CHAPTER 34

Since Rosalind and Jack's engagement announcement, Niall and Lauren hadn't rowed once. Lauren was reeling from the news and trying to come to terms with the fact that her plans had been fruitless.

They were sitting up in bed, she pretending to read a magazine while she thought about the future, Niall pretending to read a book though he was thinking of the image of Blanche riding across country looking the spit of Elizabeth all those years ago.

"Lauren?"

"Uh huh?"

"Don't you think it's odd that Troy has arrived back from London with a bride just like I arrived back with Elizabeth from London all those years ago? Kind of like history repeating itself. It's kind of funny, isn't it?"

"Hilarious! Now, shhh, I'm trying to concentrate."

Blanche spent the morning in Castleford going from boutique to boutique. She knew what she was looking for and finally found it. A two-piece sky-blue suit, as near as possible to the one she saw Elizabeth wearing in one of the photographs. After that she went to the salon and got her hair styled in the same fashion as Elizabeth's in that photo.

Niall stood in the impressive lounge of the new house at the wall of windows that looked out to the sea. He saw Blanche's car pull up.

An excited Troy had been showing his father around.

"Well?"

Niall saw the excitement in his son's face, almost pleading for him to give him praise.

"It's a fine job, son," said Niall.

"Really?" Troy could hardly believe the praise.

"Yep, I wish I was moving in here myself!"

"Hello?" called Blanche as she entered the house.

"In here!" called Troy.

Blanche walked through the large hall and paused to steady herself. Then, poised, she walked into the huge lounge smiling.

Niall stared almost in disbelief. For a moment he thought she was Elizabeth.

"Dad loves the house!" declared Troy.

"Really?" Blanche smiled at Niall.

"Don't you, Dad? . . . Dad?"

Niall tore his eyes away from Blanche. "It's gorgeous, Troy."

Niall and Blanche were out riding.

"You're a great horsewoman," complimented Niall.

"Thank you. You're sure you don't mind coming out riding with me today?"

"No, it's my pleasure. When are your parents coming up?"

"Oh, a week before the wedding. That's soon enough. My mother tends to fuss, so a week is plenty."

Niall laughed. "Planned anywhere for the honeymoon?"

"London, maybe," said Blanche.

"London?" Niall was surprised. "But Troy hates London."

"Oh, he doesn't really. He loved when he was there last, from what I could see. Loved working in the pubs."

"Troy did?" Niall looked incredulous.

"Yeah. He came up with some great ideas. Modernised the music, which attracted in a new younger crowd. Introduced new drinks. Small changes, but they made a difference. Did he not tell you?"

"No – no, he didn't. Then again – I didn't ask."

"Oh, you should ask, Niall. He just needs a little encouragement from you. But he loves the business."

Blanche rode on ahead, leaving Niall looking after her.

Jack came through the study door at Winterfield holding a large folder.

"Dad – the bank's been on and we need this signed –" He stopped abruptly as he saw Troy sitting beside Niall at his desk.

"Oh, you're busy, will I come back later?" asked Jack, looking at Troy.

"No – no. Come on in," said Niall. "Just going through a few things with Troy. Actually, I want him to know about this deal we're setting up, so bring in that file and we can talk Troy through it."

Jack stood stock still, staring at Troy in confusion.

"Jack?" prompted Niall. "Let's make a start."

"Oh, okay." Jack approached the desk with the file, feeling confused.

Blanche and Troy were in the new house looking at the cream leather couches that had been delivered that morning.

"What do you think?" asked Troy.

"Fabulous. Suits the room perfectly."

"Great. Well, I'd better head. Dad asked me to go for a meeting up at the house at three."

Blanche smiled. "Are you enjoying all these meetings?"

"Dad takes his time to really explain everything to me, much to Jack's irritation."

"Why's he irritated?"

"I don't know. Maybe because me being there is slowing down the whole process so much. You know how clever Jack is with all this stuff – he hasn't much patience."

Blanche walked over to him and put her arms around him. "You've every right to be there as Jack has. Fuck him! He's been used to having things his way too long around here."

CHAPTER 35

McEvoys was a large department store in Castleford. Upstairs in the ladies' department, which was practically empty, Jack was sitting rather glumly on one of the long luxurious couches provided, as Rosalind tried on different outfits for Blanche and Troy's wedding. Beside him was a big paper shopping bag containing the suit he had just bought downstairs.

Rosalind was looking at herself in a full-length mirror. She was wearing a yellow dress.

"What do you think of this?" She spun around for him.

"It's a bit too flouncy."

"Is it? Hmmm." She glanced at him, noting his sour expression, then went back into the dressing cubicle. "You're looking a bit depressed?" she called out to him.

"I can't get rid of Troy out of the meetings," Jack complained. "Dad is suddenly insisting he sits in all the time. And he knows fuck all about anything!"

"I blame that bitch Blanche. I've seen the way she licks up to him all the time."

"Do you think so?"

Rosalind came out in a sophisticated black dress.

"I think so. What do you think of this one?" she said and she did a turn.

"Nah, doesn't really suit you, Rosalind."

She sighed and walked back into the dressing cubicle.

"I know what she's doing. She's trying to manipulate Niall. Trying to get him on her side," she called out.

"And why is she doing that?"

"Why do you think? So that she and Troy won't be pushed out of the business, out of Winterfield."

"Well, her charm offensive seems to be working," said Jack.

"Bullshit! We're going to push her out. In fact, we're not going to give her any leeway to get in the door. Starting with her wedding day. We're going to take over that day and everyone will see we're the real stars of the show around here." Rosalind walked out wearing a white satin dress, figure-hugging, that flowed all the way to the floor, with a white stole.

"What do you think of this one?" she asked with a big smile.

"You can't wear that!" said Jack, his eyes widening.

"And why?"

"Isn't there an unwritten rule that you can't wear white to a wedding, let alone a full-length white dress?"

"Well, if the rule isn't written down then I don't obey it. I think this dress will do just nicely for Blanche's wedding."

Blanche was waiting anxiously at the front door of Winterfield for her parents to arrive. She was filled with a strange mix of excitement and dread. She had changed so much since she had last seen them, and gone through so much. She felt she understood them a lot more now than that spoilt girl who was impossible to control. But would they understand her?

Then she saw her father's Jaguar coming up the long drive.

Eagerly she walked outside and down the steps of the house onto the forecourt.

The Jaguar pulled up and she felt her heart jump at the sight of her mother and father, who were smiling at her. Her mother stepped out of the car, a picture of understated elegance, a stylish scarf around her neck.

"Mum!" said Blanche and suddenly she was in her mother's arms, holding her tightly.

"Well, this is a welcome!" said Harriet, embracing her back.

And then she was hugging her father.

"Come on in, let me introduce you to everyone!" smiled Blanche.

"It took us absolutely ages to get down here," stated Harriet, taking a sip from the teacup in her hand. They were in the front lounge. "The roads really are atrocious. The government really needs to do something about it."

"Absolutely! More tea?" Lauren asked, raising the pot.

"No, I'm fine, thank you. We've booked into the Castleford Arms as you suggested, Blanche," said Daniel.

"It's a bit olde worlde," said Harriet. "Perhaps a little too much so. I don't think your Aunt Camilla will appreciate it. Is there anywhere else to stay?"

"Well, there's The Roadhouse. The new place on the Dublin Road," said Niall.

"Oh, is that that ghastly new building on the outskirts of town that looks like a prison? No, I think we'll stay in The Castleford Arms, as bad as it is."

"I do hope you'll be comfortable," said Lauren.

"So!" said Harriet, looking at her daughter beside her. "What have you been doing here all these days?"

"Oh, just preparing for the wedding. There's so much to organise."

Harriet sat nodding and smiling.

"And there's the house," said Troy. "The new house. She's been furnishing that place beautifully."

"Funny, you never showed an interest in soft furnishings before," said Harriet. "And as for weddings, you were allergic to them from what I remember." Harriet looked at Blanche knowingly – an obvious reference to her living with Billy.

"Well, people change, don't they?" said Blanche.

"Not that much! You'll be telling me you've started cookery lessons next!"

"Blanche was always an independent spirit," said Daniel, smiling at his daughter.

"Well, I suppose we better get back to the hotel," said Harriet. "I could do with a little lie down after all those bumpy roads. I mean, *how* do they expect to exploit the natural beauty of these areas if the bloody roads are so bad!" Harriet put down her teacup and stood up.

The others rose and they all moved to the front door where they said their farewells.

"Good to meet you," said Daniel. "No doubt we'll be getting to know each other very well over the coming week."

Lauren, Niall and Troy stood at the door, watching Blanche hug her parents goodbye down on the forecourt.

"I'd say she's all fur coat and no knickers," said Lauren.

Harriet released her daughter. "So, what time is dinner booked tonight?"

"Eight thirty. We'll collect you from the hotel," said Blanche.

"And what delightful little eatery is being shown to us tonight?" asked Harriet.

"Just a local seafood restaurant."

"Can't wait!" Harriet didn't hide the sarcasm. She looked up at the sprawling house as she got into the car and paused for a second before saying, "It's all very . . . *Beverly Hillbillies* – isn't it?"

"Well – that was – adequate," said Harriet, as she pushed her finished plate away.

They were seated in a booth in Tiffanys, a restaurant on the hill, with views of the sea in the distance. The lighting was low, and quiet jazz music played.

"What's the name of this place again?" asked Daniel.

"Tiffanys," answered Troy.

"It's far from Fifth Avenue this place is," said Harriet with a smirk.

"Mother!" snapped Blanche.

"Sorry!" Harriet grimaced.

"Come on, Troy," said Daniel, standing up abruptly. "You said you wanted to take a look at the jag. I'll even let you take a drive in it. Ladies, we'll be back in ten minutes."

"Eh, okay," said Troy, standing up and following Daniel out of the restaurant.

Blanche leaned forward to her mother and said: "Can you please try and keep that tongue of yours in check? You are being exceptionally rude!"

"I said I was sorry," said Harriet. "Look, if I'm being a little off form, it's because I'm finding all this very hard to take seriously."

"Well, you better take it seriously, because a week today I will be married to Troy."

"And last Christmas you were living with this Billy character. And then you were heading off to become the next Twiggy. And after all this, you've ended up down here in the back of the beyond with these Launcelots who we've never even heard of before."

"I wouldn't look down my nose at the Launcelots, Mum. They are a very wealthy family who could buy and sell you and Dad many times over."

"Well, you can't buy class, love . . . I mean Troy seems a nice enough boy, but has he really got enough to interest you for a lifetime? And that's what a marriage is, Blanche – a lifetime."

"Mum, I agree with you. You do have to protect yourself in this life. There are a lot of sharks out there who will just use you and destroy you if you let them. I know that now. I've met enough of them to recognise a prince when I meet one. And Troy is a prince. I'm very happy with him."

"Then I'm glad for you . . . I just hope there's enough here to keep you content and fulfilled for the rest of your life."

CHAPTER 36

Blanche stood at the top of Castleford Church as the organ music blared out and held her father's arm a little tighter. They began to walk down the aisle. And now as she moved closer to her husband, she couldn't get Billy's face out of her mind. She passed her mother, smiling carefully at her. She passed Niall and Lauren, Niall looking very happy, Lauren uncertain. She passed Rosalind, in a dress whiter than her own, smiling nastily at her. And then there was Jack, the best man, standing at the top of the church, who wasn't smiling at all, but whose eyes bored into her. She felt she could read his unsmiling eyes. They told her she was a fraud, that if she followed how she really felt she would be with him and not Troy.

Then she reached the altar and stood beside Troy who was smiling with unconditional love at her. And everybody else's expressions and thoughts didn't matter any more.

There had been a marquee put up in the gardens at the back of Winterfield, and the guests drifted in and out. Harriet stood sipping from a champagne flute as she looked about her at the round tables with the perfect linen and beautiful flowers. She watched Blanche busily going around talking to people and thanking them.

"She looks beautiful, doesn't she?" said Lauren coming up beside Harriet.

Harriet was elegant in a charcoal-coloured suit, Lauren glamorous in a pink dress with matching large summer hat.

"Yes, she does," agreed Harriet. "Good idea to have a marquee, when the best on offer is The Castleford Arms." She pulled a face.

Lauren looked at her pointedly. "You don't seem too happy with this marriage?"

"Look, Troy seems perfectly lovely. But I had dreams for Blanche. We invested so much time in her education and I hoped she'd be a solicitor or a doctor. She's certainly brainy enough, if she could only apply herself. I've just seen her make wrong decision after wrong decision, and now she's getting married and seems to be settled to do nothing else for the rest of her life except be a wife and mother."

"Well, it's all we've been all our lives, isn't it?" Lauren asked.

"It's different now – there are more opportunities for a girl these days. Anyway, there's no point talking about it, Blanche will do what she wants at the end of the day. Beneath that beautiful exterior is a strong character."

Lauren looked on as Blanche charmed Niall. "I didn't think that at the beginning, but I suspect you may be right." She thought about how Blanche had worked Niall around her little finger.

The speeches were being made after dinner. Rosalind and Jack sat stony-faced as they looked on.

"You know your father hasn't come near me all day!" Rosalind snapped at Jack.

"Well, it looks like he's found himself a new favourite girl, and she's called Blanche."

"Don't you see what she's doing? She's pushing us out, Jack!"

A cheer went up around the marquee as Niall stood up to make a speech.

"Nice to see so many of our friends here today. I think you all got as much of a shock as we did when Troy arrived back from London with a stunning young woman and declared her to be his fiancée. We kept asking Blanche – are you sure?" he said, causing an outburst of laughter. "But she did seem sure, and I'm glad she's sure. Because I've never seen Troy look happier and Blanche has enriched all our lives immeasurably."

"Oh please!" Rosalind grunted into Jack's ear.

"As a little token to Blanche, to welcome her into the Launcelots, I have a little present for her." He suddenly shouted across the marquee. "Seán, bring her in!"

Seán suddenly came through the main entrance of the marquee leading a beautiful horse through the tables onto the dance floor.

"I know how much you love horses, so I'm giving her to you," said Niall, smiling at Blanche.

Thrilled and moved by the gesture, Blanche got up and hugged Niall, whispering, "Thank you."

Rosalind threw her eyes to heaven. "I hope it does a big dump in the middle of the dance floor!"

"Will you shut up, Rosalind!" snapped Jack. He was growing angrier, looking at his brother, father and stepmother and Blanche together – and he the outsider looking on. He had always felt an outsider, but always had Niall's full attention so it didn't matter. But, like Rosalind, Niall had hardly spoken to Jack all day either.

As the evening wore into night, there was a band playing out by the swimming pool and people were dancing out on the patio. Blanche looked around at everybody and everybody seemed to be having a great time.

"So, you've danced with everybody here . . . except me," said a voice to her right.

She turned around to see Jack. "Are you asking?"

"I'm asking."

She nodded and they walked out amongst the other dancing couples and began to dance. The female singer of the band was singing 'Here You Come Again'.

"Everybody has been saying what a great day it's been. Me and Rosalind have a lot to compete with," said Jack.

"I'm sure you two will rise to the occasion. The photographer said that, considering Rosalind's choice of white outfit and considering she decided to position herself right next to me in the front row for the group photos, it's going to be hard to tell at a glance which one of us is the bride."

"I think Rosalind has coped very well today, considering."

"Considering what?"

"Considering you married the love of her life today."

She studied him. "And you're still going to marry her at Christmas even though you know that."

"I might as well. I hear it's all the fashion to marry people you're not in love with."

"Don't, Jack, not tonight, please."

"I felt like an outsider today. You organised it for me to feel like an outsider."

"You weren't made feel like an outsider, Jack. Everyone has been living in your shadow for so long around here, you just need to realise that it's not all about you."

"Do I indeed? I know what you're really after, Blanche. Me out and you in charge."

Blanche stopped dancing and stared at him. "I think I'd better go and join my husband."

It was nearing midnight, but Blanche was having such a good time, she felt she could go on forever. After all the hardship of the last year, she now felt she was where she wanted to be. As she looked at Troy, she thought about what her life would have been without him. Living in that small flat in London, working in the bar, struggling and frightened. That night, once the wedding was over, they would go and spend the first night together in their new house. Tomorrow they were heading to Capri for their honeymoon. As she looked up at Winterfield, she thought that in a way she had grown to love the house. It was her sanctuary, her escape from a cruel world and cruel people.

"Time to throw the bouquet, Blanche," Lauren shouted.

"Oh yeah, I nearly forgot!" said Blanche.

All the single women lined up and Blanche went and stood in front of them. Rosalind stood in the front of the women, her arms folded, looking unimpressed.

Blanche smiled at her and nodded, taking note of where she was standing. Then she turned around and threw the bouquet into the air behind her, aiming as best she could at Rosalind. She swung around just in time to see it come down through the air, so near to Rosalind that all she had to do was reach out and take it. But Rosalind kept her arms folded and casually stepped out of the way and the bouquet landed on the ground beside her.

Rosalind then walked over to Blanche.

"I wanted you to catch it, as a peace offering between us," said Blanche.

"Forget it. I don't take your sloppy seconds . . . even if you've taken mine. Have a nice life with Troy . . . bitch."

Jack was looking on, swigging from a champagne bottle. He ran down to the back of the garden and jumped up on the garden wall. He steadied himself and looked at the straight drop down the cliff to the shingle beach below with the waves crashing over it.

"Hey, band!" Jack shouted. "Play something dramatic!"

People stared down and saw Jack walk along the wall, holding the bottle of champagne.

Blanche got a fright when she saw him.

Niall marched down from the patio to the garden. "Jack, get down off that fucking wall right now, you drunken fool!"

"Oh, attention at last, Dad!" Jack said as he continued to walk casually along the wall.

Lauren suddenly ran down the garden as well. "Jack, please get off that wall! You're being really stupid. That's a straight drop down!"

"Oh, Mama, your concern is touching."

The band had stopped playing and people were gathering down in the garden, looking on.

"Oh, Troy, get him down, please!" begged Blanche.

"What's everyone concerned about? I have perfect balance. Band – I said play!"

The band members looked at each other and very hesitantly began to play.

This encouraged Jack to be more reckless and he began to walk up and down more quickly.

"Where's Troy?" demanded Jack.

Troy came out from the crowd and hurried to the wall.

"Come on, Jack, get down, you're pissed."

"No, I'm not – I'm just enjoying myself. Taking risks – I love taking risks! But you don't, do you? You like playing it safe."

"Come on, get down."

"I'll get down – if you get up!" said Jack.

"What?"

"Come on – I dare you. Let's see, once and for all, if you're as good as me. Come on up on the wall!" Jack's voice was teasing and goading.

"No, Troy! Don't listen to him!" cried Blanche.

"If I get up on the wall, will you get down?" snapped Troy.

"Of course!" smiled Jack.

Troy went quickly to the wall, paused for a second and then jumped up.

"Now – can we get down, please?" said Troy, glancing at the sheer drop on the other side.

Jack took a swig from the champagne bottle and then held it out to Troy.

"Go on – have a drink. And a toast – to your beautiful bride!" urged Jack.

"This is ridiculous," snapped Troy, taking the bottle quickly and raising it to have a quick drink.

"Very good!" Jack clapped his hands. "Now, let's go for a walk along the wall!"

"Fuck off, Jack – you're always a fucking show off!" Troy raised his voice "Everything always has to be about you, trying to grab attention. Walk on your fucking own!" Troy went to jump down from the wall, but suddenly he lost his balance and stumbled.

The crowd gasped.

"Troy!" Blanche screamed.

Jack lurched forward and grabbed Troy, pushing the two of them off the wall to the safety of the garden.

Blanche went racing to them and helped Troy up from the ground.

"You fucking asshole!" Blanche screamed at Jack.

Jack sat up and watched Blanche and Troy walk off back into the quiet crowd.

It was three in the morning. The wedding had become subdued after Jack's antics on the wall and Troy's near-fall and the guests had started drifting home. The family were gathered in the lounge after the last of the guests had gone. Niall was pacing up and down furiously.

"What the fuck were you thinking?" Niall demanded of Jack.

"I don't know." Jack had sobered up and was looking forlornly at the floor.

"I'll tell you what you were thinking. You were showing off – as per fucking usual. Look at me, the great Jack Launcelot. I can walk on air! Well, you could have ended up killing yourself and your brother into the bargain."

"I'm sorry!" Jack said.

"In front of all our friends and neighbours. Troy nearly fucking fell! You know I've turned a blind eye to your carry-on over the years, Jack. The drinking, and being wild around Castleford. I've spoilt you. And you think you can get away with anything."

"Niall – it's not Jack's fault," said Rosalind. "Nobody forced Troy up on the wall."

"Of course it's his fault. Troy was only trying to get Jack down. He's put Jack up on a pedestal for years. We all have. And you don't deserve it, Jack. You were so jealous of Troy and Blanche today that you decided to grab all the attention for yourself by doing that stupid stunt."

Jack stood up aggressively. "I said I was sorry, didn't I?"

"That's not good enough, Jack. You think you can do whatever you want in this life. Your mother would be so ashamed of you. I'm so ashamed of you."

Jack stared, his eyes filled with angry tears. "Right then, I'll be off. I don't want to shame you any more."

"Niall – tell him you don't mean it," urged Rosalind.

Niall stared at Jack in silence.

Jack stormed past his father, though the lobby and out the front door.

"Jack!" Rosalind went racing out after him.

Troy went over to his father. "Dad, go after him, tell him you didn't mean that."

"I did mean it, Troy. I've let him get away with everything over the years, and this is the result."

"Jack! Where do you think you're going?" Rosalind called as she ran after him, catching up with him as he reached his car.

"I'm getting the fuck out of here."

"*What*?" Rosalind nearly screamed.

"You heard what Dad said in there. I can't hang around here any more. It's over for me."

"It's not! Everyone will simmer down."

"I'm through with this place. In a way it's been suffocating me for years. I want to leave. I'm bored with it and I need to get out there into the big world and live my life on my own terms."

"But I don't want to go out into that big world, Jack. I love it here, I don't want to leave!"

Jack stared at her, with a look of sympathy on his face.

"Oh!" said Rosalind quietly as realisation dawned. "You don't mean to take me with you."

"I'm sorry, Rosalind. I don't think we could survive together for long without this place to bind us together."

She stretched her hand out to the house. "But look at what you're walking away from, Jack. Are you mad?"

Jack sighed. "No. I'm just tired of fighting for it. Apart

262

from Dad, the rest will be happy to see me go. Now I've lost Dad's respect . . . See you, kid." Jack reached forward and kissed her check tenderly before getting into the car and driving off.

Rosalind looked at the car disappear from view and then she turned and marched into the house. She stormed into the sitting room and up to Blanche, who was still dressed in her wedding dress.

"He's gone! He's leaving, not just me, but Winterfield! And it's all your fault! We were fine before you arrived here, disrupting everything. Making everyone fired up against each other and jealous. I know what you've been doing, working Niall up against Jack. Well, you've got what you want, he's gone. You have everything now. If Troy had fallen down the cliff – it would have been your fault! You might as well have pushed him yourself!"

Blanche struck out and slapped Rosalind across the face.

Rosalind stared in shock, then turned and ran from the house.

Troy went up to Niall. "Dad, go up to the lodge after Jack, stop him from going."

Niall said nothing and didn't move.

"Then I bloody will!" Troy walked out.

They heard Troy's car drive off.

"Jack!" shouted Troy as he entered the lodge.

Jack was coming down the stairs with a large suitcase.

"Jack, what are you doing?"

"I'm getting outta here."

"Listen, everyone is in shock, and everyone will calm down – there's no reason for you to go anywhere."

"But I want to go, Troy. I want to leave. I was only

staying for Dad, and if he's turning on me then there's no reason for me to stay. Anyway, I thought you'd be happy – I'm leaving everything to you, Troy."

"But I don't want it, Jack. Look, I know you and Mum haven't been seeing eye to eye for a long time, but there's not been any problem between us, has there?"

"You're a nice guy, Troy. But if you knew what I'd tried to do to you, you'd realise I'm not that nice."

"What are you talking about?"

"Nothing, it doesn't matter now."

"And what about Rosalind? She's heartbroken."

"She's heartbroken after you, Troy. I was just a revenge job for her, and I don't want to get married under those circumstances."

"But you are the brains behind the farm and the pubs. I just won't be able to run things without you."

"You'll manage just fine . . . And you'll have Blanche to rely on."

Blanche had gone up to the new house on the coast road. She stood at the wall of windows, looking out at the sea, the patio door opened, blowing in an early-morning breeze.

She heard the front door open and Troy walked in.

"Dad said you'd come up here," he said, walking over to her and embracing her. "He's gone, Blanche, Jack has left for good."

"Troy, I've been thinking of what Rosalind said and maybe she's right."

"That's nonsense."

"Is it? I knew what I was doing, Troy. Everyone kept saying that you would be forgotten about and Jack would take over. And I was fighting so that we wouldn't be left behind. I was pushing you forward to those meetings and something snapped in Jack." And flirting with him behind your back, she thought.

"Look, I think Jack wanted to leave here long ago, he told me so tonight. In a way he's too clever and talented to spend his life here."

"You see, this was the problem. Everyone holding Jack up as some kind of Superman. Even he couldn't cope when he was challenged."

"And who challenged him?" asked Troy.

"I think I did," said Blanche quietly.

PART 3

CHAPTER 37

2010

Troy Launcelot walked up the steps of Winterfield House and rang the doorbell but there was no answer. It was a Saturday afternoon and a sunny day. Maybe she wasn't at home, he thought, as he strolled around the side of the house and out to the back gardens. Then he saw her. She was sitting in the middle of the lawn on a large blanket playing with their grandchild. She was casually dressed in jeans and an oversized shirt and with her dark hair flowing down her back. He stood transfixed. It was almost as if he was transported back in time and was looking at Blanche playing with their own children when they were babies in the back garden of their house in Castleford on the coast road. He watched her for a while, and she seemed wonderfully content and happy. He couldn't remember when he saw her like that. He walked down the steps and onto the lawn.

"Hi, Blanche," he said as he strolled over to them.

Blanch got a start and looked up, "Troy! What are you doing here?"

"Just thought I'd drop by for a visit," he said, sitting down on the blanket and embracing his grandchild.

"Well, you could have phoned first."

"I did, and you didn't answer the phone."

"Well, you could have rung the doorbell."

"I did – and nobody answered."

"So you just decided to barge in anyway?" She looked at him wryly.

"Well, how else can I get to see my grandchild? You're keeping him that far away from everybody at this stage."

"Oh, don't start, Troy!"

"I thought I'd let you know that I got a visit from a certain Mr Lee Dwyer."

Blanche looked up, alarmed. "And what did he want?"

"Quite a lot. He's who you're up against."

"I know, I've had the dubious pleasure."

"He wants me to come over to his side, and give evidence against you."

Blanche sighed. "And what have you decided?"

"I haven't yet . . . I did tell him that I think me and you have seen a lot of courts already."

"That's true."

He looked at her meaningfully. "I don't want to fight with you again, Blanche."

"Which means you're taking my side?"

"It means, stop this before it goes too far."

"If it wasn't for me, who knows what would have happened to him!"

"I know you acted rightly at the time, Blanche. But think what this court case would do to you. I've heard Dwyer is digging very deep into your past. He could drag out things that could destroy you."

"Well, two can play at that game. I've employed a brilliant new lawyer who is digging away in Mr Dwyer's past. Do you know he used to be a member of a far leftist

269

group when he was in university? His vendetta against me is obviously an attack on big business."

"So what if he was member of such a group? As we know only too well from Amelia, young people join many kinds of groups that they later change their minds about."

"Or don't as in the case of Amelia," added Blanche.

"Discrediting Dwyer is not going to help you get custody."

"No, but it might just get the bastard to back off."

"You know what I was thinking about recently? When you first came to Winterfield. Remember?"

Blanche shrugged. "Yes, what of it?"

"Just how happy we were then. And in the first years of our marriage, when we had the children, remember?"

She smiled at him. "How could I forget?"

"For a moment I was back there. When I came around the house and saw you."

Blanche sighed. "You can never go back, Troy. And I don't think I would want to, even if I could."

"I think I would," he smiled at her.

"What – after everything?"

He nodded. "Yeah. It was the happiest time of my life. And I think if you were honest, it was for you too."

CHAPTER 38

1981–1983

The months after the wedding passed slowly. Blanche and Troy arrived back from honeymoon in Capri to a very different Winterfield. Jack left a huge hole around the place, and Niall seemed to be different and spent a long time staring out at the sea.

It was wonderful, though, just her and Troy together in their lovely new house. She hadn't realised how stressful all the politics up in the big house at Winterfield had been until she left it. But now she could close her door and forget about everything. Troy was in the office all the time, as he attempted to take over the business in Jack's absence. The early days were hard for him, because he was thrown in at the deep end. He called on Niall all the time, and Niall tried to advise, but he didn't seem as interested any more.

Blanche was stretched out on the couch at home watching a movie when she heard Troy's car pull up. She looked at her watch and saw it was nearly eleven.

She heard him come into the house.

"In here, love!" she called.

He walked in and gave her a hug and a kiss.

"Where have you been?" she asked.

"In the office, where else? I'm trying to get to grips with the books that the accountant is screaming for."

"Are you not finished them yet?"

"No – I don't think I'll ever get them finished."

"Can't your father help?"

"He is helping, but I don't know, he just seems pre-occupied. You know, I think he's been relying on Jack for so long that he's not sure how to run things fully himself any more. I think that's the problem."

"I doubt your father would ever forget how to do anything. I guess he's just retired now and is handing the responsibility over to you. Can I help at all?"

He smiled at her and kissed her forehead. "No, hon, I'll struggle through."

Lauren was walking down Castleford's main street when she saw Rosalind with a group of work colleagues.

"Rosalind!" she called.

Rosalind spotted her and said to her friends, "You head on in and I'll join you in a minute."

Her friends headed into a pub and Rosalind walked over to Lauren.

Lauren kissed her cheek.

"I haven't seen you for ages, Rosalind, where have you been hiding?"

"I've been getting over a broken engagement from your stepson, Lauren."

"I know. I'm sorry how it all panned out."

"Are you? You got what you wanted, didn't you? Troy taking over and Jack out of the way?"

Lauren ignored that. "Why don't you come up to the house any more? We miss you."

"I'm not going near that place, not while she's there."

"Blanche?"

"Yes. Anyway, there's nothing for me to go up there for. One son is married, one has done a runner. I need to build my own life now away from Winterfield and away from the Launcelots. See you, Lauren."

It was twelve o'clock that night and Rosalind was driving home when she spotted the police car behind her, flashing at her to stop.

"Fuck!" she snapped as she pulled over.

The local sergeant, Philip Lawlor, got out of his car and came over to Rosalind.

"What's the problem, Philip?" asked Rosalind.

"You can't drive in a straight line, Rosalind, that's the problem . . . Ah, for fuck's sake, the smell of alcohol off you! Get out of the car, Rosalind."

"How dare you speak like that to me, Philip Lawlor!"

"Come on, get out, Rosalind. You father would never forgive me, if I let you drive on like that."

Philip opened the car door and pulled Rosalind out.

"Don't manhandle me!" she snapped at him as she stumbled and then she hit him across the face before falling to the ground.

"For fuck's sake, Rosalind. Come on, let's get you down to the station."

The Launcelots were having Sunday lunch at Winterfield.

"She got off with a fine," said Troy, having recounted the gossip he had heard about Rosalind's drink-drive arrest.

"Poor Rosalind," said Lauren.

"What was she doing drinking and driving for anyway?" said Blanche. "Not only was she endangering herself, but other people as well."

Lauren looked at Blanche pointedly "She's nursing a broken heart, poor lamb, that's what she was doing."

"Well, why doesn't she nurse it while not being a threat to herself or others?"

"There's a hard streak in you, Blanche Launcelot," Lauren snapped.

Niall looked at Blanche and said: "Would you pass the vegetables there please, Elizabeth."

There was a moment of confusion around the table.

"That's Blanche, Niall, not Elizabeth. Elizabeth has been dead for decades," said Lauren coldly.

Niall shook his head and looked sheepish. "I know that," he said.

That night Lauren was brushing her hair in the mirror when Niall came into the bedroom.

He stood staring at her. "You win, by the way."

She turned around and looked at him. "What are you talking about now?"

"I was in with the solicitor today. And Troy is my heir. He gets the business and Winterfield. You win." He walked into the bathroom.

Back home on the coast road, Troy was saying to Blanche, "That's so weird, Dad calling you Elizabeth. I've heard him say it before." He got into the big bed and put his arms around his wife.

"I guess."

"Doesn't it bother you? He's obviously mixing you up with her."

"No. I think Elizabeth plays on his mind a lot, and even more so since Jack has gone. He's missing him a lot."

"We all are."

"Are you?"

"Yeah. He was my brother and the life and soul of the place."

"But he used to overshadow you all the time."

"We all play different roles in families, Blanche. You get used to it. You don't know that being an only child."

She guessed he was speaking the truth. She did find all the family politics of the Launcelots strange. That's why she and Billy were like soulmates. They were both only children, and each understood what made the other tick. She quickly erased all thoughts of Billy as she put her arms around her husband.

"You know, I'm a bit worried about Rosalind," he said. "I hear she's out drinking a lot. I might stop by her place and check on her." He kissed her neck.

She pushed him away abruptly and looked at him. "You will not! I'm not having my husband drop in on his ex-girlfriend who's still in love with him to become a shoulder to cry on! Thank you very much."

"Blanche! Have a heart!"

"And what heart did she have. She went out of her way to make trouble for me from the moment I arrived. I'm sorry if she's drinking, but I don't want her coming between us, Troy."

Rosalind was in a booth on her ownk in Martin's Bar and Diner on the outskirts of town, a large vodka and tonic in front of her. Her arrest for drink driving had mortified her. To have it reported in the very paper that she worked for! She had only started going out drinking because her parents were nagging her to stop drinking all the time. And now she had been publicly shamed, not once but twice. First with her broken engagement and secondly now with drink driving. Soon, she wouldn't be able to hold her head up at all in Castleford. That's why she had started to come out to Martin's. This seedy old joint, nobody respectable would ever come here, except when Jack used to come slumming. She could drink on her own, without anybody bothering her, and just get a taxi home. She needed this after what had happened. She needed just to be by herself and try and think things through with a little help from alcohol. One minute there was Troy, then there was Jack and now there was nobody. And all because of Blanche.

"Mind if I sit down here?" asked a voice.

She looked up. It was Seán Ford.

"Yes, I do mind, now move on," she said, taking a large gulp of her drink.

He sat down opposite her.

"What did I just say?" she snapped.

"Thought you could do with some company."

"Well, you thought wrong," snapped Rosalind.

"Read all about your little misdemeanour in your paper last week," said Seán with a leer.

"How nice for you," she said in a bored fashion, not even looking at him.

Aretha Franklin's 'Respect' was blaring out of the juke box.

"Why don't you come up to Winterfield any more? It's not the same without you around. There's only that old Blanche swanning around as if she owns the place. Well, I guess she does now."

"Bully for her."

"You know you've always got a friend in me, Rosalind."

"Friends like you I can do without."

"You're drinking on your own in Martin's. I think you need all the friends you can get."

"I've loads of friends, I'm just taking a little time out, that's all. Everyone should be able to do that."

He reached over and stroked her hand. "Of course they should."

She pulled her hand away.

"It's time I was going home," she said.

"Are you driving?"

"Hardly, after what happened. I'm going to order a cab."

"Why bother? I'm driving your way, why don't I give you a lift? It will save you the fare."

"I don't need no favours from the likes of you."

"Just trying to be friendly. I'll be waiting outside," he said, getting up and walking out. She looked after him before downing her drink, and following him out.

Blanche was sitting in the lounge in the new house reading through the morning newspaper, when she stopped suddenly on seeing a photo of Shay.

Her heart began to beat quickly on seeing his face again. She looked up at the headline that read 'Top Photographer Killed in Mystery Fall'. She quickly read through the article which said he had been found in his studio having fallen through a glass door. She stared at his smiling face and then crumpled the paper and buried her head in her hands, wondering who had got to him.

"Oh Shay!" she whispered in anger at the futility of it all, remembering the quotation: *He that lives by the sword shall die by the sword.*

CHAPTER 39

It was December and Blanche stood at the glass windows of the house looking out at the stormy sea. Troy had been away to the pubs in London and she was expecting him back any moment. He had been away for three weeks and she had missed him. He had suggested she go with him, but she hadn't wanted to. London still brought back hard memories for her.

As she stroked her stomach a smile came across her face.

"Blanche?" called Troy as he came into the house.

He walked in and they embraced and kissed.

"I missed you!" he said.

"And we missed you," she said.

He smiled at her and then he thought for a moment. "We?"

Lauren was decorating the giant Christmas tree in the hall at Winterfield as Troy came in.

"That's a beautiful job, Mum," he said, looking up at all the familiar decorations and tinsel on the tree.

"You know, I was kind of sad putting it up this year. Rosalind always came up and helped me to do it, ever since she was a little girl."

"No word from her?"

"No. I'm going to insist on having lunch with her before Christmas. How's Blanche?"

"She's good, apart from the morning sickness."

"It's going to be very different in Winterfield this year. You married to Blanche and a baby on the way. No Rosalind and no Jack . . . We got a Christmas card from Jack this morning."

"Really?" Troy was excited.

"It's in on the mantelpiece if you want to take a look. Nothing personal in it. Just wishing everyone a happy Christmas and giving a forwarding address. He's in New York."

"That would suit him, he'd love it there and they'd love him."

"Your father wouldn't even look at the card. I'm worried about him, Troy. He seems to be losing interest in everything. We used to fight like cat and dog, and now he couldn't be bothered to argue with me over anything. He's so disappointed in Jack and he's shut him out."

"Well, maybe the baby will get him back to his old self again," suggested Troy.

"Hopefully," she sighed.

He leaned forward and kissed her cheek. "I'd better get into the office. The work is stacked up."

Lauren tied Rosalind down to having lunch the day before Christmas Eve. They met in a restaurant in town, full of office parties breaking up for the holidays.

They ordered a beef dinner and idly chatted about local

gossip. Afterwards they sat at the table, both drinking gin and tonic.

"So, will you come up to the house over Christmas?" asked Lauren.

"No thanks," said Rosalind.

"Niall will be so disappointed. You know how he dotes on you."

"Really? He never bothered trying to contact me over the past few months."

"You've had a hard few months, love." Lauren reached over and rubbed Rosalind's hand.

Rosalind took a swig from her drink and nodded. "And I'll have a hard few months ahead as well."

"Yeah?"

Rosalind looked around and then leaned forward and said quietly. "I'm pregnant, Lauren."

Lauren blinked a few times. "Oh, Rosalind! You need to let Jack know immediately. He's in New York, I can get you his address."

"It's not Jack's. Sure I'd be showing by now if it were!"

"What? Well, who's is it then, for fuck's sake?"

Rosalind sat back and sighed before saying "Seán's."

Lauren face clouded in confusion as she tried to think who she meant.

"Seán who works for you," confirmed Rosalind.

"Seán Ford! You're joking! How the fuck did that happen?" Lauren was truly shocked.

"I was lonely, he was there. He's a good drinking buddy and one thing led to another. He always had a thing for me, if you remember."

"Yes, but it was unthinkable. I can't believe it! Does he know?"

"No."

"And what are you going to do, Rosalind?"

"I just don't know."

Lauren drove into one of the new housing estates on the outskirts of Castleford and parked her Mercedes outside one of the houses. She walked to the door and rang the bell.

Looking back she saw some kids had gathered around the Mercedes.

"If there's a scratch on that car when I come out you're all dead!" she snapped at them.

The door opened and there stood Seán, looking very surprised to see her.

"Mrs Launcelot!"

"Hi Seán," she said, walking past him into the house and giving him a dirty look.

She knew he rented the house and, as she looked around, she saw it was kept in good order.

"Is there something the matter, Mrs Launcelot?" asked Seán, following her into the sitting room.

"I'll say – Rosalind Dawson is pregnant and you're the daddy."

She watched as he paled before her.

"So, what you going to do about it?" she asked.

"I – eh – are you sure?"

"Sure I'm sure."

"But it could be anybody's!"

"Could be but it isn't. It's yours. As shocked as I am to hear it."

"Well, why hasn't she told me?"

"She doesn't know what she's going to do herself. But I'm going to tell you what you're both going to do, before it gets out and destroys that girl for life and her poor parents along with her. I'm going to have a quick word with the Monsignor and you're going to be married at the earliest opportunity, do I make myself clear?"

"Yeah!" he nodded.

Lauren called over to the Dawsons on Christmas Eve. She gave presents to Rosalind's parents, kissed them on both cheeks and wished them a happy Christmas.

"We're expecting a few guests over for some mince pies and mulled wine this evening, will you stay?" asked Rosalind's mother.

"Eh, yes, I'll stay for just a little while, thanks."

Rosalind's mother went into the kitchen to attend to the mulled wine while her father went to make a phone call and Lauren seized her opportunity.

"I have it all set up, Rosalind. Seán is willing to marry you and I'm trying to set a date for the wedding," said Lauren quietly.

"Lauren! I don't want to get married to him!"

"Too bad. You are!"

"Lauren, I haven't decided what I'm going to do yet. I don't have feelings for Seán, he was just a bit of company!" Rosalind's eyes filled with tears.

"Well, you should have chosen your company more carefully! Look, Rosalind you've no choice."

"I could bring up the baby by myself."

"Don't be ridiculous. You'd never be able to hold your head up again and neither would your parents. You've made your bed, Rosalind, and now you must lie on it."

Blanche and Troy decided not to go up to Winterfield House on Christmas Eve but to spend it in their own home. As Blanche looked into the blazing fire, she marvelled how much her life had changed in a year. She looked out the wall of windows to the moon shining over the sea and thought about herself this time last year. A model living a fast life, living with Billy. The toast of the town. She wondered where Billy was that Christmas Eve and whether he would think of her.

Blanche was dreaming. She was driving through the night trying to get back to Billy and then she was going into his house and finding him on the floor covered in blood. Then she was on her own in that hostel in Earls Court and then walking the streets with no money. And then there was Shay in front of her, smiling wickedly at her.

"Nooo!" she was suddenly screaming.

"Blanche!" Troy turned on the light beside their bed and held her tightly. "It's just a dream. It's fine. You're safe."

"Oh, Troy! I was so frightened."

"It's only a dream."

"I never want our child to not be safe, Troy. I never want our child to not be secure and safe."

Everyone noticed that Lauren was distracted on Christmas Day. Niall was as well, but everyone was getting used to that with him. The day passed nicely. Dinner was served and there was much talk about the fact there would be a baby this time next year.

That night Niall went to bed early. Lauren and Blanche and Troy were in the lounge having a drink.

"You alright, Mother?" Troy asked Lauren.

Lauren looked at them and then got up, closed over the doors and came back.

"I just have to tell somebody. Rosalind is pregnant by Seán – our Seán, before you ask." Lauren took a big gulp of her whiskey.

283

"Seriously?" asked Troy.

"She's in a terrible state."

"Oh well, I guess that makes sense – a bitch having a bastard," said Blanche with a shrug.

Lauren glared at Blanche. "Can you not show just a little bit of compassion here? It's alright for you with your loving husband and secure home being pregnant, but imagine how Rosalind feels!"

Blanche sighed and sat back. It was obvious that Rosalind would always have this hold over the Launcelots, and they couldn't see her for the manipulative nasty woman she was.

"So what's she going to do?" asked Troy.

"I've arranged for her to have a quick wedding with Seán. At least it will put an air of respectability on the whole situation."

"That's the most ridiculous thing I've ever heard. I take it she doesn't love him, does she?" said Blanche.

"She's not in love with him, no. But that doesn't matter, it's about the child from now on," said Lauren.

"So you're sentencing her to a life with a man she doesn't love and from the look of Seán a man who is not going to make either a great husband or father just because of respectability?"

"You know, Blanche, you might go through life doing what you want. Living with some guy up in Dublin just because it might be fun. You know, around here, life isn't all about models and glamour. We take things seriously!"

"So seriously that you'd force the girl into an unhappy marriage?"

"I'm not forcing her into anything. I'm trying to help her. She's been let down badly by this family. First by you, Troy, and then disgracefully by Jack."

"And you would have been quite happy to have Troy in

an unhappy marriage with Rosalind as well, just because it served your purposes, Lauren," said Blanche angrily.

"At least I would be sure that Troy was in a marriage with someone who truly loved him."

"Meaning I don't?" Blanche's eyes widened.

"You tell me! But I can tell when someone is really in love with somebody and I'm just not sure about you, Blanche."

"Mum! Would you shut the fuck up!" Troy nearly shouted. "Don't you think we've had enough falling out and upset this year without you two falling out as well?"

They sat in silence for a while.

Lauren cleared her throat. "I'm sorry, Blanche. I spoke out of turn . . . Of course I know how much you love Troy. I've just been under pressure recently with everything and . . ." Lauren spoke apologetically, but her eyes viewed Blanche coolly.

"Apology accepted, Lauren. Don't worry about it."

There were huge snowfalls that January. The whole country seemed to come to a halt as drifts several feet high piled up.

Lauren stood at one of the long windows and looked out at the snow-covered landscape stretched out under the darkening sky. She spotted Niall strolling towards the house.

"I can't remember when we had snow as thick as that," said Niall, coming into the lounge. "What a day! That bloody Seán didn't show up again for work. He's getting worse, I'm going to have a serious talk with him."

"No need. He won't be coming back to work here any more. He's gone over to work at the Dawson farm."

"What's he gone over there for?" Niall was shocked.

"He married Rosalind today and so it makes sense for him to work his own farm, don't you think?"

"Rosalind married Seán!"

"Uh huh. And just think, Seán is going to get that lovely Dawson farm. You know, the one you had your eye on for years . . . The one you hoped would be joined to Winterfield when Rosalind married Jack. Now it's Seán's. Funny how things turn out, don't you think? Not that you've even noticed Rosalind not being around any more. You're too distracted with Blanche, or Elizabeth as you keep calling her."

And Lauren walked past him and out of the room.

CHAPTER 40

Blanche and Troy's son, Carl, was born on the 15th of July 1982. Rosalind and Seán's daughter, Gabrielle, was born the following day on the 16th of July.

Blanche sat in the hospital, holding her first-born surrounded by her family.

Lauren and Niall stood at one side of the bed smiling proudly, while Harriet and Daniel stood the other side, just as proud. Troy sat on the bed beside Blanche, smiling broadly. The room was full of flowers and teddy bears and there had been a constant stream of visitors.

"He's the image of his mother," said Harriet.

"No, he's not! He's the image of Troy," said Lauren.

There was a knock on the door.

"Hi, is it okay for us to come in?" asked a woman and a man carrying more flowers and teddies.

"Hi, Jessica, hi, George, come on in!" said Blanche.

Lauren watched the new visitors come happily in. Blanche had a way with her alright, she thought. She had quickly charmed all the Launcelots' friends and made many more besides.

Lauren excused herself from the room, walked down the corridor and stopped a nurse. "Hi, darling, what room is Rosalind Ford in?"

"Room 315, Mrs Launcelot."

Reaching Room 315, she knocked on the door and let herself in.

There was Rosalind, stretched out on the bed, a cot beside her. There was only a small amount of flowers compared to Blanche's room and she was on her own.

"Hi, darling, how are you?"

Rosalind struggled up. "Thanks for the flowers, Lauren."

Lauren looked into the cot at the baby.

"She's beautiful, Rosalind."

"I know."

Lauren sat down beside the bed. "You're very lucky."

"Am I?" Rosalind scoffed.

"Where's Seán?"

Rosalind laughed bitterly. "You tell me! He's only been in once to see his daughter, and the smell of drink off him was making me sick so I just told him to get out."

"Oh Rosalind!" Lauren reached out and clasped her hand.

Lauren studied the once exceptionally pretty features of Rosalind, now tired and puffed out. It was hardly possible to recognise her as the spoilt, sociable, lovable girl she once was.

"Where are your parents?"

"I sent them home as well. They're exhausted."

Lauren nodded. Her parents had found it very hard to accept their princess had married Seán Ford. And since they had married, Seán had moved into their house. For a family who prided themselves on being a cut above, it was a terrible comedown for them.

"I don't know, Lauren. I really don't think I should have married Seán. I mean, he's a serious drinker. Sometimes he can be nice and loving, but other times he's just a lout."

"How's he working out on the farm?"

"Oh, as if he's Lord of the Manor! Dad hasn't said anything, but I know he's horrified that his beautiful farm is going to fall into Seán's hands."

"Well, look, Rosalind, you've got a child to think of now. Do you understand me? You need to take charge and keep your family going. For the sake of little Gabrielle, if nothing else." She knew Rosalind had been moping about over the past few months, feeling sorry for herself.

"I know, Lauren. The newspaper said they'll keep my job open for me, and I think I'll need it for my sanity if nothing else."

"Good."

"You're right, Lauren. I need to get back control. It's just not going to be easy."

"Nothing is, darling."

By the end of the year, Blanche was pregnant again. Their daughter Amelia was born in September 1983.

CHAPTER 41

2010

As Blanche looked at her ex-husband play with their grandchild on the blanket in the back garden that afternoon, she felt too that she was being transported back to when they were first married.

He looked over at her and smiled and then saw she looked sad.

"What's wrong?" he asked.

She sighed. "What's right? I'm just thinking about where we are now compared to when we started off. Us divorced, never speaking. The kids, all gone their separate ways. How did we go from being such a close family unit to this, Troy?"

"Maybe you should be asking yourself that question," suggested Troy.

"So, it's all my fault, is it?"

"I'm not saying that. You just made decisions."

"I was forced to make decisions, Troy. I've always been forced to make decisions. I would have been content to live in Castleford for the rest of my life, being a good wife and mother. I was forced into being somebody else."

"There's an element of truth in that. But you're also deluding yourself. Castleford was not enough for you, it never was. You tried to convince yourself and everybody else that you were happy with your life as it was. But I knew you weren't deep down. I could see it in your eyes. You wanted more."

"Oh, Troy! I wish things had worked out differently."

He looked at her and he almost felt like giving her a hug, she looked so sad.

"I won't get involved in this case, Blanche," Troy said eventually.

"Really?" She looked up at him.

"No, I'm going to leave you two to fight it out. If Dwyer contacts me again, I'll say I won't be helping."

"Thank you, Troy." She nodded her appreciation.

"That's not to say that I approve of what you're doing, but we've too much history for me to go against you."

CHAPTER 42

1984

Blanche loved the summers at Winterfield. And as that summer of 1984 began to draw close she was looking forward to the long hot days and long evenings. Carl was nearly two years old and his sister was nine months. Blanche was pretty happy with her life. She had a girl that came in to help her with the children. She also had a cleaner and a cook. She loved spending time out on the beach with the children. Troy was very busy with work and he seemed to love to come home to his family. As he took over the business he became more stressed, but he tried not to show it. He made frequent trips over to London. Back in Castleford they had a lot of friends and were always out to dinner or around to friends' houses.

She was out having lunch with some girlfriends one day in one of Castleford's restaurants. They were all the wives of local businessmen and politicians. As the wife of Troy Launcelot, they had all sought her friendship. She would listen to their idle gossip and small-town talk, and be slightly bored by it all. Brooke O'Hara, the glamorous wife of their bank manager, was recounting some tale of some fashion mistake she had seen somebody make, as they all drank their Bacardi and Cokes.

Just then Rosalind came into the restaurant with a colleague from her paper.

"Hi, Rosalind," said Brooke and a couple of the other women at the table.

"Ladies," acknowledged Rosalind unsmilingly as she walked past them to a table in the far corner.

Brooke sat forward and spoke in a hushed tone, "I hear the husband is up at that dive Martin's every second night."

"I hear he's got another woman," said another lady who lunched.

"Well, let's face it, he's hardly up at Dawsons much. Rosalind's poor parents can't stand the sight of him."

"Well, she and her family were going around as if they owned this town for long enough. It's quite a comedown for them," said Brooke.

Blanche glanced over at Rosalind, deep in conversation with her colleague.

They barely acknowledged each other if they ever passed in town. It was true what the others were saying: Rosalind had tumbled down Castleford's society and she knew it and that was why she didn't bother even trying to be friends with these women any more.

The ladies' conversation moved on to the deepening recession and how their husbands' businesses were being affected. As Blanche glanced out at her brand-new Mercedes and thought about their holiday in Italy the following week, she realised how lucky they were that the recession wasn't affecting them.

That night, after Blanche put the children to bed, she returned to the sitting room to catch the news. But it was all about unemployment figures and she found it depressing so she switched it off and instead started to unpack all the shopping bags full of new clothes she had bought for their Italian holiday.

She heard the front door bang and Troy walk across the hall and into the lounge.

"Hi, darling," she said. "I got you some clothes for the holiday and want you to try them to make sure they fit. I'll return them if they don't." She walked over and kissed him. "You should have seen Amelia today! She was so attempting to get out of her cot. She's so determined, and the defiant look on her face!"

Troy went over to the drinks cabinet and poured himself a whiskey. He held the glass tightly and knocked back the drink, before filling the glass again.

He then went and sat down on the couch and stared into his drink.

"And as for Carl! He was asking for you all day." She glanced over at him and saw that he was very pale.

Suddenly he put his glass down on the floor and buried his face in his hands.

"Troy?" said Blanche, dropping the clothes she was folding and running over to sit beside him. "Troy! What's the matter?"

He looked at her and she saw his eyes were red and he looked completely stressed.

"I've lost it, Blanche. I've lost it all!"

"Lost what?"

"Everything! The business, the pubs, the farm, Winterfield. Even the house here, it's all gone!"

She stared at him, trying to comprehend what he was talking about. "I don't understand . . ."

He buried his face in his hands again. "Blanche, the bank is taking it all away from us."

She pulled back and looked at him in horror. "How is that possible?"

"I don't know how it happened, Blanche! The pubs have been losing big money for the past three years. And I couldn't do anything to stop the loss so I kept mortgaging the estate here to fill the gap."

"Fill the gap! But what about all the luxury cars and holidays we've been having?"

"It all been funded by borrowings, Blanche. And now the bank won't give us any more time. They are foreclosing on everything. Next week."

"But what will we do? Where will we go?"

"I don't know."

"What savings have we got?"

"Nothing. We've spent it all."

She looked at him with increasing horror. "And what do your parents say about all this?"

"They haven't a clue. They know nothing of it. Dad hasn't bothered with the business since – well, since Jack left. He just left everything in my hands. And Mum never bothered with it either."

"But Troy – it will kill them if they have to leave Winterfield. If they lose everything they've built in their lives!"

"I know," he said.

And as she continued to stare at him in horror she realised he was even more frightened and lost than she was.

The next day Blanche and Troy drove up to Winterfield.

"We can't say anything to your father about this," Blanche had advised. "Not the way his mind has been recently. He won't be able to handle it."

"Well, he'll know next week when we're all turfed out," said Troy.

"That can't happen."

"Blanche . . . being in denial won't help."

"I'm not."

Lauren listened as Troy tried to tell her the news in the lounge. Blanche had to step in to keep finishing his sentences as he seemed frightened to.

"*What?*" Lauren screamed as they came to an end. "*How did you let this happen?*"

"I don't know, Mum. It just seemed to all run out of my control. I couldn't manage it. Money stopped coming in from the pubs and we were spending so much with nothing coming in. I just kept borrowing."

"We were hoping you might have some funds that we don't know about. Something to keep things going until we can get a grip on this?" asked Blanche.

"No! All we have is tied up in the estate and the business. I've only my jewellery and that won't keep things going for long."

"But what are we going to do?" asked Troy. "We have to leave here next Tuesday."

"Leave for where? We've nowhere to go!" said Lauren.

Blanche felt a terrible panicky feeling envelop her. The feeling of being poor, of having nothing, of being desperate.

"And what is Jim O'Hara saying about all of this? He's been our Bank Manager for years. In fact he wouldn't have got the job only we recommended him."

"He's the one pulling the plug on us, Mum. I've tried to talk to him and he won't move."

"You're obviously misreading him." Lauren got up,

crossed over to the phone, picked up the receiver and dialled the bank.

"Hi, it's Lauren Launcelot here. Can you put me through to Jim, darling . . . but it's urgent . . . I can wait for him . . . I see . . . Well, can you get him to give me a call as soon as he can? Thanks." She hung up the phone. "He's in a meeting."

"He's only saying that, Mum. He won't talk to you. He's not the friend he pretended to be."

Lauren sat down and stared into space. "Niall was right all along . . . Jack should have been left in charge of the business."

Troy stared down at the ground and said, "I'm sorry."

"Look, I'm good friends with Brooke O'Hara, Jim's wife," said Blanche. "Let me have a word with her and see."

Blanche waited in the lounge of the Castleford Arms. She glanced at her watch and saw that Brooke was half an hour late. Finally she arrived, all glamorous and dressed up to the nines.

"Hi, Blanche!" she said, sitting down opposite her and ordering a Bacardi and Coke.

"Brooke, thanks for meeting me," Blanche smiled at her.

"No problem at all." Brooke studied her for a while and then leaned forward and in hushed tones said, "Jim told me about you losing everything. I'm so sorry. I haven't told the others yet."

Blanche nodded. "Thanks, Brooke." She took a deep breath. "Brooke, you know this has come as such a shock to us. I just wondered if there was something you could do to help?"

Brooke sat back abruptly and put her hand to her heart. "Me? But what could I possibly do?"

"Well, you could have a word with Jim for a start. He won't take our calls. And he's such an old friend of the Launcelots, I'm sure if we could just sit down and have a chat we could come to an arrangement."

Brooke gave a little laugh. "As if Jim ever listened to me!"

"But this will ruin us, Brooke. We have nothing. No savings. Nothing."

Brooke nodded as her drink arrived. "I know. I'm sorry."

But she didn't look one bit sorry, thought Blanche.

"It's a pity Jack wasn't left in charge. This wouldn't have happened with him . . . now he was a man!"

Blanche stared at her, suddenly realising she was enjoying their downfall.

"I'm sorry for wasting your time, Brooke," said Blanche, standing up.

"Oh, going so soon? Oh, and Blanche, how many bedrooms are there in Winterfield exactly?"

"I don't know," said Blanche, confused.

"You know the house is due to go up for auction the following week? It's a big house to run, I think, but it must be lovely to live there." Brooke took a sip of her Bacardi and Coke and smiled at Blanche.

Blanche almost was in a trance as she drove back to their house on the coast road. This was unthinkable. Yesterday she was planning her luxury trip to Italy, now she and her family would be out on the street next week – literally.

She walked past Troy's car as she let herself in.

In the lounge she found Troy on the phone.

"Who were you on the phone to?" she asked after he had hung up.

"Another bank, to see if they would lend us some money – not a chance."

He reached out to his tumbler of whiskey and took a gulp. There was a terrible sick feeling in Blanche's stomach.

"Any luck with Brooke?" he asked.

"No luck at all. She actually seemed to be enjoying it. She said Winterfield is going on the market in a couple of weeks . . . I got the distinct impression the O'Haras were going after it to buy it."

"Of course. Jim O'Hara has always been jealous of us. Pretending to be Dad's friend through the years. And now he's kicking us out and he'll buy Winterfield at a knock-down rate as a repossessed property. The bastard!"

"Troy – what are we going to do?"

"I don't know, Blanche!"

"Troy, I know what it's like to have no money and no roof over your head. It's terrifying and nobody gives a shit about you when you're that far down."

Troy sighed heavily and stared into his drink.

"Come on, darling, follow me," Blanche said to Carl. He toddled alongside her as she held Amelia and they walked into the house at Winterfield. She walked out to the back and found Niall there enjoying the sun.

She often brought the children up to their grandfather. Niall got great joy in seeing them. His mind had continued to wander occasionally and Lauren and Troy tried to keep anything stressful from him. She shuddered to think how he would react when he found out that he had lost Winterfield. And where would he and Lauren go?

299

"Kiss your grandfather," Blanche said to Amelia as she bent down to allow Niall to kiss her.

"How are you, little fella?" said Niall as he gave Carl a hug.

"Where's Lauren?" asked Blanche as she sat down beside him.

"Out shopping. Where else?"

They chatted for a while, mainly about the children. She enjoyed his company.

"What's going on, Blanche?" Niall suddenly asked.

"Sorry?"

"Something's going on. I can tell by Lauren and Troy. The two of them are walking around like the walking dead. They don't tell me anything any more. Think I can't handle it. Do you think I can handle it, Blanche?"

She stared at him, not knowing what to say. "To be honest I don't know if you can."

"Is it serious?"

"Yes, Niall, very." Tears sprang to her eyes.

"It's the business, isn't it?"

She nodded and he sighed loudly.

"Tell me."

"I can't. It's not my place."

He gazed searchingly at her, then leaned over and took her hand. "Blanche, you need to do whatever has to be done. Don't rely on anybody. Do it yourself. You're the only one strong enough now Jack is gone."

"But I can't do anything, Niall." Now the tears were rolling down her face.

"Yes, you can," said Niall.

CHAPTER 43

Blanche walked into the bank and approached the reception.

"Hi, I'm here to see Jim."

"I don't think you have an appointment, Mrs Launcelot, do you?"

"I'm sure he'll see me."

"I'm afraid he's in Dublin today," said the receptionist.

Blanche spotted him walking into his office. "Really? I'll just have a word with his twin brother then, will I?" Blanche walked across the bank's lobby to Jim's door, knocked on it and opened it.

"Blanche!" he said, looking up.

The receptionist arrived behind her. "Sorry, Jim, I couldn't stop her."

"It's alright – come on in, Blanche," said Jim.

"Thank you," Blanche said, closing the door behind her and sitting down.

"Look, Blanche, I know what you're here for and there's nothing I can do. And I think it's pretty lousy for Troy to send his wife in here to do his dirty work."

"He'd come himself if you would only agree to meet him."

"There's nothing more to be said. The Launcelots can't dig themselves out of this hole, Blanche."

"I believe Winterfield is going up for auction in a couple of weeks."

"It's going to be divided up and sold off in lots, yes."

"Winterfield House would be a splendid home for a senior bank manager and his glamorous wife, don't you think?" she tested him and she saw him flush.

"If the property doesn't have any other interested parties we might bid for it, nothing illegal in that."

"And there will be no other interested parties, not in today's depressed market I daresay . . . After all Niall did for you over the years."

"Business is business . . . it's nothing personal," said Jim.

There was something in the way he said it. It didn't ring true. It seemed very personal, looking at him now. But why would it be? The Launcelots had only been good to him. No reason in the world why he should hold a grudge.

'It's a pity Jack wasn't left in charge . . . now he was a man!' Suddenly Brooke's words in the Castleford Arms flashed through her mind. Beautiful, glamorous Brooke who seemed to flirt as if it was her second nature.

Blanche wasn't sure, but it was worth a shot.

"How long was Jack sleeping with Brooke, Jim?" she asked.

Jim's face went bright red and his hands clenched into fists.

Bingo! thought Blanche.

"So – you're getting revenge on Jack by taking away Winterfield, is that it? You might even be trying to impress Brooke by getting Winterfield. Make her love you again, make her forget Jack – is that what all this is about?"

Jim looked as if he could erupt. "It's about you fucking Launcelots living and acting like royalty and unable to pay your fucking debts! Now get the fuck out of here!"

Blanche shook her head, leaned forward and spoke calmly. "No, Jim. We're not losing everything next Tuesday. You're going to extend our loan for eighteen months. And if you don't I'm going to tell everybody in Castleford that your wife was screwing Jack. I will holler it from every corner of this town. I will bring Jack back from New York and get him to holler it in every bar. Your wife will be known as the town slut, Jim, and you will be destroyed. And you never know, with Jack back in town – he and Brooke might take up where they left off. No doubt they will if I am to judge by some comments she made to me about him recently."

Jim jumped to his feet. "I'll kill you," he hissed. "I'll kill you!"

Blanche sat back. "No, you won't, Jim. You'll extend our credit facilities by eighteen months and then nobody will ever hear what I've just said about your wife and Jack, alright?"

She looked at his red face, his bulging eyes. Every muscle in his body was tense to breaking point. And she knew she had won.

Blanche walked down the street to her car and sat in. Only when she was safely in the car did she recognise her heart thumping madly and she rubbed her face. But she was holding the loan extension letter and that was all that mattered.

"I got it! I got it!" Blanche yelled as she entered the lounge at home.

"Got what?" asked Troy.

She flung the loan offer letter from the bank at him. "An extension of the credit for eighteen months."

"How did you manage that?" demanded Troy, a huge smile breaking across his face.

"I don't know – but I did it!" She could hardly catch her breath from excitement.

Troy lifted her up into a tight hug. "Oh, my baby! My baby!" he shouted.

Blanche managed to get some sleep that night and got up early the next morning. She saw to the children, fed them and clothed them and left them with the help. The phone rang in the hall as she raced past it and she scooped it up.

"Hi, Blanche, it's Joan here," said a sweet voice on the phone. It was one of the businessmen's wives she had befriended. "Just wondering could you pick me up from the house for our game of tennis today. My car's on the blink."

"Oh, Joan, I completely forgot about our tennis! Do you mind if I cancel?" Blanche made a few more excuses and then hurried from the house and up to Winterfield. Tennis and lunches! She felt she was going to have a little more on her plate than those pastimes over the next while.

Troy was at the desk in the office when she arrived, a mountain of books opened in front of him.

"What are you doing here?" asked Troy, surprised to see her.

"I've come to help? What do you think?"

"You! But how can you help?"

"In the same way I got us eighteen months' extension on our credit. By using my brain."

He laughed, sitting back. "Seriously, darling. What experience have you got of business? I think you can best help me by making sure the kids are alright, don't you?"

Blanche stared down at her husband. "No, Troy. We can't go on the way we have been, or else we'll be in the exact same situation in eighteen months, if not worse. Now there's too much at risk here, all our futures. The children's futures. I want to know what's going on, Troy."

He stared at her and then sighed. "Pull up a chair."

Blanche and Troy didn't raise their heads from the books for the whole day, eating a sandwich at the desk for lunch. Blanche got Troy to explain how things worked, and she slowly got a handle on it.

Blanche looked at her watch and saw it was nearly seven. She sat back and rubbed her temples.

"Troy, this is a disaster. We'll never be able to repay all this debt and all the pubs are about to go under . . . Why didn't you see the alarm bells ringing ages ago and do something? Say something?"

"I was trying my best, Blanche!" he snapped at her.

She studied her husband and his stressed face. She remembered when she was working in the pub in London. She remembered what Dolores and the others had said about Troy. They hadn't respected him. They had respected Jack, but not Troy. They just tolerated him and tried to fob him off. And she remembered Troy in London. Keeping to himself, pretending to look busy with the books, but not really interested in what was going on. As she thought about it, she realised it was no wonder it had turned into a disaster.

The door opened and in walked Lauren holding a few shopping bags from boutiques. "Troy darling, do you want some dinner?" Her face dropped when she saw Blanche sitting at the desk in front of all the open books.

"What's going on here?" she demanded.

"Blanche is just helping me go through some of the books," explained Troy.

Lauren marched over to the table and slammed a couple of books shut.

"Well, she shouldn't be! These are our private matters, not just for anybody to go through!"

"Mum! She's trying to help!" said Troy.

"Trying to help herself more like. Seeing what's in the honeypot!" Lauren's eyes blazed.

"Some honeypot!" said Blanche. "There's nothing in it!"

"She's my wife," said Troy. "She has a right to know what's going on."

"In all my years married to Niall, I never once went looking through the business books!"

"No, you were too busy shopping!" snapped Blanche.

"Don't you speak to me like that!" said Lauren.

"Lauren, it's time that you and Troy and everyone else stopped living in cloud-cuckoo-land. If I hadn't gone into the bank and sorted out a credit extension we would be out on the streets tonight."

"So . . . what are the results of your 'inquisition'?" demanded Lauren sarcastically.

"We need to take drastic action immediately. Me and Troy need to get over to London and figure out what's going on."

"*You're* going to London?" Lauren was incredulous.

"Yes, I am," insisted Blanche.

"I – I don't think there's any need for you to go, Blanche," said Troy.

"Troy, you can't manage this on your own. That is glaringly obvious. So I'm going too and that's final."

CHAPTER 44

Blanche felt London had changed a lot in the three years since she had left. There was a new confidence about the place by 1984. She knew that the city was on the cusp of a boom. People felt they could make money and were out to do so. People who had never dreamed of buying shares were putting their names down for the British Telecom privatisation. Everyone wanted to buy their own house which was pushing up property prices.

Blanche and Troy went to the house in Kensington, unpacked and headed out for dinner that night. They had left Carl and Amelia with Lauren, and Blanche was filled with guilt about that. But she kept reminding herself of what the alternative would be. Anyway, she wouldn't be away for long. Just enough to see what was going on and advise Troy on the action that needed to be taken. They went to an Italian restaurant in Knightsbridge and again she was struck by the growing confidence of the people dining there.

"Okay, what I'm going to do is visit all the pubs tomorrow as a customer and see what's going on," said Blanche. "That's the beauty about me being here. They all know you, but they haven't a clue who I am, except Dolores. I'll be able to observe undetected."

"And what exactly will you be observing?"

"How the places are being run, of course!" She sighed and raised her eyes to heaven.

The first thing Blanche noticed was that the areas the pubs were in were undergoing a transformation. They had previously all been very rough working-class areas but now they'd had a huge influx of new people living there. And these peoples seemed young and affluent. The tattered old townhouses that had been all divided up into flats and bedsits were now being bought by young professionals and entrepreneurs and being restored into beautiful homes.

The Launcelot pubs looked grubby and old-fashioned in their new surroundings. And when she visited the insides of the pubs they were even more depressing. A couple of old men sitting at the bar, staring into their Guinness while 'The Fields of Athenry' played from a broken-down jukebox. The bar managers looked rough and mostly uninterested.

"It's no wonder we're losing so much money, Troy."

They were sitting on the floor of the lounge having a Chinese takeaway and a bottle of red wine.

"The places are ready to fall down! They look decrepit at this stage. And they're not in keeping with the people who now live there. The places have become gentrified. There's no room for those sad old pubs any more."

Troy was intrigued at the animation in his wife.

"Well – look what the cat dragged in! If it ain't me old barmaid!" said Dolores as Blanche walked into her pub.

"Dolores!" Blanche felt happy to see her again.

"Look at you now – Lady Muck!" Dolores said, running her eyes up and down Blanche's grey suede suit. "I wouldn't recognise you from the frightened girl who arrived in here looking for a job. Remember?"

"How could I forget?" Blanche smiled at her.

They sat down at a corner table with toasted cheese and ham sandwiches and Cokes.

Blanche looked around the pub. "I recognise those fellas at the bar, they used to drink here when I worked here!"

"I know. They're a loyal lot. I'm grateful for them – especially in these hard times."

"But they don't spend much," said Blanche.

"Well, they don't have much to spend, love."

"Do you get any of the new people that moved into the area coming in?"

"What d'you mean? Those fucking yuppies? No, thanks. I don't serve vol-au-vents!"

That night Blanche paced the lounge at home smoking.

"We can't let it go on the way it's going, Troy! We are bleeding money. We're not running a business, we're running a day centre for old folk to while away their afternoons!"

"But what can we do?"

"The areas have become wealthier and we need to attract in those wealthy young professionals."

"But they're not wanting to come into our places, are they?"

"Not as they are. We need to re-invent them. Turn them into something nice, change the drinks we serve, serve something more than toasted cheese sandwiches. Get rid of some of those managers who look as if they would put customers off."

"A lot of those managers have been with Dad for years."

"Yes, and they nearly cost him his business."

Troy looked at his wife cynically. "And where do you

propose we get the money for all these changes. We're broke, unless you forgot."

"That's the tricky bit," sighed Blanche.

Blanche spent the next day thinking hard. That evening she was on the typewriter all evening, typing as best she could, with the last year's set of accounts opened beside her.

"Dare I ask what you're doing?" Troy came behind her and inspected all the neatly set lines of figures she was working on.

"I'm doing a bit of creative accountancy," she said, continuing to type.

"Huh?"

"I'm just re-jigging the figures on the accounts a little."

He leaned forward and peered at the figures.

"Blanche! What the fuck are you doing? You're changing the accounts to show the pubs made a profit last year!"

"I know. It's the only way we can get a loan out of an English bank. We know they won't touch us with the accounts the way they are."

"But Blanche, that's fraud!"

"No – it's survival."

The next day she went to a printer and took the cover of a real set of accounts with their accountant's logo and details and had it bound on her new paperwork. Then she met an estate agent who did an evaluation of all the pubs. As she waited in the estate agent's office for the evaluations to be done, the secretary popped out the back. Blanche seized the moment and dashed behind the girl's desk, grabbed some of the headed paper that was there and stashed it inside her bag. That night she retyped the evaluations on the headed paper giving the properties a much higher value.

Then she made an appointment with an English bank for the following day. She decided not to tell Troy about the appointment as he was so against what she was doing. Besides, he was a bad liar and she felt he would give the game away.

She dressed in a business suit and made her way to the bank. As she sat in the reception she was overcome by nerves and felt like being sick. She forced herself to remain calm. She thought about Samantha Armstrong at the model agency in Dublin. She thought about the cool businesslike demeanour she always portrayed.

The bank manager, Rupert Golden, flicked through the set of accounts and nodded. He then flicked through the fake evaluations of the pubs she had done.

"It all looks pretty impressive Mrs Launcelot. These pubs are in up and coming areas."

"And we want to take advantage of that and modernise the pubs."

"I think we can secure you the funds you're looking for," smiled Rupert.

She smiled back. It was as simple as that.

"Well, a simple 'well done' would be nice!" said Blanche that night as she excitedly told Troy about the loan approval.

"You never even told me you were going to the bank today."

"No, because you would have tried to stop me, wouldn't you? And I was nervous enough about going."

"I can't believe you've done all this. All this fraud!"

"And I can't believe you let the business get in such a mess that I had to!"

"And what happens when the bank back in Ireland and this new bank come looking for their money back?"

"We'll have turned the thing around by then."

Blanche and Troy visited all the pubs and told the managers and staff they were closing down for refurbishment. Then they told most of the managers they would not be needed on re-opening. Troy sat through the meetings with the managers, all ashen-faced and stressed as the news was broken.

"But I've been working for your father for thirty years, Troy – *thirty years!*" shouted one, Tommy Green.

"I know, but there's nothing I can do," said Troy, looking equally as upset.

"This place has been operating on a huge loss for five years, Tommy," Blanche spoke softly.

That night Blanche could hear Lauren hollering down the phone to Troy.

"I got a call from Tommy Green, who's under the impression you've fired him," shouted Lauren.

"I have," confirmed Troy.

"*What?* Well, you can just re-instate him tomorrow. He's not going anywhere, Troy. He's been with your father longer than I have! Get him back on the job tomorrow."

"It's impossible, Mum. He won't fit in with the new surroundings."

"This isn't you speaking, Troy. You've a good heart. It's Blanche! Put her on the phone!"

Troy looked over at Blanche who was sitting on the couch. Blanche shook her head vehemently.

"I can't, she's in the bath."

"Well, if I was over there – I'd drown her in it!"

CHAPTER 45

Blanche and Troy worked tirelessly over the next few weeks. They were up at the crack of dawn, going to the pubs and overseeing the builders as they carried out the refurbishment work and not getting home until midnight. Blanche was good at saying what she wanted and deciding on the different designs, Troy was good at making sure the work was carried out. At the beginning Blanche was a bit intimidated by the working men and told everything to Troy who relayed it to the builders. But after a while she got more confident and spoke to them herself. As the pubs shaped up into modern glamorous bars, she contacted recruitment agents and herself and Troy did a series of interviews with young bar managers. They carried out the interviews in one of the bars as the building work went on around them.

"I didn't like him," said Troy as he watched a young good-looking man swagger out. "He's far too sure of himself."

"Troy – he's perfect! Young, confident – the women will love him. He's hired!"

Every Friday night, they would fly home and spend the weekend with the kids. Rather than listen to Lauren's constant berating, Blanche avoided collecting the kids herself and would wait at the house for Troy to bring them home.

And every Sunday night when they had to fly back to London, they felt their hearts wrench as they had to leave them.

"It's only for another couple of weeks," said Troy to Blanche as they flew back to London. "We'll have the pubs up and running by then and we can go back to Castleford permanently."

She nodded and smiled.

The week the pubs were due to open Blanche and Troy went and inspected the work and they were really shaping up and looking amazing. However, two of the pubs were way behind schedule.

Troy was arguing with the builder in charge of these two pubs.

"We warned you we needed to have it ready for the opening on Friday, and there's no way you're ever going to get this finished by then," said Troy.

"Well, we're going as quick as we can," shrugged the builder.

"Not a chance it will be ready by Friday!" said Troy.

Blanche looked up from the drawings laid out in front of her. "Can't he hire more staff in to get it finished?" She said.

"He says he's working at full capacity," Troy sighed again.

Blanche looked over at the builder. She never liked him, he had a dishonest look and had lied to them all along about the speed he was working at.

Suddenly she was marching over to him.

"Mr Folgar," she said.

He looked at her, surprised. They hadn't exchanged more than a few words before.

"Mr Folgar, you did assure us you would have the work ready by the 25th, did you not?"

"I can't remember what we said."

"Well, I do . . . we had an agreement and you've broken it and so I'm going to have to discount your price."

Folgar started laughing. "No fucking way!"

She was becoming increasingly angry at his attitude. "Well, then you're fired."

"You can't just fire me. Who's going to finish the job for you?"

"The other builders from the other pubs are ahead of their schedules so I'll just get one of them to finish, and they will be finished by Friday."

The man stared at her in anger. "Leave it with me, and I'll make a couple of calls," he said.

Blanche went back to the table she was working at and sat down.

"You're shaking," Troy said.

She didn't realise she was until he said it.

Two hours later a team of labourers arrived in and joined Folgar's other workers.

Folgar came over to Blanche and Troy. "The job will be finished by Friday afternoon," he assured them.

Blanche and Troy looked up as the new sign reading 'Launcelot' was put up over a pub. Previously all the pubs had individual names.

"Are you sure it's a good idea, changing all the names to Launcelot?"

"Definitely. I think branding is going to become very important. We're creating a chain here, giving the pubs all the same look, menus and image. If we give them the same name then we've created a brand."

Troy sighed, wondering where she got all her ideas from. He had watched her transform the pubs with such energy and drive that he could but marvel at her. But he couldn't wait to return to their lives as they were, and how they should be.

Blanche looked at Dolores wearing the new manager's uniform the Friday night of the opening. It didn't sit comfortably on her. Dolores was one of the few original managers who had been kept. In reality, Blanche felt Dolores was certainly not the young trendy image the Launcelot bars needed, but felt she couldn't get rid of her due to the fact she owed her so much.

"I feel like a fucking penguin!" snarled Dolores, looking down at the smart outfit she was wearing.

"You look wonderful," lied Blanche.

Dolores stared around at the beautiful new pub and sighed. "I don't recognise the place."

"Good! A lot of money has been spent so you wouldn't."

Dolores looked at the new cocktail menu. "A Sex on a Beach! I never heard of such a thing! We'll be closed down by the vice squad!"

"Dolores, you don't have to worry about it. The new bar staff are all trained in making all the cocktails."

Dolores picked up the new food menu that Blanche had put together with the new chefs she had employed.

"I don't even know what half of this shit on this so-called gastro-pub menu is!"

"Again, you don't have to worry, the new chef will take care of everything."

Dolores looked at Blanche. "So what exactly am I supposed to be doing here then?"

Blanche looked puzzled and then just smiled at her.

The doors opened at seven. The pub was full by nine. Blanche was dressed in a black cocktail dress and she surveyed the crowd with excitement. They had attracted in the young professionals and they were busy ordering bottles of wine and cocktails.

Suddenly seeing they were short-staffed, Blanche went behind the bar and started working there.

Troy came out from the office in the back.

"Were you speaking to the other managers?" she asked.

"Yeah, and all the pubs are doing really well. Congratulations, Blanche, your ideas worked."

She leaned forward and gave him a hug.

CHAPTER 46

Three weeks after the Launcelot chain of pubs was launched, Blanche found she was as busy as ever. And she loved it. She loved the interaction with the new managers as they discussed different strategies. She loved seeing the pubs full every night. And they started doing a brisk lunchtime trade with people coming in to try out the new pub menu. The more she stayed working there, the more she realised she had been bored with her life back in Castleford. Those tennis matches, those lunches, those endless discussions with the local wives about fashion and hair styles, Lauren's continual disapproval. She realised she didn't want to go back to that life.

It was a Monday night and Troy and Blanche were getting ready for bed.

"Well, everything seems to be up and running," said Troy. "I suppose our work is done now and we can go home."

"What do you mean, our work is done? It's only just beginning. Troy, how long do you think the profits will be up if we go back to Castleford? The places will slip back quickly enough if we're not here to keep an eye on things."

"We?"

"Yes, Troy. Me and you. It's too big a job for you to do on your own."

He looked at her, confused and annoyed. "So what are you suggesting?"

"I'm saying we have to bring Carl and Amelia over here to live with us as we continue to manage the business."

"Oh no!" he smiled. "We're not moving to London, Blanche. I don't even like the place."

"You've no choice, Troy. We're in too much debt and we'll lose everything when the credit extension expires. We have to roll up our sleeves and work as hard as we can to keep this show on the road."

"But, I don't want to live here. And I don't want to bring my kids up here."

"Well, the way things were going, you were going to end up bringing them up on the streets!"

"It wouldn't have come to that."

"What! You and Lauren are not facing reality here, Troy! Do you not remember we had a few days to clear out of Winterfield."

"Of course I remember how it was. I was living with it for months before I told you. I just don't want this life for us."

"We can't have the luxury of sitting back and living the life we had in Castleford any more, Troy . . . And you know, this might be for the good. Ireland is in such a deep recession, I can't see any end to it. And London, it's just beginning to happen here, I can feel it and see it and we can be part of that . . . I want to bring the kids over and start living our lives here, Troy. We've actually no choice."

"It's only temporary. As soon as we have the business back on top and the debt under control, we'll be back for good," Troy assured Niall and Lauren.

319

"What can I say – needs must," said Lauren, lighting up a cigarette. "But it's going to be very lonely around here without you guys."

For a moment Blanche thought Lauren might cry. But the moment passed quickly; Lauren was too tough to show tears.

Carl came running into the room and jumped into his grandmother's arms.

"And I'm going to miss the children so much."

"It will be nice though, having a long holiday like that," said Niall. "London's lovely this time of year."

Lauren glanced over at Niall and then at the other two with a concerned look.

That night, Niall was asleep by the time Lauren had finished brushing her hair. She slid into the bed beside him and, resting on one arm, gazed down at him.

She spoke softly. "You know, if you got your way and Jack was in charge, Troy would be staying here with us and I wouldn't be losing him. Jack would be handling everything." She stared at his sleeping form. "Oh, Niall, I miss our arguments. I wish you'd come back to me the way you were."

She sighed and turned off the light.

Blanche got into her new routine quickly in London. She would be up early and herself and Troy would spend the mornings with the children. Then a childminder came in and they would head into the pubs and start going through stock-control, menus, rotas and all other management issues.

They would be home for dinner with the children and have them in bed by seven thirty. Then they would be back to the pubs, working until after closing time. And Blanche loved it. She loved the excitement of running the places, of making decisions that would improve the Launcelot brand.

Blanche based herself in the original pub that she had worked in with Dolores. Perhaps it was because it was most familiar to her. Or because she didn't have the heart to let Dolores go and felt she neither fit the part nor was able to run the trendy new establishment it had become. Blanche was very hands-on there.

One night a large group of young men arrived in with an assortment of young glamorous girls. They occupied a corner table and ordered bottles of champagne and food from the evening menu. They were loud and arrogant. Roxy Music's 'Burn Both Ends' was playing loudly.

"For fuck's sake," snapped Dolores. "Who do they think they are? Fucking footballers and their glamour model girlfriends! I'm going to go over and ask them to shut up or get out!" Dolores started making a beeline for them.

Blanche grabbed her arm and pulled her back. "No, you don't. I don't care how much noise they make when they keep ordering champagne by the bucket." She turned to Troy. "Who are they?"

Troy peered over at them. "The blonde guy is Jamie Tonkins, he's just been signed by Chelsea. The dark guy is Freddie Gordon. You know, the guy who scored at the World Cup."

Troy continued to name the men. But as Blanche listened it was the quiet middle-aged man who sat amongst them who was attracting her attention.

The players seemed to be from different clubs and so she thought the middle-aged man must be the common denominator.

"Any idea who the older man is?" she asked.

Troy squinted over. "That's Ronnie Richards. He used to manage Arsenal, but has gone out on his own now as an agent."

She kept an eye on the table all night, going over and checking everything was alright for them and making sure they weren't annoyed by any fans. True for Dolores, they were very rowdy.

"Here, love – this champagne is off," declared Jamie Tonkins as she walked by the table.

She glanced down at the three-quarters drunk bottle and smiled at him. "I'm sorry about that, Mr Tonkins, I'll replace it for you straight away." She walked away with the ice bucket. "Jennifer, a new bottle of champagne over to that table immediately."

"He's taking the piss! There's nothing wrong with that champers! He's just looking for a new bottle free, cheap git!" said Dolores loudly.

"Shhhh! He'll hear you!" hissed Blanche.

"That's the idea. In the old days, he'd be out on his ear!"

Blanche studied them for the night, making sure their every whim was seen to.

By the end of the night, the manager Ronnie Richards got up and walked over to the bar.

"Bill, please," he requested of Blanche.

Blanche smiled at him and handed him the hefty bill.

He reached into his jacket for his wallet.

"Don't worry, it's taken care of," said Blanche.

He looked up at her, surprised. "By whom?"

"By me. I'm Blanche Launcelot," she said, reaching her hand across the bar.

He looked at her suspiciously and then shook her hand

and introduced himself. "Ronnie Richards. And to what do we owe this free evening?" he asked.

"Could I have a drink with you – if you've got five minutes?"

He looked her up and down and shrugged. She poured them both a glass of wine and went to an empty table.

He studied her intently as she smiled at him.

"I take it from your surname you own the joint?" asked Ronnie.

"This one and another nineteen like it," said Blanche.

He nodded, impressed. "Not just a pretty face, then . . . You still haven't told me why I don't have to hand you over a grand tonight for all that drink and food."

"From what I hear, you've started your own business as an agent, managing football stars."

"Not just footballers, all sports people, and the odd glamour model as well."

"Excellent, and we've just launched the Launcelot chain of pubs and wine bars. I would just like you to keep us in mind if you send your stars out on the town. I will provide them with an excellent venue, a fun night, make sure they won't get annoyed by other punters, protect their privacy, and throw in the odd bottle of free champagne as well."

"And what do you get out of it?"

"My pubs get a reputation of being where your stars like to hang out."

"I could just nod my head, not pay the bill, and walk out of here laughing and you might never hear from me or any of my stars again."

She shrugged. "That's a chance I have to take."

He reached into his wallet, took out his card and handed it to her.

"Ring me next week." He got up and joined his players and they finally all left.

On Monday Blanche was in the back office of the pub looking down at Ronnie Richards' card. She picked up the phone, steadied herself and dialled the number.

She got through to a secretary.

"Hi, could I speak to Ronnie Richards, please."

"Who will I say is calling?"

"Blanche Launcelot. He knows me."

"One second, please."

Blanche waited for more than thirty seconds before the secretary came back on the phone.

"I'm afraid he's in a meeting. Can I take your number and he'll call you back?"

Blanche gave her number and waited expectantly for him to call her back. He never did. She felt crushed.

CHAPTER 47

As the summer turned into autumn, business continued to boom and Blanche made sure money started to go back to the bank in Ireland to start paying off the debt. With the expanding business came her expanding confidence as the decisions she made continued to pay off.

Dolores came to her one day in the back office of the bar.

"Just letting you know I'm finishing up on Friday," said Dolores.

"What?" Blanche said, sitting back and looking confused. "But why?"

"Come off it, love. You don't need me around here. You've got shut of all the other old managers in the other bars. You're just keeping me on because you feel some loyalty to me. And I'm not charity case."

Blanche looked at her in the new bar manager's outfit. It didn't sit any more comfortably on her than it did on opening night.

"I don't want you to go, Dolores. I admit I feel a debt to you because you looked after me but –"

"I needed a barmaid, love, and now you need a bar

manager, a young and glamorous one. See ya, kid." Dolores began to walk out.

Blanche was overcome with sadness watching her leave, and some kind of strange fear.

"Wait! Dolores!" Blanche got up from her chair and raced after her. "What will you do? Where will you go?"

"I haven't decided yet."

"Listen, okay, if you're not comfortable in the pub here any more, why don't you work for me in a different capacity?"

"I don't understand."

"I'm mad busy here with the pubs and the children. Will you look after the children for me and run the house when I'm at work? I've a childminder in at the moment, and she's great, but I don't know her like I know you. Would you consider it?"

Dolores sighed. "It's the best offer I've got all day."

Dolores moved out from over the pub and got a flat nearby. Blanche then renovated the upstairs of the pub, turning it into an office for herself and Troy.

"Blanche, there's a guy downstairs to see you," said the new bar manager. "Looks like a businessman."

"Didn't you ask his name or business?"

"Eh, yes, but he said just to tell you he was here."

Blanche was annoyed but intrigued. "Okay, I'll be down in a few seconds."

As she came into the bar Wham's 'Freedom' was blaring from the new music system. It was six o'clock and the bar was just beginning to fill up. The manager pointed out the man at a corner table.

It was Ronnie Richards.

Blanche was taken aback but she walked over to him casually.

"Hi, remember me?" he said.

"Yes." She sat down opposite him. "So, what can I do for you?"

"I must apologise for not ringing you back that time."

"Slightly rude of you, but however."

"Well, *I* didn't ask you to pay that bill for me."

"I know. But I'm sure you haven't come in here because you suddenly felt guilty about your rudeness."

"I need a favour," he said.

She was intrigued and confused. What could Ronnie Richards possibly want from her? And how had he the nerve to ask her?

"Like what?"

"I just want you to say if anyone asks you that Jamie Tonkins was here last Friday night, all night until the bar closed."

"Jamie Tonkins?"

"Yes, the premier league footballer."

"I know who he is! But why would I say he was here?"

"That doesn't concern you."

"If I'm going to lie I think it does."

"Jamie was involved in a fight in town. Some tosser picked on him and Jamie had to defend himself. The man is now pressing charges. There were no other witnesses. So it's his word against Jamie's. It will destroy his career."

"And you're trying to tell me that I'm the only alibi you could find?"

"I need somebody who's not already known by Jamie, otherwise the cops will say it's a cover-up."

"Which is exactly what this is," Blanche pointed out.

"Will you help me or not?"

Blanche sat back and lit up a cigarette. "And what do I get out of this?"

"I'll put your pubs on the map. I'll have them filled with footballers and models and actors every night. Your pubs will be the places to be . . . Deal or no deal?"

Blanche thought for a while before saying, "Deal."

The police visited the next day and came up to her office.

"Sorry for bothering you, but I just want to see if this man was here on Friday night last?" said the detective, handing over a photo of Jamie Tonkins.

"This is that footballer," said Blanche.

"Jamie Tonkins, that's right."

"Friday night – yes, he was here."

"From roughly what time to what time?"

"He came in early, around six, and I think he was one of the last to leave, very late."

"Thank you for your help."

True to Ronnie Richard's word, the celebrities suddenly started to arrive into the Launcelot pubs. They got a name as the places to be very quickly. It wasn't long before Blanche was organising doormen and restricting access.

CHAPTER 48

Troy and Blanche flew back to Ireland the day before Christmas Eve. They were returning to London for New Year. They were planning big parties in all the pubs for New Year's Eve and it was bound to be a big money-spinner.

They stayed at the main house that Christmas and Blanche really enjoyed putting her feet up and relaxing.

Niall was playing with the children by the Christmas tree and Blanche and Troy sat with Lauren in the sitting room looking on.

"So things are looking up then?" quizzed Lauren.

"We're making inroads with the debt," said Troy.

"That figures, I even passed Jim O'Hara in town the other day and he managed to smile at me. Bastard," said Lauren. "Well, do you think you'll be home for good by the summer then?"

"That's the plan, anyway," said Troy.

Blanche felt herself getting irritated. "Do you honestly think we'll have that mountain of debt paid off by the summer?"

"No, Blanche, but we'll have everything on the right road so we can get back to our lives."

"Troy! This is our lives! Those pubs are our lives, and our children's future. Now I know you want to come back here and potter around the farm all day but that's not an option at the moment!"

Troy suddenly lost his temper and leapt to his feet. "This has been all about what you want! I think it should be about what's the best for our family from now on!"

She stood up and faced him. "I'm doing what's best for our family. It's you that's being selfish!"

"Ever since I met you it's been about what you want! You never even asked my opinion about all the changes in the pubs. Or doing that deal with the bank manager over there. Or getting so close to that Ronnie Richards. He's so involved with us at this stage, he might as well have shares in the business . . ."

As Troy raged on, his words became more distant until she couldn't hear him. She could only see his angry face and then that faded away as well and all she could see was blackness.

Blanche struggled up in the bed and looked around the bedroom.

"Easy! Take it easy!" said a man's voice.

She looked up to see the doctor from Castleford.

"What happened?" she asked.

"You fainted," said Troy softly, coming into view.

"Nothing serious, just a little tiredness and too much going on for a woman in your condition."

"My condition?"

"You're pregnant, my dear. Congratulations," said the doctor as he smiled at her and walked out of the bedroom.

Troy came and sat on the bed. He smiled at her and reached down and held her. Blanche could hear the television on downstairs, 'Do They Know It's Christmas?' playing loudly on it.

"It's such wonderful news. I'm so delighted. Another baby! It's just what we need," said Troy.

"Is it?" asked Blanche, trying to comprehend it.

"Of course. This is a sign of what we need to put first: us not the pubs."

And as he held her tightly he couldn't see the tears falling down her face.

Blanche stood at the patio doors looking out at the back gardens of Winterfield. A light snow had fallen and Troy was out in the garden with Carl and Amelia, the three of them wrapped up warm against the cold. She folded her arms and leaned against the heavy curtains.

"Aren't you going to join them?" asked a voice behind her. She turned quickly and saw Niall standing there.

"Eh, no. I better not. The doctor has ordered me to stay indoors for the next couple of days." She touched her stomach.

"You don't look too happy about the good news."

She studied Niall. Sometimes he could be the strong bright-as-a-button man he always was, and then other times he would drift away and not make sense. He seemed his old self today.

She turned and looked out the window at Troy playing with the children.

"Troy's delighted," said Niall.

"I know he is. He thinks this is going to turn us back into the family we were. The one he wanted and yearns for."

"And you?"

"I thought our family was complete. I didn't expect or

want any more children . . . that sounds terrible, doesn't it?"

"No. Just honest."

"I'm trying so hard to be happy about this baby. But it just won't come." She turned and stared at him suspiciously. Everyone tiptoed around Niall these days, trying not to cause him stress which the doctor warned could cause his memory loss. She smiled at him. "Don't mind me, Niall. Everything's fine."

He put his hands on her shoulders. "Look, Blanche. I know my mind isn't what it used to be. But I know what's been going on. I know we nearly lost everything and I know you've been working around the clock to keep things afloat."

"Oh Niall! It's been so hard." She started rubbing her forehead. "And trying to make Troy and Lauren see what has to be done. I feel as if they're working against me. Trying to keep me out, wanting me to be the little wife and mother and leave business to them."

He smiled at her. "I know what it's like to have Lauren work against you, as does Jack." He tightened his grip on her shoulders. "Now you listen to me, Blanche. I told you before and nothing has changed. If you leave things to Troy we will lose everything. There's only you that can keep us going . . . now that Jack's gone."

"How can you have such faith in me?"

"I just know. I knew what you were made of the first time I saw you. It's like a horse: you know who's a winner and who's not. And you're a winner, Blanche. Be happy with this baby, but don't let him get in your way of keeping our family on top. Make him part of it. Do you understand me?"

She nodded.

"I miss Jack so much," he said. "I wish I'd handled everything differently."

They flew back to London the next day. On New Year's Eve Blanche got ready to go into work. Troy walked in and saw her putting on her make-up.

"What are you doing, Blanche?"

"Trying to get ready. The pubs are going to be packed tonight."

"You're not going in!"

"Of course I am. It's every hand on deck tonight, we're going to be short-staffed."

"Blanche, you're pregnant. You need to take it easy."

She stood up and looked at him. "Dolores is going to be here any minute."

"So you're going into a smoky drunken atmosphere for the night and leaving the babies with Dolores?"

"I'm doing this for them, Troy."

He shook his head and looked down at the floor.

She went over to him and held him and spoke softly. "I went to see my own doctor today and he said there's no reason I can't continue working as long as I don't overdo it . . . Come on, we're running late."

PART 4

CHAPTER 49

2010

Lee Dwyer had got an early morning flight from Dublin to London, and a taxi to take him straight to the city. He had set up the appointment to meet Ronnie Richards the previous week and had spent some time talking to him on the phone about the case. Ronnie Richards was a name over the years that had become almost as well known as Max Clifford or Simon Cowell. A Svengali agent for footballers, singers, actresses and anyone who had a story to tell and sell to the media, the more lurid the better. From the telephone conversation Ronnie Richards had had with him it was also obvious he had a deep dislike for Blanche Launcelot and was more than willing to tell any information that could further the case against her. Lee wasn't sure how useful he would be, but he needed all the help he could get. The taxi pulled up outside the Gherkin building where Ronnie Richards' head-quarters were located. Lee looked up at the huge oblong skyscraper and made his way into reception. He looked at the panel on the wall that listed all the businesses based in the building. Ronnie Richards was on the 18th floor.

Ronnie's office had the unique wall of triangle windows that gave the Gherkin building its distinctive appearance.

There sat Ronnie at his desk, breathtaking views of the city behind him. Lee judged him to be in his mid-sixties, silver-haired and slightly overweight, with eyes that were sharp and intense. As well as being a very well-known agent he was also a very rich man with extensive investments in the stock market and property.

"Take a seat," instructed Ronnie.

As Lee sat down, he wondered how many starlets and footballers had sat in the chair, crying their eyes out, being advised or being screamed at by this formidable man.

"Blanche Launcelot," mused Ronnie, sitting in his chair and swinging from side by side. "Now, that's someone I haven't spoken about for a while."

"As I explained on the phone, any help you could give my client to help win back custody would be appreciated."

"I wouldn't trust Blanche Launcelot to look after a dog, let alone a child. And what about her husband, what does he make of all this?"

"Troy Launcelot won't get involved."

"Yeah, he was a nice lad, too nice for her. She ran rings around him. She ran rings around us all." He leaned forward and lowered his voice. "Nobody would ever have heard of her if it wasn't for me. I made her who she is. And what did I get in return? The bitch double-crossed me. Not once – but twice!"

"When did you meet her first?"

"The eighties – it was a great time." Ronnie gave a little chuckle. "London was booming, even if the country was shit. All you needed was some courage and hard work and money and connections and the world was your oyster. Blanche had all those things, a lot of them thanks to me. It was Thatcherism, it was city boys, it was stockmarket booms and property booms – it was loadsamoney, and it was us."

CHAPTER 50

1985–1987

As Blanche's pregnancy progressed, she began to feel terribly guilty at her initial thoughts of not wanting the child. She cut down her hours in the evenings and started going into the office during the day to do her work and have meetings with the managers. Working alongside her husband had only confirmed her opinion that he wasn't very good at business. She had got into the habit of not consulting with him, because it just meant too many arguments and disagreements. She often thought he disagreed with her for disagreement's sake, and that could infuriate her. She had Carl at a local nursery school where he was thriving. He seemed a very independent child and very bright. Amelia was showing a stubborn streak which could get on Blanche's nerves, when she was tired from the pregnancy and work. Dolores continued to be a blessing in the house and seemed to worship the two children. It was funny because Dolores still spoke to Blanche as if she was her barmaid. And she was that good around the house, that Blanche chose to ignore the odd glass of rosé Dolores helped herself to during the day.

It was June 1985, and Blanche was in her office over the pub going through the accounts. She was due to give birth in just three weeks. Troy sat opposite her. Madonna's 'Material Girl' was belting up from the bar downstairs.

"We're making great inroads paying off the debt to the bank in Ireland," said Blanche. "If we keep on going as we are, we might even have it all paid off by the end of the eighteen-month credit extension." She sat back and rubbed her face in relief.

"And what about the English bank that gave us the loan for the refurbishment?"

"I've spoken to them and they are quite happy to give us as much time as we want to pay it back."

"Probably because you fed them more fraudulent figures," accused Troy.

"No, I didn't have to this time, Troy, because the figures are good enough on their own. Anyway, I think we should concentrate on payment of that bastard Jim O'Hara. I wouldn't trust him not to try and foreclose on us again. Agreed?"

He shrugged.

Blanche gave birth to Roger Launcelot on the 4th of July. As Blanche held the baby in the hospital she marvelled at how much he looked like her. Carl was the spit of his father, and she didn't know where they got Amelia from. But Roger was so like her. She felt even more guilty about not wanting him initially as she held him close to her.

There was a big party for Roger's christening back in Winterfield in September. All the Launcelots' old crowd, were over for the party, which was held out by the pool. As Blanche went through the crowd with everyone cooing over Baby Roger she came face to face with Jim and Brooke O'Hara.

339

"He's so gorgeous!" sang Brooke as she peered at Roger.

"Isn't he?" said Blanche.

"And how are you, Blanche? We miss you so much here!" said Brooke.

Really? thought Blanche. "I'm fine – busy – you know."

Jim lowered his voice. "And well done on the repayments, I didn't think you'd do it. I believe you made a final payment last week. Your loan is paid off." He smiled happily at her.

"Actually, I was going to drop in on you before we headed back to London, Jim. What time suits?"

"Any time, Blanche. Any time you want, just drop in and I'll always be available for you!"

"Thanks, Jim, we could always rely on you." How things had changed, she thought, now that they were in a strong financial position again.

Blanche moved on through the crowd and went over to Lauren. Bruce Springsteen was belting out 'Born In The USA'.

"Such a wonderful day. Reminds me of the old times here at Winterfield." Lauren looked wistfully around the crowd.

"I wonder how many of them would have come to our help if we lost everything like Jim O'Hara was threatening?"

"You know, you've become so cynical, Blanche. I'd like to think a lot of them would have come to help us."

"I wonder."

"Besides, I don't know how many of them would be in a position to help. The recession is getting worse and worse, the country is on its knees."

Blanche nodded, and felt relieved that London was booming. She suddenly spotted Rosalind by the pool, laughing and throwing her hair back as she spoke to Troy. A beautiful little girl was beside her playing with Carl.

"What's *she* doing here?" demanded Blanche.

"Rosalind? I invited her."

"I didn't want her here."

"Rosalind is our oldest and dearest friend. I couldn't not invite her, Blanche. Besides, she's gone through a terrible hard time."

Blanche looked at the still beautiful Rosalind who was laughing and flirting with Troy.

"She doesn't look as if she has."

"Well, you know, I think she's turned a corner at last. But it's been hard for her. That marriage hasn't been a bed of roses."

"You mean the one you arranged for her?" Lauren as usual seemed to be in denial – in this case her role in wrecking Rosalind's life seemed to have escaped her memory. "Where is the lovely Seán?"

"Who knows? Probably down at that Martin's dive getting drunk. She's been left to raise that lovely child, Gabrielle, almost singlehandedly. Her own poor father passed away last year. I think it was all too much for him. Seán's been drinking the farm dry. Poor Rosalind keeps going, though, holding things together. She's a wonderful mother to Gabrielle, she keeps the farm going, keeps her job at the newspaper and she's going to run for the County Council in the future. She's just a trooper!"

And you're as fond of her as ever, Lauren, thought Blanche, regardless of the fact you all but ruined her life. Observing Rosalind throw her head back in laughter and touch Troy's shoulder, she mused that she had emerged from her trials the same old Rosalind.

"Look at the two children," said Lauren, nodding over at Carl and Gabrielle playing. "Don't they look a picture? Just think in another world, in another life, if things had worked out between Rosalind and Jack, they might have been cousins!" Lauren looked at Rosalind and Troy laughing together and said, "Or in a different world, a different life, they might even have been . . . something closer."

"Carl!" Blanche suddenly shouted at the top of her voice. "Carl! Come on here and have some cake!"

Carl ran away from Gabrielle and over to his mother.

CHAPTER 51

"Thanks, Jim, for meeting me," smiled Blanche as she sat down opposite Jim O'Hara in his office.

"Any time, Blanche, you're welcome here," he said, beaming a smile at her.

"Well, that's good to know. Jim, we're closing down our accounts here."

The smile dropped off his face. "What?"

"All our accounts, both business and personal. We're moving to the bank across the road."

"But – Blanche – you've been banking here for years!"

"I know, but I just feel it's time to move on . . . it's nothing personal," she said and smiled at him.

Blanche then arranged to have lunch with Emily Parker, the head of the Tennis Club in Castleford.

They spent an hour chatting about local gossip, reminding Blanche of how bored she had been with her old life, and then Blanche handed over a cheque.

"What's this for?" asked Emily, impressed by the amount.

"It's a donation from the Launcelot family to the Tennis Club."

"But this is more than generous! Especially during these hard times." Emily was smiling from ear to ear.

"There's just one stipulation, Emily. I want Brooke O'Hara removed from the committee of the club."

"What? But why?" Emily was shocked.

"I can't go into it."

"But Brooke is our best player, and her life revolves around the club!"

"I can't go into details, Emily, but it is a stipulation that Brooke is not on the committee if you want to cash that cheque."

As Emily studied the cheque, she shrugged. "I guess I've no choice. The club is in debt."

Blanche drove back to Winterfield, pleased with her day's work. Leaving Jim O'Hara and his bank was a good business move; he had tried to destroy them, his loyalty couldn't be counted on. Removing Brooke from the tennis committee was petty, she knew. But that smug look on Brooke's face when she was planning to buy Winterfield and have them kicked out was reason enough.

CHAPTER 52

It was October and Ronnie Richards' 45th birthday and he was having a party at his house on Bishop's Avenue.

"I don't want to go to this," snapped Troy as he fixed his bow tie in the bedroom mirror. It was a black-tie event.

Blanche started to sing 'Thank God I'm a Country Boy'.

"Oh shut up, Blanche! Your idea of fun might be mixing with this bunch of twits, but it's not mine!"

She came over to him and straightened his tie. "There will be loads of good contacts there tonight, it will be good for business," she said.

"You know, that's how you justify everything – by saying it's good for business," he accused.

"And aren't I right? Look at the books! We're making good profits, aren't we?"

"So fucking what? Where's our quality of life? You can barely make it back in time to have dinner with the children these days."

"That's a bloody lie. I'm always here for them, nearly every evening. And if I'm not, then I take the next day off and spend that time with them."

"There's no space for our children to grow up in. All

they have is that fucking small garden and a park down the road. I want them to grow up with what I had, the freedom and space of Winterfield."

"Really? So that they are so cocooned from life that when things fall apart they do what you did – stick your head in the sand and hope everything goes away?"

He stared at her in anger and ripped off his bow tie. "I'm not going to bloody Ronnie Richard's bloody birthday party. You can go on your fucking own."

"Right! I will!" She turned and walked out of the room.

Blanche went across the landing and looked in on the children who were already asleep and went downstairs. Dolores was sitting in the lounge, Wogan on the television, and a glass of rosé on the coffee table in front of her.

"Will you be alright?" asked Blanche.

"Yeah, haven't I got Terry for company?" she smiled, nodding at the television. "Where's Troy?"

"He's not going." Blanche pulled a face.

"What? Do you still need me to baby-sit then?"

Blanche looked down at Dolores, comfortable on the couch, the opened bottle of rosé and a box of chocolates in front of her.

"Oh, yes, you stay put. He's fairly tired. I'd say he'll have an early night."

There was a beep outside.

"That's my taxi, see you later."

As the taxi journeyed down Bishop's Avenue, Blanche was feeling guilty for leaving Troy. She shouldn't have been so cutting to him. But his lack of understanding of the ways of the world infuriated her sometimes. She looked out the window at what seemed to be the never-ending Bishop's Avenue with its palatial houses, each one bigger than the last.

"The Arabs are buying up all these gaffs now," said the taxi driver.

"Probably the only ones who can afford them," said Blanche, as she wondered just how much Ronnie was worth.

The taxi turned into the drive and there was Ronnie's mansion in front of her. She got out, paid the driver and walked up the steps to the door.

Inside, she immediately met Ronnie.

"Oh Ronnie, happy birthday!" she said and kissed his cheek.

"Where's Troy?"

"Can't make it I'm afraid. He's ill."

"Come, I want to introduce you to some people," said Ronnie as he took her arm and they walked through the crowd.

"Blanche, this is Stephen Waldron."

Stephen was the owner of one of the London premier football clubs.

"Blanche is one of our young entrepreneurial business-women," said Ronnie with a smile.

Blanche rang home and Dolores explained that Troy had come down for a while and then said he was going to bed. Blanche had planned on going home but decided to stay at the party for another while longer. After all, if Troy was asleep, what was the point of rushing home?

She went and mingled with the crowd and Stephen Waldron was entertaining company all night long.

"I've just signed Jamie Tonkins in a multi-million-pound deal," Stephen told her.

"Good for you – I don't know much about football but my husband insists he's one of the best."

"He's going to be the next Georgie Best or Kevin Keegan," insisted Stephen.

"Well, here's to your investment then," she said, smiling and holding out her champagne glass.

He chinked his glass against hers.

Looking at her watch and seeing it was nearly one, Blanche decided it was definitely time to go home.

"It's been really nice meeting you," she said to Stephen.

"Going already?"

"I'm afraid so. I've got three children under five and they will have me up at seven in the morning, I daresay."

Stephen looked at his watch. "Gosh – it is late. I think I'll head myself. How are you getting home?"

"Taxi."

"To where?"

"Kensington."

"Well, that's on my way. I'll give you a lift. I insist."

"Ronnie speaks very highly of you," said Stephen as he drove Blanche through the London streets in his Bentley.

"Does he? I'm flattered."

"He always says if you want a good, discreet fun night out then head to one of the Launcelot clubs."

"He's very good at sending us clients . . . Take the next left – that's my street."

Stephen kept on driving, took the next right and pulled over in the quiet street.

"You took the wrong turn," said Blanche.

He turned and faced her and smiled. "No, I believe I took the right turn." Suddenly his hand was on her leg and he was leaning over and kissing her.

"Stephen!" she snapped and pulled back. "What are you doing?"

"What do you think I'm doing?" His hand travelled further up her leg.

"I'm a married woman!"

"Aren't they all?" He went to kiss her again.

She pulled back and slapped him across the face.

"Get your bloody hands off me!"

He looked at her, shocked. "Come on – you've been giving me the signal all night."

"I can assure you I haven't!"

"Who do you think you are? Running a couple of back-street bars and thinking you're something. You're nothing, love. Young entrepreneur businesswoman my arse! Do you really think Ronnie respects you? He thinks you're just a bit of fluff who was once helpful to him."

"What are you talking about?"

"You lied to protect our investment – Jamie Tonkins. Told the coppers he was in your place and got him off that hit-and-run charge."

"What?"

"I know Ronnie fed you some story about him hitting some deranged fan to defend himself. In actual fact our Jamie was pissed at the wheel and knocked some old fella down. We reported the car stolen and Jamie in your crummy pub, so it couldn't possibly be him driving the car, we told the cops. As I said, Jamie Tonkins is a multi-million-pound investment. And we can't let a little thing like a hit-and-run jeopardise all that, can we?"

Blanche opened the car door and got out. She started to walk quickly down the street. She heard Stephen Waldron drive off. She walked briskly into her own street and into her home.

"You lied to me, you fucking bastard!" screamed Blanche as she stormed into Ronnie Richards' office.

The secretary came rushing in after her.

"Will I call the police?" asked the secretary.

Ronnie looked up from his desk. "Now how many young women come screaming into my office every week saying I lied to them, Jane? If we called the police every time, they would be very busy boys, wouldn't they?"

Jane, the secretary, nodded and exited. Ronnie looked at Blanche coolly.

"Your slimeball of a friend, Waldron, told me all about Jamie Tonkin's hit and run. He wasn't attacked by some fan. He was drink driving and ran over an old man."

"Merely a technicality, Blanche."

"No, it's not. This is a very serious offence that you involved me in."

"Yes, and what of it? The old man made a rapid recovery, and I deposited some money through his letterbox. Jamie got off and signed a multi-million-pound deal, and your pubs have been filled with celebrities ever since. A win-win situation in my opinion."

"I can't believe you set me up!" said Blanche, her eyes blazing.

"Oh, come on, Blanche. So you didn't mind telling a white lie, but you did mind telling a serious one?"

She felt rage burn inside her. "I've been made a fool of in the past, Ronnie, and nobody is going to do that to me again, do you understand? I wonder what the police will make of all this?"

Ronnie's gaze was calculating.

"Sit down, Blanche," he said.

"No!"

"I said – *sit down*!" he shouted.

She paused and then sat down. He took out two cigarettes,

threw one at her and put the other in his mouth. Then he took out his lighter and lit both the cigarettes.

"Now what good would going to the police do? Except destroy all of us involved – including you, Blanche. I tell you what I'm going to do. I'm going to forget about all this and so are you . . . I shouldn't have lied to you, but I didn't know you then like I do now. I think my friendship has been very beneficial to you – but this is only the beginning. I want to really make you into something. You're just pissing around in them backstreet pubs. You stick with me, and I'll introduce you to the best stockbrokers, the best investors in the City. They'll take whatever money you have and multiply it. Whatever deals they offer me, I'll cut you in on the action. This city is just taking off, Blanche. Join me and take off with it too."

CHAPTER 53

It was spring 1986 and Blanche and Ronnie were drinking in a wine bar up near the Stock Exchange in the City. They had just met with a team of Ronnie's stockbrokers and they had been talked through an investment deal concerning a company that had just gone on the stock market. Ronnie was investing a sizeable amount and Blanche was matching him penny for penny. The pubs continued to churn out the money and Blanche, since she had made her agreement with Ronnie, was investing frequently.

The bar was packed with stockbrokers ordering champagne.

"Tossers!" said Ronnie, looking over at them as they danced around. He opened a bottle of champagne and filled both their glasses. "You happy with the deal?" he asked.

"Your brokers say they can quadruple my money in four months. If it's true then I'm more than happy," said Blanche as she took a sip of champagne.

"It's only the start, Blanche," Ronnie promised.

"Blanche – it's Ronnie – buy British Airways shares. There's going to be some announcement of record profits."

The phone rang again. "Blanche – buy sterling quickly. There's going to be a rush on the pound."

An hour later the phone rang again. "Blanche, get your broker to buy shares in a company called Regent – it's a mining company – seemingly they've just discovered a huge gold mine in South America."

"Mrs Launcelot – this is Jane, Ronnie's secretary. He asked me to advise you to sell all Lybian oil shares. With the whole Gadaffi issue there might be a trade embargo – if not a war!"

Blanche was flabbergasted with the speed at which Ronnie could get information. He was so connected with everybody in the stock market. She followed all his advice word for word, and continued to plough all the profits from the pubs back into the stock market as Ronnie advised. And as the Big Bang revolutionized the London stock market, shares began to soar. Very soon the value of the stocks began to dwarf the value of the pubs as they continued to rise and rise.

CHAPTER 54

Troy pulled up outside Carl's school and Blanche got out and walked him to the door, gave him a kiss and sent him in. She returned to the car.

They had already dropped Amelia off at her nursery.

Troy headed to the City where they had an appointment with Ronnie Richards.

"I wonder what Ronnie Richards wants this time?" mused Troy.

"I wonder," agreed Blanche as she put on some lipstick, looking in the wing mirror.

"Some new highfaluting new idea of his no doubt."

"No doubt." Blanche put away her lipstick.

"I'm sorry, I just can't warm to the guy."

"I know that. But maybe you do warm to all the profit we have made on his advice on investments."

"Yeah – but what's he getting out of it? I mean, why is he bothering to help us so much?"

Blanche thought about her role in the Jamie Tonkins cover-up and shuddered, thinking about Troy's reaction if he ever discovered what she had done.

"I guess he's just a nice man," said Blanche.

"Hmmm – from what I hear Richards doesn't do anything unless there's something in it for him. Do you know what I think? I think Ronnie Richards just likes playing the big powerful man. I think he loves playing Svengali. He loves taking starlets and turning them into stars, models and turning them into actresses, footballers and turning them into legends. I think he gets a power kick from it. And I think that's what he's enjoying doing with you!"

"With *me*?" Blanche was mystified.

"Yeah – he has taken you under his wing and enjoys transforming you into a big businesswoman."

"You're being ridiculous . . . our relations with Ronnie have been mutually beneficial."

Troy glanced at his wife. "Of course he might just like a bit of ornamentation around as well."

Blanche turned and looked at Troy, her eyes blazing. "Don't be a bloody bastard, Troy!"

Seeing her anger and feeling guilty at his comment, he drove in silence for a while.

"This bloody traffic! Is it ever quiet in this city!" he snapped as a car pulled out in front of him. "I can't wait to get home for Christmas!"

Blanche didn't respond, thinking it might not be a good time to mention her plan for staying in London for Christmas.

Finally they got to the City and into the side street where they had arranged to meet Ronnie.

Ronnie was already there.

"Hi, Ronnie!" said Blanche getting out of their car.

"Blanche . . . Troy! Right. Before you say anything, just look up at that building and tell me what you see." Ronnie pointed to the disused Victorian building behind him.

"I see broken windows, I see graffiti, I see filth!" said Blanche.

355

"Well, I see potential!" said Ronnie.

"As what exactly?" said Troy, looking unimpressed.

"As a new venture for the Launcelot pubs," said Ronnie.

"A new venture?" asked Blanche, bemused.

"Yes, it's perfect. This is within walking distance to the Stock Exchange – all the stockbroker firms are based around here. You open a wine bar here, and the place will be packed each night with these tossers ordering champagne."

Ronnie took out a key, opened the front door and they walked in. Inside it was derelict and full of rubbish. But there was plenty of light coming in from the long Victorian windows.

"I think we've enough on our plate at the moment, thanks, Ronnie, trying to keep all our other pubs going," said Troy.

But Blanche was busy inspecting everything, and now set off up the old central staircase.

Ronnie ignored Troy and followed Blanche, Troy trailing behind. "Blanche, you've been in enough wine bars up here at this stage with me to see how much these guys spend on their social life."

"Have you?" asked Troy, looking at Blanche, surprised.

"This is a goldmine ready to take off, and a great opportunity for you to expand your pubs from the suburbs into the very heart of the City. It will make your name."

Just then it started to lash down with rain outside.

"And what's your interest in this?" said Troy.

"I'll be honest with you. The guy who owns the building owes me money. He's broke, I shift this building, then I get paid," said Ronnie.

"Look, thanks, Ronnie, for thinking of us, but we'll pass. As I said, we've more than enough on our plate at the moment." Troy shook his hand and made his way downstairs.

Ronnie looked at Blanche and shrugged.

"Don't show it to anyone else," whispered Blanche. "I love it and I want it." She smiled at him and followed Troy out.

"Not a chance!" shouted Troy that night as they argued about it back home.

"Why not? It's a wonderful opportunity for us. You heard Ronnie, it could make us big in London."

"I don't want to be big in London, I want to be back in Winterfield where we belong! The deal was we would stay in London until we got the pubs back on their feet and we've done that, and more than that we've made all those great investments in the stock market you're always telling me about. Now it's time for us to move home and start getting our lives back to normal."

"What is normal, Troy? Drifting boringly around Winterfield?" she shouted at him.

"I want to go home, Blanche. I want to bring my kids up in Winterfield where they can be free, not in this place where they have to be watched all the time."

"And what will happen to the business?" she demanded.

"It was here long before you were on the scene and it will be here long after you're gone as well!" His words were cutting.

She stared at him, hurt. "Niall was right – Jack should have got the business, because it's wasted on you!" she spat.

"You're a bitch!"

"So what if I am?"

His eyes filled with tears and he went and sat down on the couch and buried his face in his hands. She stared at him and her heart melted. She went to him and put her arms around him.

"I'm sorry, Troy. I shouldn't have said that. I just don't

understand your rush home, when there is so much opportunity here."

He looked up at her. "You and the kids mean everything to me. I just want us to be happy."

"But don't you understand? We are!"

He put his face in his hands again.

She held him tight. "Let's give it another two years and then we'll go home."

They bought the building the next week. The new wine bar was opened by Christmas.

CHAPTER 55

True for Ronnie, The Launcelot Wine Bar in the City took off like a rocket and as 1987 began the place was packed every night with traders, stockbrokers and City boys. Downstairs was a huge glamorous wine bar and upstairs was turned into a restaurant. Blanche made sure to maintain and highlight all the building's original Victorian features.

She worked hard at being nice to Troy and including him in everything. They made the journey home for Christmas even though she didn't want to.

In the new year Blanche was sitting in her office over the pub and going through the figures. Troy sat at his desk across the office from her. All she could think about was the new wine bar in the City. She loved being down there and the buzz of the place.

"You know, I was thinking, Troy," she said.

He looked up, concerned. He didn't like when she thought too much; she usually came up with a new hair-brain scheme.

"Uh huh?"

"Why don't we base ourselves at the new wine bar? I mean, the third floor is empty there and we need more office space. And we'd be more near the loop there, especially when we're so heavily invested in the stock market."

"More near Ronnie Richards, you mean, and his mates, who I'm very wary of," he said, looking cynically at her.

"Oh, Troy, you're wary of everyone who doesn't come from Castleford! Come on, it's a much better idea than being stuck here all the time. We'll be at the push and thrust of everything."

He sighed. "I'm sure it's a terrific idea, Blanche. You're out socialising with them anyway. Easier for you to just go down from your office to the bar than make the trek across the city."

"I'll ignore your sarcasm, Troy." She returned to her paperwork.

Blanche had the third floor at the wine bar renovated into offices, and set up separate ones for her and Troy. It was getting awkward sharing an office with him, as sometimes she had to taper her telephone conversations so as not to alarm him with the investments and deals she was organising. He was so easily alarmed.

As she looked around the office, she felt sad leaving. But you can't stay still forever, she thought. If you stay still, you get overtaken.

Blanche walked quickly down the road, Amelia holding one hand and Carl holding the other. It was September and Amelia had started the same school that Carl was at. Blanche glanced down at her watch and realised she would be late for a meeting.

They passed a young person begging on the street.

"Any spare change, miss?" the young man asked.

Blanche quickly walked on. She usually gave some change to the growing army of young people who seemed to be sleeping rough on the street and she gave to charities each month. But that morning she was in too much of a rush to start looking for her purse in her bag, especially with the children.

"Mum, why is that man sitting on the street?" asked Amelia.

"Because he doesn't have any money, love. Now, come on, we're going to be late."

"But why doesn't he have any money?" asked Amelia.

"I don't know, maybe because he doesn't have a job. There's lots of reasons."

"But what will he eat?" persisted Amelia.

"I don't know, Amelia! Now come on!"

Suddenly Amelia stopped in the street and refused to move.

"Please give him some money," she begged.

"Darling, I haven't time to go back, now come on!" Blanche insisted.

Amelia was suddenly crying. "He won't have any lunch otherwise!"

"Amelia you're being naughty, now come on!"

Amelia refused to budge.

"Oh for goodness sake!" snapped Blanche, turning and heading back to the homeless man with the children. She reached him and searched for her purse, found £10 and gave it to him.

"Satisfied?" asked Blanche to Amelia, as she turned and they walked off. Amelia was smiling.

Blanche was shown into her chief stockbroker Jeremy Harkin's office.

"I'm so sorry I'm late, Jeremy. My children were being particularly difficult this morning!"

He got up and gave her a kiss on the cheek. "No problem, Blanche."

He pulled up a chair for her and she sat down. She studied him. He was in his mid-forties, with an Oxford accent, and slicked-back black hair, with a permanent 'cat that got the cream' look about him. She had got on with him since Ronnie introduced them and tended to do most of her investment through him at this stage.

"So how's everything doing, Jeremy?"

"Your portfolio of investments is performing out-standingly, I'm delighted to say. All the stock you have invested in has jumped better than we could have expected, and the yields are terrific. And they show no signs of stopping." He smiled at her happily.

Ronnie and a group of his investment friends had lunch with Blanche at the wine bar. They were having a celebratory lunch over another investment that had paid big dividends.

The champagne bottle popped and Ronnie filled all their glasses.

"To our continued success!" toasted Ronnie.

Blanche clinked his glass along with everyone else's to a background of Hue and Cry's 'Labour of Love'. It was three in the afternoon and she looked around. The place was packed with traders, ordering champagne. A huge group of brokers were at the bar, making a lot of noise as they continually ordered more rounds of tequilas.

She wondered who was doing all the work back on the exchange, and she presumed they had all made so much money that morning that they could spend the rest of the day celebrating. They all looked pleased with themselves, *too* pleased with themselves.

After lunch she headed upstairs to her office and turned on the television in the corner. She caught the business news and as ever she saw the stock market had risen again that day, as it had every day for months.

She sat at her desk and suddenly felt uneasy. Everything was flying too high. She took out her filofax, found Jeremy's number and phoned him.

"Jeremy, Blanche Launcelot here."

"Blanche! How are you?"

"Good. Jeremy, I want you to sell all our stock."

"I'm sorry?"

"Everything! Every last share, sell them as quick as you can!"

"I don't think I understand. You want to sell your portfolio?"

"Yes."

"But why the fuck would you want to do that? It's performing excellently and the projections are –"

"I'm sorry, Jeremy, I don't want to argue about this. I want everything sold immediately. *Now.*"

Blanche had a sleepless night. She began to regret the decision to sell everything and said nothing to Troy about it. Why had she panicked? Was she afraid of success? After all her hard work, did she really not want success? She just remembered being with Billy and, when everything was going wonderfully, everything fell apart. Or when she was back in Castleford living on a cloud, only to find they were on the verge of bankruptcy. She was obviously carrying a fear of failure and it had made her act irrationally. She had panicked and decided to sell for no reason at all.

The next morning she rang Jeremy to tell him to reverse her decision and to stop selling.

"Good morning, Blanche." Jeremy was cold as ice on the phone to her. "I've followed your instructions and sold everything."

"Everything?" She felt panicked.

"As per your instructions, Blanche. All monies are being deposited in your bank accounts this afternoon. All very substantial monies at that."

"Oh, okay, thanks, Jeremy," She felt like a fool. "Em, Jeremy, don't tell anybody I've sold everything, not even Ronnie."

"As per your instructions, Blanche," Jeremy said and hung up the phone.

Blanche rubbed her face. What was she thinking of, selling everything on a whim? It could take years to build up a portfolio like that again with the way stock prices had gone. Ronnie would think she was such a fool if he found out.

The next Monday Blanche was at her desk when there was suddenly a lot of shouting and commotion downstairs. She got up and walked quickly out of her office onto the landing and down the stairs towards the bar. The place was in a state of panic with customers running out of the place and talking loudly on their very large chunky mobile phones.

"What's going on?" she demanded of a man as he rushed by her.

"The stock market! It's crashing!"

She raced back to her office and put on the television to see the unfolding crisis. Troy came racing in to her.

"Blanche! Get on to the brokers! Everything's crashing – quickly!"

"Relax! Don't worry. I sold everything last week."

"What?" He was confused.

"We've no stock left, we're safe."

He stared at her with a mixture of relief, confusion and distrust.

That evening she left the bar which was completely empty. Walking down to the tube station, she stopped at a shop and bought the *Evening Standard*. Written across the front page in a huge headline was '*Black Monday – Stock Market Crashes*'.

CHAPTER 56

Blanche sat opposite a pale-faced Ronnie Richards at a table in the wine bar. Apart from them, the place was empty.

"Everyone at home nursing their injuries," commented Ronnie as he raised the tumbler of neat whiskey and took a gulp.

Blanche took a sip from her glass of red wine and nodded.

"It's bloody wipe-out!" continued Ronnie. "Everyone's gone down. Nobody saw it coming, things were going so great."

"Did you – eh – lose much altogether?" Blanche looked nervously at him.

"A fucking huge amount. Like yourself I'd invested every bit of spare capital into stocks. Some of them stocks will never recover." He shook his head sadly.

Blanche bit her lower lip, wondering how she could tell him she'd sold everything before the crash.

"Is Troy taking it badly?"

"I – eh – you know Troy. Doesn't say much about these things."

He studied her. "You're taking it remarkably well, Blanche.

I thought you'd be screaming and tearing the place apart. How much did you lose in total?"

She sighed, took a cigarette from the packet in front of her, lit up and then sat back in her chair, deciding to bite the bullet.

"I didn't lose a penny, Ronnie."

"Huh?"

"I sold everything last week."

Ronnie's eyes pierced her. "I don't understand you."

"I rang Jeremy and told him to sell all our stocks and shares."

"But Jeremy never said anything to me."

"I asked him not to."

Ronnie sat back in his chair and stared at her, a dark cloud encompassing his face. "You got a tip-off about what was going to happen and you never told me?"

"No! Nothing like that."

"Why did you sell then?"

"I just got a funny feeling."

He sat forward and spoke slowly. "But you must have made a fortune selling when you did."

She sighed and nodded. "We came out very well."

"While the rest of us came out with nothing . . . oh no, Blanche, I don't think you had a 'funny feeling'. I think you're a very clever little bitch. And whoever informed you what was going to happen warned you not to tell anyone else, because the panic would start too early."

"No, Ronnie, I swear. I'm telling the truth."

"So the fucking barmaid is now a financial wizard!"

"I just went on instinct . . . Ronnie, if you need some money to help you out, whatever you want you can have. You've been very good to me and I want to help you if you need it."

367

"Need help from you?" He raised his voice. "I fucking pulled you out of a backstreet pub and made you what you are. I don't want any help from the likes of you!"

He downed his drink and stormed off.

Blanche walked slowly down their street after catching the tube home that evening. She walked up the steps and let herself in. She walked through the hall to the kitchen in the back where pandemonium was breaking out as Troy attempted to feed the three children.

"Where have you been? I've left messages for you at the wine bar. Dolores is sick and I'm on my own here," snapped Troy.

Blanche threw off her coat and took up Roger who was crying and began to soothe him.

Amelia was crying at the table.

"Oh Troy, Amelia's going through a funny phase and won't eat meat – take it off her plate and I'll cook something else for her," said Blanche.

"Mum, I won at football at school," said Carl.

Blanche went over to him and kissed him. "Okay, darling, you can tell me all about it after dinner."

Troy whipped the plate away from Amelia. "If you returned my calls, then you could have been here on time to help me make them dinner."

"I didn't get your messages, Troy," Blanche snapped at him.

"No? How convenient for you!" His voice dripped sarcasm

"Oh shut up, Troy!"

"Don't tell me to shut up in front of the children! Or ever for that matter!"

Blanche stared at him, put Roger down and went racing into the lounge.

A couple of minutes later Troy followed her in and found her crying softly on the couch.

"Blanche? What's wrong?" He rushed over to her and put his arms around her.

"Everything! I'm trying so hard to make everything a success and I'm losing everything in the meantime. I'm losing your love, I'm not there for the children as much as I should be. I'm losing my friends. And all I really want is for us to be safe and secure."

He put his arms around her and held her tightly as the tears flowed. "You're not losing my love, Blanche, you never will. I adore you. And I appreciate all you've done so much." He rubbed her back as he spoke.

She pulled back from him. "I'm sorry, Troy, for not being the wife you wanted."

"You are the wife I want, every day. And I'm sorry for not being more supportive of you . . . Now come on, what's all this about? You shouldn't be crying, you should be laughing – you're about the only person not bankrupted by the crash."

The next day Troy went to see Ronnie in his office.

"What can I do for you, Troy?" Ronnie looked at him sceptically.

"Look, I know about your run-in with Blanche, and she's really upset."

"She's upset! Do you know how many millions I've lost?"

"But it's nothing to do with her . . . Blanche has done many things, Ronnie, but she didn't lie to you. If you knew Blanche like I know her, then you would know this is nothing out of the ordinary for her. She amazes me constantly. She does things without saying, she pulls off things you'd never imagine she'd be able to do without any fuss. Blanche sold those shares on her own initiative. Your problem is you underestimated her, Ronnie, and I've learned never to do that."

Blanche was at her desk when the phone rang on her desk.

"Blanche, Ronnie Richards is down in the bar to see you."

Surprised, Blanche said nothing.

"Blanche?"

"Eh – I'll be down in a minute, Jenny."

She steadied herself, left the office and walked down the stairs. She mentally prepared herself for another tongue-lashing. He had probably come to finish off what he had been too angry to say before.

The downstairs bar was almost empty; everyone was still reeling from the shock of the crash. Ronnie was at a corner table. Her high heels clicked across the teak floor over to him.

"May I sit?" she asked.

"It's your bar," he answered. Seeing she looked nervous, he said, "Take a seat, Blanche."

He studied her. In a way he saw her for the first time. He was used to beautiful women, he managed enough of them, but he now realised Blanche was very strikingly beautiful. She had mentioned she had modelled back in Dublin, but he never gave it a second thought. As he looked at her now, he wondered why she didn't try to make it big. He had kept her on side because of the fear she would expose him over that whole nasty Jamie Tonkins business. And then he had kind of got used to her being around. She was in awe of him, and he enjoyed people being in awe of him. She had been handy when he was making up investment cartels; the

Launcelots seemed to have a lot of spare cash coming in and Blanche was more than willing to invest it in anything he suggested. But the fact that she had sold everything at the height of the market showed there was a lot more going on in her head than he had ever credited.

"I want to apologise, Blanche. I was very rough on you the other day. I now realise you didn't have a tip-off."

She looked at him warily. "What made you change your mind?"

"Troy visited me and explained things."

"Oh – I didn't ask him to!"

"I know. So I'm sorry. Friends?" He offered his hand across the table.

She smiled at him and shook his hand. "Friends. Jenny," she called over to the barmaid. "Bring us over a nice bottle of Chilean red please."

"I just wish you'd told me that you were selling, and I could have got out in time as well."

"You would have just ignored me and called me a silly girl, and maybe even talked me out of it."

"True."

Jenny opened the bottle and poured them two glasses.

"So, seemingly I *have* got a new financial whiz kid on my hands. What are you going to do with all that money you're sitting on?"

She shrugged. "You usually advise me. What do you think I should do?"

"No – seriously. What do you think would be a wise move?"

She sat forward and started talking quickly. "Well, I want to open more wine bars. More up the West End. This place was such a success, and I think it might be quiet for quite a while, but I think a Launcelot Wine Bar would be very successful around Leicester Square with all the tourists and theatre crowds."

He nodded, surprised. "Indeed . . . go on."

"And property, Ronnie. I can't believe what the house down the road sold for recently. I think property in London is just going to go up and up, commercial and residential."

Ronnie took a sip of his drink. "Tell me more – and incidentally, I might need to take you up on that offer of a loan."

Blanche let herself into their home and went into the front lounge where Troy was reading a book. She went over to him and kissed him.

"Ronnie told me you paid him a visit."

"Uh huh."

"Why did you bother? You don't like me hanging around him or his crowd. Wouldn't it have been easier for you if we fell out?"

"I don't want you being unhappy, Blanche, and you were unhappy about the falling out. And I don't want him thinking that you acted dishonestly when you didn't."

"I told my mother I was marrying a prince – and I was right."

CHAPTER 57

2010

Lee listened intently as Ronnie recounted his tales from the eighties.

"Drink?" asked Ronnie.

"Eh, yes, please."

Lee expected to be asked if he wanted tea or coffee but Ronnie got up and went over to a cabinet and opened it. It was filled with decanters full of different alcohols.

"Whiskey alright?" questioned Ronnie.

"Eh – just a very small one," said Lee.

Ronnie returned with two crystal glasses of whiskey and soda, placed one in front of Lee and then went and sat back behind his desk.

"It's intriguing stuff. To hear how she built her empire," commented Lee.

"Ah, she was only getting started. She was sitting on a pile of money after the market crashed in 1987 and for the next two years she invested heavily into the London property market. She had an instinct for a good buy and soon, rather than her following me and my investor friends, we were following her. She'd find out about an apartment block being built in the Docklands and have us down there looking at it and suddenly we were all buying off the plans. Next thing we'd be investing into retail buildings in Oxford Street, residential in Mayfair. That was all throughout 1988 and 1989. And the prices of everything just kept soaring. I was pretty broke after the crash and so I had to borrow heavily from the banks to invest into the property, but with the rising property prices I was suddenly back with a lot of equity. You know this was the time when everyone in London was having dinner parties where all they discussed was how much their house had gone up in the previous week while they listened to Sade singing 'Smooth Operator' on their brand new CD players. And they didn't come any smoother than Blanche. She was expanding the Launcelot chain as well. She opened wine bars in the West End, targeting all the markets. Leicester Square for the cinema goers, Covent Garden for the theatre goers, Regent Street for the tourists, Knightsbridge for the shoppers, Heathrow for the travellers. They were springing up all over the place. I think it was 1989 that she bought her first hotel. She bought a decrepit old hotel in Kensington and turned it into a boutique hotel. By the end of the year she opened her second hotel out by Heathrow."

Lee took a sip from his drink. "So if everything was going so well, how did you end up becoming enemies?"

Ronnie smiled and sat back. "I suppose things started going wrong between us in 1990. It was the night of her thirtieth birthday in April. I hosted a party for her."

CHAPTER 58

1990–1991

The limousine drove through the streets of London towards the Embankment. In the back sat Blanche and Troy. It was a Saturday afternoon, it was Blanche's thirtieth birthday and Ronnie was throwing a party for her on his yacht. She fingered the diamond ring on her finger that Troy had given her as a birthday present.

"Do you really like it?" Troy asked her, taking her hand and holding it.

"Yes, of course I do. It's too much."

"You deserve it." He smiled at her.

Blanche nestled back into the cream leather seat and smiled. The last couple of years had been exciting, exhausting, rewarding and satisfying. It was almost as if she had a golden touch and everything she bought went up in value. Of course the property market in London had gone up in such dizzying jumps that it was hard to lose on investing in property, and she had made a huge amount of their money from selling just before the '87 crash.

But more than that, on a personal level, she was content.

For years Troy had resented Blanche and her new-found role in the business. He resented living in London. He resented a lot. But in time he had mellowed. He still disliked living in London, but made regular trips back to Winterfield to see his parents and his friends. There was general agreement that they would one day move back, when the business was secure. But as the business expanded there was always something new to secure. And then there were the children, their pride and joy. Carl was eight that year and seemed to be a natural-born leader. He excelled at sports and school and was very popular. Amelia was a bit of a handful. She was due to turn seven that year and seemed to have a permanent defiant look on her face. If Blanche told her to put on a white dress, she would come down in a red one. Everything had to be explained to her or she refused to co-operate. The previous week she had come home distraught because one of her school friends was leaving the school as her parents could not afford the fees.

"But that's just not fair!" Amelia had shouted. "Why should I get to go to the school but she can't just because of money?"

Blanche had tried to explain that that was just the way of the world, but Amelia would have none of it. Her teacher had contacted Blanche and made a complaint that Amelia had taken it on herself to arrange a collection to raise the girl's fees and was getting all the other children to hand over their pocket money. There had been much anger that night, with Blanche trying to point out that Amelia had no right to interfere with this girl's situation. And all Amelia could keep asking was – why?

Nice things didn't seem to impress Amelia. She wasn't a greedy child in the least. On the contrary, Blanche would ask what happened to a lovely doll she'd got the previous

Christmas and Amelia would just say "Oh, I got bored with it, so I gave it away."

Then there was Roger, who was about to be five and had a way of twisting people around his little finger to get just what he wanted. Unlike Amelia, Roger did like nice things.

His birthday and Christmas lists were always excessively long. And as soon as he saw anything his brother or sister or friends had, he wanted it immediately. Blanche and Troy tried not to spoil him, but he had a certain way of looking at you or talking to you that always got him what he wanted. Blanche even spotted it with him and the parents of his friends or indeed their own friends: he would go to work on them and suddenly they were eating out of his hand. He always got the biggest slice of cake, the most sweets, the biggest present. He'd had three different teachers, and somehow had managed to end up each one's pet.

Blanche squeezed Troy's hand tighter as the limousine pulled up outside Ronnie's yacht on the Embankment on the Thames. They got out of the car and their smiling host greeted them as they walked onto the gangplank.

A band struck up with 'For She's Jolly Good Fellow' as Ronnie came up and kissed both her cheeks.

"Happy birthday, Blanche!"

Shortly afterwards Ronnie gave the signal and the yacht pulled away from the Embankment. It was a beautiful afternoon and evening. As the sun shone down on the open decks, the guests enjoyed a feast of food and drink.

As the evening progressed Ronnie made a speech.

"We've all known Blanche for quite a while now and we've found her to be a trustworthy, reliable friend. If you ever have a problem, go to Blanche, because she'll find a way around it quicker than anyone else." He smiled at her and raised his glass.

As the night wore on the band played, the saxophone booming out through the night air. Blanche stopped counting how many times they had sailed past Canary Wharf.

Around midnight, Blanche spotted Troy coming out of the toilet looking very pale.

"Are you alright?" she asked.

"No, I feel pretty shit. I was never that great on boats." Ronnie came over.

"Ronnie, poor Troy needs land, I'm afraid!" said Blanche.

"We're docking in ten minutes — some of the guests want to go home," said Ronnie.

"Good." Troy looked relieved.

"Sorry we have to go so soon," said Blanche.

"Blanche, there's no need for you to leave, I'll be fine. You stay another while."

"No, Troy, I'll come with you."

"Blanche, it's your thirtieth, I want you to stay and enjoy it," insisted Troy.

The yacht docked an hour later at one in the morning, and Troy gratefully left. Over the next couple of hours, the rest of the guests dwindled until only Blanche was left.

"I want this night to go on forever." She smiled at Ronnie.

"Well, you don't have to go home yet."

She laughed. "What? A party for two?"

"Why not?"

"Alright then," she smiled.

They stood at the rail as the yacht took off for another cruise down the Thames, the night air blowing a breeze through Blanche's hair.

"I hope Troy is feeling better," said Ronnie.

"I'd say he'll be fine now he's on dry land."

"He's a fine man."

"Yes, I'm very lucky . . . I hope he feels as lucky."

"Of course he does, why wouldn't he?"

"I don't know if I'm that good for him."

"What? You're great for him. You run the businesses, you're a great mother and wife, what more could he want?"

Blanche looked over at Ronnie and sighed. "Somebody to connect with maybe."

"You don't connect?" Ronnie was surprised.

"Not in the way Troy wants to connect. When I talk I think sometimes he hasn't a clue what I'm saying. And he doesn't understand that I don't want the same things in life as he does. I don't adore Troy in the way I should. I never have. And deep down he knows that, and he never allows himself to think about that because if he did . . . well, I think it would break his heart."

"So why did you marry him?"

"I was very scared and very lonely and he was very lovely . . . Troy came along like a knight on a white horse. And he loved that role, but I don't let him have it any more. He would have been better off marrying a local girl back in Castleford who would adore him for who he is."

Ronnie got up and came over to her as she rubbed her forehead. He put his hands on her shoulders.

"Don't be hard on yourself, Blanche. Loads of couples want different things in life – you just have to get on with it."

She looked up at him and smiled. "You're a good friend, Ronnie."

He smiled back.

And then the smile dropped from their faces as they stared at each other and inched forward to kiss.

Blanche opened her eyes and looked around the ornate bedroom. The early morning light was streaming through the windows. She sat up in the satin sheets and saw Ronnie, face down beside her sleeping. She grabbed her watch and saw the time was seven in the morning. She quietly slid out of bed and tip-toed over to her clothes that had been tossed on to the floor and slipped into them. Then, picking up her shoes and bag she quietly left the room. She walked down the corridor and up the stairs onto the deck, blinking in the sunshine. She hurried down the gangplank and onto the pavement of the Embankment and started walking down the street looking for a taxi in the early morning traffic.

Blanche sat at the kitchen table at home, the patio doors open in the early morning Sunday sunshine. Her face was buried in her hands as she relived what had happened between her and Ronnie. Trying to understand why she had done it. The champagne, the party, the spark she'd always felt for Ronnie, the lack of spark she often felt for Troy. And then other thoughts swirled in her head: the children, her home, her feelings for Troy. How she had jeopardised her whole family and life over a stupid one-night stand. She wasn't a stupid young model flying around Dublin, naïve to the world. She was a thirty-year-old wife and mother, a respected businesswoman.

And a whore. Tears began to flood down her face.

Troy walked in in his dressing gown, yawning.

"What time did you get in at?" he said. "Blanche?"

He saw the state she was in and came quickly over to her.

"What's wrong, love?"

She said nothing, just continued to sob.

"Tell me what happened," he demanded.

The tears continued to flow as he cradled her.

Carl and Amelia came in.

"What's wrong?" cried Carl as he came running over.

"Nothing. Your mum's just a bit tired and emotional after her big birthday."

Amelia started hugging Blanche and Carl joined in. Blanche continued to cry. They stayed like that for a long while.

The phone ringing persistently in the hall forced Troy to finally get up.

Blanche held on to Carl and Amelia tightly as Troy went into the hall to get the phone.

After a while Troy came back into the kitchen and just stood in the doorway staring at them. Blanche managed to look up and wiped away her tears as she saw Troy looking ashen-faced.

"That was Lauren. Niall has died," Troy finally said.

They all flew home that evening.

CHAPTER 59

"We're having the funeral on Friday. It gives Jack a chance to get home from New York," explained Lauren as she dabbed at her eyes with a handkerchief.

"Oh, good – you managed to get in contact with Jack?" asked Blanche.

Lauren looked over at Blanche coolly. "Of course we got in contact with him."

All the friends had drifted home and Blanche and Troy were alone with Lauren after they'd put the children to bed. They had decided to stay in the main house at Winterfield, rather than their own, so they could be with Lauren.

Blanche studied Lauren. She was now sixty-seven and still cut a glamorous figure.

"The last year has been particularly difficult. Niall used to drift between reality and his own world a lot. But this last year he was hardly here at all. Rosalind has been a treasure, of course. Helping me out here. As if she doesn't have enough on her plate. She's a County Councillor now. The marriage to Seán is as good as over. I don't think they even live together any more. It's all so sad – the way things can work out." Lauren was crying again, and Troy went over and put his arms around her and he was crying too.

Blanche forced herself not to cry. She wanted to be strong, but as she thought about Niall she was overcome with grief. He had been so nice to her, and welcoming when nobody else was at Winterfield. And he had given her so much advice and support, telling her not to listen to Lauren and Troy but concentrate on the business. He understood her and appreciated what she was doing. It was to her that he had entrusted his business.

"So when are you moving back here?" said Lauren, looking at her son and then at Blanche. They looked at her blankly. "I can't run this estate on my own. I need you back here, Troy."

"We'll talk about it during the week," said Troy.

"There's no talking about it. You have to come home. I have it all worked out. Winterfield House is far too big just for me to rattle around in, so you can all move in here. And I'll move up to the old lodge."

"But you don't want to leave your home here," said Troy.

"It's only down the road – and besides, I'll be up here all the time anyway."

Blanche closed her eyes in horror at the thought.

Blanche seemed to drift without thinking over the next couple of days. She tried to keep the children occupied and out of the way. Troy was very quiet and Lauren had a stream of visitors. With all that was going on, she hardly thought about Ronnie Richards at all. And when he did come into her mind, she felt extremely agitated. What was she going to do? And on top of everything was the prospect of meeting Jack again after all this time.

It was the day before the funeral, and Jack was due to arrive in time for dinner. Blanche felt apprehensive. She hadn't seen him in nine years. He would be now thirty-eight. She wondered what he would be like now. Had living away from Winterfield changed him? Had life been good to him? Her mind went back to when he told her he had fallen for her and how she had rejected him, and rejected her own attraction to him. And hadn't she been right? Look what a fool she was when she followed her attraction. Look how she had ruined everything now with Ronnie.

Lauren was like a cat on a hot roof, her nerves not helped by the fact that Jack was two hours later than he had promised and she was afraid the roast goose would be overcooked.

As Blanche played with the children in the front lounge, she kept one eye out the window for any approaching car. Then there was a sudden deafening noise outside and she and the children rushed to the window. They saw a helicopter hover over the house.

The children rushed outside and Blanche pursued them in alarm. Outside she grabbed them and hung on as they watched as the helicopter did much manoeuvring, then descended and landed on the front lawn.

Troy and Lauren appeared on the steps.

"Who on earth is that?" said Lauren.

"Do you really have to ask?" smirked Troy.

The blades of the helicopter spun slowly to a halt, and Jack jumped out.

Then they watched him help a tall blonde out of the helicopter.

"And who's *she*?" said Lauren.

Jack looked fit and tanned. He looked affluent. He seemed as confident as ever, in fact even more so.

He hugged everyone warmly, and fussed over the children.

"Blanche!" he said when it was her turn, as if greeting an old and fond friend. He enveloped her in a hug, then drew back and smiled at her. She smiled back. All the bitterness he had towards her nine years ago seemed forgotten. And as she looked at the stunning blonde waiting to be introduced, Blanche imagined Jack probably had too many distractions to be bothered with any resentment towards her.

"Oh, I'm sorry!" said Jack as he turned and, taking the blonde by the hand, led her forward. "This is Sheryl Hutton."

"Hi, everybody!" said Sheryl in a pronounced American accent.

"This is just like old times," said Jack, smiling around the table as they sat down to eat.

"With one exception," sniffed Lauren as she looked at Niall's empty place.

"Yeah," Jack nodded sadly.

"Jack is like always talking about Ireland and Winterfield, and the wonderful time he had growing up here," Sheryl said, smiling around at everyone.

Lauren smiled back and smoothed her hair. "We had some great times."

Blanche raised her eyes to heaven. So everyone was deciding to forget all the bitterness and play happy families?

Troy was carving the roast goose and passing each plate to Lauren who was adding a selection of vegetables and potatoes before passing the laden plate on down the table.

When Sheryl's plate reached her, she looked down and

said, "Oh, I'm sorry, Lauren. Would you mind just taking all the carbs off this?"

"I'm sorry?" said Lauren, taken aback, and then copped on. "Ah . . . why don't you just give Sheryl an empty plate, Troy, and she can help herself to what's on the table." She indicated the array of foods in front of them.

"Great!" smiled Sheryl.

"So how's everything in New York, Jack?" asked Troy. "How's work? Is it true you're in the theatre now?"

"Yeah, I guess I am," said Jack. "When I arrived in New York, I did anything and everything. You name it, I did it. I did washing-up in a kitchen of a nursing home, I worked in a video store, worked in a casino – I even drove a cab. Finally I ended up working in a theatre, just doing odd jobs. Got to know a few people, worked hard, next thing I'm assisting producing plays. Next thing I'm producing plays."

"That's really exciting," said Blanche, impressed.

"Ah – it's less exciting than it sounds."

"No, it's not, Jack. Don't be so modest. Jack is one of the hottest producers around at the moment. He has the Midas touch. Every play he touches turns to gold," Sheryl informed them.

"You always had the Midas touch," smiled Troy.

"Where are you from, Sheryl?" asked Blanche.

"New York born and bred. Upper East Side."

She spoke with the confidence of somebody brought up with wealth, thought Blanche.

"In fact I was Miss New York 1983!" Sheryl added with a broad grin.

"Oh – that's interesting!" said Lauren.

"And are you in the entertainment field then as well?" asked Blanche.

"Heavens no! I'm an investment banker on Wall Street."

"Right!" Blanche nodded while still smiling.

"Uh huh. That's the whole irony of me being a beauty queen. I have a first from Harvard in Economics. I came top of my year. And I just entered Miss New York as a lark, and next thing I end up winning the darn thing! Still, it's good for my resumé. I always get an interview, because they want to take a look at me. And of course then when they meet me, I inevitably get the job."

"Of course," nodded Blanche. "And where did you two meet?"

"We met at an afters party for one of Jack's plays." She reached forward and held his hand. "Mutual friends had told me about this gorgeous Irish guy who was a hot new producer taking Broadway by storm. So I just had to meet him!"

"And where do you live in New York?" asked Lauren.

"Down at the tip of Manhattan at South Sea Seaport," said Sheryl.

"You hear so many stories about the crime in New York, all the attacks and murders," said Troy. "It's fairly dangerous, isn't it?"

"Oh, yeah, like there's a terrible crime wave. But, you know, I don't worry too much. I spent a year training at a martial arts school. I have a black belt in karate, so I can take of myself."

That night Blanche walked in the gardens with Jack and Sheryl.

"What a beautiful pool! I can't wait to take a swim in it," said Sheryl as they walked around it. "I like to take a swim every day."

"Sheryl was the New England Champion swimmer

387

in the 50 metres when she was at Harvard," explained Jack. "She leaves me lagging behind any time we swim together!"

"You're getting better though!" said Sheryl, yawning. "Um, I think I'll head to bed. It's going to be a long day tomorrow." She leaned forward and kissed Jack's lips and then smiled at Blanche before heading off inside.

"She's seems incredibly . . . em . . . accomplished," said Blanche as they continued to the end of the garden.

"She is!" said Jack.

"You certainly wouldn't have met anybody like her around Castleford."

"For sure . . . I hear you've accomplished quite a lot yourself, and you're the big businesswoman these days."

"Not really. I did what I had to do. Sheryl seems very directed, I just stumble from one thing to another. But with a lot of work and good luck, things come right . . .You know, I was very worried about meeting you again. I thought you might be a bit bitter or something."

"Nah. The best thing I ever did was get away from here. I was meant for the wider world, not this place. That's probably the reason I was always in scrapes here and running into trouble. I was looking for excitement."

Blanche looked at him enviously, and remembered him inviting her to join him on a journey of excitement all those years ago.

"I came back to see Dad last summer and we kind of made up."

"Oh, I'm so glad, Jack. He was heartbroken after you."

"I hope he managed to remember that we did make up."

"I'm sure he wouldn't forget that. It would mean too much to him. I'd better be going to bed too. As Sheryl said, it's going to be a difficult day tomorrow."

"I'm not looking forward to seeing the whole of Castleford again," said Jack with a grimace.

"You'll be the centre of attention, as always," said Blanche.

"That's what I'm afraid of. Not looking forward to seeing Rosalind again either."

"I can imagine. I believe things have been tough for her over the years."

CHAPTER 60

The next day was long and exhausting. After the funeral the guests came back to Winterfield where there were caterers providing an array of food.

Rosalind looked as pretty as ever, thought Blanche, though she was carrying more weight and now had a voluptuous figure. She was there without Seán and seemed to stick close to Lauren all day. Her beautiful daughter was with her, and stood attentively close to her mother, until Rosalind urged her to go out the back and play with the other children. Despite Rosalind's near-decade of bad luck, she seemed to be her old social butterfly self as she chatted to everyone. Blanche even observed Rosalind smiling and waving over at Jack a couple of times. As predicted, Jack and his beautiful companion were the centre of attention.

Blanche spotted that some of the silver trays holding canapés were empty and she went to gather them up and take them back to the kitchen.

"Let me give you a hand with that," said Sheryl as she took some of the trays.

The two women headed out into the hall and down the side of the main staircase on their way to the kitchens.

"Everyone's holding up alright," said Sheryl.

"Yes, thanks for all the help, Sheryl."

"No bother," she smiled as they entered the kitchens.

The caterers were busy preparing more trays of canapés and Sheryl observed them for a minute before suddenly going over to them.

"Hey, guys, let me show you how you can spice up those canapés. After college I spent a year at the Betty Stafford School of Catering in Manhattan. I came top of my class – you should see my soufflé! Being an expert chef is such an advantage as you go through life, don't you think?"

The caterers stepped out of her way. Blanche rolled her eyes as Sheryl began to take over. She left her to it and made her way back to the hall.

Jack was coming down the stairs and Rosalind was waiting for him at the bottom. Instinctively Blanche pulled into the side of the stairs, out of Rosalind's line of vision.

"Hello, Rosalind," Blanche heard Jack say kindly.

There was no response from Rosalind.

"You look well," said Jack.

"I wish I could say the same for you!"

"Don't be like that, Rosalind."

"You dump me practically at the altar and publicly humiliate me. You fuck off to New York. Then you arrive back years later in a *helicopter* with a plastic *whore* of a surgically enhanced Barbie doll, and all you can say is – '*Don't be like that*'?"

"I'd hoped you wouldn't still be bitter."

"Oh, I am bitter. And twisted. And nasty. You made me so!"

"Look, Rosalind, it would never have worked between us. I did us a favour. You were on the rebound from Troy, and I was on the rebound from – well – life."

"Don't prattle that American psycho-babble shit at me. You ruined my life walking out on me like that. I had to turn to drink as a crutch, and then to food and even to Seán Ford!"

"We got engaged as an act of revenge. It would never –"

"Did you honestly think you could just arrive in here and flutter your eyelids and all would be forgiven, and I would fall at your feet like all those other wives you screwed in there? *Fuck you!*"

At this point Blanche was embarrassed to see Sheryl emerge from the kitchens. She threw a glance at Blanche lurking by the staircase but walked past her to confront Rosalind.

"Hi there, is there some aggro in the air?" she asked.

"Oh and here's Sherry Trifle, or whatever her name is," said Rosalind.

"My name is Sheryl, honey. With an 'l'."

"I don't care if your name is Slut with an 'l'!"

Sheryl stepped back, raising both hands in the air. "I'm sorry but I don't do conflict."

"*Well, I fucking do!*" said Rosalind.

With Rosalind's voice rising, Blanche feared some of the guests might hear so she stepped forward to join the others.

"Now, come on – this is not the time or the place," she said.

Rosalind turned on Blanche. "*You!* Don't *you* tell me what to do! I'm from here. I'm not a blow-in like you. And we were all happy here before you arrived!"

"Rosalind, I'm very sorry that life has been difficult for you. But you can't blame other people for your unhappiness."

"Why not? You *are* responsible for my unhappiness. And anyway, what the fuck would you know about unhappiness? You can't even see unhappiness under your nose, in your own family."

"I don't know what you're talking about."

Jack and Sheryl were standing back out of the line of fire at this stage but were listening avidly.

"You ruined poor Troy's life!" Rosalind hissed. "Forcing him to live in London all these years. You know he hates the place."

"We had to live there for the business!"

"Yes, I heard you explain everything away with 'what's good for the business'. That's why you ignore your husband's unhappiness. That's why you leave your children with some old lush while you work all hours, or attend posh parties. I've heard all about you. It was a sorry day for Troy the day he met you!"

"I don't have to listen to this," said Blanche as she walked past Rosalind towards the front door.

Rosalind followed her, spitting fury. "And you left poor Lauren here on her own to mind poor Niall, as he slipped further into senility every day! And she had to run this whole farm single-handed! You know, when Troy comes home on holiday on his own, he's down in the town drowning his sorrows with his old friends, spilling his problems out!"

Blanche hurried down the front steps, as Rosalind continued to hiss a stream of accusations at her. Her tormentor at last went back into the house but Blanche's heart was beating quickly as she made her way through the gardens and into the fields beyond, Rosalind's vile accusations ringing in her ears.

The moon was shining and she felt calmer as she made her way down to the beach.

Where had Rosalind got all that stuff from? Obviously it was from Lauren. The two of them were as thick as thieves still – that was obvious. And Lauren's disapproval of her obviously ran far deeper than she had ever imagined.

And then there was Troy. Had he confided in Lauren the details of his marriage? Or even worse got drunk in some Castleford watering-hole and said too much to friends? She felt terribly exposed. And worse, wasn't what Rosalind said the truth after all?

Since Niall's death, she had refused to think about the night she had spent with Ronnie Richards. But there was a huge mess in London awaiting her. What happened between her and Ronnie threatened her whole family. If Troy ever found out, it didn't bear thinking about. She had betrayed him and their children and now she would have to make things right. She would put them first.

By the time she got back to the house, all the guests had gone home and it was almost in darkness. She slipped into the house through the patio doors at the back.

She opened the bedroom door quietly so as not to wake Troy. But he was sitting at the window looking out at the moonlit landscape.

"Where were you?" he asked, looking up at her and smiling.

She went over to him and kissed his forehead. "Just went for a walk, clear my head. You okay?"

He nodded and smiled.

"Everyone's gone to bed . . . Sheryl's been great. She great at distracting people from things." He managed a laugh. "Do you know she's fluent in Italian and German? She spent a year living in each country."

"You know, I'm sure if you counted up everything Sheryl has spent a year doing, she would be one hundred and twenty-three years old!"

They both laughed.

"Darling, I've been thinking – will we move home?" Blanche asked tentatively

394

"Back to Winterfield – to Castleford?" Troy was confused but excited.

Blanche nodded. "I'm ready to move back, if you are."

He held her close. "Oh, yes, I am."

Sheryl sniffed at the aroma of a glass of red wine in the drawing room at Winterfield and then took a tentative sip.

"I would say Chateau de Ville? Late seventies vintage – probably 1978. Am I correct?" She looked at Jack expectantly.

"Correct – as usual," he said.

"I spent a year working in a winery in the Loire Valley – I became an expert at French wines during my tenure there," explained Sheryl to the rest of the family.

It was the day that Niall's will was being read out, and the Launcelot solicitor Henry Redmond had just arrived. Lauren was chatting to Henry as she led him through the hall into the drawing room where everyone was waiting. She glanced up at the portrait of her predecessor Elizabeth hanging majestically on the wall as she had since before Lauren had arrived there. She was waiting for Jack to leave and then she would have the portrait removed.

"Lauren, could I have the portrait of my mother that's hanging in the hall?" Jack suddenly asked.

"Oh! Yes, of course you can, Jack," said a startled Lauren.

"Good afternoon, everybody," smiled Henry as he entered the room and sat down on the couch, putting his briefcase on the coffee table in front of him. He took out paperwork and said, "I know Jack is heading back to the States so I'll keep this brief, and just give you the main points. I believe you all know already the exact nature of the will, as Niall made it no secret."

Blanche looked at Lauren, Jack, and Troy who all

nodded. Nobody had bothered to tell her any details previously. She was just spending every waking hour keeping the show on the road. She began to feel annoyed at being uninformed.

"Jack, you are to receive the forty acres on the Castleford road beside the sheds. I believe it was your father's wish that you build a holiday home for yourself there. You are also to receive all of your late mother Elizabeth's jewellery and personal possessions and also considerable monies due." Henry looked over at Lauren and Troy. "The rest of Niall's estate, Winterfield and the business in London, properties etc. is to be divided evenly between Lauren and Troy."

Everyone sat in silence for a while and nodded.

Sheryl suddenly said with a big smile, looking at Lauren, "I guess the second honey gets the money!"

CHAPTER 61

Blanche sat nervously in the Launcelot Wine Bar in the City. She kept looking over at the door, waiting for Ronnie to arrive. She had put off phoning him when they got back to London but she couldn't put it off any longer, and besides there was business to attend to. The glass door of the wine bar opened and in walked Ronnie. There was a knot in her stomach as he approached her table and sat down. She was overcome with shame at the memory of what had happened between them.

"How was Ireland?" asked Ronnie. His eyes searched her face for some sign of how she was feeling.

"It was difficult. I'll tell you all about it later."

"Funerals generally are . . . And how are you?" His eyes connected with hers.

She looked down at her gin and tonic quickly, then up at him again. "I've never been unfaithful to Troy before, Ronnie."

"I know that."

"I was probably just another girl in your bed but –"

"No, of course you weren't!" He reached over and grabbed her hand reassuringly.

She quickly pulled back her hand and then looked straight into his face.

"We're moving back to Ireland, Ronnie."

"Oh – I see!" He sat back in his chair and continued to study her. "Is this because of what happened between us?"

"Not entirely. With Niall gone, Troy really is needed at home. Winterfield is a big estate, and it's not fair to leave it all to Lauren to run. And, besides, Troy is not happy here and I can't ignore his unhappiness any more."

"I understand. I'll miss you – I kind of got used to you being around."

"And I've got very used to you. You've been very good to me. I wouldn't be where I am without you."

"So what are you going to do about the business?" asked Ronnie.

"I've a good management installed in all the bars and the two hotels, and so I'll just move the headquarters to Ireland and run things from there. And we've decided we're going to sell all our property investments here."

"I see. You'll do very well on your property portfolio – with this boom in the London property market."

"I know. We've been very lucky. So we're going to put it all on the market and liquidate everything."

"I would like to have first refusal – myself and our other investor friends."

"I was hoping you would say that. It would make sense for you and the others to buy me out as we're mostly invested in the same property."

The rest of 1990 was very busy as the family planned their move back to Ireland. There was so much to be seen to, in order to ensure the business would run smoothly, as Blanche looked into transferring the headquarters of the business to

Ireland. The Launcelot property portfolio was by this time very extensive and many evaluations were done as Ronnie and his friends put in place the finance and started to buy out all their properties. Blanche was shocked to see just how much the properties had gone up during the boom, as the money began to pour into their bank accounts.

The week before Christmas the house in Kensington was filled with boxes as they packed everything to move home that week. The children didn't seem too upset by the move. Blanche and Troy had been at the solicitor's that morning, signing the last of their property portfolio over to Ronnie. They were going to keep the house in Kensington as a base for when they had to travel over. Although Blanche imagined that once Troy got back to Winterfield again he would never leave it and it would be mostly her coming over on her own.

CHAPTER 62

It was strange living in Winterfield House; Blanche had always felt like a guest there. And even stranger living in the country after London. The quietness, the darkness of the night without any light pollution, the having to get into your car every time you wanted to go anywhere.

Troy seemed like a new man back home in Castleford, and their marriage became much better as the year wore on. Lauren too was delighted to have them all home, if still always cool with Blanche. But Blanche had become cool with Lauren as well after Rosalind's outburst since it was obvious that Lauren had showed no loyalty to Blanche.

Every day Blanche sat at Niall's old desk in the study and worked from there, constantly on the phones to the different managers in London.

By the autumn, profits were beginning to nosedive in the bars. Financially they were sitting on substantial monies from the sale of all their London property, but she wanted to know what was going on in the bars.

"It's nothing to do with anything we're doing," explained her most senior manager. "A big recession has started and people aren't spending like they were last year."

She wouldn't do what Niall and Troy had done in the early eighties and just ignore the problem. She went to London and made sweeping changes, reducing costs, personnel and even temporarily closing down three bars that were not making a good turnover.

She was sitting in her office over the wine bar in the City, going through books one afternoon. She was due to return to Ireland the following day.

Suddenly the door of her office swung open and there stood Ronnie Richards.

"Ronnie! I was going to call you later to see if you wanted to meet for a drink tonight."

"I heard you were back."

"Yes. Sorry I didn't call you earlier but I'm just here for a week and I'm trying to go through everything to do with the business. This recession seems very bad, doesn't it?"

He slammed the door behind him and walked slowly to her desk. He hadn't shaved and looked rough.

"Ah, yes – this recession. But do you know what's worse? The property collapse!"

Blanche blinked a couple of times as she looked at his angry face.

"Do you see what's happened to the London property market, Blanche?"

"I know it's not been doing too well, but I haven't kept a close eye on it because I've been busy with settling the children in school and –"

"It's fucking collapsed!" he shouted, making her jump. "It's fucking wiped out! We've lost millions! I've lost millions!"

"Well, maybe you should try to sell now and recoup your losses and –"

"Nobody is buying! Everybody is selling! There's no point trying to sell everything because nobody will fucking *buy*."

"I'm sorry to hear that, Ronnie."

"Not half as fucking sorry as I am! All those properties I bought from you last year have halved in value."

"I didn't realise it was so bad or so swift –"

"Oh please, Blanche. You've played me for a fool once, don't play me for one again."

"What are you talking about?"

"Like in '87 after the market crashed and all you were doing was acting on instinct selling all your stock! I suppose it was just luck that you sold all your property last year at the height of the market, wasn't it?"

"Well yes! We were moving home –"

"I don't know who your source is but they warned you about this property collapse in the same way they warned you about the market collapse."

"That's ridiculous!"

"And then you sold it on to me and set me up with the loss while you sit on your millions, you bloody bitch!"

Blanche felt threatened by his anger and realised there was no point in even trying to reason with him as it would only agitate him further.

"And you even slept with me to smooth over the whole deal, you tramp," he sneered.

"Okay, Ronnie, I want you to get out of my office and out of my building," she demanded, as tears sprang to her eyes.

"You wouldn't even own this building if I hadn't shown it to you. You've ruined me and I'm going to get you back one day for this. And don't bother sending your husband to try and make up this time, or I might just have to tell him what a slut he's married to."

"*Get out!*" Blanche shouted.

Ronnie turned and walked out of the office, slamming the door after him, leaving Blanche sitting in stunned silence.

Part 5

CHAPTER 63

2010

Lee Dwyer put his foot down as he sped down the motorway. The sun was shining and he squinted as he drove under a sign that instructed to take the next exit for Castleford. He indicated and turned off the motorway. He followed the directions that had been given him and drove past a series of large housing estates and on to the town. A big sign stood beside one of the housing estates: *A Launcelot Development*.

Castleford had become a commuter town over the past decade, the opening of the new motorway making it an easy journey for people to Dublin. He drove on through the town and passed the new hotels, council offices, stores. He imagined it was a very different place from the town Blanche Launcelot had arrived in nearly thirty years previously. He passed a manufacturing plant on the outskirts with a big notice at the entrance: *Launcelot Industries*.

He made his way out along the coast road, until he turned into a large gateway and drove up the short driveway to a well-maintained Georgian house. He got out of the car and looked around at the beautiful location, then made his way to the front door, climbed the steps and rang the doorbell.

A minute later a woman in her mid-fifties answered,

blonde hair swept back and well groomed. Her figure was bordering on being overweight, but she still cut a glamorous figure.

"Rosalind?" Lee asked smiling.

"Ah – you must be Lee!" Rosalind smiled back and shook his hand. "Come on in!"

He followed her into the hall.

"What a lovely house!"

"Isn't it? It's been in my family for generations. My family the Dawsons were the main family around Castleford since time began. Certainly long before anybody heard of the Launcelots . . . Come on through to the kitchen. It's always been my favourite room."

He followed her through into the Clive-Christian-designed kitchen, where an array of cakes, biscuits and buns had been laid out on the table.

"Coffee or tea?" questioned Rosalind.

"Eh – tea please," said Lee as he sat down. "I hope you didn't go to all this bother for me?"

"It's no bother," she said, smiling.

She brought over the teapot, then went to the double-door fridge and took out the milk. He noticed the fridge was packed with cakes: plates of chocolate éclairs, doughnuts and French Fancies were sitting on the shelves.

As he watched her pour their tea, he realised she must have been a great beauty in her day.

"You obviously know what I'm here for, Rosalind. We're going to court to try and recover custody. And so I'm interviewing people like you, who know Blanche, to try and build up a strong case against her."

"Too right! I think it's outrageous that she got custody in the first place. Just because she has money, she thinks she can buy anything she wants – including her grandchild!"

Rosalind cut two huge slices of cake and placed one in front of him.

"It's imperative that the child is taken off her as soon as possible, before she ruins more lives the way she did everyone else's!" she said.

"So you'll co-operate with me as best you can, like my client suggested you would?"

"Of course! I can't wait to! If I knew what was going on the first time it went to court I'd have weighed in then! Blanche destroys everything she touches. She destroyed this town, she destroyed my family, she destroyed her own children! That's Blanche!" She bit into the cake, taking a big mouthful of sponge, cream and jam.

CHAPTER 64

1993

The middle-aged man looked around the packed Town Hall in Castleford before he announced: "I hereby declare Rosalind Dawson Ford elected to the Town Council!"

A cheer went up as Rosalind turned to the other candidates, shaking their hands and kissing their cheeks as they offered their congratulations. She stepped up to the microphone and looked out at the cheering crowd. Near the front she spotted her mother and daughter Gabrielle clapping wildly. She smiled at them and blew them a kiss, and felt her eyes fill with tears as she remembered the struggle to get where she was now.

It was never a love match between Rosalind and Seán Ford. It wasn't even a marriage of convenience. It was a marriage of necessity. And anybody who knew them knew that was the case. With her stomach getting bigger every day, and a scandal the likes of which Castleford had never seen before on the cards, Rosalind was complicit if not grateful when Lauren Launcelot arranged a quickie marriage for her. It broke her parents' hearts. For their princess to end up saddled with the alcoholic reckless Seán Ford was too much for them to bear. But, as Lauren had pointed out, an illegitimate grandchild and a daughter's ruined name would be worse.

Rosalind had an image of them building a dream home somewhere on the Dawson farm the way Troy and Blanche had built their first home on the Coast Road. And indeed they got planning to build a nice house and even got as far as putting in the foundations and walls up to the windows. And then worked stopped as Seán lost interest in it and the money they got from the bank for the mortgage approval started dripping away as Seán kept dipping into it for his drinking and gambling. Suddenly they were left with a mortgage for a house that did not exist. They had been living with Rosalind's parents, but the strain of them living with Seán was proving too much. Seán would arrive in drunk at night and suddenly there would be a screaming match between Rosalind and him and Baby Gabrielle would start crying. Seeing the stress it was causing her parents, Rosalind and Seán moved out and rented a house in an estate in Castleford. Seán had taken over the running of the Dawson farm. He had always been a good farmer, and when he was good he was very good. But then he would suddenly not turn up on the farm for six weeks and everything would go to pieces.

Rosalind kept her job at the newspaper which was her salvation, as they badly needed the money and it gave her something to do and kept her sane. A lot of her old friends turned on her, not wanting to be associated with somebody like Seán. There were many who took delight in her downfall. Lauren was a good friend always and they stayed close.

Rosalind would sit in the rented house, looking out at

the children playing on the street on their estate and start crying, thinking of how different her life could have been. Imagining herself living up at Winterfield. She began to drink, but it wasn't a good combination with Seán drinking as well and the two of them would end up having screaming matches in the night. Food became her next comfort.

And of course through it all was her beautiful daughter, who was her reason for living. Seán would disappear off to Martin's Bar constantly and rumours were circulating that he was seeing other women. One night, Rosalind looked at Seán's dinner in the oven slowly burning away for three hours and no sign of him. Suddenly she got up and put Gabrielle into the back seat of the car. She took the dinner out of the oven and put it on the front seat of the car beside her and she drove through the town to Martin's Bar. She parked outside the bar and got out and, holding the plate of dinner, marched up to the door. She pulled the door open and hurled the plate into the bar. Hearing a loud crash, she then turned and drove home. The incident became a legend around Castleford.

By the time her father passed away, she'd had enough and the marriage was over in all but name. She and Gabrielle moved back into the home place. Seán still ran the farm, when he could manage it, and she made sure he saw Gabrielle every week. She worked hard at the newspaper and then one day, when interviewing a town councillor, she realised she was twice as smart as him and decided to turn her attention to local politics.

The night Rosalind was elected to the Town Council, Seán was as ever at the bar in Martin's.

"Congratulations, Seán, on your wife's election victory," said the barmaid with a smirk. "You must be proud!"

"Shit, Melanie, nothing that girl does makes me proud. All she's trying to do is crawl back to the top of the shit-heap in this town."

Melanie smiled at him and leaned over the bar. "Don't take this the wrong way, honey pie, but that's some climb for her – with a husband like you!"

CHAPTER 65

Blanche took the bacon from the grill and placed it beside the scrambled eggs on the plates laid out in front of her. She was in the kitchen in Winterfield House and Carl, Amelia and Roger sat at the kitchen table waiting for their breakfast. Amelia was finishing off her homework while Roger was crayoning a colouring book.

Troy came in, reading the front of the local newspaper.

"I see Rosalind made the front page," he said, throwing the paper on the table. "*'Rosalind Ford Elected to Town Council'*."

"Of course she got the front page – she works for the newspaper!" said Blanche, ignoring the paper.

"Still – no mean feat being elected," said Troy, taking up his knife and fork and cutting into his bacon.

"Wasn't this her third or fourth attempt to get elected?" questioned Blanche.

"*Miaow*!" laughed Troy.

"Amelia, put away that homework, you should have done it last night," said Blanche.

Blanche glanced at her Cartier and realised she was running late. She had a business meeting in Dublin that morning and was meeting her mother for lunch after, with another meeting in the afternoon.

She took her own seat at the table.

"Isn't that Gabrielle's mother?" questioned Carl, taking up the paper and looking at it.

He was now eleven, and in the same class in school as Rosalind's daughter. A fact Blanche didn't like.

"Amelia, please eat your breakfast!" demanded Blanche.

"I'm sorry – I've told you. I've given up meat permanently," Amelia said, pushing the plate aside.

"Amelia!" snapped Blanche. "Will you stop this nonsense and eat your breakfast!"

"I'll eat the eggs, but I'm not touching the bacon."

Carl reached over and took the bacon off her plate. "Your loss!" he said with a laugh.

"Amelia, I don't have time to be dealing with your latest fad this morning, but we are going to chat seriously about it later," said Blanche.

"Chat away – I won't change." Amelia shrugged defiantly.

Eight-year-old Roger smiled wickedly at Amelia. "Where do you think all the cattle that Daddy has on the farm end up? Only on people's plates!" He laughed nastily.

Amelia turned to her father and glared at him. "Murderer!"

Sighing in exasperation, Blanche got up and went to her office. A little while later, she arrived back with her brief-case, and took all the dishes and stacked them in the dishwasher.

"Come on, everybody – to the car!" said Blanche. "Now I'll be late home this evening, so you head up to your grandmother's after school."

As the children headed to the car, Troy enveloped Blanche in a hug and kissed her.

"So you're definitely going ahead with this deal?" he asked.

"Yes – I don't think we can lose." She kissed him back and smiled. "I'll see you later."

Blanche dropped the children off at the school and set out for Dublin. In the couple of years since they had moved back to Ireland, Blanche hadn't expanded the business in any way. She concentrated on the wine bars and two hotels in London, making sure they weathered the recession. But something had caught her eye over the past six months. An old rundown hotel in Ballsbridge. She had fallen in love with the location and the building and felt it might be a good move.

She met the owners of the hotel, two men in their fifties, at eleven and did another tour of the place.

"Gentlemen, I am interested in the premises," said Blanche, as they wandered into the tired old lounge bar with peeling wallpaper and stained carpets. "But your asking price is out of the question. Your turnover just does not justify your asking price."

The two men looked at her, irritated.

"I'm prepared to offer a deal. Two hundred thousand below your asking price and I'll have contracts signed within a week and the deal closed in one month."

They stared at her and then at each other. She knew the hotel had been on the market for a year with no interested parties, and they were losing money by the week.

An hour later, Blanche drove into town smiling. They had accepted her terms and now she was filled with excitement. She parked the car on Baggot Street and made her way to the Shelbourne Hotel. Her mother was already there in the restaurant when she arrived. They kissed each other and Blanche sat down.

"How did your meeting go?" asked Harriet as they ordered Caesar Salad and the waiter opened a bottle of white wine for them.

"Excellent!" She clapped her hands together. "We're buying the hotel! I've been wanting to buy something in Dublin for a long while and this is perfect. I know I can turn that place around. And, besides, I think Dublin is just going to take off. There's a feeling in the air in the same way there was in London ten years ago. I want to be part of that."

"How are the children?" asked Harriet.

"All doing well. Amelia is doing my head in. She has a new cause every week."

"Yes, she's very spirited."

"And you know Carl is due to start secondary school next year. I'm thinking of enrolling him in a private school in Dublin. Troy of course wants to send him to the local secondary school in Castleford, but I don't want that. I want him to get a proper education so he will be able to take over the business.

"Good thinking," agreed Harriet. "And Roger?"

Blanche smiled. "What can you say about Roger? He has everybody eating out of his hand."

Roger was in the kitchen with his grandmother while Amelia and Carl played outside on the back patio. She cut him another slice of cake.

"Thanks, Gran, Mum doesn't let us have that much cake. She's says it's bad for us."

"Such nonsense! What's childhood about if you can't indulge yourself? What else has your mother been saying this week?"

"She . . ." Roger paused as he finished off the slice of

cake, "she says Rosalind Ford is a stupid cow who doesn't deserve to be elected."

"Really!" said Lauren with a frown. "Don't you listen to her. Rosalind is one of my closest friends and a wonderful woman. Where's your mother today that she couldn't pick you up from school?"

"She had meetings in Dublin."

"Oh yes, playing the big businesswoman, no doubt. Did you happen to hear what she was doing in those meetings?"

"Something about buying a hotel," said Roger.

"Lord save us! Will that woman never stop?" As she heard Carl and Amelia come into the house, she reached into her pocket, took out a £20 note and handed it to Roger. "That's for you, darling, and don't tell the others I gave it to you."

Roger put the money in his pocket and kissed his grandmother.

"This isn't the way home!" complained Roger.

The autumn sunshine shone down on the golden-leafed trees around them as they walked through a field.

"Yeah – well, we're just going to meet Gabrielle first to play with her," said Carl.

A young blonde girl was sitting on a fence and waving enthusiastically over to them.

"Hi there!" said Carl as he sat up on the fence beside her.

"Hi, Gabrielle," said Amelia, smiling as she sat up the other side of Gabrielle.

Roger looked into the sky, bored.

"I brought you some sweets from my gran's," said Carl, taking some sweets from his schoolbag.

"Ah, thanks, Carl," smiled Gabrielle who then distributed the sweets amongst them all.

"Come on, let's go play down by the beach," said Gabrielle and they all went running through the fields.

An hour later and Roger was whining. "I'm missing TV, I wanna go home," he demanded.

"Actually, we'd better be getting home," Amelia said. "See you tomorrow, Gabrielle! Come on, Carl."

"You two head go ahead, and I'll walk Gabrielle home," said Carl.

"Alright, see you a bit later. Come on, Roger."

Amelia and Roger headed to the road while Carl and Gabrielle walked off through the fields.

"Why do we always have to hang around her for? She's boring," complained Roger as they walked down the country road.

"Gabrielle is our friend, that's why. And we like her."

"I don't like her." And he didn't. He didn't like how, when Gabrielle was around, his brother and sister concentrated on her rather than him.

"You've no reason not to like her," said Amelia as she slowed her walk and began to survey the huge field full of cattle on the right that was part of the Winterfield estate.

"It's just so unfair!" said Amelia as she surveyed the animals. She thought hard for a minute and then suddenly she opened the gate wide, ran into the field and started to hunt some of the cattle out onto the road.

"Amelia! What are you doing?" Roger was horrified.

"I'm making sure they don't end up on somebody's plate!"

"I'm going over to your gran's tomorrow for dinner with my mother," said Gabrielle to Carl as they walked.

"Are you?"

"She's cool. She's always so nice to me."

"Yeah, she's pretty cool alright."

"When my mam was growing up she was always over at Winterfield playing with your dad and his brother."

"I know – my dad tells me," smiled Carl.

They looked at each other awkwardly. Both knew that there was a problem between their mothers, but they couldn't understand why. Both had asked to have the other over to their house to play but the request had always been slapped down by both Blanche and Rosalind. That's why they arranged to meet in the fields to play or down on the beach.

"What are you doing tonight?" asked Carl.

"I'm meeting my dad tonight. We're going to McDonald's."

"Lucky you," said Carl. He always felt a bit awkward when Gabrielle's father was mentioned. He knew her parents didn't live together and he had heard people talk about Seán Ford and they never had much good to say about him.

Gabrielle started to sing her father's praises. The only person who had good things to say about Seán Ford was his daughter, thought Carl.

"It must be hard – your parents living in different houses," suggested Carl.

"I'm used to it. I kind of prefer it."

"Why would you prefer that?" Carl looked confused.

"Just because – look, not everybody's parents get on like yours, Carl. Sometimes they are better off apart – that's what my mam says." The beautiful Dawson house came into view down the road. "Anyway, I'd better go or I'll be late for my father. See you tomorrow!"

"Yeah, see you tomorrow, Gabrielle." He watched as she hurried down the road.

CHAPTER 66

That night at dinner Blanche was in great form as she explained to Troy all about the new hotel.

"And there's this huge garden out the back – I think we could get planning for a big extension out there and make the hotel twice the size it is now."

"Brilliant!" smiled Troy. He had learned to leave all business to Blanche. He trusted her completely. She always seemed to know the right move and what to do in any event. She managed the business effectively and profitably and, what's more, she thrived on it.

The phone rang and Troy got up and walked into the hall to answer it. He returned a minute later, hastily putting on his coat.

"What's wrong?" asked Blanche.

"All the cattle somehow got out and are straying all over the place. A car on the road had to swerve to avoid one and ended up in a ditch."

"Oh no!" said Blanche.

"I'd better hurry, I'll see you later. I feel one big law suit coming our way with this car accident."

Roger looked over at Amelia who was concentrating on the food on her plate.

Later Blanche was stretched out on the couch in the drawing room, reading through paperwork about the hotel, when she heard the front door open and close. She sat up as Troy came in.

"We managed to get all the cattle back in the field."

"And what about the car?"

"I said we'd pay for the damage to the car. There was nobody injured."

"How did it happen?"

"I don't know. The gate was left open. It could have caused a serious accident. I'm going up to bed. I'm exhausted."

"I'll be up in five minutes," said Blanche and she started tidying away her paperwork.

She headed up the stairs and, as she walked down the long corridor, she heard crying coming from Roger's room. She gently pushed the door open and went and sat on his bed and held him.

"What's wrong, darling?"

"I can't tell you!"

"You can tell me anything."

"No! I can't!"

"Come on now – I'm your mum and you really should tell me if anything is troubling you."

Roger raised his tear-stained face. "Oh, Mum! Amelia left the gate open and that's how the cows got out."

"Oh!"

"Please don't say I told you!"

"No, I'll say nothing, darling. Now, don't you worry about it and go to sleep." She kissed him and tucked him in. As she walked out of the room, Roger smiled.

Blanche walked down the corridor to their own

bedroom. Troy emerged from the bathroom. He looked shattered.

"I think I know who the culprit is for leaving the gate open," said Blanche.

"Who?" demanded Troy.

"Amelia. It's probably because of her vegetarian stance."

"I'll give her vegetarian stance!" erupted Troy as he marched to the door.

"No, stop, Troy!" Blanche blocked his way. "I'll sort it out."

"But Blanche, somebody could have been killed. Her oddness is getting dangerous!"

"Calm down. I said I'll deal with it, okay?"

It was Saturday afternoon and Blanche went up to Amelia's bedroom door, opened it and walked in. Amelia was stretched out on her bed reading a book, while East 17 harmonised on her CD player.

Blanche crossed over to the CD player and turned it down. Amelia ignored her and kept on reading.

Blanche studied her daughter. The girl had a striking face with brown hair and intelligent blue eyes. Blanche sat down on the bed.

"Amelia?"

"Uh huh?" Amelia didn't look up from her book.

Blanche started stroking her daughter's hair. "As I put the roast in the oven I was remembering the little scene at the breakfast table yesterday – not eating the bacon, and being mad about the cattle on the farm." Blanche spoke gently. Her daughter was nothing if not honest.

Amelia snapped the book shut and stared ahead.

"Amelia – you didn't let those cattle out on the road, did you?" Blanche kept her voice soft.

Amelia turned around and looked defiantly at Blanche. "And what if I did?"

Blanche sighed and closed her eyes. "Oh, Amelia, that was a very stupid thing to do. The people in that car could have been injured, or worse."

"I don't care!" Amelia was suddenly crying.

"You don't mean that. You're the most caring girl. You'd hate for those people to be injured." She took her crying daughter in her arms and soothed her.

"I wanted to save the cows."

"Oh Amelia. You can't change the world like that – why are you always swimming against the tide? Why do you make life hard for yourself? Why are you always fighting everything?"

"I just do what I feel is right."

"Oh – I'm not saying you're not right. But you can't change the world just because you want to."

Amelia pulled back and wiped away her tears. "Well – I can try!"

Lauren sat in the dining room at the lodge with Rosalind and Gabrielle. A big chocolate cake that Rosalind had brought sat on the table and Lauren began to cut slices.

"None for me, thanks," said Rosalind. "I'm on a diet, trying to regain my figure now I'm on the Council."

"I'm just so delighted about you winning that seat," smiled Lauren, giving Gabrielle a slice of cake.

"I've been walking on clouds since. I really think things are coming together at last."

"And how's Seán about it?" Lauren lowered her voice slightly as she looked at Gabrielle.

"Hasn't said two words to me about it," said Rosalind

nonchalantly, sitting back in her chair. She believed in speaking openly in front of Gabrielle about everything. She took up a fork and reaching over to the cake took a forkful and ate it.

"I – eh – I was taking a walk the other day past your land. Some of those fields are going to waste, Rosalind." Lauren's voice was full of concern.

"I know. The hay wasn't cut this year. Seán didn't organise it." Rosalind spoke in a bored tone, as if she had given up trying to push him. She reached out and took another forkful of cake.

"But you can't let the farm go to wrack and ruin, Rosalind. If Seán won't look after it, you need to get somebody in to run it."

"What can I do, Lauren? I have a guy who comes in to keep the livestock tended to, but Seán won't let me bring in somebody to run the farm. I want to get on now with my own life, my new life. He's dragged me down for long enough." Rosalind took another chunk of cake.

Lauren shrugged and sat back. But it's still your farm, thought Lauren.

"It's all so changed around here. Nothing worked out the way we wanted," said Rosalind.

"I guess I wanted Troy to get everything and he did," sighed Lauren. "I just didn't expect somebody like Blanche to be part of the bargain."

"And how is the bitch?" Rosalind took a further piece of the cake.

"Buying a hotel up in Dublin is her latest adventure."

Rosalind looked surprised. "Can you afford that?"

"Seemingly. Blanche is very good at making money."

Rosalind pulled a face and reached for the cake again.

"Rosalind!" Lauren reprimanded. "I thought you were on a diet! You should have just taken a damned slice at the beginning! You're after taking much more cake picking away at it. Little pickers wear big knickers!"

CHAPTER 67

Blanche employed a team of architects in Dublin and they got to work to draw up a huge extension for the hotel in Ballsbridge. The planning was passed in early 1994 and Blanche wasted no time hiring in a construction firm to carry out the work.

"I'm looking to have this place open by June, and I want no delays!" Blanche demanded and had written it into the contract. She smiled to herself when she thought about how tentatively she had dealt with the builders when they were converting the pubs all those years back in London.

One evening after work, she met Troy and they walked down to the cinema on O'Connell Street and watched *Schindler's List*. They walked through the streets afterwards arm in arm to an Italian restaurant in Temple Bar. The theme from *Riverdance* seemed to be bellowing out of every pub they passed.

"I had an appointment today with Blackrock College," said Blanche as she took a mouthful of lasagne.

"Oh – why?"

"Well, I enrolled Carl there for the autumn," said Blanche.

"But he's already enrolled in the secondary school in Castleford!" said Troy.

"I know, but I don't want him going there. He's a bright and intelligent boy and I just think he can do better than Castleford High, or whatever it's called!"

"Not a chance!" shouted Carl.

"Look, Carl, this is a wonderful opportunity for you. The best teachers —"

"Forget it!" said Carl. "I'm not going to some snobby old school up in Dublin, and that's it!" He turned and ran from the living room.

Troy looked over at Blanche. "Well, that's that, I guess."

Blanche sighed. "Once he starts there he'll love it."

"Blanche, if the kid doesn't want to go then nobody is going to force him, end of story."

"You know he's spending much too much time with that Ford girl."

"Rosalind's daughter?"

"The very one. According to Roger they meet up all the time after school, and hang around in the same crowd at school."

"What's wrong with that? Me and Rosalind were like that growing up."

Blanche drew heavily on her cigarette. "My point exactly."

The Launcelot Hotel in Ballsbridge opened the end of May, ahead of schedule. The night before it opened its doors, Blanche stood in the refined grandeur of the lobby. Now the hotel was the very picture of elegance and sophistication. There was to be an official opening the next day and Blanche had hired a public relations firm to organise it.

The opening was scheduled for two o'clock the following afternoon and the PR firm had organised all the newspapers and magazines to be there along with a good sprinkling of dignitaries and minor celebs.

Blanche was dressed in a slinky silver gown, and Troy was smartly dressed in a black suit beside her.

"Another mission successfully launched!" Troy whispered in her ear as he chinked his wineglass against hers.

"Yes," she said smiling as she looked proudly around the full hotel lobby.

The opening had cost a lot, but she was hoping that the elegant bar and restaurant would attract the in-crowd and become a place to be seen.

"Blanche?" called a voice.

Blanche looked around and saw Samantha Armstrong standing there. Blanche felt a strange combination of nervousness and surprise. It hadn't dawned on her that when the PR company said they were inviting the in-crowd to the event that people from her long-distant modelling days would still be on the social scene in Dublin.

"I thought it was you!" Samantha looked as surprised as Blanche felt.

Samantha must be in her mid-forties by now, thought Blanche, but she still looked as glamorous as ever. She suddenly felt as intimidated as the nervous young girl who met the model boss all those years ago.

"What are you doing here?" asked Samantha. "And where have you been all these years?"

"I – eh –" Blanche looked at Troy's intrigued face. "Samantha, this is my husband, Troy Launcelot."

"Launcelot?" Samantha said as the penny dropped. "You own the hotel?"

"Yes," said Blanche.

Samantha looked impressed. "Blanche was one of my best models when I was an agent."

"You've left the agency business?" asked Blanche.

"Yes, years ago. I went and became a magazine editor. I'm the Social Editor of the *Sunday Review* now."

"Oh – you've moved on quite a bit then!" said Blanche

"As have you!" Samantha turned around and called over to a photographer. "Zac, when you have a second!"

Zac came over straight away.

"I want a photo of Blanche and Troy. And then you and me, Blanche, are going to sit down and have a drink and you're going to tell me exactly what you've been up to."

"Oh, no – I don't want any photos of me taken," objected Blanche.

Zac smiled at her as he positioned her for a photo. "Samantha runs the social scene in this city and nobody says no to her."

Samantha and Blanche found a booth in the bar and the cocktail waiter poured them two Martinis.

"Will there be anything else, Mrs Launcelot?" asked the waiter.

"No, that's fine, Joe," said Blanche.

Blanche was in two minds meeting Samantha again. She was stirring up a lot of old memories, some very good and some very bad. She was curious as to what had happened to people.

"I never forgave you for walking out on me back then, and just when I was about to launch you big-time," said Samantha, raising her Martini to her lips.

"I had a lot of things on my mind at the time and had to get away," explained Blanche.

"Man trouble? With Billy Forrestal?" probed Samantha.

"Something like that." It was odd speaking to somebody who knew Billy. "Have you ever seen him around in Dublin?"

asked Blanche, the burning curiosity not even letting her wait to ask.

"No – he never came back from Australia that time. Everyone said he ran away with a broken heart after you dumped him."

Blanche sat back and sighed. "I heard he went away with a girl."

Samantha shrugged. "I don't know about that."

Blanche decided to change the subject. "And how're the girls? Jill?"

"Jill married a surgeon and now lives in some considerable style in Dalkey."

"And Gail?"

"Gail married a horse-breeder and lives on a stud farm that I believe takes up half of Tipperary. Most of the models ended up marrying well and are ladies of leisure. A bit like you, by the looks of it."

"Oh, I'm no lady of leisure. I run the business."

Samantha looked over at Troy who was talking to some men at the bar. "Who exactly are you married to? I've never heard of Troy socially before."

Blanche laughed out loud. "No, you wouldn't have – not unless you went into the Castleford Arms."

Samantha looked even more curious. She knew everyone on the social scene, but she was aware that there were a lot of business families around the country who kept to themselves. She imagined Troy was one of them.

"And this is your first hotel?" she asked.

"Well, we have a couple in London, and the wine bars."

Samantha nodded as the whole picture fell into place. "The Launcelot Wine Bars! I've been in them more than once. So that's Troy's family. And you work in the business?"

"As I said, I run the business."

"I see." Samantha digested all the information.

"What happened to that model, what was her name – Darla?"

"Darla!" Samantha threw her eyes heavenwards. "I had to fire Darla from the agency not long after you left. She's a rip-roaring alcoholic now, I believe. I haven't seen her in years. And her boyfriend Shay had a terrible accident – it was all very suspicious – the Guards never got to the bottom of it."

Blanche shuddered, thinking of how she had got caught up in that murky world, and the near miss she had.

The next day Blanche opened a copy of the *Review* to be greeted with a huge photo of her and Troy under the heading: *'Former Model Becomes Hotel Tycoon'*. Blanche quickly read the article beneath the photograph.

'Former 80s model Blanche Fitzclarence is pictured with her husband Troy Launcelot at the opening of their new hotel, The Launcelot, in Ballsbridge. The new hotel is the first Irish premises to be opened as part of the Launcelot Bar and Hotel Group.'

Blanche made the journey into Dublin most days to oversee the running of the new hotel. Bookings were swift and it was booked out for the first six months solid. The bar and restaurant were always full and it did become a destination spot for Dublin's in-crowd. Blanche found herself being put on invitation lists around town, but she rarely went to any of the events she was invited to. She felt she was an object of curiosity to Dublin's microcosmic social scene. The ex-model turned millionaire. And she didn't want to be seen as a vacuous social butterfly with money. But Samantha insisted they do lunch on a regular basis, and it was good spending time in an old friend's company again.

Then Blanche was contacted by an auctioneer about a hotel up for sale near Dublin Airport. She viewed it and put in an offer, which was immediately accepted. She couldn't believe the low price of real estate in Dublin and had a feeling it wasn't going to stay low for long, so now was the time to buy.

After finalising the contracts with the solicitor one morning in December, she finished early and headed back to Castleford to collect the children. She collected Amelia and Roger from their primary school before driving on to the secondary school. As she drove along, cigarette in hand, and the window opened, she was wondering what to organise for Troy's fortieth birthday party the following year. She would like the two of them to head to somewhere exotic for a couple of weeks. She was half-thinking of asking Jack to join them as a surprise. He was living in Los Angeles now.

Carl and Gabrielle came out of the school together.

"I'll see you tomorrow," said Gabrielle as she headed to the school bus.

"Why are you getting the bus?" asked Carl. Gabrielle was usually collected from school by her mother or grandmother.

"My dad was supposed to collect me this evening, but he's held up and my mum has a late Council meeting," said Gabrielle.

"Well, we'll give you a lift home – we're going past your door," offered Carl.

"No, I'm fine, thanks." Gabrielle shook her head as she saw Blanche pull up in her black Mercedes. Blanche had always intimidated Gabrielle and she had never spoken to her. She was a bit of a legend around Castleford, known for her glamour and no-nonsense manner, and of course being a Launcelot. And Gabrielle had heard Rosalind call her every name under the sun.

"Come on. You'll be home in ten minutes with us, or an hour on that bus. No contest really." Carl grabbed Gabrielle's arm and led her over to the Mercedes.

"Mum, it's okay to give Gabrielle a lift home, isn't it?" said Carl, opening the front passenger seat and directing Gabrielle in.

Blanche looked at the pretty blonde. "I'm not sure – have you checked with Gabrielle's parents?" She felt very uncomfortable.

"Sure! They are tied up and so she'd have to get the bus otherwise," Carl said, pushing Gabrielle into the front seat and slamming the car door. He then jumped into the back beside Amelia and Roger.

"Hi, Gabrielle!" smiled Amelia.

"Hi," said Gabrielle, looking back and smiling at the others.

Blanche was even more intimidating up close, Gabrielle thought, as they drove off.

"And how are you finding your new school, Gabrielle?" said Blanche.

"It's cool so far," Gabrielle said.

"It's no problem to Gabrielle, she's top of the class," said Carl.

"Good for you! Maybe you three in the back should take a leaf out of Gabrielle's book and work a bit harder!"

Blanche sped out the coast road. She tried to make small talk with Gabrielle but found it very strained. The child had obviously been indoctrinated against her.

That night the phone rang in the hallway.

Blanche was on the couch with Troy, his arm around her, watching television.

"I'll get it," said Blanche, jumping up and heading into

431

the hallway. She expected it to be some last-minute problem with the contract for the hotel at the airport.

"Hello?"

"Good evening – this is Councillor Ford," said the abrupt voice on the phone.

"Who?" asked Blanche, confused.

"Councillor Ford!"

Blanche recognised the voice. "Oh – Rosalind!"

"I'm just ringing to say I do not want you giving a lift to my daughter in future. I don't want you anywhere near my daughter. Understood?"

Blanche saw red. "I gave the girl a lift because I was passing by her door and my son suggested it."

"Well, tell your son to keep his suggestions to himself. I don't want my daughter anywhere near the likes of you! Understood?"

"Completely understood! I hope I never have to speak to you or see your daughter again!" Blanche slammed down the phone.

Raging, Blanche stormed into the lounge, grabbed a cigarette, lit it and started pacing up and down.

"What's wrong?" asked Troy.

"That was that bitch Rosalind. You know we gave her daughter a lift home? She rings me up and says I'm never to do such a thing again!"

"Why?"

"How the fuck would I know what's going through that mad bitch's head? That's the last time she ever speaks to me like that. She has been nothing but abusive from the moment I stepped foot in Castleford. I've had enough! And if she crosses me again she'll be sorry."

CHAPTER 68

The plane touched down at San Juan International Airport in the Caribbean. It was spring 1995 and it was Troy's fortieth birthday. A car met them and drove them out from the capital of Puerto Rico through the beautiful countryside to the El Conquistador Wyndham Estate. Their car turned off the main road and the driver waved to the security, then drove along the avenue that led through the golf course to the main hotel. The car pulled up outside the entrance of the hotel and the porters came to take the luggage. Troy and Blanche stepped out and walked into the coolness of the giant lobby, a refreshing relief from the Puerto Rico midday sun.

As they were booking in a voice said, "Excuse me, could you tell me the direction to Castleford?"

Startled, Troy turned around to see Jack standing there smiling.

"What the fuck are you doing here?" shouted Troy, smiling broadly.

"A little surprise organised by your wife," smiled Jack as he hugged both of them.

Blanche kissed Jack's cheek and looked around, expecting

to see Sheryl. Instead a dark-haired beauty with sallow skin and a rangy body stood beside Jack.

"Oh – and this is Marcy," said Jack.

"I thought he was still with Sheryl," Troy muttered to Blanche sometime later, when they were out of the other couple's earshot. "Who's Marcy?"

Blanche shrugged. "You know Jack. Always full of surprises."

The hotel was built on the edge of a cliff face, looking out to the sea. At the back of the hotel was the lounge area and swimming pool, and then a series of cable cars could bring guests down the cliff face to a restaurant that was built halfway down. The cable cars continued down to the bottom where there was a private port where yachts were moored, with another restaurant and bar. The Wyndham Estate also had a private island with a regular service of a yacht to bring hotel guests out to the private beaches there.

That evening, after unpacking in their hotel room, Blanche and Troy took the cable car all the way down to the port where they had arranged to meet Jack and Marcy for dinner.

The restaurant was open-air and looked out on rows and rows of yachts.

Jack waved over to them and they joined them. Marcy was sitting with her legs stretched out on a neighbouring chair. Her long rangy body was dressed in flared black trousers and a tight black T-shirt, her long black hair casually pushed back. Blanche guessed her to be in her late thirties. She was smoking a cigarette and drinking a Margarita.

"When did you get in?" asked Blanche, once they had ordered shrimp for starters.

"We flew in from LAX yesterday," said Marcy. "We nearly missed the flight. I had a meeting at the studio that ran overtime."

As the conversation continued, it transpired that Marcy was a studio executive at Universal. It was the same studio that Jack was now producing films for. Blanche found Marcy to be incredibly relaxed. She had an easygoing manner and her Californian accent was unrushed. But Blanche imagined behind that cool exterior was a tough studio boss.

"So you're living in Malibu now?" Troy asked Jack.

"Yep, we have a beach house there, don't we, darling?" Jack smiled at Marcy.

As the food arrived and everyone tucked in, Marcy didn't bother taking her feet down from the neighbouring chair, and continued to smoke, casually reaching out for some shrimp when the notion took her.

They filled Jack in on all the gossip back home.

"So Rosalind is now a politician?" asked Jack, surprised by this revelation.

"Well – a County Counsellor," said Blanche.

"Rosalind in power! Oh no!" laughed Jack.

Blanche and Jack glanced at each other, both remembering the tongue-lashing they had received from Rosalind at Niall's funeral.

Marcy opened a silver cigarette case and placed a rolled-up cigarette between her lips and lit up. Blanche and Troy gave each other a look at the strong smell of marijuana.

"Oh – I'm sorry – did you want one?" Marcy asked.

"Ah – no, thanks!" said Blanche, looking around. As the restaurant was open-air, nobody at the other tables seemed to notice.

They finished their dinner and then drank white wine and beer into the night.

Troy was getting quite drunk and suddenly he blurted out, "Hey – Jack – whatever happened to Sheryl?"

"Troy!" snapped Blanche, horrified by his lack of discretion.

Jack glanced at Marcy who had a look of amusement on her face.

"Sheryl ended up marrying some billionaire businessman and lives in Palm Springs," said Jack.

Marcy choked on the smoke she had inhaled and started laughing.

"That's not quite the full story, is it, Jack?" said Marcy.

"Shut up, Marcy!" Jack gave her a warning look.

"Sheryl is living in Palm Springs alright," said Marcy, laughing. "She's spending a year in the Palm Springs Correctional Institution for white-collar crime!"

"*What*?" said Blanche and Troy in unison.

"Marcy!" warned Jack. "I don't think Troy and Blanche need to know."

"Why not? The whole of Palm Springs knows. Sheryl was the vice president of one of her husband's firms and was found guilty of orchestrating tax evasion and received a year-long prison sentence!"

"A year in prison?" said Blanche eventually. "Oh well, at least it's another year-long accomplishment for her CV!"

The four started to laugh, Jack laughing the loudest.

Blanche was so impressed by the grandeur of the Wyndham estate. Every detail was taken care of. The resort spelled luxury. And as the week passed, an idea began to form in her head.

"Troy?" said Blanche on their last night. They were in their bedroom after dinner. The patio doors were open and a cool breeze wafted in.

Troy came in from the balcony. "Yeah?"

"Don't you think that the countryside around Winterfield is every bit as beautiful as here at the resort?"

"You're probably asking the wrong person – I think Winterfield is the most beautiful place in the world," he said with a laugh.

"I've been thinking . . ." And she began to speak in that quick manner that marked her Eureka moments – the manner he had come to dread. "We could build something like this at Winterfield."

"What are you talking about?"

"We could build a hotel and golf resort at Winterfield. A world-class resort that would attract premier golfers from all around the world."

"That's the daftest thing I've ever heard!"

"No, it isn't! It makes perfect sense. I mean, we're sitting on a goldmine! This could really put the business into a new league."

"Winterfield is a farm. It's not going to be turned into a tacky golf course for fat Americans."

"You're being ridiculous!"

"It would ruin the place. It's the most stupid thing I've ever heard," Troy was becoming angry and his voice was rising.

"It wouldn't take up the whole farm, just about a quarter. I've been planning it. If we used the south part of the farm, you wouldn't even be able to see the new hotel from Winterfield House."

"You're fucking priceless! You have the whole thing planned! You're not ruining my farm with one of your stupid schemes!"

"Why can't you just support me once? Why do you fight me on every fucking thing?" Blanche's voice became raised too.

"If you came up with a good idea occasionally then maybe I would support you!"

Blanche's eyes filled with tears. "How can you say that after all the hard work I've put into the business over the years and all the ideas that have paid off so well? You and Lauren never give me any credit for what I've done."

"Well – you remind us enough!"

"And you resent me for it. You resent me for not staying at home and being a good little wife and mother. The truth is I'll never be the wife you want me to be."

"No – you won't. Not while you continue with this relentless drive to be on top of the world!"

"You don't accept me for who I am. I accept you for who you are. I know you don't want the pressure of running the business and I accept that –"

"No – you love that!"

"Well, somebody has to keep the show on the road. And I made a promise to Niall that I would."

"What are you talking about now?"

"Niall asked me to run the business. He said that you and Lauren didn't understand what it took to run things and told me to follow my instincts. Niall would have loved the idea of Winterfield being turned into a golf resort."

"Don't fucking tell me what my father would have wanted!" shouted Troy.

"Oh – forget it!" shouted Blanche as she marched out of the room and slammed the door.

Blanche stormed out of the elevator on the ground floor and walked quickly through the giant lobby and into the casino. It was two o'clock in the morning and the place was nearly empty. She marched up to the bar.

"A double whiskey with ice, please," she ordered.

She took her drink and turned to survey the casino, forcing herself to calm down. Then she spotted Jack at a roulette table. He was on his own. She walked over to him.

"Do you mind if I join you?"

"Be my guest," he said, tapping the stool beside him.

"What has you up playing roulette at this time of night?" she asked.

"I'm an insomniac."

"Really? And I used to think that all those late night parties you had were just down to you being a playboy."

"Well – that too. Each condition complements the other."

"I can imagine." Blanche sighed and took a long drink from her whiskey.

"Trouble in Paradise?" asked Jack.

She sighed again. 10cc's 'I'm Not in Love' was playing on the casino's sound system.

"You were smart never to get married," she said.

"I actually did – briefly."

"*What?*"

"It was 1985. I met this fabulous girl called Candy. She was the first person I really cared about since . . . anyway, just after we got married, we headed off to Las Vegas on honeymoon. I love to gamble, so we betted all my money in card games in the casinos, and I won. I won a fortune. We couldn't believe it. We thought we were millionaires. We booked into the presidential suite in the hotel and celebrated through the night. I went to buy a cigar in the early hours and walked down the street to a store. When I got back both she and the money were gone. Last time I saw either."

"Oh Jack! I am so sorry." She reached out and touched his arm.

"Well, you know what they say – lucky in cards, unlucky in love . . . but you've been successful in business and love."

"Have I?" questioned Blanche. "I often think that he doesn't understand me. And, you know, I often don't understand myself. I've a wonderful husband and three beautiful children. Pity about me – I guess I'm just a restless soul. But I hate making Troy unhappy."

"That's bullshit, Blanche! You forget – I knew Troy long before he met you. And he was never as happy as when he met you. When he met you, his life came together . . . So much so that I was insanely jealous . . . I often feel really ashamed that I made a move on you. You were brother's fiancée, and I had no right."

Blanche looked at him curiously. "So you just said those things at the time? You know, that you were in love with me etc etc. Because you were jealous?"

"I was jealous – and I really wanted to get out of Castleford and was frightened to do it on my own. I thought you were my ticket out."

"I see." Blanche looked straight ahead and then downed her drink. "I'll see you tomorrow, Jack." She got up off her stool.

"Blanche – are you okay?"

"Yeah – I'm just very glad I had the good sense to see through a charmer like you at the time and didn't destroy my life running off with you. See you in the morning, Jack."

Blanche crept into the bedroom, expecting Troy to be asleep, but she saw him sitting out on the balcony. She walked out to him.

"I'm sorry, Troy, for shouting at you and for not listening to what you want," she said, putting her hand on his shoulder.

"Did Niall really say that?" asked Troy.

"It doesn't matter."

"He did, didn't he? So, come on, tell me all about this plan of yours for turning Winterfield into a golf resort."

"No, seriously – forget about it."

"Start from the beginning – what kind of a hotel would it be?"

CHAPTER 69

Roger sat in the lounge in the lodge with Lauren.

"A *golf resort*?" shrieked Lauren.

"Yes," said Roger, tucking into the cake in front of him. "Down in the south of the farm. They are planning to build a huge five-star hotel and golf course."

"And when were your parents planning on telling me about all this?" demanded Lauren.

"I think tomorrow over Sunday dinner," said Roger.

"Don't take this the wrong way, kid, but your mother is a nut. What does she think this place is – Vegas?"

"They've already employed a big firm of architects in Dublin," said Roger.

Lauren sighed and sat thinking while she looked at her grandson.

"Okay, Roger – I'm going to box clever on this one. I'm not going to say one negative thing about it, as Blanche is expecting me too. What good will it do if I object? There will just be arguments and fights between me and Blanche and Troy. And there's no need for me to object, because she hasn't a chance of getting planning for this resort – not with Rosalind on the Council."

Troy was down at the stables with Carl, training him how to ride a horse that was mettlesome. Roger looked on.

"Can I have a go?" asked Roger.

"No, Roger, I've told you you're too young for this horse, now get back!" snapped Troy.

"But I want a go!" demanded Roger.

"Roger, will you stop being a pain and move out of the way!" said Carl.

One of the farm hands came into the stable yard.

"Troy – there's a problem with the Hereford herd – one of the cows looks very poorly."

"Okay – I'll head up. Come on, Carl!"

Troy headed over to his car, Carl close behind him. Roger followed them and went to get into the back.

"Roger, you're not coming. Go on home," said Troy.

"But I want to go!" said Roger.

"Roger. You'll be bored silly up there and wanting to go home as soon as we arrive. This is serious stuff, now head on home."

Troy and Carl drove off while Roger stood kicking a stone in frustration. Carl was now fourteen, three years older than Roger, and Roger was beginning to feel left out. Roger had always managed to get his father to do just what he wanted, but lately Carl seemed to be getting all the attention. Being that much older Carl was being invited along with his father while he got left behind. Roger took up another stone and fired it at a stable window, breaking it. He would have to think of a way of getting his father's attention and pushing Carl out of the way.

Blanche got a call on her mobile from Carl's school. She

was in a meeting with the architects in Dublin. They were working on the extensive plans for the golf resort which were going to be submitted to the council.

She drove straight to the school in Castleford where Carl was waiting in the headmaster's office with a black eye.

"What's all this about?" demanded Blanche as she anxiously looked at her son's bruised face.

"I'm afraid Carl has been fighting, Mrs Launcelot. But he refuses to say why."

"Carl – why were you fighting?" demanded Blanche.

Carl looked stubbornly and forlornly down at the floor.

"This is the second fight Carl has been in over the past two weeks, Mrs Launcelot. I think we have a problem."

Carl was interrogated all evening by Blanche and Troy, but he refused to give details and was sent to bed. Blanche went into the kitchen and started cleaning up. She massaged her temples. She was tired from all the planning for the resort and now she was very worried about Carl.

Roger came into the kitchen.

"Can I have some ice cream?" he said, opening the fridge.

"No, Roger, you've already had dessert."

Roger ignored her, took out the ice-cream tub and started to eat.

"Mum, I know something and I don't know whether to tell you," he said with a worried look.

"Of course you should tell me," said Blanche, closing the dishwasher.

"I know why Carl's been fighting." Roger looked up at her, all doe-eyed.

Blanche sat down beside him. "Well – go on," she urged.

"The other kid was hassling Gabrielle."

"Gabrielle? Gabrielle Ford? Rosalind's daughter?"

"That's the one," said Roger, licking the ice cream off the spoon. "This fella started calling Gabrielle's father an alcoholic and other things and next thing Carl jumps in and he's fighting him." He scooped up another spoon of ice cream.

"And was that the same as the other fight he was in?" asked Blanche.

Roger nodded.

Troy was singing 'You've Been Talking In Your Sleep' as Blanche walked into the bedroom.

"As long as you aren't singing in your sleep, I don't care!" said Blanche, pulling a face at Troy's bad singing. "Troy, I've got to the bottom of the problem. Carl is fighting to protect the honour of Rosalind's daughter. Instead of concentrating on his exams and enjoying life with his friends, he's fighting over that silly girl."

"Where did you find that out?"

"It doesn't matter. But I know what I'm going to do about it. Carl is leaving that school next week and I'm enrolling him in a private school in Dublin where he can concentrate on his studies and get away from bad influences like Gabrielle Ford!"

CHAPTER 70

Rosalind could hear a lot of commotion outside her office in the Council building in Castleford.

It was early 1996 and the spring sunshine was melting away the winter.

One of her colleagues popped his head into her office. "The submission for the Launcelot Hotel and Golf Resort has come in. Seemingly they are spectacular. Are you coming down for a goo?"

Rosalind yawned. "I might as well take a look at this pipedream." She stood up and followed him out. There was a Council meeting on Friday and Rosalind was going to shoot down the planning for it straight away. This was one baby that was never even going to get off the ground, thought Rosalind happily.

At the Council meeting Rosalind spent fifteen minutes listing the reasons why the hotel and golf resort should not even be considered for planning.

"And so, ladies and gentlemen, I request the immediate turning down of this insane planning submission for this tacky Disneyland," Rosalind said, looking confidently at her fellow councillors.

"I don't think it's as easy as that, Rosalind," said John Fallon, the Council head. "This development would bring millions into the town in investment, jobs, tourism. I think we can't dismiss it so easily. We need to have a proper assessment of it. And we need to get the town's opinion as well as our own."

Rosalind looked around the table irritably as the rest of the councillors agreed with him.

Blanche was in her office at home one evening when Amelia walked in holding up a paper with a lot of scribbled signatures on it.

"This is a petition that I've got all the children at school to sign. It's an objection to your hotel and I'm going to post it into the Council."

"What?" Blanche said. "Don't be so ridiculous, Amelia, and hand that to me."

"No. It's a democratic mandate from my school objecting to your plan to ruin our town with your rotten hotel."

"Amelia, you are messing with things that you do not understand. Now, you hand me those papers immediately!" Blanche's voice was raised in anger.

"No! There are a hundred signatures here and the council is going to get them!"

With that, Amelia turned and walked defiantly from the room.

Carl had by now completely settled into his new school in Dublin. At the beginning there was much shouting and sulks and silent treatment. But slowly he stopped complaining. He quickly made friends in the new school and suddenly he was on the soccer and the rugby teams. The commute to Dublin meant he wasn't home till much later and he had a lot more homework to do. But he didn't seem to mind. He made the journey into Dublin and back most days with Blanche as she went to work or on the bus.

"Eh – Mum, I was just wondering – this weekend – my friend Jake at school has invited some of the guys down to his family's holiday home in Kinsale. Is it alright if I go?"

Blanche smiled. "Of course it is!"

He nodded and smiled back and walked out.

She sat down happily. The move to the private school had been a wonderful move for Carl. He was totally wrapped up in his new school and friends and it was a great environment for him to be in. She knew what was best for her children. And if they listened to her, they would avoid the mistakes and hard knocks she had endured while she learned the hard way.

That Friday evening, Gabrielle sat expectantly on the fence by the beach where she had arranged to meet Carl. Time passed slowly and she kept looking at her watch as there was no sign of him. Finally, she got down and slowly walked home. She entered the house and walked into the kitchen where Rosalind was baking.

"Hi, darling," said Rosalind as she put the finishing touches to the cake. She looked up and saw Gabrielle's red face and teary eyes. "Darling! What's wrong?"

Rosalind came quickly to her daughter and put her arms around her. Gabrielle started to cry softly.

"It's Carl – I had arranged to meet him this evening, and he didn't show up."

"Oh darling!" Rosalind hugged her tightly.

"I've hardly seen him over the past few weeks, and we were so close. He hated going to that new school, and I kept telling him to try his best there. And now he's off with his posh new friends and has forgotten all about me."

Rosalind sighed loudly. "Well, he's a Launcelot, isn't he? They are all fine and well until something comes along and distracts them, and then off they go without so much as a backward glance. Life has taught me the hard way about them. And he's her son on top of it all. He didn't lick it off the stones. She takes what she wants, without giving thought to anybody else, and it sounds like her son is just the same . . . Now, I want you to forget about him, Gabrielle. You're the brightest girl in the school, and the prettiest. You're going to have a wonderful life, without the likes of Carl Launcelot dragging you down."

CHAPTER 71

The proposed resort was a very emotive issue in Castleford over the next several months. Despite Rosalind's best efforts, she was unable to dismiss the application as there seemed to be as many people in favour of it as were against it. Finally a town meeting was called in the Town Hall in the run-up to Christmas 1996, at which the Launcelots could explain the reasons why the resort would be good for the town and the opposition could give their reasons why it wouldn't. The opposition was to be led by Rosalind.

As Troy pulled up outside the Town Hall the evening of the meeting, Blanche felt very nervous.

"Give me a meeting with hardnosed businessmen any day rather than try to talk to all these locals," she said, pulling frantically on her cigarette.

"They won't bite you!" smiled Troy, reaching over and squeezing her hand.

"That's easy for you to say. You're one of them. I've always been an outsider."

"And aren't I here with you every step of the way?"

Inside, the hall was packed and on the stage were two

tables. One was occupied by Blanche, Troy and their team of architects and some local politicians who supported them. On the other table were a coterie of different interest groups led by Rosalind.

The evening passed in lively debate. Finally Rosalind gave her speech. She spoke for a full half an hour.

"And so, ladies and gentlemen, to conclude. This monstrosity that is being proposed would ruin our town forever. We would suffer from pollution, and destruction of the natural beauty of the area. We would have traffic chaos. And for what? Just so one family can get richer. Thank you." Rosalind sat down.

"Mrs Launcelot, would you care to speak?" the meeting's scrutineer said.

Blanche steadied herself and stood up. She looked out at the sea of faces in the hall, all looking at her with the same curious expression as when she had arrived in the town all those years ago.

"Rosalind is right. This development would change Castleford forever," began Blanche. "She's right as well about there being a lot more traffic and the place being flooded with tourists. But, how many of your sons and daughters had to emigrate during the eighties to get jobs? How many of your businesses and jobs were lost in the past? If you don't stay up, you get left behind. And this resort will put Castleford on the map. It will provide long-term jobs for up to 400 local people, not to mention the many jobs during construction. The knock-on effect for all local businesses with the amount of money the tourists bring –"

"Money!" Rosalind suddenly shouted as she jumped to her feet. "Money, money, money – that's all you care about. You're not from here. You don't care about here. All you care about is making more money, and not for the people who live in this town but for yourself!"

"I'm trying to create a huge profitable business here that will mean everyone will benefit, you stupid woman!"

"Oh, your concern is so touching. You're a blow-in, never had any time for us in Castleford. Always thought you were too good for the place."

"That's a lie!"

"Is it?" Rosalind smiled at her nastily. "Why then did you take your son out of the local school and put him into some rich kids' private school in Dublin?"

"I'm warning you, Rosalind, do not get personal!" Blanche's voice rose and her eyes glinted dangerously.

Rosalind was smiling triumphantly. "Answer the question, Mrs Launcelot. Why did you take your son out of the school here? I'll tell you why – because you looked down on the school, and you didn't think it was good enough for your precious son. And you then expect us to think you care a damn about Castleford?"

"That's not true!" Blanche shouted.

"Well, tell us then. Why did you take him out of school?" Rosalind sneered at her.

"To get him away from your daughter!" Blanche snapped over at her.

The hall erupted in noise and protest.

Rosalind's mouth dropped open, but before she could think of anything to say, the scrutineer stood up quickly.

"Please, everybody, be quiet! I think we've gone off the issue here. Now we've heard everyone speak and so we are going to put it to a vote. How many people are against this development? Please raise your hands."

A sprinkling of hands shot up around the hall.

"And those who are in favour?" asked the scrutineer.

The huge majority raised their hands.

"Come on, let's get out of here," said Blanche to Troy and they made their way through the congratulating crowd and out to the car.

"How fucking dare you!" shouted Rosalind, marching over to their car. "You basically called my daughter a tramp in front of the whole town."

Blanche stood her ground. "You shouldn't have got personal with me, bringing Carl into the equation!"

"I've had enough of you!" shouted Rosalind and suddenly her hand shot out and she grabbed Blanche's hair, pulling her to the ground, breaking her pearl necklace and causing all the beads to bounce down the road.

Troy was over in an instant and grabbed Rosalind, shouting, "Let go of her!"

Rosalind released Blanche.

Blanche got up and smoothed back her hair and then laughed a cold laugh.

"I guess that proves when you lie down with a dog like you have, you get covered in fleas."

"Let me go!" Rosalind demanded of Troy.

He did as she asked and Rosalind stormed off.

"You okay?" asked Troy, putting his arm around his wife.

"I'm fine," nodded Blanche, and she got into the car and Troy drove them away.

It was only when they got out of the town onto the coast road that Blanche burst into tears.

CHAPTER 72

Planning permission was granted for the new Winterfield Hotel & Golf Resort in January 1997. Within six months the place was full of diggers and JCBs clearing the area for construction work to commence.

Rosalind drove frantically to the lodge one morning.

"Lauren!" she called loudly, entering the house.

"In here, Rosalind," Lauren called from the drawing room.

Rosalind raced in.

"What's the matter, honey?" asked Lauren, seeing Rosalind's stressed and tearstained face.

Rosalind threw the letter she was holding at Lauren. "Read that! Oh, Lauren, I don't know what to do! The bank is foreclosing on the farm! I'm going to lose the farm!" She paced up and down frantically.

Lauren quickly read through the letter. "Oh Rosalind! How did it come to this?"

"It's all Seán's fault. He ran the place into the ground and drank the place dry! He kept re-mortgaging the land!"

"And what does he say about this?"

"I can't get hold of him. Oh, Lauren – what will I do?" Rosalind was shaking.

Lauren got up and put her hands on Rosalind's shoulders, steadying her.

"Just you relax. We'll lend you the money to keep them away."

"Oh Lauren! Could you?"

"Of course we will." said Lauren, hugging her.

"So, I've told her we'll lend her the money," explained Lauren, at lunch the next day in Winterfield. "I mean – how long have the Dawsons and Launcelots known each other? We can't let them lose their farm!" Lauren spoke as if it was a fait accompli.

Blanche looked over at Troy and raised an eyebrow.

"I'm sorry, Lauren, but we can't lend Rosalind that money," Blanche eventually said.

"I beg your pardon?" Lauren looked at Blanche incredulously.

"It's out of the question. We've far too much going on to be giving money away to neighbours who we never see."

"I see this particular neighbour all the time! And we wouldn't be giving it away, we're lending it to Rosalind."

"Lending! Ha!" dismissed Blanche. "We'd never see that money again, Seán Ford would have it drunk down his gob and the farm would only be repossessed again this time next year anyway, and we'd have lost our money into the bargain."

"No, Rosalind is going to appoint a farm manager to pull the farm out of this," explained Lauren.

"She's never going to pull the farm out of that situation," said Troy. "They owe too much and besides Seán is the problem – he won't let anyone else on to that farm."

"Speaks the expert! Anyway, I'm afraid your opinion doesn't matter – I've told Rosalind we'll give her the money, so that's an end to it."

"Well, I'm afraid that's just not possible, Lauren," Blanche said.

"I think you're forgetting who you're talking to. This is my money we're talking about, and I can do what I want with it."

"No, you can't. It's the company money, and I veto it being thrown away on lost causes . . . and, besides, I don't want Rosalind Ford to have the money. Not after the way she's acted to me over the years . . . and especially after our last altercation."

Lauren looked at her disdainfully. "I heard about your catfight. Fighting on the street like trash. It's hardly ladylike and you sullied our good name."

"Mother! Rosalind attacked Blanche! I was there and saw it all," Troy insisted.

"Well, if you go around upsetting people all the time, then what can you expect?" said Lauren.

Blanche threw her eyes up to heaven and raised her voice. "No matter what – you're never going to believe that it wasn't my fault, are you? It's always my fault! If Rosalind had spent more time looking after her business instead of trying to stop mine, then she might not be losing her farm next week!"

"You know we were in a similar situation ourselves a few years ago," said Lauren.

"Yes, and we worked every hour of the day to get out of it. We didn't go begging to neighbours."

"Niall would insist we help the Dawsons!" Lauren insisted.

"No, he wouldn't, because he wasn't a stupid sentimentalist like you. He would have insisted we take care of our own business first. Now – I'm sorry. I've a hotel to build." She got up and walked out.

Lauren looked out after her. "What kind of a woman did you marry?"

Troy reached over and squeezed his mother's arm. "You can't blame her. Rosalind attacked her physically. She's lucky the Guards weren't called. There's too much bad blood under the bridge at this stage to get involved with Rosalind financially . . . besides, Rosalind can keep the house, can't she? It's only the land she's losing."

Blanche studied a map of the Dawson farm. It was directly adjacent to the new hotel and golf course. Its acquisition would greatly enhance the resort by expanding the golf course into it. And since it was being repossessed, it would be going at a cheap price. When the land went for auction the following week, Blanche bought the land.

Lauren was now officially not speaking to Blanche since she had bought the Dawson farm, describing it as an act of high treason. Troy was very uncomfortable with the purchase as well, regardless of the fact that she pointed out the farm was lost anyway to Rosalind, so they might as well have it rather than anybody else.

It was the beginning of the Easter holidays 1998 and Blanche had been for a meeting with the foreman on site to offer the workers double time to work through the holidays. She switched on the news and it was all about the Good Friday agreement.

There was a lot of noise in the house. Carl had four of his friends staying over for the Easter weekend.

Carl suddenly came bounding into her office.

"We're all heading down town for a while. Roger's insisting on coming too."

"Okay, enjoy!" smiled Blanche.

Carl was now sixteen, and Roger had just started at the same school, and was anxious to keep up with his brother.

Gabrielle had got a part-time job working in a café in Castleford. Since the farm was lost, everyone at the Dawsons' had been very upset. Her grandmother had just gone very quiet, repeating that she was glad her husband hadn't been there to see the farm, one of the county's finest, gone. Rosalind had been stuffing herself with cakes, and when Seán called over there had been a screaming match between the two. Gabrielle had to eventually separate them and demand they shut up.

After that, Gabrielle had called around to her father's house a couple of times, and found him quiet and uncommunicative.

As she looked out the window of the café, she suddenly saw Carl Launcelot walking down the street with a group of his friends and Roger.

"Oh no!" she said to herself as she watched them come to the café and sit at one of the tables out on the pavement in the evening sunshine. There was nobody there to serve them but her. She steadied herself, took her notebook and pen and went out to them.

"Yes – what can I get you?" asked Gabrielle in a businesslike fashion.

"Gabrielle!" exclaimed Carl in surprise. "What are you doing here?"

"Working – what does it look like?" she snapped.

A snigger went around the table.

"What do you want?" she asked again.

"Em – just a Coke for me," said Carl.

She took all their orders, and a couple of them asked for beers.

"Can I see your ID?"

"Just serve them!" said Roger disdainfully.

"Unless you can prove you're over eighteen, no alcohol," said Gabrielle sharply.

"Cokes are just fine for everyone," said Carl, going red.

"Ignore her," said Roger. "She's just trying to get on a power trip, because her family is a failure."

Gabrielle stared at Roger in anger.

"Roger! Shut your fucking mouth!" shouted Carl.

Gabrielle turned on Carl. "I don't need you to defend me, so you can shut your mouth as well!"

"Gabrielle – don't fall out with me over what he said!"

"I'm not falling out with you over what your little shit of a brother said. I'm falling out with you because you're an arrogant bastard from an arrogant family, who's taken away what we love so much!" Tears stung her eyes.

"The farm? That was just business, Gabrielle. If we didn't buy it somebody else would!"

"Spoken like your mother. She must be very proud of you! What's that farm to you? Just another opportunity to make more money!" She was shouting now.

The owner of the café came out and said, "Gabrielle – I think you'd better go home."

"Gabrielle! Calm down – I've never seen you like this before," pleaded Carl.

"And you never will again," she said. "Because I never want to see you again, Carl Launcelot." She took off her apron, threw it on the table and walked quickly down the street.

"Gabrielle! Come back and talk to me!" Carl pleaded.

"Oh, let her go!" said Roger, sitting back, looking bored. He turned to the others and spoke loudly enough for Gabrielle to still hear. "She can't help it – her father is a drunk and her mother a fat cow."

"Roger – shut the fuck up!" Carl shouted as he watched Gabrielle storm off into the distance.

PART 6

CHAPTER 73

1999–2003

The building of the Winterfield Hotel and Golf Resort was fraught with difficulties. It didn't go to schedule, and there were constant interferences from the Council, courtesy of Rosalind, that held up progress. Blanche fired the first construction company for not meeting schedules. She then fired the second one. Eventually, she decided it made sense to buy a small construction firm and do the building themselves. It would be much more economical. Troy got involved on the construction side and seemed to enjoy that.

Meanwhile, The Launcelot Corporation was riding the back of the Celtic Tiger very well and making good profits. Their real estate value was multiplying as the Dublin and London property market made great gains. They opened a new hotel in Galway and another one in Killarney. And when Blanche was approached to become a main investor in one of the giant new shopping centres being built around Dublin, she jumped at the chance. The company was like a juggernaut buying up everything from shops in Grafton Street to apartments along the Liffey. As soon as something was bought, it had jumped in value the following week.

The three children were now in school in Dublin. Carl had an eager interest in the business and began to do business studies in UCD when he completed the Leaving Cert in 2000. Amelia had no interest in the business, and if anything was very anti the business. She was captain of the debating team at school and hugely interested in world affairs and human rights. Roger, his teachers insisted, was the brightest boy in the class, but his grades managed to be consistently at the bottom. Blanche and Troy tried everything with him to improve his grades, but finally had to agree that he just wasn't academic. He tried his best, but he couldn't improve his results, they accepted. He said he didn't want to go to university anyway but go straight into the business, and Blanche was delighted that at least he knew what he wanted to do in life, unlike Amelia.

They still had some problems with Roger. First of all there were the exam papers that came into his possession from the headmaster's office. After a school investigation, Roger's story that they were planted in his schoolbag was accepted. Then there was the other situation where Blanche and Troy were summoned into the school to be told that Roger had been accused of bullying another boy. Finally, it was agreed that Roger hadn't been the main culprit but had just been hanging around with the wrong crowd. One of his best friends was expelled for smoking and another for drinking. And even though there was a smell of both nicotine and drink off Roger, the headmaster could not pinpoint anything on him directly. And the headmaster soon realised that, unless you had direct evidence, it was best not to summon the busy Blanche Launcelot into the school. She didn't suffer fools gladly and had a habit of turning situations around that made the school look culpable.

Rosalind's mother passed away not long after they lost the farm. It was just Rosalind and Gabrielle at home now. Rosalind rarely saw Seán any more; she had no reason to. Gabrielle made sure to see him at least once a week. Gabrielle worked exceptionally hard for her Leaving Cert, and came out with one of the best results in the country. She had applied to do medicine, and started her degree in the autumn of 2000. Lauren was delighted for her.

Lauren continued to live at the lodge at Winterfield. She cut a striking and glamorous figure for a woman in her seventies. And Troy and Rosalind were always there for her. But they avoided each other, their once-close friendship a thing of the past. They had to keep distant now after what happened with Blanche.

The hotel and golf resort were due to open in 2003 and Lauren had arranged for Gabrielle to get a job on reception for the summer. Lauren was delighted that Gabrielle had matured into a beautiful and confident young woman who would make an excellent doctor on graduation.

Lauren remained on civil but cool terms with Blanche.

In spite of herself, and although she would never show it, she was impressed with how Blanche had given a name to the family that was said in the same breath as Smurfit and O'Reilly.

Blanche was finding it hard to keep an eye on all the components of the company and so had set up a headquarters for the business in a glass-towering headquarters in the IFSC. Her office was on the top floor, offering majestic views across the city.

CHAPTER 74

2003

It was the day of the opening of the Hotel and Golf Resort at Winterfield, and Blanche was in her office conducting a series of meetings with department heads. She wanted to leave early so she could get herself ready for the big opening that night. She had hired a Public Relations firm to run the opening of Winterfield Hotel that night and everybody who was anybody would be there. She was flying in some international stars to sing at the event. She was very nervous. It had been such a long process to get finished, and finally she was there.

The door of her office opened and in walked Troy.

"Oh, sorry!" he said, seeing she was with somebody.

"No, you're alright, Troy, come on in. I think we're finished here, aren't we?" she said to the executive on the other side of the desk.

"I think we are – good luck with tonight!" He smiled at her and exited.

Troy came over to her, smiling and waving a copy of a magazine. There was a photo of Blanche on the front cover under the headline *'Blanche Launcelot Launches World Class Resort'*.

Blanche took the magazine and leafed through the interview.

"It's all good, charting a meteoric rise," smiled Troy.

She looked at the front cover. She felt exposed and uncomfortable. It was strange – as a former model, she should be used to seeing herself in print. But she didn't like people knowing that much about her.

"It took me ages to get over here. There's a massive demonstration against the Iraq war and all the traffic was diverted," said Troy.

"We better make a move shortly then – we don't want any delays in getting back to Winterfield," said Blanche.

He smiled down at her. At forty-three, she still looked amazing, and after twenty-two years of marriage, he was as attracted to her as ever.

He sat on her desk, bent down and started to kiss her, then his hand went to the back of her dress and started to pull down the zip.

"Troy!" She objected with a laugh. "We don't have time for that!"

"We'll make the time."

"And my secretary is just outside the door!"

"So?" He continued to kiss her and she kissed him back, pulling him towards her.

The phone rang on her desk. She reached for it, while continuing to kiss Troy.

She broke away from her husband. "Yes, Stella?"

"Mrs Launcelot, I've a Sergeant Collins on the phone and he says it's fairly urgent."

"Who? Oh, okay, put him on." She sat forward while Troy continued to kiss her neck.

"Mrs Launcelot?" said the Sergeant.

"Yes?"

"I'm sorry to bother you, but I have a young woman in custody claiming to be your daughter."

"My daughter? I don't think so," she said, allowing Troy's kisses to seduce her, sure that it was a case of mistaken identity.

"She was arrested today at the demonstration."

Blanche sat forward abruptly and pushed Troy away. "A demonstration?"

"I'm afraid so."

"Okay, tell me where she is and I'll come on down." She scribbled down the details.

"Amelia's in jail" asked Troy incredulously.

"Yes. She's really done it this time! And today of all days! Come on!" She grabbed her handbag and coat and they left. "I'm really going to kill her this time!"

CHAPTER 75

"Now Mrs Launcelot!" said the hairdresser, smiling. "You know, you really needed a haircut badly."

"Really?" said Lauren, giving the girl a withering look. "Well, that's why I came to you – you cut it badly last time!"

Lauren got up and paid and walked out onto the busy Grafton Street. She walked up to Shanahans where she was due to meet Roger for lunch.

"Hi Gran," said Roger when she arrived into the dining room, getting up and kissing her cheek. "You look nice."

"Thanks, I've just been to the beautician's and the hairdresser's. Thought I better make a bit of an effort for this big opening tonight."

Lauren and Roger were due to drive back together to Winterfield. Roger had just come from his final Leaving Cert exam.

"And how did the exam go?" she enquired.

"Accountancy was never really my strong point," said Roger, glancing through the menu.

"Were any of them?" questioned Lauren with a smirk.

Roger shrugged. "What's the point in going to college? I know what I want to do. I'm going straight in to work in the business."

Lauren observed the eighteen-year-old boy. He was the spit of his mother, with the same black hair, green eyes and chiselled face. He looked nothing like Carl, who with his fair looks continued to look more like Troy. She would have thought she would have been more naturally drawn to Carl, as he looked so much like her side of the family. But even though Carl was nice and honest and you always knew where you were with him, she couldn't help but have Roger as her favourite.

"Steak, please, rare." Roger smiled up at the waiter.

"And mine will be well done," commanded Lauren, then turned her attention back to her grandson. "So – any news?"

Roger looked sheepish and his face went red as he studied the tablecloth in front of him.

"Roger?" Lauren pushed.

"I shouldn't really say." Roger looked embarrassed. "But I guess you'll find out sooner or later. Dad just rang me and Amelia has been arrested."

"*What?*"

"She was on that anti-war demonstration and seemingly she assaulted a policeman."

"Ohhh!" Lauren gasped in horror. "The hooligan! I just can't fathom her."

"I don't think anyone can. There was a huge big row between her and Mum the other day. Again. She started accusing Mum of being greedy, expanding the business so much. And Mum said that she was doing it all for us and Amelia shouted back that she didn't want anything of it."

"She's a selfish girl, that one."

"And then Amelia said that when it comes to her turn

to inherit anything she will just give it all away to charity, and Mum said that the company would collapse if she did that, and Amelia said she would be delighted to see The Launcelot Corporation collapse and that corporations were what had half the world living in poverty."

"Oh, don't tell me any more about that silly girl and her daft ideas," said Lauren. "Well, I'll tell you one thing – she's not getting a penny from me when I'm gone, since she has no respect for money. And she won't get one bit of my half share of the company!"

Roger nodded as the steaks arrived and then he looked up and said with a smile, "I was always your favourite – wasn't I, Gran?"

"Really Amelia – of all days! With the opening of the resort tonight!" Blanche was furious as she sped down the new motorway to Castleford from Dublin.

"I really don't care!" Amelia spoke unrepentantly. "I think an illegal war in Iraq is just a little bit more important than the opening of a new playground for the rich and famous, don't you?"

"You might as well be talking to the wall, Blanche," sighed Troy.

"Well, of course I wouldn't expect any support from you, Dad!" snapped Amelia.

Troy turned around angrily. "You slapped a Guard across the face. It's inexcusable!"

"He was manhandling my friend. I had to go to his defence."

Blanche glanced at her daughter in the rear-view mirror. "Your friend being Jason, of course?"

"Yes – Jason was been pushed by the Guard."

"Easily known he'd be tied up in this," said Blanche.

"Not that it takes much encouragement to get Amelia going," added Troy.

Carl drove himself and his girlfriend Vicky to the opening. Roger sat in the back seat.

"I can't wait to see all the celebrities tonight," said Vicky. "Is it true Bono is going to be here?"

Carl shrugged. "He's invited anyway. The PR department have been working round the clock making sure the guest list is perfect."

"If he is there, don't embarrass us by asking for his autograph, Vicky," warned Roger.

"As if!" tutted Vicky.

Roger looked at Vicky. Carl had been going out with her for a few months. She was in his class at UCD. Her father was a respected judge. Blanche and Troy loved her. She was very pretty and very nice, unassuming and easygoing. They made such a lovely couple, everyone said. Yawn, thought Roger.

They approached the huge gateway into the resort and a fleet of expensive cars were queuing to go in, their invitations being checked by security at the gateway.

"Hi, Carl, go on through," smiled the security man as he waved them on.

They drove along the road that ran through the lush golf course which seemed to stretch for miles in either direction.

And then the hotel came into view. A palatial neo-Georgian white building, the sea in the background. A series of spotlights were focused on the hotel, changing colours every few seconds. Two helicopters were circling the building.

"Well, she did it, the old girl," said Roger as they were directed to a parking spot by a valet.

"After much blood, sweat and tears," added Carl, as they got out of the car.

It was nearly eight in the evening, and the event was black tie. Guests were all making their way in, dressed in tuxedos and gowns.

Vicky held Carl's hand as they walked across the huge courtyard and up the steps into the hotel.

"Champagne, sir, madam?" They were greeted with silver trays of champagne glasses.

The inside of the marble lobby was filled with guests chatting while they took in the grandeur of the building. To the left was a giant white marble staircase. Above them hung a spectacular chandelier from the thirty-foot-high ceiling. There were glass doors that led to restaurants and lounge bars, and at the back of the lobby were a series of French windows that led out to manicured lawns that overlooked the sea.

"Is that *that* girl?" Roger asked, pointing over to one of the receptionists. "What's her name? Gabrielle?"

Carl followed Roger's pointing finger. "Yeah – it is too. Haven't seen her in years. Come on, let's go and say hello."

Roger and Vicky followed Carl over to Gabrielle.

"Hello, stranger – remember me?" said Carl as he approached her.

Gabrielle looked up with a start. "Yes, hi, Carl."

"Remember Roger?"

"Hmmm – how could I forget?"

"And this is Vicky. What are you doing here? I heard you'd gone off to do great things at university?"

"Your grandmother sorted me out with a job here for the summer – it's handy because it's so near home."

"Well, let's sit down and have a drink later, okay?" said Carl.

"Well, I'm on duty all night. But I'll see you later," nodded Gabrielle.

Blanche stepped back from the full-length mirror in their bedroom and gave herself the once-over. She was dressed in a slinky black dress that flowed to the floor, leaving her arms and back exposed. Her shoulder-length hair gleamed and she had a light tan, while the diamonds on her ears and fingers sparkled.

"You look marvellous, darling," said Harriet.

"I feel I'm going to be scrutinised," said Blanche. "A lot of people there would like to see tonight be a big disaster. There was a lot of opposition to this resort."

"Nonsense – they should put a statue of you up in that miserable town. You've put this backwater on the map."

"Once I get tonight out of the way, I'm going to give full attention to my children. Roger has failed the Leaving Cert, that's a given – he didn't even try! And as for Amelia and being arrested! She getting serious with this boyfriend called Jason, who will only lead her into bad ways. I'm going to put a stop to it."

Harriet burst out laughing.

"What's so funny?" demanded Blanche.

"Oh Blanche – you've become me! Going on about unsuitable boyfriends and failing exams! And take it from me, you can't interfere in their lives, you have to let them make their own mistakes."

Carl spotted Gabrielle and went over to talk to her, leaving Roger and Vicky together.

"Oh there's that singer, I love her!" declared Vicky as she spotted a star nearby.

"You're so easily impressed," dismissed Roger. "You'd

473

want to lose that. Mum hates people who are easily impressed."

Vicky looked at Roger irritably. "I'm not going out with your mother, Roger – it's Carl I'm seeing."

"Yeah, that's lasted longer than I thought."

"And what's that supposed to mean?" snapped Vicky.

"Nothing," he smirked at her and they stood in silence for a while. "All I'm saying is I hope Carl appreciates you." He paused, gazing at her. "Would you like to go for a walk on the beach?"

"Why would I want to do that?" she said, studying him.

"Carl would never find out." He smiled at her and touched her arm.

She suddenly burst out laughing. "Oh Roger! Are you coming on to me? Oh, Roger, I don't date Leaving Cert students!" She saw two young girls looking over at Roger and whispering to each other. "Why don't you try those two over there – I think they might be more your scene."

His light hold of her arm became a tight grip.

"Roger!" she objected.

Carl arrived back at that moment and Roger quickly released Vicky's arm.

"Anyway – I'd better find Mum and Dad!" Roger smiled at them and disappeared into the crowd.

Vicky looked after him. "Carl – your brother –" she began, her voice filled with concern.

"Yeah?"

She studied Carl's happy face. "Your brother is quite a guy."

Carl laughed. "Isn't he?"

Blanche made her way through the crowd in the hotel holding Troy's hand. She was being swamped with praise and admiration.

474

"You know, this is going to take over from the K Club, it's going to be up there with Sandy Lane as a first-class resort," a captain of industry assured her.

"Thank you," smiled Blanche, feeling the overwhelming satisfaction of having her dream become a reality.

Then Blanche came face to face with Amelia, her slender body lithe in an emerald dress, her brown hair falling loosely around her shoulders. She stood beside her boyfriend Jason whose hair was longish, to his shoulders.

"Jason!" Blanche managed to smile at him. "How nice to see you. Although I don't remember you being on the guest list."

"He's my guest. If you wanted me here, then you must also want Jason."

"Well, of course Jason is welcome. I just didn't think he would be comfortable here on such an extravagant night."

"I'm here for Amelia. We won't be staying that long," Jason said unsmilingly.

"Well, have a few drinks and you never know – you might even enjoy yourself! See you later." Blanche winked at him and moved on.

"Mum – you look great," said Roger, kissing her cheek.

"Thank you, darling." Blanche kissed him back.

"Em – don't know if I should tell you this – heck – I'll tell you anyway. Rosalind Ford's daughter is working out on reception – she's been employed for the summer."

Blanche's face clouded over. "How did that happen?"

"Lauren was behind it, seemingly."

Blanche sighed. "I wish she'd stop interfering. I don't want anything to do with that family."

"Carl's already arranged to have a drink with her later."

Blanche tutted. "Okay, thanks Roger."

A manager from the hotel came up to her. "Mrs

Launcelot, I'm afraid there's a bit of a problem down at the main gate. There's a woman who insists on seeing you, she says she's a friend. Darla O'Brien?"

Blanche stood still and it was as if the loud noise of people talking and music around her faded away.

"Mrs Launcelot?" pushed the manager.

"Get security to bring her up to my office."

"Yes Mrs Launcelot."

"Oh and Jim, there's a Gabrielle Ford working on reception. I don't want her working here. Can you get rid of her?"

"Yes, Mrs Launcelot. I'll give her her cards after tonight."

"No, Jim, get rid of her straight away."

Blanche was in her office on the second floor of the hotel. She stood smoking at the open window, looking out at the sea under the darkening sky.

There was a knock and a security man opened the door. She could hear somebody enter the office and the door close. She steadied herself and then turned around to see Darla standing there. She got a shock. The once-beautiful model was now prematurely aged with grey-blonde hair and lined skin.

"Hello, Blanche," said Darla, her voice now throaty from a million cigarettes.

"Long time no see," said Blanche.

"I never thought I'd see you again. And there you suddenly were on the front of that magazine in the newsagent's. I just had to come and see you."

"I'm touched – now what can I do for you?"

"No beating around the bush then – eh? I thought it would be obvious. I just want a small share of your good fortune."

"How much?"

"Well, how much is your reputation worth? You tell me. I could blast away your reputation in a second. What would all these society people think if they knew about your involvement in a terrorist organisation?"

Blanche laughed loudly. "I had no involvement in a terrorist organisation. You were the one involved with that shower, as I remember."

"Well, you did take part in a kidnap attempt on a British diplomat, didn't you?"

"I think you'll find that there was no diplomat kidnapped and no record of an attempted kidnap."

Blanche crossed over to a safe, opened it, took out a wad of money and handed it to Darla.

"This isn't blackmail, Darla. I think that would be giving you too much credit. It's charity. Don't spend it all at once. And if you feel the need to talk to people about my past, you'll find I'm a very bad enemy, not that anyone will believe you anyway. I'm not a frightened young girl any more."

Darla stuffed the money into her handbag and looked embarrassed.

Blanche nodded and said, "I think we're through here." She crossed over to the door, opened it and said to the security man waiting outside, "Can you escort this lady off the premises?"

"Goodbye, Blanche," said Darla as she exited.

"Goodbye. And don't ever come near me again."

Gabrielle grabbed her coat and handbag and walked quickly through the foyer to the exit.

"Hey, Gabrielle!" called Carl, catching up with her. "Are you on your break? Let's grab a drink and have that catch-up."

"No, I'm not on my break. I've been fired," snapped Gabrielle.

"What? But why?"

"No explanation given."

"There must be a mistake – come on, I'll sort it out."

"No! I was insane to come and work here anyway. Too much bad blood. Too much water under the bridge. I'll see you, Carl."

"Wait! Gabrielle!" He went to go after her, but suddenly Vicky arrived and distracted him.

Gabrielle continued down the grand steps of the hotel and walked across the forecourt that was filled with expensive cars. She stopped and turned around. Through the glass doors she could see all the people in their finery dancing and enjoying themselves to the music. She saw Carl put his arm around Vicky and they kissed. She saw Roger laughing with two girls. She saw Blanche descend the grand marble staircase and join Troy and kiss him. She saw a dishevelled middle-aged blonde woman, clutching a handbag, being escorted to a battered old car by a security man and told to leave immediately.

"Well, at least you're not being escorted off the premises," Gabrielle said to herself.

As she looked at them all, she raised her eyes to heaven. Then with a sigh she got into a waiting taxi.

Gabrielle entered the local nightclub in Castleford and looked around for her friends. She spotted them at a table and waved over to them as she made her way through the crowd.

"Well? What's it like?" demanded her friends as she sat down with them.

"The hotel is spectacular," shrugged Gabrielle. "Everything you can imagine and more."

"What are you doing back so early? I thought you were working the night?" said her friend David.

She shrugged again. "I got my marching orders. No reason given. I guess the Launcelots are everything my mother said they were."

"What are you going to work at for the summer now?" asked David.

"A friend will get me a job in Dublin, working in a pharmacy. I only took the damned hotel job so I would be near Mum for the summer. Because, after my final year in med school, I am out of here and I'm not coming back."

"Don't say that, Gabrielle," said David.

"I'm serious, David. I've had it with this town and everyone in it. No matter what I do in life I will always just be Seán Ford's daughter in this town, with all the stigma attached to that. I'm getting far away from here – as far away as possible."

CHAPTER 76

2004

Roger loved working at the Launcelot Corporation. He spent the first few months just spending time in each department to give him an overview of the company. It was strange because he was starting at the same time as Carl was. The difference was Roger didn't even have a Leaving Cert, whereas Carl not only had a degree in Commerce but a Master's in Business Management. So, Carl was immediately at an advantage due to his age and education.

Roger threw himself into his social life and was out partying every night with his work colleagues. He would often arrive in late dying of a hangover. All the company thought he was great *craic* and warmed to him, unless he did his boss's son routine.

Carl liked to keep work and social life separate, sticking with his university crowd for socialising. His relationship with Vicky came to an end when she moved to Paris. And then he started to see a girl called Susan. Roger thought Susan was a Vicky clone and he often called her Vicky, to her great annoyance. And yes, she was pretty and bright and sociable, and came from the right background, and

Blanche loved her. Roger loathed her. He often wondered what Carl was doing getting into these deep meaningful relationships when he could be out having a great time like him. The Launcelot name meant he got into any party or gig he wanted to, and his name along with his looks made him a natural magnet for girls.

He went out with some girls from work. He went out on a date with a young publicist called Katy from the legal department and ended back at her place. The next day at work he was in a queue at the staff canteen waiting for a coffee and Danish, when Katy came up to him in the queue.

"Hi!" she said with a big smile.

He turned and looked her up and down, gave her a disdainful look, said nothing and walked off. Seemingly she had spent the afternoon crying in her office. Carl had come into him, looking annoyed.

"You shouldn't poke the payroll!" Carl had warned him. "And if you do, then don't act like a bastard the next day. It's not good for the company morale!"

"Oh, Carl – relax! Stop getting so uptight!"

"I'm serious, Roger. Mum and Dad didn't spend all their lives building this company up for you to make a mockery of it all. It's not your private playground – it's a serious place of work."

Roger had been annoyed that Carl had spoken to him like that. Carl, who was invited to all the boardroom meetings. When Roger had confronted Blanche to as why he wasn't invited to boardroom meetings, she had simply said, "You will, when you have a Master's in Business Management as well."

He was furious. He knew what she was playing at. She was trying to force him to resit his exams and go to college. Not a chance, he thought.

But Roger knew he was smarter than the rest. He looked at

his parents, and though officially it was Troy that owned the company, he was completely in Blanche's shadow. Roger wasn't planning on going through life being in Carl's shadow as his father lived in his mother's. Lauren owned half the company and she had as good as said that he was going to get her share. That would put him firmly in charge. And as for Amelia, with her causes and her demonstrations, she wasn't even in the running. But in the meantime, Carl was cramping his style, and he needed to get him out of the way for a while, so he could establish himself properly in the company. Carl had been given a key role in the glamorous business-development sector, whereas Roger had been stuck in the retail department, dealing with clients in the shopping centre, most of whom he just wanted to tell to fuck off.

Throughout 2004 Blanche was busy trying to buy a hotel on Lexington Avenue in New York. She finally managed to acquire it. She was very excited about it; it was their first acquisition in America.

Roger was in her expansive office on the top floor of the headquarters in the IFSC. He sat on her desk.

"So – I've decided I want to go and work at the new hotel in New York," declared Roger, swinging his legs.

Blanche looked up at him. The last thing she needed in New York was her party-mad son on the rampage.

"Roger, darling, you are not going to New York – period."

"But I think it's very important for me to be there."

"Roger, you're nineteen years of age. I think the hotel can survive without you. What's far more important is those licensees for the shops in the shopping centre which I asked you to have signed about a month ago and which I'm still waiting for."

"But you always said that back in the eighties when you

were facing ruin, you had to be there on the spot in the bars in London. You said you needed to be on the spot."

"Well, that's true."

"So you've just bought a huge hotel in New York and you're just going to leave it in the hands of managers?"

"What do you suggest? That I drop everything here and go live there? Hardly."

"No – send me, then I can keep an eye on everything and report back to you."

"The only thing you would be keeping an eye on is pretty girls and nightclubs, Roger." She looked at him in amusement. She loved his enthusiasm, but since he had come to work there it was clear his dedication and ability were much lacking.

Roger sighed loudly. "Well, if not me then – Carl! Send Carl! I just think it is vital that one of us should be there during this initial period."

Blanche sat back and thought. It mightn't be a bad idea to send Carl. She would like somebody she could completely trust on the spot there. And the experience would only add to his already impressive ability. Maybe she might suggest it. He would have to leave his new girlfriend Susan. But she had a strong notion that he didn't have such strong feelings for her as he'd had for Vicky.

She picked up the phone. "Stella, can you get Carl to pop up to my office?"

By the end of the afternoon, it had been agreed that Carl would be based in the New York hotel in the New Year for the foreseeable future.

"Ah – I'm really going to miss you!" said Roger to Carl.

"Yeah, me too," said Carl.

Roger went out to celebrate that night. He called in sick for the rest of the week.

CHAPTER 77

2005

Blanche was at breakfast in Winterfield, reading an article headed '*Launcelot Heiress in Shannon Protest*'. The article was accompanied by a photograph of Amelia. The article read: '*There is one member of the media-shy Launcelot family who seems very happy to court as much publicity as possible in highlighting her different causes. Twenty-two-year-old Amelia Launcelot, the ardent anti-war protestor, was leading the demonstration at Shannon airport yesterday when American Senator and businessman, Warren Gardner, touched down on Irish soil for a week-long visit. Senator Gardner, an aviation tycoon, is a close aide to President Bush, and spent some time in Shannon meeting American troops who were on a stopover to Iraq. Ms Launcelot led the very vocal protest with chants such as "Down With American Imperialism". Mr Gardner's car was then pelted with eggs as he left the airport.*'

Blanche threw the newspaper across the table to Troy.

"I can't bear to read any more," she said.

Troy glanced through the article and tutted.

"I don't know what we're going to do with her," he said.

"Maybe we make life a little too easy for her. Maybe we should take back that apartment she has the use of for a start," suggested Blanche.

Ever since Amelia had turned twenty, she had been given the use of a company apartment.

"That would only make her more militant," warned Troy. "Besides, I want to know where she is."

"True. I just know that she has that Jason living there with her, and it makes my blood boil to think he is living off us while he protests about our corporate greed at the same time." She turned a worried look on Troy. "I wonder what she would say if she knew that Warren Gardner is going to be a guest of ours this evening?"

"Hi, sis, nice article in the paper today," said Roger down the phone to Amelia. He was in his office at work.

"You could at least try and hide your sarcasm," she said.

"According to a couple of my mates, you were seen partying away in Renard's until three in the morning last night."

"So?"

"So you spent your day protesting, and your night partying? I wish I had your life!"

"From where I'm standing your own life looks fairly cushy. At least I have a purpose to my life."

Roger yawned. "Making the world a better place? Anyway, listen, Jane Fonda, I just want to tip you off. Stay away from Winterfield tonight, okay?"

"Why?" Amelia demanded.

Roger sat in silence.

"*Roger!*" shouted Amelia.

"Look, I just don't want any hassle for anybody. Not for

Mum and Dad and not for you – okay? So just keep out of the way."

"I've never kept out of the way in my life. Now tell me, what's happening at Winterfield tonight? I won't utter a word. Have I ever betrayed your confidences in the past?"

"No – I guess not – but this is something serious, Amelia. Warren Gardner and a group of his political and business friends are coming for dinner."

"*What? That no-good-son-of-a-bitch-facist!*"

"Promise me you won't say I told you anything!" pleaded Roger.

"Don't worry." Amelia hung up the phone. She sat on the couch, looking out of the glass-encased balcony at the water below. Jason came in from the hall, a terrycloth towel around him, drying his hair.

"I've told Gavin we'll go to his party tonight," said Jason.

"I won't be able to make it. Something else has come up."

Roger stretched back in his swivel-chair and put his hands behind his head, smiling. He really had the run of the place now. Everyone kept saying Carl was doing sterling work in New York – *sterling*. Amelia was constantly *persona non grata*, and she definitely would be after whatever shenanigans she would now perform that night. Blanche wasn't due into the office that day due to the Senator's visit that evening, and Roger was half-thinking about knocking off early.

There was a knock on the door and in walked Louis. Louis was a French guy who worked in the legal department and had become good friends with Roger. Roger found him to be very clever, cunning, slightly dangerous and very good fun.

"You around tonight? I've got a couple of girls lined up to go out on the town. We can start with dinner at Bang," suggested Louis.

"Sorry – can't make tonight. Got a family thing on at home."

"Ahhh!" Louis looked disappointed, and then he took an envelope from his pocket and, opening it, sprinkled a liberal supply of cocaine out on the glass-topped desk.

"Maybe we have a little party now then – no?" Louis said with a smile.

CHAPTER 78

The guests were due at seven that evening, and Blanche was doing a final check of the dining room to see that everything was in order. The table had been elegantly dressed by the catering staff at the hotel, with lilies decorating the room. She had brought in the best chef and catering team from the hotel group. Senator Warren Gardner was a powerful and important man. He was also a man who had become a friend of the Launcelots over the past year. So much so that he was now inviting them to buy a twenty per cent stake in his airline. It was a deal that had Blanche salivating, and that night's dinner, although dressed as a social event, was really a business meeting to put the seal on the deal.

Blanche was dressed in a gold knee-length dress with a plunging neckline. She wore her black hair piled up high, with strands escaping, curling down the sides of her face. She wandered out of the dining room, across the hall and into the drawing room, where Troy was sitting watching television drinking a whiskey.

"How can you be so relaxed?" she said almost irritably.

"Because you already have the deal in the bag. Tonight

is just the icing." And with the hand holding the crystal of whiskey he pointed over to the television screen and said, "Remember him?"

Blanche glanced over at the screen and saw Ronnie Richards on a panel of judges on some British talent show.

"How could I forget?" she said, looking at Ronnie as he cruelly tongue-lashed some poor young singer's performance. He was a regular on these television shows now.

"I'll never figure out how you two fell out so badly. The two of you were like two peas in a pod," said Troy.

Blanche felt herself go red as she remembered their night of passion on the yacht. "He ludicrously thought I single-handedly masterminded the London property crash to rip him off!" She took the remote control and turned off the television.

Troy looked at his wife, as always trying to figure her out. She seemed to have this mechanism that made her go forward, never looking back. He admired this ability, and it also frightened him.

Blanche made sure all the staff were in their places by seven. She had security at the entrance to Winterfield House and also positioned around the house. Senator Gardner was to have a Garda escort due to his prominence, but she still wanted to have ultimate protection.

Blanche stood in the hall between Troy and Roger as the cavalcade of cars came sweeping up the avenue to the house. She nodded to the concierge at the door and he opened it swiftly. Blanche stepped forward smiling onto the outside steps. Warren Gardner emerged from one of the middle cars as his team came from the others. The accompanying Gardaí took their positions around the house along with Mr Gardner's own security.

"Senator!" greeted Blanche as Warren reached the steps.

"It's Warren, please," he said smiling and, taking her hands, as he kissed both her cheeks. "And Troy." Warren proceeded to shake Troy's hand.

"And, Warren, this is my son Roger, I don't believe you've met," said Blanche.

"Indeed I haven't. Unlike your other son, who I've met on numerous occasions over in New York. He's a very impressive young man."

Roger felt himself burn with anger over the Senator's comments.

"What a marvellous house," said Warren.

"Isn't it? It dates back to the nineteenth century. Of course it's been modernised over the years . . ." Blanche continued to talk as she took his arm and led him into the house.

The evening was going wonderfully. Blanche's army of caterers attended to the guests' needs continuously. Blanche sat at the head of the table, Troy at the other end, Warren to her left and Roger to her right.

"Thank you, Blanche, for that very generous donation to my humanitarian foundation," said Warren.

"You're very welcome, Warren."

"Hey, Warren, it's a pity you can't stay here the night. I'd like to get the opportunity to beat you in a round of golf," said Troy to some laughter.

"And I'd like nothing better. We passed the hotel and golf course on the way here – it looks very impressive. Maybe next time. Unfortunately time is short on this trip and I promised our ambassador I would stay at the embassy."

After dinner the guests relaxed around the table, drinking port and smoking cigars.

"To me, it makes perfect sense," said Blanche. "We're looking for an airline to invest in, and you're looking for an investor. We have recently sold a portfolio of properties in Dublin and London and so we are cash rich. And after the hard times the airline industry has had since September 11th, you need an injection of cash."

"We've had a number of approaches from interested parties," said Warren, "but I have to say I couldn't imagine anybody I would prefer to be a business partner with."

"After taking over a landmark hotel in New York, we are now planning to expand – opening a five-star hotel in both Paris and Budapest. I think our hotel business and the airline could greatly benefit each other."

Warren nodded and continued to smile at Blanche, while thinking that she was a shrewd operator. By being an investor in an airline, she would have access to all the passengers for her hotels.

Just then the front door slammed and they heard the sound of high heels clicking across the marbled hallway.

Blanche looked around, startled, to see her daughter enter through the double doors. Dressed in backless high-heeled sandals, flared jeans, a white top, and a burgundy fitted jacket, she looked stylish but out of place among the lavish dresses and designer suits of the guests.

"Hi!" said Amelia. "Sorry I'm late!"

Warren looked at the beautiful young woman, with her brown hair cascading past her shoulders and looked at Blanche for some direction.

Blanche shot Troy a look of dread and he shrugged his shoulders at her.

"Warren, this is my daughter Amelia," said Blanche, unable to hide her unease.

Warren rose to his feet and approached her, taking her hand. "Enchanting!" he said.

"Well, I'm not really – not when you get to know me." She winked at him and looked around the table. "Oh, they forgot to set a place for me. Never mind, I won't be eating anyway." She went to the side of the room, grabbed a chair and carried it to the table. "Shove up, Roger!"

Roger looked at Blanche, and then made room for Amelia to pull the chair into the table and she sat down.

"Have we met before? I feel you look familiar?" asked Warren.

"I was in Shannon yesterday. You probably saw me screaming in your car window as you sped by. Although I didn't throw any of those eggs personally. Being a pacifist I don't agree with anything like that."

"You were on that demonstration?"

"I was leading that demonstration, my dear Senator. And I feel very privileged to get this opportunity to deliver my thoughts to you personally on the subject." She spoke loud and harshly. "Senator Gardner, you are the representative of an illegal war. You are responsible for the suffering of a nation and your own troops."

The murmur around the table grew in loudness.

"Amelia!" hissed Blanche.

"You are a war criminal, Senator Gardner!" Amelia's voice was rising all the time over the muttering and shocked reactions around the table.

Roger stood up, took Amelia's arm and tried to take her away from the table. She shook him off.

"I look forward to the day when you stand trial for crimes against humanity!"

One of Warren's aides was on his mobile phone to the Guards outside and suddenly the Guards and Warren's security were in the room as all the guests including Warren rose to their feet.

"Warren, I can't apologise enough," said Blanche.

Warren nodded at Blanche and then Troy. "Thank you for your hospitality." And then he, his aides and security quickly exited the house.

Blanche crossed over to the window and saw Warren quickly enter his car and watched while all the cars disappeared down the avenue.

Blanche turned to Amelia and shouted, "You stupid, stupid girl!"

"I don't want to hear your excuses. How can you sit down and eat with a man like that. Do you know what he's responsible for?" demanded Amelia.

"Amelia! He is, or was – our friend. You don't know anything about him! He's actually trying to stop the war!"

"So he says! I've seen the legislation he's signed off on."

"You've messed up one of our biggest business deals!" snapped Troy.

"Don't tell me you were going to go into business with that man! I'm so glad I arrived when I did – I'm glad I've fucked it up! There would have been blood on your hands as well as his! Mother, there is more to life than money!"

"That's easy for you to say – you've always had it – thanks to us!"

"I just hope that one day you'll understand what I've saved you from," said Amelia.

"The only thing I want to be saved from right now is *you*!" shouted Blanche.

Amelia threw her hands into the air. "I think I'll head back to Dublin." She walked out of the house and they heard her car start up and drive off.

That night, when they were going to bed, Blanche's mobile bleeped indicating a text had come through. She opened the text. It read – *'Blanche, thank you for a wonderful night. On retrospection, I think I'll take a rain check on the merger. What's that expression? – You can choose your friends, but unfortunately not your relatives – Warren.'*

CHAPTER 79

Carl looked around the sumptuous Fifth Avenue apartment filled with young socialites and thought of what *The Wall Street Journal* once wrote: '*Money is something that can buy you anything except happiness, and bring you anywhere except heaven.*' As the son of the owner of one of New York's swishest hotels Carl was openly welcomed into this select group. Blanche had established many contacts and friends in New York, and they all welcomed him with open arms.

It had been good, he supposed. He had a ready-made network waiting for him when he moved to Manhattan. But he wasn't sure if he really liked them. He often thought, if he wasn't who he was, they wouldn't have been quite so welcoming. They were wild and hedonistic, and he was sure Roger would love their scene. He just wasn't sure if it was for him. Looking at his watch, and seeing it was nearly one, he decided he would head home early.

It was autumn and Carl strolled down the street in the warm night air, Central Park to his right. He hadn't been back to Ireland since he moved here several months ago, and he was looking forward to going back at Christmas and catching up with everybody. There was some major falling out between his parents and Amelia. Maybe he could act as peacemaker. And then there was Lauren. She was now eighty, and though in fine spirits and health, he wanted to see her and spend some time with her. She was –

The whack to Carl's head seemed to come from nowhere in the middle of his train of thoughts and he blacked out as he hit the ground.

When Carl came round, there were two policemen there, one kneeling on the pavement beside him. Carl attempted to get up.

"Just stay there, son, and don't move – there will be an ambulance here in a couple of minutes," assured the policeman.

Carl reached to the back of his head which was throbbing with pain, and felt the stickiness of blood before passing out again.

"The doctor will be here in a few minutes," said the nurse.

Carl was lying on a bed with curtains around him. It seemed like hours had passed since he had come to the hospital. He had received stitches and painkillers.

"Hopefully the doctor will discharge you," said the nurse with a reassuring smile.

Carl closed his eyes. He just wanted to get home now and away from this nightmare.

The doctor arrived – he could hear her outside the curtain, talking to the nurse.

"What have we got here?"

"He was mugged. They came up from behind and he was hit on the back of the head."

The curtain swished and Carl opened his eyes.

Gabrielle was staring down at him.

He wasn't sure if he was hallucinating from the drugs.

"Gabrielle?" he managed.

She looked as shocked to see him.

"Hello, Carl," she said and switched into professional mode. "Now let me see that wound."

"I thought this city was supposed to be cleaned up," he said.

"You still shouldn't take any chances . . . This looks worse than it is."

"How long have you been over here?" he asked.

"A few months." She continued to inspect his head.

"I didn't know."

"Why would you have?" Gabrielle turned to the nurse. "Okay, he can go home but under instructions to come straight back in if he experiences any dizziness, extreme drowsiness or other such symptoms." She glanced at Carl to see if he was taking this in.

"Yes, doctor – I'll give him the leaflet about concussion." The nurse left.

Carl sat up in the bed and he and Gabrielle looked awkwardly at each other.

"You're based in this hospital?" he asked.

"Yes. And I've just come to the end of my shift – so I'd better be going."

"Eh – alright then."

"Somebody is waiting for me, you see – how are you going to get home?"

"I'll just get somebody from the hotel to collect me."

She looked thoughtfully at him and seemed to hesitate. Then she said, "No need. We can drop you off."

"I really appreciate this," said Carl as he walked slowly through the hospital reception beside Gabrielle. He glanced at her appreciatively. She was looking really good, he thought.

She was wearing a smart grey suit, expensive-looking leather shoes and carrying a slim briefcase. Her blonde hair was now shoulder-length.

"Well, I couldn't leave you to make your own way home."

The glass doors of the hospital automatically opened, and they walked out.

"Just over here." She indicated a red Ferrari parked to the side of the hospital.

"Hi!" said the man in the driving seat, who looked to be in his thirties.

"Malcolm, this is a friend from home – Carl. He got mugged last night and I met him in Casualty. I said we'd give him a lift home," explained Gabrielle.

"Oh! Sure!" Malcolm's mouth broke into a smile. "Where to?"

"Lexington Avenue. I hope I'm not putting you out," said Carl, climbing into the back seat.

"Of course not!" said Malcolm.

Gabrielle sat in beside Malcolm and kissed him on the mouth.

"How are you feeling now?" asked Malcolm, looking at Carl in the rear-view mirror as they made their way through the New York traffic.

"I'm okay, just a thumping headache."

"He was hit over the head during the mugging," explained Gabrielle.

"Nasty business." Malcolm reached over and rubbed Gabrielle's leg.

"Do you work together?" asked Carl.

"Yes, Malcolm is a consultant at the hospital," said Gabrielle.

"Although not for the next week. We've both got some time off and we're heading up to Newport for a few days."

498

They got to Lexington Avenue and Malcolm pulled the car over. Gabrielle jumped out to enable Carl to climb out from the back.

"Thanks for the lift," Carl said to Malcolm.

"Any time!"

"Well, that was all so unexpected!" said Gabrielle, smiling at Carl.

"I'm still a bit dazed."

"You need to take it easy for the rest of the week."

"Yes, doctor! Um . . . we must meet up for a coffee or something."

"Eh, Gabrielle, we really need to get on the road if we're to beat the traffic," called Malcolm.

"Take care of yourself, Carl." Gabrielle got into the car and they drove off.

CHAPTER 80

Amelia pulled up in her Mini in front of the Launcelot Headquarters and put the flashers on before jumping out.

"Hi!" she smiled at the security as she strode in.

"Miss Launcelot, I'm afraid you can't leave your car there!" said one security man, embarrassed.

"Oh, I'll only be a couple of minutes. Be a doll and keep an eye on it for me, won't you?"

The security man shrugged helplessly.

"Hi, Stella, is my mum busy?" asked Amelia as she strode past her to Blanche's office door.

"I'm not sure – hold on and I'll check!" cried Stella as Amelia ignored her, opened the door and marched into Blanche's office.

Blanche was on the phone and looked up to see Amelia walking towards her with a big smile on her face.

"I'll call you back," said Blanche as she hung up the phone. "I was going to ask do you ever knock. But I think both I and Senator Gardner know you make a habit of showing up uninvited."

"Oh, don't go on about that old chestnut again, Mum. I told you, I forgive you for hanging out with that awful man . . . anyway, you didn't hang around for long. I read in the newspaper today that you've signed a deal to take a large percentage of another American Airline. Anyway, I'm here to ask for a favour. A group I'm involved in is setting up an animal sanctuary on the west coast and I'd like a donation from you."

Blanche started laughing. "You are priceless, Amelia! Where do you think the money comes from? My ill-gotten gains!"

"Okay – can we skip the lecture and get to the bottom line. How much are you willing to give?"

"Not a cent! Not until you start acting like a responsible adult!"

"If caring for the environment, animal welfare and human rights is not being a responsible adult, then tell me – what is?"

"I'm sorry, Amelia, but go and work and raise the money yourself to give to your animal sanctuary!"

Amelia gave Blanche a filthy look and marched out. Seething, she walked through the building and entered Roger's office.

"Come on and I'll take you out to lunch," said Amelia.

"Sounds good to me," said Roger, standing up and putting on his suit jacket.

"I don't think I'll ever understand Mum!" she said.

"I don't think she'll ever understand you!" said Roger as they walked down the corridor. "How's the Crusty?"

"Don't call Jason that."

As they went past Louis's office, his door opened and he came out.

"Oh, Roger! I was just going to ask you if you wanted to go for lunch?" he said.

"I'm afraid I've got a prior appointment, old boy," said Roger. "This is my sister, Amelia."

Louis turned and gave her an appreciative look up and down. "My pleasure," he smiled, taking her hand and shaking it.

Amelia flushed and just nodded as she took in the devastatingly handsome Frenchman with the golden-blond hair. Roger immediately spotted Amelia's reaction to Louis. In a way he wasn't surprised – Louis seemed to have that effect on most women he met. He had thought confident and opinionated Amelia would be immune to Louis' charms – but no.

"Tell you what – why don't you join us?" suggested Roger.

Amelia looked extremely uncomfortable with the idea.

"I would be delighted to – if you have no objection, Amelia?" Louis' blue eyes bored into hers.

She shook her head lightly and smiled.

"I know something you don't!" said Roger in his mother's office that afternoon.

"And what's that?" asked Blanche.

"Amelia fancies somebody!"

"Unfortunately, I know that already – that dull do-gooder Jason."

Roger shook his head. "Uh huh – she fancies someone else."

Blanche lit a cigarette and sat back, observing her son who was wearing that mischievous look that so suited him.

"I doubt it. She hasn't even looked at anybody since she met that scruff."

"You know Louis Chavannes, my friend from Legal? He came to lunch with us today and she could hardly speak in his company! She kept blushing and going quiet. And when he asked her something she even stuttered!"

"Amelia? Hardly!"

"I know. I could hardly believe it myself. She was like a different girl around him."

Blanche absorbed the news. After Roger had gone, she picked up the phone and rang Human Resources.

"Celeste, can you bring me the file on Louis Chavannes – as quick as you can."

Blanche had read Louis' file with great interest. Aged twenty-eight, a graduate of the Sorbonne in Paris, he had worked at a number of blue-chip organisations in Paris before moving to Dublin two years before. His file noted that he was driven, ambitious, sociable and popular. She picked up the phone to Celeste in HR.

"Is he as good as his file says he is?"

"He's one of our rising stars, Mrs Launcelot. One to watch. Slightly arrogant, if I had to say anything negative."

"His family background?" Blanche's interest was further pricked.

"From what I hear, he's from some aristocratic background. His next of kin are his parents and their address is some chateau."

"Give me their address and names," said Blanche.

Within an hour Blanche had discovered exactly who Louis's family was. She contacted a friend in Paris who made some quick enquiries and rang her back.

"The Chavannes family is very old and respected," divulged her contact. "Plenty of breeding, not too much spare cash. Louis, I believe is the third son. Excelled at law in university. A bit of a party boy, I believe."

Blanche called Louis's manager and told him to send him up to her at three in the afternoon. She then phoned Amelia.

"I've had second thoughts about your animal sanctuary and am willing to give you a small donation," said Blanche.

"I knew your conscience would get the better of you!"

"Call in to me at three fifteen today. And don't be late because I have a meeting at three thirty and the cheque will be leaving with me. And I might not be feeling as generous tomorrow."

At three on the dot, Louis Chavannes knocked, then confidently opened the door and walked towards her smiling.

She studied him intently and decided he was everything that had been described.

"Madame Launcelot," he smiled and gave a little bow when he reached her desk.

"Take a seat, Louis," said Blanche.

As he sat he spotted his HR file in front of her.

"How long have you been working for us, Louis?" she said, opening his file.

"About eighteen months."

"And you enjoy it here?"

"Of course, I would not stay otherwise."

"Why did you move to Dublin?"

"That's easy. The salaries are much higher here – I followed the money," he said with a smile.

"Money is important to you then?"

"Of course – is it not to everybody?"

"Not to everybody, no . . . what are your thoughts on politics?"

"Politics?" He shrugged. "They are quite inconsequential to me. They play no great role in my life."

Blanche smiled. "Good. I do find fanatics very boring, don't you?"

She waffled on about his experience and potential

504

prospects until the door opened on the dot at three fifteen and Amelia confidently strode in as per usual.

"Oh! I didn't realise you were with somebody," said Amelia.

As if that would stop you anyway, thought Blanche. She studied Amelia intently as she approached the desk and watched for her reaction when she saw it was Louis there.

"Hello again!" he said, standing up and smiling at Amelia.

Amelia blushed and her eyes widened on seeing Louis.

"Oh, have you two met?"

"How are you today, Amelia?"

"I'm – I'm, fine – thanks," said Amelia.

Blanche opened her drawer and took out an envelope. "I think this is what you're looking for, Amelia." She handed over the envelope.

"Thanks, Mum."

"Is there anything else?" asked Blanche.

"Em – no . . . I'll see you . . ." She smiled at Louis.

"Yes – see you!" said Louis.

Amelia walked quickly out of the room and Louis sat down again.

Troy drove Blanche back to Winterfield that evening after work.

"I tell you – Roger was absolutely right. Amelia is completely taken by Louis. There she was – all coy and blushing, like a love-struck schoolgirl!"

"Amelia – coy and blushing! That doesn't sound like my daughter," said Troy.

"I know! And he's the most delightful young man. Charming, ambitious, well-mannered. I think he's exactly what Amelia has been looking for!"

"Blanche –" warned Troy.

"No, seriously, Troy, I think a lot of Amelia's problem is that radical Jason that she's going out with. And this is a golden opportunity to get her away from him."

"Well, I don't think we should get involved."

"Too late, Roger has invited him to Winterfield for the weekend, and Amelia is due home too!"

Amelia raced her Mini Coupé up the avenue towards Winterfield House on the Friday night. One of the concessions she had granted her mother for the donation to the animal sanctuary was that she spend the weekend with them at home. There would be some guests there, and she was to be on her best behaviour. She was hoping to sneak back to Dublin on the Saturday night. The car screeched to a halt, and she jumped out and ran up the steps and through the front door.

"Hello!" she called as she walked through the hall.

"In here!" called Blanche from the drawing room.

Amelia strode into the drawing room.

"Good evening, everybody!" she said.

Louis was seated with his back to her as she came in. He stood up and turned around to her smiling.

"Oh . . . hello there!" said Amelia, stunned to see him.

He smiled broadly at her.

She didn't return to Dublin on the Saturday night.

CHAPTER 81

Carl sat in his office in the hotel on Lexington Avenue and picked up the phone to the Marketing Manager.

"Can you arrange to have a $500 voucher for the restaurant sent up to me immediately, please?"

Carl hadn't been able to get Gabrielle out of his mind since he met her again. He wished he'd got her number. Having said that, he wasn't thinking straight after getting bashed on the head and her *'I'm a smasher'* consultant boyfriend was impatient to whisk her off to Newport.

Once he got the voucher delivered to his office, he took out some hotel notepaper and wrote: *'Gabrielle, just a token to thank you for looking after me in the hospital and for giving me a lift home the next morning. Look forward to catching up with you soon – Carl.'* And he wrote his phone number underneath.

It was a busy day at the hospital, and Gabrielle was quickly going through her post. She was very surprised to get Carl's voucher and note. She spent a while studying the letter, before crumpling it and the voucher up and throwing them in the bin.

Blanche summoned Louis to her office on Monday morning.

"Did you enjoy the weekend, Louis?"

"Very much so, Mrs Launcelot. I would like to thank you for your hospitality."

"Am I mistaken, or was there something going on between you and my daughter?"

Louis managed to look affronted. "I can assure you, Mrs Launcelot, that there was nothing inappropriate between me and Amelia."

"More's the pity . . . I've been studying you, and I like you, Louis. And more importantly, I think Amelia likes you. And more importantly still, I think you are what she needs."

"I don't think I understand, Mrs Launcelot."

She sat back and lit a cigarette. "Amelia is a very good girl who has fallen in with, in my opinion, bad company. I'm not going to beat around the bush, Louis. Not only would I approve of a relationship between you and Amelia, I actively encourage it."

"I think I'm flattered, but I'm not sure Amelia thinks that way about me."

"Don't try false modesty, Louis. You know she's taken with you and I want you to act on that."

"Although I would be flattered to think Amelia would like me in that way, I could not predict what might happen."

"Good, Louis, good. Discreet to the end. I can assure you that your position will not be affected here in one way or the other if you choose not to pursue . . . eh, the matter . . . but if you do, I think you'll find your career will sky-rocket here. And what's more, if your relationship should ever develop into a marriage, there will be a personal gift to you of €1,000,000 and a substantial house of your choice on the day of your wedding."

Louis stared at her, his eyes wide. "Like a dowry?"

"More of an insurance, I would call it – and besides, I would want my daughter setting up home in comfort."

Louis sat there, deep in thought.

"Amelia is big on gestures. You should do something dramatic to show you're interested in her. She's in Geneva at the moment, as you know. I can have our reservations department book a flight for you."

Amelia was at a conference in Geneva, but as she tried desperately to concentrate on the subject – Women's Rights' in the Third World, she found it impossible to think of anything but Louis. Her mind went over every detail of the previous weekend in Winterfield. Louis had been the perfect guest all weekend, and had been completely attentive to her. They had gone out sailing together with Roger, played golf at the resort, dined in the restaurant in the Resort Hotel on the Saturday night. She felt elated in his company, in a way she had never felt before.

She was due to fly to Geneva the next day, and on the Sunday night he had requested her mobile number and asked if he could phone her when she got back. She had felt incredibly guilty when she had met Jason back at the apartment on the Sunday night; not that anything had happened, but just because of how she was feeling for somebody else. Now she wondered would he phone her when she returned to Ireland the next day.

As she walked out of the conference, her mobile rang.

"Hello, Amelia Launcelot here," she answered.

"Amelia, it is Louis here."

"Louis! Hello!"

"Are you still in Geneva?"

"Yes, I'm not due back until tomorrow."

"Guess what? I'm in Geneva too."

"*What*?"

"When are you finished with your conference? I can meet you."

"I'm just finished now!"

"Excellent. Give me the name of your hotel and I shall meet you there in an hour."

Almost shaking with excitement, Amelia rushed back to her hotel and quickly got ready, then got the lift to the lobby. Louis was waiting for her there carrying a large hamper.

"Have you had lunch? I hope not!"

"No, I haven't!"

"Excellent, then I hope you are very hungry. Come on."

The hotel she was staying in was on President Wilson Avenue that ran along Lake Geneva in the centre of the city. They walked along the promenade, looking out at the city around the lake with the snow-capped Alps in the distance. In the middle of the lake, the famous fountain dominated the scene, shooting water hundreds of feet into the air. They got to the pier that ran out into the centre of the lake and walked along it, passing the many sunbathers. They walked right to the end of the pier, which gave them a spectacular view of the fountain.

"I think here is good for a picnic, no?"

Louis knelt and opened the picnic hamper. He spread a tablecloth and she sat down and took the food out while he opened a bottle of red wine.

"Louis! I don't know what to say!"

He poured her a glass of wine and handed it to her.

"Why are you here?" she said, smiling broadly.

"I couldn't wait until tomorrow to see you," he said, staring in her eyes.

"This is unbelievable. So you flew over and went to all this trouble because you couldn't wait twenty-four hours?"

"I'm a very passionate man, Amelia. I don't think, I react."

Louis was stretched on the end of the pier, looking up at Amelia.

"And how was your conference?" he asked.

"Very good. You know, in the emerging markets their laws are not as regulated as ours, and this organisation that I'm involved in is trying to push these countries into bringing in equal-rights laws so women are not exploited."

His eyes glazed over as she spoke, and she felt she had lost his interest, which panicked her.

"You're not interested in women's rights?" she asked.

"Frankly, if I can be honest, no. Not so much women's rights specifically, but political agendas I find very boring."

"But how can you find them boring? Making the world a better place!" Amelia was flabbergasted.

"In my experience people who try too hard to make the world a better place have not got a very happy world in their own lives. Is this you, Amelia?" He reached over and very delicately began to stroke her arm.

"I'm - I'm happy," she stuttered.

"Are you sure? Have you stopped long enough to ask if you're happy with your life? Never mind what is happening out in Saudi Arabia, but what is happening in your heart." His hand reached over and touched her chest and he whispered, "In here."

Her heart was beating quickly and she felt herself shaking. Her hand was shaking and he reached down and put his hand on hers.

"Why are you trembling, Amelia?"

She shook her head. "No reason!"

He turned her hand over and held it softly. "I wonder sometimes if people from great wealth like you do not feel they deserve the fruits of it, so they grow up over-compensating, trying to do all these good works like you do, instead of making sure they're happy."

"The great wealth has really only come in the past few years or so. We were nearly broke in the eighties. And things were tight for a long time. That's why Mum is so driven, I think, to make sure it doesn't happen again. But when we were growing up we weren't flying around in private jets – we had a normal enough upbringing, with Mum making breakfast and putting the roast beef in the oven on a Sunday."

"I cannot see the great Blanche Launcelot in this role you describe," he laughed and held her hand tightly.

"Well, it's true. She knows how to accumulate wealth, does my mother. But that's not why I commit my life to good causes." She started to laugh. "According to my father, I was just born awkward!"

"I think you were born perfect. But I worry that while you try to make all these strangers happy, you forget about your own happiness and what could make you happy." He reached up and played with her hair, then moved his hand to the back of her head, gently pulled her down to him and kissed her lips.

She pulled back abruptly, startling him.

"I'm sorry! I can't do this!" she said.

For a moment, she saw his face completely change and darken as if a cloud had passed over it. But then his affable smile was reinstated.

"But I thought this was what you wanted. I thought

there was an amazing chemistry between us, a connection," he said.

"There is! But I'm seeing somebody else, and I just couldn't do this to him."

"There you go again, putting other people before your own happiness. That is your problem, not thinking about what you want! For once, why don't you just put yourself first? Think about your own needs rather than other people's. Because you know, life is very short, and it passes by very quickly."

They stared at each other intently for ages.

Then she slowly lowered herself down to him and kissed him.

CHAPTER 82

2006

As the days turned into weeks, Carl became more perplexed that Gabrielle never phoned him, if for nothing else but to thank him for the voucher. He flew home for a quiet Christmas. Roger and his friends tried to get him to go out, but he wasn't in the mood as his thoughts were preoccupied with Gabrielle. Back in New York, it finally got the better of him, and he found himself sitting in a coffee shop across from the hospital, studying the people as they came in and out. Just as he was leaving the coffee shop to go home, he saw Gabrielle walk out of the hospital, wave to a couple of friends and continue walking down the road. She was wearing a stylish chocolate coat, tied at the waist, brown leather boots and her hair was tied back in a bun.

He rushed across the road, darting between the cars as they beeped their horns loudly at him.

"Hey – Gabrielle! Wait up!"

She turned and looked at him in surprise. "Carl! What are you doing here?"

"I just wanted to see you." He hesitated and decided to

514

take the plunge. "I was puzzled . . . I sent you a voucher and note saying thanks, and I thought you might get in contact with me to have a catch-up."

"Oh!" She turned and starting walking at a slower pace down the road, with him walking beside her.

"There was absolutely no need for the voucher."

"Still – I was very grateful."

"It's forgotten," she said, picking up her pace somewhat.

It was rush hour and the cars beside them on the road were bumper to bumper as the drivers kept blowing the horns incessantly.

"I thought it might be nice for us to meet up. We're both from Castleford in this huge city on our own."

"I'm not on my own, I've got a great network of friends and I've got Malcolm."

"Oh, it's fairly serious between you and Malcolm then, is it?"

"Sorry, I don't mean to be rude but that's none of your business really."

"I was only trying to be friendly!"

She turned and faced him. "Why would I want to meet up? I have a happy life here. There's no point in meeting up just because we're both from Castleford."

"We were good friends once."

"In another lifetime. Before you headed off to your posh schools without giving me a second thought. I waited for you for months to contact me, and you never did. You just went off with your rich friends without a backward glance."

"I'm sorry, Gabrielle. I didn't think of it that way. I was just really busy at the time."

"And then your little shit of a brother calls my father names in the high street that evening. And your mother denounces me on the stage in the local hall, saying she didn't want her darling son hanging around somebody like me."

"I know – I'm sorry about all that, Gabrielle."

"And to top it all, I took a job in your hotel to be close to my mother for a summer. And I get fired on my first night! And you didn't even bother to try and sort it out – you were too busy socialising with your rich girlfriend. So I'm sorry if you are feeling alone in New York, but you deserve it. What goes around comes around. I have a great life here, please let me get on with it." She turned and walked quickly down the street, leaving him staring after her.

Carl walked on, staring straight ahead, hardly aware of his surroundings, hands in his trench-coat pockets, thinking about what she had said.

When he got home, he closed the door and sat down on the couch. Despite the network of friends he had here, he was lonely. And she obviously saw that. She could see it in him straight off. He remembered how close they had been for years. Everything she said was true. He had dumped her without a second thought, getting on with his busy hectic life. What did they say? Life is what passes you by while you're busy making plans.

Gabrielle was walking down a corridor at the hospital when her pager bleeped. She was wanted on main reception and made her way there. She was very surprised to see Carl standing there.

"Carl, I'm at work and I'm extremely busy. What do you want?" she asked impatiently.

"I'll only take up a moment of your time. I just really wanted to apologise. What you said was absolutely true. I never even realised at the time the consequences of my actions. I just want to say I'm truly sorry for anything I did in the past." He nodded at her and turned and walked out.

Carl was at his desk in his office at the hotel when the phone rang on his desk.

"Yeah?" he answered.

"A Gabrielle Ford is on the phone. She says she knows you," said reception.

He was very surprised. "Put her through."

"Carl?"

"Oh hi! Great to hear from you!"

"I was just wondering if you wanted to meet up for a drink sometime?"

"I'd love to!"

Carl steadied himself as he entered the bar he had arranged to meet Gabrielle in. She had picked a trendy bar in mid-Manhattan on a quiet street. It was a Saturday afternoon and the bar was quite empty, and so it was easy to spot Gabrielle immediately sitting at a table. He walked across the wooden floor and sat down opposite her with a smile.

"Hi," he said.

"Hi there."

They made small talk for a while – discussing the weather, crime, good social spots in Manhattan, the price of accommodation in New York.

"Where are you living?" asked Carl.

"I have an apartment in Chelsea. It's not huge, but it's a great location. Right beside the famous Chelsea Hotel – you know where Arthur Miller wrote his most famous play, and Sid killed Nancy amongst many other strange things going on."

"Right – sounds interesting!"

"What about you?"

"I live in a suite at the hotel."

"Oh! You live in a hotel room? I don't like the sound of that."

"Well, it's a bit more than just a hotel room," he said in defence.

"Oh, I'm *sure* it is – we couldn't have you in anything less than opulent!" Her voice dripped sarcasm and she smirked at him.

He studied her slightly mocking face. "It's handy for work as well. I just have to get a lift downstairs to the office."

"Sounds wonderful! It also sounds cold and impersonal and businesslike, but maybe that's what you want."

"And I guess your apartment has got *Home Sweet Home* written all across it?"

"Well, at least it's a little more homely than a hotel room – sorry, *suite*!"

They studied each other intently.

"And do you share your lovely home with the lovely Malcolm?" he asked.

"No, at least not yet. And he is lovely, incidentally, for the record."

"Oh, I don't doubt it for a second. He's got '*I'm a smasher*' written all over him."

"I'm sorry?"

"'*I'm a smasher!*' – he exudes it on meeting him. He seems very confident. And, I suppose, why shouldn't he be? He saves people's lives, he's handsome, he's charming, and he drives a Ferrari to boot. As I said – a complete *smasher*!"

"I hope you're not trying to take the piss out of him?" She looked slightly annoyed.

"Would I?" He raised his beer glass and took a drink, viewing her cautiously.

The afternoon passed into the evening and then into the night. Each of them couldn't help but be sarcastic to the other whenever the opportunity arose. They both enjoyed the sparring.

"So how long are you going to stay in New York?" questioned Gabrielle.

"I'm not sure. I'm really over here for the hotel during this initial takeover period. I guess I'll go back to Ireland when I'm needed there. What about you?"

"Oh – I've no plans to head back home. I like living here too much. Nobody here judges you like they do back home. I'm just me here and all people care about is who I am, without carrying baggage from the past."

"Nobody judges you at home either."

"Easy for you to say, coming from your family. No matter what I'll ever do at home I'll always be Seán Ford's daughter. Big bad Seán Ford."

Carl felt awkward, feeling her anger on the subject. "I guess things were hard for you growing up."

"I wouldn't swap Seán as my father for anything. He's everything everyone says he is – a terrible drunk, a womanizer, not a penny to his name . . . But he always treated me like his princess." She stared into her beer, and quickly wiped the sudden tears from her eyes. "I'd better be going – all this talk of home is making me maudlin. There's a reason why I stay away from Irish people over here. Another drink and we'd be singing 'Fairytale of New York'! Come on, let's go." She reached over for her coat and handbag.

They left the bar and walked through the streets for a while, talking about memories of growing up in Castleford, laughing at incidents at school.

Gabrielle put her hand out to call a cab and one pulled up beside them.

"Anyway – it was really good catching up again," she said as she opened the back door of the cab.

"I really enjoyed it. And I'm glad we managed to sort things out after all this time."

"So am I," she smiled at him.

She got into the cab and it drove away. He stared after her.

"Well, that's the last time I'll see her," he said loudly before hailing a cab for himself.

Carl's phone rang on his office desk.

"Hi, it's Gabrielle – Ford."

He sat up straight. "How are you?"

"You sound surprised to hear from me?"

"I am, I guess. I didn't think I would again."

"Well, I just was feeling sorry for you in your big hotel suite on your own and wondered if you wanted to come by mine for dinner tonight? Nothing special – chilli con carne is about as far as I can go, I'm afraid. Having said that, it might be a welcome change from hotel food."

"Sounds like a great idea. What's your address?"

Carl came out of the subway station and walked down the block to Gabrielle's apartment block. He buzzed and she let him in. He walked through the narrow lobby to the elevator at the end and went up to her apartment. She was waiting for him at the door, dressed casually in pale-blue jeans, a white shirt with the collar up and her hair loose to her shoulders.

"You found it alright?" she said.

"Yeah, no bother at all," he said, handing over a bottle of Californian red wine and stepping inside.

"Are you hungry?" she said, taking his coat and hanging it in a small cupboard in the hallway.

"Yeah."

"Good – because I think I've cooked too much food!"

A small corridor ran from the front door, with a bathroom to the right and a small kitchen to the left, into a large room with high ceilings and two long windows that offered a view of the New York skyline. The apartment was very homely, its large comfy white sofas on wooden floors and a large dining table between the two windows. He spotted a door that led to the bedroom.

"Open the wine, will you? The bottle opener is on the table."

She disappeared into the kitchen.

"So how was your day?" she asked, talking loudly from the kitchen.

"Very busy."

"What actually do you do all day?"

"Ah – meetings, checking stock-takes, hiring. No day is the same."

"Sounds interesting!" she said with a smile, coming out of the kitchen holding two plates of chilli con carne aloft.

"And how was your day?" he said, taking a seat at the table.

"Crazy. Absolutely crazy. I had three ERs. I had a cardiac patient assigned to me in serious trouble."

He studied her while she ate. He couldn't imagine their working days being more different.

"I was surprised to hear from you again."

"Why?"

"I don't know. I just thought you weren't interested in pursuing a friendship again after all this time. For all the reasons you mentioned."

She looked up at him and laughed. "Pursuing a friendship? You can be a bit intense, Carl."

He looked up at her, irritated. "And you can be very offhand and dismissive."

"Well, I'm not with anybody else – you must just bring it out in me." She put a forkful of chilli in her mouth.

Frank Sinatra's 'Fly Me To The Moon' was playing on the music system. Carl was seated on one sofa while Gabrielle lay out on the other.

"Does your mother come to New York much?" questioned Gabrielle.

"Every few months. She would probably have to come over a lot more if I wasn't based here."

"And your father?"

"No, he doesn't bother that much."

"I was always a bit scared of your mother. I remember her arriving up at school in her Mercedes, dressed glamorously and smoking a cigarette. And she had been a model and was this big businesswoman – she completely intimidated me."

"I think she does that to a lot of people."

"Does she see much of your grandmother these days?"

"Lauren? I think they try to keep out of each other's way. They clash a bit."

"Hmmm – that's what I heard."

He studied her, wondering what else she had heard about his family – all delivered from Rosalind's point of view.

"And what else have you heard, Gabrielle? I feel we're skirting around things here. I'm feeling resentment from you, and I thought we'd dealt with our issues."

"Oh, we've dealt with *our* issues, but there's still all our *families'* issues hanging heavy in the air that we haven't even touched upon."

He felt his irritation turn to anger. "And those issues are?"

"Well – your father leading my mother on for years and then dropping her, for a start. And then there's your uncle who dumped my mother almost at the altar. Then there's the little issue of you buying our farm and turning it into a golf course. Do you know how many windows of our house have been broken by stray golf balls? We have to duck every time we hear someone shout '*Fore!*'"

Carl nodded. "And your family are just sitting there, the victims in all this, are they? Do you know your mother mounted a campaign against mine from the moment she stepped into Castleford? She did everything she could to split up my parents and drive my mother out. She made a scene at my grandfather's funeral. She's responsible for that wedge between my mother and Lauren. She actively encouraged Lauren to dislike my mother over the years. She used her limited political powers to do everything she could to try and stop us building the golf resort hotel –"

"Carl!" interrupted Gabrielle, sitting up.

"And then . . . and *then* your mother physically attacked mine in the street! Don't sit there pontificating at me. It's time you and your family grew up and took responsibility for your own lives and your own fuck-ups."

Carl slammed down his glass and stood up.

"Carl – okay! I'm sorry. Calm down! I take your point."

"No. The only reason you wanted to meet up again was to settle old scores! Well, settle them on your own."

He went and took his coat and stormed out.

Over the next couple of days Carl thought about little else than Gabrielle. He was glad he told her some home truths. But he felt bad that he had overreacted. He resigned himself to the fact that he definitely wouldn't hear from her again.

By the Friday he realised that if he left it any longer, it would be too late to make contact again and he couldn't bear that. He resigned himself to go over to her apartment that night. As he came out of the subway, he was preparing exactly what he would say. Somebody was entering the apartment building as he approached it, and he followed him in. He made his way up to Gabrielle's floor and knocked loudly on the door. A few moments later she opened the door. She looked stunned to see him.

"Carl!"

He stepped inside. "Look, about the other night. I'm sorry – I overreacted. And you know this is ridiculous, we shouldn't be carrying this fight on to the next generation. It's just sometimes I feel you're teasing me for a reaction. Anyway – I'm sorry!"

She stood there, looking awkward and uncomfortable.

Suddenly a voice from the apartment called out, "Who is it, baby?"

Carl glanced down the corridor and glimpsed Malcolm lying out on the couch in boxers.

"It's – just Carl."

"Oh!" said Malcolm, looking surprised. "Hi, Carl! What's up – been mugged again?" He gave a little laugh.

Carl went bright red with embarrassment.

"Ah – I'll head off. See you."

Carl walked out and heard the apartment door close after him. He got in the lift and fell back against the wall, leaning his head against the mirror, feeling like a complete fool.

It was nine in the evening, the lights in the suite were dimmed and the lights of New York shone a million twinkles from the different buildings outside the windows. Carl was sitting in the living room which was large and expansive, decorated with burnished opulent antiques. Walnut double doors led through to the bedroom. It had been a week since he turned up at Gabrielle's apartment. What had he been doing? It had looked like he was stalking her or something. The phone rang on the coffee table in front of him.

"Mr Launcelot, it's reception. There's somebody here to see you – Gabrielle Ford."

"Oh – send her right up."

He jumped up and quickly turned up the dimmer and the lights of the chandelier shone brightly. He smoothed down his hair and went to the suite's double doors and opened them. A minute later the elevator opened and Gabrielle stepped out.

"I thought I'd surprise you for a change," she said, walking into the suite. She looked around, taking in the grandeur of the gold ornate ceilings and gold thick-pile carpets.

"I'm sorry about just turning up unannounced at your place. I hope it didn't get you into any trouble with Malcolm," said Carl.

"No – why should it?" She sat down on the ornate chaise longue. "I'm sorry I didn't invite you in. You just took me off guard," she said. "Look, you're right in what you were saying – I was trying to make you feel bad about everything. About you dumping me as a friend years ago, about the imagined wrongs inflicted on my mother by your family. And I'm wrong to feel like that. I've had a great life and that's all in the past. Just meeting you brought it all back and made me bitchy. I'm sorry."

He nodded.

"So I just wanted to say that and to say goodbye really."

525

He was taken aback. "You don't want to see me again?"

"No, it's not that at all. Far from it. But Malcolm has been offered a very important position in Boston and he's asked me to go with him. There's an excellent post waiting for me there as well."

"Oh, I see! When are you going?"

"The end of the week," she said, standing up.

"Just when I was getting to know you again," he said ruefully.

"Maybe we're just not meant to know each other," she smiled.

She started walking towards the door and then stopped and turned and looked at him. And she suddenly wasn't the high-powered New York doctor with the smart mouth and the attitude but a vulnerable girl in Castleford again.

"Carl – I won't go, if you ask me not to." Her voice was a whisper.

They stared at each other and he moved towards her.

"Of course I don't want you to go."

He put his arms around her.

CHAPTER 83

The invitations, 550 of them, were couriered out from the Launcelot Public Relations Departments.

'Mr & Mrs Blanche & Troy Launcelot are delighted
to request the pleasure of your company at the wedding
of their daughter Amelia to Mr Louis Chavannes
at the Castleford Catholic Church at 1 o'clock
on Saturday September 1st 2006 & at a reception
to follow at the Winterfield Hotel & Golf Resort.
Black Tie. No Children.'

Blanche took a call from Samantha Armstrong as she sat at her desk in her office.

"Blanche, thank you so much for the wedding invitation! I want to know every detail about the wedding. I want to know everything about this Louis Chavannes for my social column. Please tell me he isn't one of those long-haired Crusty types Amelia has a penchant for?"

"No, he's far from it. We're delighted with him. And if

you contact Tara in the PR department she'll give you a full briefing."

"Lovely. Incidentally, I was in New York last week and was staying in your hotel –"

"Where else would you be staying?"

"Indeed, and I bumped into Carl there who was very cosied up with a beautiful young woman."

"Oh, he's keeping that quiet! It's the first I've heard about it. Did you catch her name?"

"No, he didn't say – I thought it odd at the time."

"I see. Well, I'm over there next week on a flying visit. I look forward to being introduced to her."

Blanche spent a week in New York staying at the hotel. Carl seemed to steadfastly avoid the subject of his new girlfriend. Finally Blanche cornered him and insisted on meeting his elusive new love on her final day before returning to Dublin. They would meet for afternoon tea at The Plaza, Blanche informed Carl.

Carl and Gabrielle walked past all the parked horse and carriages lined up across from The Plaza and hand in hand crossed the road.

"Do I look alright in this?" asked Gabrielle, smoothing down her silver-grey suit.

"That's the hundredth time you've asked me that today," said Carl.

"Well, your mother has been on Ireland's Bestdressed Women list for the past two years. It's only normal that I feel nervous!"

Carl stopped as they got outside The Plaza and held her face in his hands.

"You look wonderful. You are wonderful. She'll love you."

"Not when she finds out who I am."

"She and everybody else at home have to find out about us sometime, so they might as well find out now."

"Which one of these limos is your mother's, I wonder?" asked Gabrielle wryly, pointing to the rows of limousines parked outside The Plaza.

"Probably the biggest. Now come on!"

Holding hands, they climbed the steps up to the revolving door and entered the hotel.

They walked through the lobby and into the great dining hall, where tea was being served at all the elegant tables. Carl spotted Blanche at a central table and waved over to her.

As they made their way over, Gabrielle whispered, "I feel as if I'm fifteen again like that time you forced me into the front seat of the car your mother was driving for a lift home."

"Shut up, you'll be fine," he whispered back.

Blanche stood and kissed Carl and then turned all her attention to Gabrielle and shook her hand.

"I've heard so much about you, Gabrielle, that I feel we've already met!" smiled Blanche.

We have! – thought Gabrielle, as they all sat down.

There was something very familiar about the girl, thought Blanche as she scrutinised her.

"I'm afraid this can only be a brief chat, Gabrielle. I'm going straight to the airport from here. Flying back to Dublin."

"So I believe, Carl told me."

"Oh, you're Irish!" said Blanche, surprised at hearing her accent.

"Eh – yes," Gabrielle smiled.

"Carl didn't say, he's been so coy about you. Where are you from in Ireland?"

"Eh – Castleford," said Gabrielle, realising it had been a mistake not to pre-inform Blanche about who she was. Carl had insisted that, if he had told her, it would only give her a preconception.

"*Castleford?*" exclaimed Blanche in surprise. And then, as she studied Gabrielle's features and saw the resemblance to Rosalind and remembered her daughter's name, she put all the pieces of the jigsaw together.

"You're Rosalind's daughter?" Blanche's voice had turned to ice.

"Yes, I am." Gabrielle's face went red.

Blanche looked at Carl in shock.

Carl reached over and held Gabrielle's hand. "I know! I come all the way to New York to meet a girl from up the road! How weird is that?"

"*Very* weird!" pronounced Blanche.

The rest of the conversation was stilted, with Blanche being cool and businesslike and Gabrielle being reserved and defiant. They stuck to neutral topics, punctuated by long silences. Blanche cut the meeting short.

"I'm afraid I really better be going. Security can be so delaying at Kennedy Airport. Carl," she said, giving her son a brief hug, "I'll phone you tomorrow." She turned to Gabrielle and gave her a cold smile that didn't carry to her eyes. "And it's been so nice to meet you."

Blanche strode out of the dining hall and Gabrielle and Carl watched her go.

"It didn't go great," said Gabrielle.

"No – no, you wouldn't describe it as going great," agreed Carl.

Blanche sat seething in the back of her limo as it sped to the airport. Of all the bints he could have met in New York, he met that twit from next door. She would have to put her thinking cap on, before things got serious.

Blanche was on the phone to Carl a few days later.

"Look, Carl, you are needed here at home in Dublin. We've expanded so much and it's not fair for it all to be left to Roger. After all, you only were supposed to be in New York during the start-up period for the hotel."

"But I love New York," said Carl.

"Excellent, then you can buy one of those T-shirts that declare that sentiment at the airport on your way home."

"I just don't want to come back yet."

"We all have to do things in life we don't want to. Give yourself to the end of the month, but when you come home for your sister's wedding, I think you should come home for good."

"So what are you telling me you did then? You gave Carl an ultimatum to move home?" asked Troy as their chauffeur drove them home one night.

"Not even an ultimatum. An order. It's the only way we can get him away from that Ford girl."

"You're being absolutely ridiculous, Blanche!"

"Am I indeed?"

"Yes. You've no right to try and break up Carl's relationship just because you don't like who he's seeing."

"I've nothing against the girl personally. It's her family I have the problem with."

"It's none of our business. What are you doing, interfering? You were the same with Amelia, throwing her at Louis all the time to get them hitched."

She dreaded Troy ever finding out about her agreement with Louis.

531

"And wasn't I right? Aren't they gloriously happy now?"

"You know, you're worse than Lauren. The way she was trying to push me and Rosalind together all the time. The way she wanted to split you and me up. It's history repeating itself."

"Now you're being ridiculous – and keep your voice down," she said, nodding at the chauffeur.

"And so what, if Carl ends up with Rosalind's daughter? I think it would be great. It could bring our families together again after so much hatred."

"Oh – easily known! You probably would love the idea – you've always had a soft spot for Rosalind, both you and Lauren. Well, no – I'm sorry but it's not going to happen. She's got bad genes anyway. She's got a bitch of a mother and a loser as a father. I don't want that gene pool around me, thanks very much!"

Troy tapped the driver's shoulder. "Pull over, will you?"

The driver pulled over on the side of the motorway.

"What are you doing?" demanded Blanche as Troy got out of the car and slammed the door. She quickly rolled down the window.

"I want to get away from you and your meddling," said Troy.

"Troy – get back into the car, please!"

"No. You get away with having everything your own way in the company, and now you're trying the same in the family. And I don't want to be around you tonight."

"Troy! Will you get in!"

"No!" He turned to the driver. "Drive on!"

"Do not!" snapped Blanche.

"I said drive on – *now* – before I really lose my temper!" Troy shouted at the driver.

"But how will you get home?" demanded Blanche.

"That's my problem!"

The nervous driver started up the car and sped off.

"Well, it's obvious, isn't it? She's trying to break us up," said Gabrielle in a not-too-fussed fashion.

They were in Carl's suite at the hotel.

"So does she just think that when she clicks her fingers I'll run back to Dublin and that will be the end of us?" asked Carl.

"Well, that's what she's hoping."

"Well, I just won't go. I'll tell her I'm staying in New York."

"What – forever? You told me you were only supposed to stay here less than a year, and that you would be gone home by now if you hadn't met me. She'll insist that you go home. She *is* your boss at the end of the day."

"That can be changed too. I'll just get another job."

"What? And leave the Launcelot Empire? I don't think you can walk out on all that, do you?" She looked at him sceptically and thought for a long while. "I'll tell you what – I'll move back to Dublin with you. End of story. I can pick up another position in a Dublin hospital very quickly. And then she can't say anything."

He sat down slowly and stared at her. "You'd do that for me?"

"Of course I would. You'd be surprised what I'd do for you, Carl."

He sat thinking, studying her, realising how much she loved him and that she always had.

"Gabrielle – let's get married now."

"Married!"

"Look, when you didn't go to Boston that time, we made a huge commitment to each other, didn't we?"

533

"Yes, we knew we wanted to be together for good."

"And now you're prepared to leave your life here. Your career. I mean, I was only ever going to be in New York for a while but you planned to stay here indefinitely. And you're giving that up for me, to be with me. We knew within three or four weeks of meeting in New York that we wanted to be together. And I want to do it before we return home."

"Are you being serious?"

He was over beside her, holding her hands. "There's no point in hanging around. And if we go back to Ireland not married, we'll have to listen to everyone's crap. My parents, your parents, everyone trying to put us off. We've been living in a cocoon, just the two of us here, not thinking about anyone else. At home it would be different. But if we are married, there's nothing they can say or do. They will just have to accept us from day one."

She smiled mockingly at him. "And could you give up your Fifth Avenue debutantes and your judges'-daughters socialites, like Vicky, back home?"

"I can if you can give up your *'I'm a smasher'* consultant boyfriends. Will you marry me?"

"It's what I've always wanted."

CHAPTER 84

An article in the *Review* read:

> '*In what is being billed as the society wedding of the year, Amelia Launcelot will marry businessman Louis Chavannes today. The event, being held at the family's exclusive Winterfield resort, is to be attended by the cream of the Irish business and entertainment world. Amelia's bridesmaids are to be Miss Cordelia O'Gara and Johanna Hatton. And the best man is brother of the bride, Mr Roger Launcelot.*'

Roger stood at the top of the church beside Louis as the beautiful organ music flowed from the balcony. The church was packed to capacity and everyone was now waiting for the bride to arrive. Roger was deep in thought. Carl was due back from New York that morning but, judging from the spare seat Blanche was keeping beside her, he hadn't arrived yet and was running late. Roger wasn't one bit pleased with the thought of Carl coming back to work in Ireland. He had got very used to being *numero uno* at the company. What did the stupid bastard go and get mixed up with Gabrielle Ford for? Blanche might have been happy to leave him in New York indefinitely if it were not for that. Roger glanced to his left to look at Louis. No nervous groom there. He looked straight ahead in a confident and relaxed manner. What a turn-up for the books this had been! Louis and Amelia getting married. He remembered the thousand parties and nights out he'd had with Louis, and thought about the drugs he had consumed and other things he had witnessed. He hoped Amelia would never find out about her husband's tastes. But then Louis was too clever for her ever to find out. He sighed. He spotted a very pretty dark girl sitting in the choir stall nearby. She looked Italian. He smiled over at her. She blushed and looked to the ground. He hadn't seen her before and realised she was obviously part of the choir that had been brought in. He must look her up later.

Blanche glanced at her watch, irritated at Carl being late. He shouldn't have left it to the last minute to arrive. She felt a tap on her shoulder and she looked around to see Samantha.

"I'm impressed, not a Crusty in sight!" said Samantha as she glanced around at the immaculately dressed guests.

Blanche gave a little laugh and turned around again.

"I have to say this all a bit too soon, in my opinion," commented Lauren in a low voice to her.

"Amelia's happy and that's the main thing," said Blanche.

"And so are you. You look as pleased as a Cheshire cat . . . I don't know, there's something about Louis I just can't take to."

"So you've been saying," snapped Blanche. "But, since

you are the worst judge of character I know, that's an immediate plus in his favour."

The two women settled back into stony silence.

The car screeched to a halt outside the church and Carl and Gabrielle jumped out. Amelia and Troy were waiting outside the church.

"Come on! Come on! We're waiting on you!" shouted Troy as they raced up to the front door.

"Sorry! The traffic!" said Carl, kissing his sister.

"Just get in!" ordered Troy.

"Good luck!" said Gabrielle, squeezing Amelia's hand.

Carl and Gabrielle quickly walked up the aisle to the top of the church.

"About time!" snapped Blanche as Carl bent to kiss her. Then her mouth dropped as she saw Gabrielle beside him.

"Shove up, you've left only room for one here!" said Carl.

Blanche reluctantly pushed up to allow Gabrielle sit in the pew as well, and the result was that Blanche was squashed up beside Lauren.

"This is just wonderful!" snapped Blanche. "I can hardly breathe!"

"Oh, well, everything has a positive side," snapped Lauren who was staring at Gabrielle in confusion.

"Hi, Lauren!" Gabrielle gave her a little wave with a big smile.

Roger edged towards the dark beauty as soon as people began to file out of the church.

"Hi – I'm Roger."

She nodded shyly.

"Maybe we can have a little dance later?" he said and winked at her.

"Oh, no, no, señor, I am an Augustinian," she objected.

"Honey, that doesn't matter – I'm a Gemini!" said Roger with another wink.

"Roger!" snapped Blanche in his ear. "She's a nun."

"Oh!" said Roger. He gave the nun an awkward smile and moved off to join the crowd exiting the church.

The guests had finished the wedding banquet in the elegant function room in the Winterfield Hotel. They had dined on Waldorf Salad, Beluga Caviar, then a choice of lobster or lamb for the main course. They had toasted the couple with vintage Bollinger champagne. And sweetened the toast with a 1950's port. Ethiopian coffee to finish and rare chocolate truffles that were specially handcrafted for the event.

The family were seated at the head table which was set against a backdrop of the Georgian windows that looked out to the lawns and beyond to the sea. Carl and Gabrielle were seated at another table and Blanche continued to stare at them during the speeches.

"Why don't you try and pretend you're enjoying yourself?" Troy suggested to Blanche in irritation.

"What is she doing here? She wasn't invited to the wedding," snapped Blanche.

"I think Carl is entitled to bring the guest of his choice to his sister's wedding, don't you? I was speaking to her earlier, and she's lovely."

Gabrielle chose to ignore Blanche's constant glares.

"When do you think we'll tell them our big news?" she whispered to Carl during the speeches.

"We'll let Amelia have her day. There's a family dinner tomorrow before they head off on honeymoon. We'll make our announcement then," said Carl, smiling at her as he squeezed her hand.

The whole family were in the dining room. Blanche sat at one end of the long table and Troy on the other.

"Carl has obviously got into the habit of bad time-keeping since living in New York," said Blanche.

"I'm just flabbergasted that he's seeing little Gabrielle," said Lauren. "It was such a surprise for me."

"For us all," remarked Blanche, ignoring Troy's warning looks.

Carl walked into the dining room and Blanche threw her eyes to heaven on seeing that Gabrielle was with him.

"How's the heads?" asked Carl with a laugh. The wedding party had gone on till the early hours.

"Really, Carl, I wish you would have given us some prior notice that you were bringing somebody," snapped Blanche. "We haven't set an extra space for your friend, and this is really supposed to be family only."

Troy stood up, giving Blanche a filthy look. "There is absolutely no problem at all. We can set a place in two seconds flat and you are very welcome, Gabrielle."

Gabrielle was getting sick of Blanche's hostility – and she didn't even know they were married yet.

"Well, Mother, that's why Gabrielle is here," said Carl loudly and defiantly. "She's family now. We got married in New York."

There was stunned silence for a while, only broken when Roger laughed loudly.

Then Troy moved over to them and gave them both a hug. "Well, congratulations! Why didn't you tell us sooner?"

"We didn't want to take the attention from Amelia's big day," said Gabrielle.

Amelia was up and hugging them. "I can't believe it! Gabrielle! I'm so delighted."

Roger thought he'd better say something and so quickly got up and offered his congratulations.

Lauren was in tears as she hugged them. "It's like it was meant to be. I went from your room in the hospital when you were born, Carl, down to visit you, Gabrielle. And I've seen you grow up as I watched your mother growing up . . . Niall would be so delighted! His grandson marrying his best friend's granddaughter! It's like everything has come full circle."

"Who knows what he might say at the thought of his grandson marrying Seán Ford's daughter," muttered Blanche. Troy suddenly was by her and gripped her by the arm. Everyone was making a fuss of Carl and Gabrielle and no one noticed.

"Now you get up and get over there and you kiss them both and offer them your congratulations," Troy hissed in her ear.

"Let go of my arm, you fool!" snapped Blanche.

"I'm warning you, Blanche. You put on the happy mother-of-the-groom routine or else –"

"Or else what?" she snapped.

"You don't want to know. You tried to break them up and you ended up pushing them together. Now you can live with it." He tightened his grip further on her arm and pulled her up out of her chair.

"You're hurting me!" she warned.

"And you're not going to hurt Carl – now get over there and smile!" Troy ordered, propelling her forward.

"Wasn't too bad," said Carl as he drove into Rosalind's driveway.

"Your mother's smile looked like it would crack and she was going to burst into tears any second," said Gabrielle.

"She'll get to used to it. She has no choice!"

"And now for my mother!"

Rosalind was at the door waving and smiling. She had laid out a sumptuous feast of cakes and chocolate on the coffee table in the drawing room.

Holding hands, Carl and Gabrielle informed her that they were married.

Rosalind got a shock and started to cry. Gabrielle joined her on the couch and put her arm around her.

"But why all the secrecy? Why the rush? Are you pregnant?" demanded Rosalind.

"No, Mum! That's not a good enough reason to get married any more," said Gabrielle. Times have changed since your day, she thought. "We just decided that this is how we wanted to do it. With the animosity that exists between the two families, we felt it was the only way to do it. Imagine us trying to organise a wedding, between you and Blanche Launcelot!"

"But it's so unfair! I had to get married in a make-do quickie ceremony in the back of beyond and I wanted you to have the big fairytale wedding. Of course Blanche's daughter gets the big royal wedding and mine gets the cheap version, same as my wedding."

"Do you see, Mum, that's why we had to do it our way. You're bitter about the wedding already – there would have been war."

Rosalind dried her eyes and studied Carl.

"At least you don't look like your mother!"

"Mum!" warned Gabrielle.

Carl laughed. "Now I know where Gabrielle gets her cutting remarks from."

"I grew up with the Launcelots," said Rosalind. "They were like family to me. I know them and I know how ruthless they can be. I'll be honest with you – I would prefer if my daughter had not settled down with a Launcelot. Your ability to cause misery is too acute. But Gabrielle has made her decision – and I stand by her decision."

"Thank you, Rosalind," said Carl.

CHAPTER 85

The Social Column in the *Sunday Review* read:

> '*They say that a bird in the hand is worth two in the bush – but we wonder what two brides are worth – particularly when they are members of the super-rich Launcelot family. It has come to light that Amelia Launcelot is not the only blushing bride after her spectacular wedding last Saturday. Her brother Carl has married Castleford native and New York based Doctor Gabrielle Ford. Her family are believed to be old friends of the Launcelots – so everyone must be delighted with the union. Meanwhile happy couple Amelia and Louis are cruising the Mediterranean on a private yacht on loan from millionaire developer Charles Hunt. They are due home next week from honeymoon to start married life in a spectacular new home in the Dublin Hills.*'

Amelia enjoyed every moment of her honeymoon. It had been amazing, cruising in the sunshine, stopping off at little ports along the Adriatic for lunch and some sightseeing.

One night they could be having dinner at a restaurant on the Italian coast, a couple of days later in some tavern on a Greek island. Amelia thought how a couple of years ago she would have recoiled at such extravagance. But Louis had taught her so much. He had taught her how to live. How not to feel guilty for enjoying life. Life didn't always have to be about fighting other people's battles. And Louis was certainly an exponent of what he preached. He took the good things in life as if they were his natural birthright.

They had spent months looking for their dream home and finally came across a place high up in the Dublin Hills. The road it was on, Canyon Drive, was a twisted country road that kept getting higher and was dotted with lavish entrances into spectacular homes. There was a high-walled entrance and a sweeping cobblelocked driveway led up to their house. The house was a unique modern villa with statues built into the walls. It had been designed by the previous owner, an architect who had been shipped off to the mental asylum after his business had gone bust, the estate agent had cheerfully told them. Notwithstanding this piece of information, they fell in love with the property straight away. It was perched up on the mountains, offering breathtaking views across the whole of Dublin and out to the sea. Inside the front door was a large hallway with slate tiles on the floor and a wooden open-stepped staircase. The ceiling of the hall rose straight to the roof. In the lounge there was a wall of windows that electronically opened and led on to a small swimming pool that was situated on a patio that was literally hanging on the ledge of a cliff overlooking the city. The site was exceptionally private, as were all those on the road, as they were all a few fields apart. Which was just as well, thought Amelia as there was so much glass in the house it would be too exposed otherwise.

Amelia was due to start a PhD in History when they returned from honeymoon and she had just been in Trinity, meeting her course director. The meeting went fine and she was due to meet Louis for dinner afterwards. As she sat in Pacinos waiting for him she couldn't help but reflect how happy she was. She had never thought that normal happy marriage would have been for her. She had always thought she was too different for that and that she would be too busy fighting conventions. How easy it was to just sit back and enjoy life! As time drifted on at the restaurant, she looked at her watch and there was no sign of Louis. She took up her phone and tried to dial his number but his phone was off. After forty-five minutes went by, her mobile rang.

"Hello?" she said.

"Amelia! Where are you?" demanded an irate Louis.

"I'm in the restaurant waiting for you. Where are *you*?"

"I'm here too but I cannot see you. My mobile is dead and I'm using the restaurant phone. I can see the whole restaurant and cannot see you. Stop playing games!"

"And I can see the whole restaurant too and I can't see you. What restaurant are you in?"

"Da Pino's."

"Oh!" said Amelia, nodding her head and smiling. "I'm in Pacinos. It's just a misunderstanding. I'll walk up and be with you in five minutes." Smiling, she turned off her phone and walked up to the other restaurant. She entered Da Pino's and smiled and waved over to him. When she reached the table, she kissed him and sat down.

"Sorry about the misunderstanding," she laughed.

"I've been waiting an hour. It was a silly mistake, you need to listen more accurately to our arrangements."

"Whoa!" she laughed, puzzled by his anger. "Who said I heard you wrong? Maybe you said it wrong?"

"Because I expressly said Da Pino's. And said it three times! But then – you never listen!"

"Darling, you're slightly overreacting. A simple mistake of two restaurants that sound similar – with no huge repercussions. Now, can we order?" She took up the menu and started to peruse it.

"It was the same on honeymoon. I'd arrange to meet you at the pub at six and you are waiting in the café at seven. You never concentrate on what is being said."

Her mind was whirling. Did she never concentrate? There were a few fuck-ups on plans while they were away, but she never gave them much thought.

The waitress arrived over.

"And what can I get you guys?" she smiled.

"May I have the steak, rare, with frites and may I have the Béarnaise sauce with that?"

"Of course. And madam?" smiled the waitress.

Amelia was studying the menu and pulled a face. "There's nothing really appealing to me, I'm afraid. I'm a vegetarian."

"Oh, we have a special vegetarian dish on tonight, one second." The waitress went off to get the details.

Louis was swearing away in French quietly. She looked at him curiously. He seemed to be in terrible form.

"Always this drama at restaurants!" snapped Louis and he mimicked her voice "'*I'm a vegetarian*' – as if the whole fucking world should stop for you or something! We can never go anywhere without you causing a fuss looking for something that's not on the menu."

"It's not my fault if the menus don't cater to vegetarians –"

"*It's boring*!" he snapped.

The waitress returned and smiled. "Yes, we have a beautiful dish on tonight, a variety of Mediterranean vegetables baked in cheese."

"Sounds lovely. Thank you," said Amelia, closing over the menu.

"Sounds like *merde*!" Louis whispered under his breath.

Later, Louis looked at Amelia's dinner in disgust. "How is your cauliflower cheese?"

"It's lovely actually," she said.

He cut of a piece of his steak and held it out on a fork for her. "Here – try!"

She looked at the rare cooked meat and felt ill. "No. I don't want to."

"You know, I knew this girl in Paris who was a sworn vegetarian and she changed overnight and became a meat-lover. She used to tell the waiters – just barely touch the pan with it, the rarer the better." He forced the fork closer to her mouth.

"Louis! No! I don't want it," snapped Amelia, pushing the fork away and wondering who the girl in Paris was all at the same time. "Can we just eat, Louis? You're putting me off my food."

Amelia was upset the next day thinking about the previous evening, thinking about Louis's reaction to her vegetarianism and her supposed lack of concentration. She found it very hard to do research on her PhD and just sat in the spectacular white-themed lounge looking down at the views across the city, the laptop untouched beside her. When Louis phoned her she couldn't hide how she felt and was curt on the phone to him.

That evening he arrived in with a big smile and the biggest bouquet of roses she had ever seen, and she was back in heaven.

CHAPTER 86

Gabrielle had got a position in Vincent's Hospital. It was very strange being back in Dublin and she was having to acclimatise herself to it. Herself and Carl had gone house-hunting, and eventually decided to rent an Edwardian redbrick terrace in Ranelagh. It was handy for work for both of them. No wedding present of a spectacular house in the hills for them, as Amelia and Louis were rumoured to have received from the Launcelots. Not that she wanted it; she would hate to be beholden to them.

They travelled to Castleford most weekends to see her parents and his. The reception was always lukewarm at Winterfield, with Blanche barely hiding her disdain. And Roger was worse than ever if he was there. She wondered how nobody could see through him like she could. She held her tongue on him even to Carl, who seemed to think he was a great guy. But Roger had shown his true colours to her years ago and she knew what he was like.

They tended to stay overnight with Lauren who fussed over them no end, and it was nice to have some tender loving care after the coldness at Winterfield. Gabrielle didn't care about any of it. She had Carl, what she always wanted, and that was all that mattered.

Blanche was having tea with her mother in The Westbury. Harriet was every bit the elegant and distinguished-looking great lady, now in her seventies.

Blanche found it strange that when they were younger they never saw eye to eye, but now she found Harriet was a great ally who was sometimes the only person who understood where she was coming from, particularly in relation to Carl's marriage to Gabrielle.

"I mean I've tried with the girl, I really have," said Blanche. "But even looking at her makes me uncomfortable. I just see that awful mother of hers and her appalling father when I look at her . . . You know, Carl was the most talented of my children. He's so bright and good at business. Who knows where he could have brought the company in the future – and now he's just going to be dragged down by her, mark my words."

"Her pedigree sounds appalling," agreed Harriet.

"All the hard work I've put in, only to see it going to Rosalind Ford's damned daughter. Of course, they are all ganging up on me. The whole family. All Lauren's Christmases have come at once. At last a union between her and Rosalind! Praise be! And as for Troy, I know he's delighted. All he ever wanted was for us to stay down on the farm in Winterfield and live quietly – until we rotted away. In a way Carl is living the destiny that was meant for him."

"Are you and Troy rowing over Gabrielle?" questioned Harriet, concerned.

"That's the understatement of the year, Mother. We're shouting so much that I often think we must sound like Lauren and Niall when they used to holler at each other all night. And we're fighting about the same bloody thing. They were fighting about Rosalind and we're fighting about her bloody daughter!"

"And how is Carl fitting back into the company in Dublin?"

"Like a dream. He knows what he's doing and does it. He drives things forward and gets things done."

"Let's hope Roger's nose isn't being put out. He's been used to getting all the attention while Carl was in New York."

"You know, Roger has been nearly four years in the company now and everybody loves him. His colleagues love him, our business partners love him. You can send him out with business partners to the golf course or to dinner, and they come back with glowing references about it. But I'm afraid he doesn't actually *do* anything! In all the time he's been there, I don't think he's achieved one thing!"

"Oh dear! Have you tried to talk to him about it?"

"Yes – to no avail. He just looks at you with those big confused eyes, looking slightly hurt, and I just drop it. Because he's my son there will always be a role for him at Launcelots, but the company couldn't rely on him for survival. He may look like me but he's got his father's genes when it comes to business – unfortunately!"

CHAPTER 87

2007

Roger sat swivelling from side to side in his office, his back to his desk, looking out at all the glass office blocks of the IFSC. Since Carl's arrival back from the Big Apple, he had effortlessly taken over at the headquarters. Roger had become an afterthought. Heads of departments used to always inform him about board meetings, and he used to drop in to them if the desire took him. Now they had stopped informing him. Carl was going to them all. He made it his business to go to them all. Everyone saw Carl as the true power in the future. Carl and his twit of a wife, that drunk's daughter, who looked at him with a constant look of contempt. Who was *she* to look at *him* with contempt? They might think they had everything tied up, but they should never underestimate him. He picked up the phone and dialled Carl's secretary Diana. She was a quiet and sensible girl, but he knew she had a thing for him.

"Hello there, Diana, it's Roger here. Just wondered if you wanted to go out to dinner this week?"

"I-I-I'd love to!" she stuttered.

That evening Roger spotted Carl walking through the lobby of the building with his briefcase.

"Hey, Carl – wait up!" said Roger, jogging over to him. "Finished for the day?"

"Yeah."

They continued walking together.

"Do you fancy going for a couple of drinks in The Harbourmaster?" suggested Roger.

"Okay, that sounds good," smiled Carl as they walked through the swivel-doors onto the street. They heard a beep and saw Gabrielle waiting in her Audi.

"I thought I'd surprise you and pick you up," said Gabrielle. "Jump in, I've made a booking at Tribecca at six . . . Hi, Roger." She managed to smile at him.

"Oh !" said Carl, pulling a sympathetic face to Roger. "Another time for the drink? Sorry."

Roger forced a smile. "Sure. Maybe tomorrow." He spotted Gabrielle's white doctor's coat on the back seat. He leaned down and looked at her. "That's a lovely little coat there. Is it Chanel?"

"No – it's mine." She smiled back sarcastically at him.

Roger laughed. "Well, enjoy your meal."

"We'd invite you along, but the booking is only for two, and you know how strict they can be," said Gabrielle, not looking remotely disappointed.

"Hmmm. They used to be quite discriminatory in there – they've obviously relaxed their door policy," said Roger.

"Yeah. They might let even you in now, regardless of the fact you don't even have your Leaving Cert." Gabrielle stared at him uncompromisingly as she started the car's engine.

"How nice – how is your father incidentally?" said Roger.

Gabrielle tore off down the road. Roger stared after them. Smart bitch. He couldn't stand her. What did Carl see in her? *And* she was coming between them. He turned around, went back inside the building and got the lift up to Carl's office. Diana was still there tidying up, about to leave.

"Oh – h-h-h-hello," said Diana.

"You know, I was thinking why bother waiting until later in the week for dinner when we could go out tonight?"

"Oh – alright," she smiled. "J-j-just give me a couple of minutes and I'll smarten up." Smiling broadly, she grabbed her handbag and rushed off to the bathroom.

He quickly went around her desk, grabbed Carl's diary and went over to the photocopier and started photocopying.

The next few weeks were chaos for Carl. Appointments cancelled. Meetings being rescheduled and nobody being informed. Potential business deals falling through as one or the other party failed to show up.

"What is going on here?" demanded Blanche. "Charles Hunt contacted me screaming on the phone saying that you were supposed to meet him at the new shopping centre project and you never bothered showing up. Charles Hunt is not a man you mess around, Carl!"

"*He* stood *me* up! That meeting was scheduled for Friday and he didn't bother showing up."

"Carl, Charles is not the kind of man who gets things wrong. I've dealt with him many times and he has one of the most acute minds I've ever encountered."

"Well, he's obviously not that acute or he'd remember what day the meeting was supposed to be."

"Just forget it, Carl! I'll deal with Charles myself! I haven't spent years building up a special relationship with a developer as big as Hunt for you to go and fuck it up just because your mind isn't on the job!"

"That's not fair!"

"I don't give a damn what's fair! Ever since you met that girl you're not concentrating on your job here!"

"That girl is my wife!"

"That's your problem! I'm serious, Carl. You need to shape up. I'm not having everything I built up destroyed because you're otherwise engaged."

"You're just never going to accept her, are you?"

"I'm never going to accept sloppy work from you."

"Oh – forget it!" Carl turned and marched off.

Roger sat in his office on the phone to the secretary of a businessman Carl was due to meet the following Tuesday.

"Hello, I'm just ringing on behalf of Carl Launcelot. I'm afraid he can't make next Tuesday's meeting. If we could cancel until further notice? Thanks."

Amelia came down the stairs in her dressing gown and walked across the hallway into the kitchen where Louis was having breakfast, dressed in his suit ready to go to work.

"Hello." She kissed him and went and poured herself a coffee, yawning loudly.

"I'm not surprised you yawn so loudly. Did you sleep at all last night?" he asked.

She yawned again and joined him at the round table. "I slept alright."

"No, you didn't. You were tossing and turning, and even kicking!" He rubbed his leg.

"Oh, I'm sorry! Did I kick you?" she said and laughed with embarrassment.

"It's no laughing matter. You are a very restless sleeper. Even talking in your sleep and crying out. If this goes on, I'll have to sleep in another room."

She looked at him, horrified. "I'm sorry, I didn't realise it was such a problem."

"Well, you are! What are you doing today?"

"Gabrielle is dropping up to see me. We're having a catch-up."

Gabrielle drove up through the hills, impressed by the houses dotted around. It wouldn't be for her, the houses were too isolated for what she would want, but she couldn't help but be impressed as she turned into Amelia's driveway and followed the drive around the front of the house.

Amelia heard the car pull up, and raced out to the front door and opened it.

"Wow!" said Gabrielle as she looked up at the house as she approached the front door. "This looks like it should be in the Hollywood Hills not the Dublin Hills."

"It's fab, isn't it?" said Amelia, kissing her.

"I love this!" said Gabrielle in the lounge, looking out at the pool through the windows.

"Yes. There's a Jacuzzi in the far end of the pool and we sit in there on warm nights, a bottle of wine cracked open and the city lying out beneath us."

"Sounds very romantic! So how's married life treating you?"

"I'm loving it!" Amelia said, pouring them tea. "I never thought this would be for me. Husband, home."

"I kind of always knew what I wanted, I just didn't think it was going to happen," said Gabrielle.

"You really held a torch for Carl all that time?" Amelia was incredulous.

"I wasn't sitting there pining for him. I was having a great time, I can assure you. He was always just at the back of my mind. And everything is perfect now – except for your mother."

"Is she still giving you a hard time?"

"No, she just ignores me. But she's giving Carl a hard time. I know he's not telling me the half of it."

"She'll come around, Gabrielle. She's just become so used to getting her own way, she finds it hard when things don't go exactly as she wants them when she wants them. Once she gets to know you, she'll love you."

Gabrielle sighed. "We live in hope!"

CHAPTER 88

Grafton Street was clad in Christmas decorations, all the shop windows dressed with themes, each vying for pride of place to attract the thousands of passing shoppers laden down with bags.

It was a Thursday night and the week before Christmas and Blanche and Roger were walking down the street. Blanche was attracting looks from passers-by who recognised her.

"So what's the story for Christmas?" asked Roger.

"Same as ever. Everyone back to Winterfield."

"It's just it's a bit different this year. There have been two marriages since last Christmas."

"I was speaking to Amelia today and she and Louis are coming to stay with us for the whole of Christmas week."

"And Carl and Gabrielle?"

"That I don't know. They haven't confirmed."

"Since her mother is on her own, she might want to spend the day with her."

"Hopefully she will!"

"Hmmm, hopefully," said Roger. "Oh, incidentally I booked dinner for you and Dad tomorrow in Chapter One."

"Did you?" Blanche looked at her son in surprise.

"A little Christmas present to both of you. I think you could do with a nice night together, just the two of you."

Blanche sighed. Their arguments had got worse and worse. They seemed to annoy each other so much.

"We'll probably end up rowing again," she warned.

"Well, you could try not to." He hated when his parents fought. He was aware they always had an uneven relationship that could flare up given the right circumstances. Gabrielle arriving on the scene had provided just such right circumstances.

"And incidentally, it's Grandma Lauren's birthday this weekend. Just thought I'd remind you, if you wanted to send flowers or something. She's going to be eighty-three."

"Gosh, is the old girl that age?" She stopped and looked at Roger. "You're so good. If only all my children were as uncomplicated and thoughtful as you."

He laughed and shook his head modestly. "Anyway – I'm off to meet some friends for drinks." He leaned forward and kissed her cheek.

"Alright, love. See you tomorrow."

She continued down Grafton Street, pulling her full-length faux-fur coat tightly around her to keep out the cold. She needed to do some serious Christmas shopping and headed towards Brown Thomas. Walking into the store, she headed to the jewellery department and started pondering over the glass cases.

"Hello, Blanche," said a voice to her right.

She turned around and saw Billy Forrestal standing there. She stared at him in shock.

"Sorry – I'm after giving you a start," he apologised.

She still couldn't find any words as she stared at him. It had been so many years. He must be fifty now and yet he was still slim and fit-looking. His face was tanned and his hair was grey at the temples. But his eyes and expression were the exact same.

"Blanche?" he said again with a look of concern.

"I'm sorry – I'm just a bit shocked to see you again." Her eyes were wide in amazement.

"I've handled this all wrong. I was going to ring your office and make an appointment. But when I saw you walking down Grafton Street with that man, I just decided to follow you and say hello."

"I never thought I'd see you again," she said.

"You probably never wanted to see me again."

"No – I didn't say that."

"You look as if you could do with a drink," he said.

"I think I could."

They walked in silence through the crowded streets and made their way to The Shelbourne. They managed to find a free table in the corner. He went to the bar and ordered them two red wines. She studied him at the bar, trying to take it all in. She became self-conscious. It was twenty-five years. She was a young model when he had seen her last. How did she look to him now? He returned, put the wines down on the table and then sat down.

"I heard you were in Australia," she managed at last.

"Yes, I've been living in Sydney all this time."

"And are you back for Christmas?"

"I've moved home. I've been meaning to for a long time. But you keep putting off decisions till the next year, and the years creep by, don't they?"

"So what have you been doing?"

"Still in law. I worked as a state prosecutor for about ten years and then I moved into corporate law – it pays better." He gave a little laugh.

"But you were never motivated by money," said Blanche.

"No – it wasn't that – I just got weary of dealing with crime and bad stories all the time."

She had a flashback to him lying out on the ground in a pool of blood.

"Corporate law is a lot easier," he went on. "It's not as emotionally draining."

"I'm sure it isn't . . . Are you married?" She wished she hadn't blurted the question out so unsubtly.

"No, I'm not. But you are – I read a profile of you in the *Sunday Times* a few weeks ago. Three children, isn't it?"

"Yes. That was one of them you saw me walking down Grafton Street with."

"I see. And you're running quite an empire from what I hear. Congratulations, Blanche – life has been very good to you and you deserve it."

Why doesn't it feel like it has, she thought.

"You said you were going to ring me for an appointment – why?" she asked.

"I just wanted to get something off my chest. It seems ridiculous now – I'm embarrassed even to think it. You running your multi-national corporation and your busy family life – I'm sure you've got too many things to be concerned with."

"Go on," she insisted.

"I just wanted to say I'm sorry for not supporting you all those years ago. I'm sorry I turned my back on you. I can only imagine the fear you must have been feeling at the time. I was in shock. I was in hospital, so I couldn't think straight. And by the time I got out – you were gone."

She blinked a few times. "If anyone should say sorry it's me. You ended up in hospital because of me."

"I was a criminal lawyer. I should have realised what

pressure you were under. I didn't support you and I'm sorry."

Blanche felt her eyes go misty. "I don't know what to say . . ."

"The great Blanche Launcelot speechless? That's a first from what I hear!"

She shook her head slightly. "Where are you spending Christmas?"

"I'm with cousins. Family. I guess you'll be at home."

"Yes, in Winterfield. It's in the country."

"Well, I've delayed you enough. It's been so good to see you again, Blanche."

"And you."

He got up and put on his trench-coat.

"Are you looking for a position, a job?" she asked quickly.

"Yeah, I'm going to start looking for a job in the New Year."

She opened her handbag and took out her card.

"Ring me. I've a lot of contacts. I might be of some help."

"Thanks, Blanche." He nodded to her and smiled. "And have a happy Christmas."

CHAPTER 89

Carl and Gabrielle were having a mince-pie and mulled-wine party in their house the night before Christmas Eve. There was a roaring fire in the cast-iron fireplace as their friends filled the cosy house. They had made their arrangements for Christmas. They were travelling down to Castleford the next day and would spend Christmas Eve and most of Christmas Day at Winterfield House. Then the following evening they would go to Rosalind and spend the rest of the Christmas holidays with her.

The party was in full swing with people dancing as the lights on the Christmas tree continuously changed colour

"Do you know, I wish we were just staying here in our place for Christmas and not bothering going home at all," said Gabrielle.

"It won't be that bad," said Carl.

"It's easy for you to say. My mother is civil to you. Yours barely acknowledges me, and as for that brother of yours!"

"Roger just has a cutting sense of humour. You'll get used to him."

"It's ridiculous my mother can't just come and we all

spend Christmas together. You know, the christening is going to be a nightmare to organise."

"Christening?" Carl looked at Gabrielle, confused.

"Oh, I forget to tell you. I'm pregnant."

Lauren was in Castleford on Christmas Eve doing last-minute Christmas shopping. She got into the car that was waiting for her. She had been provided with a car and a driver by Troy and Blanche which she found very handy as she wasn't as comfortable with driving as she used to be. She was going straight to Winterfield House and she couldn't wait for Christmas and to have all the family around.

As the car passed a boutique she asked the driver to pull over.

She got out and looked at the green gown full of feathers in the window. She went in.

"Good day, Mrs Launcelot," said the boutique owner with a big smile "How can I help you?"

"I wonder could you take that dress you have on display out of the window for me?"

"Of course – I'll fetch it straight away," said the owner.

"Good – it's disgusting. I've been passing it every day for the past month and it's making me sick." Lauren turned and walked out of the shop, got into the car and told the driver to continue to Winterfield.

As the car drove through the town Lauren continued to marvel at the changes in Castleford. If Niall could see the place now, she thought, as she passed by one of the new housing developments with the word 'Launcelot' in giant letters on the advertisement board.

Blanche had been almost in a trance since she had met Billy again. She couldn't think of anything else. Seeing him again had thrown her for six. It was Christmas Eve and as she went around making sure the house was ready for the whole family that was about to descend on them, it was the image of Billy that dominated her thoughts.

She put the Christmas music on, and the fire was blazing in the drawing room. Lauren had already arrived and was in the kitchen checking on the dinner for the following day. The thought of being stuck with Gabrielle for the next twenty-four hours filled her with dread. Is this what her life was? Sandwiched between a mother-in-law and a daughter-in-law who despised her and a husband who tolerated her. She wondered what Billy was doing now. She heard a car pull up in front of the house and went to look out the window. Louis and Amelia were climbing out of his Range Rover. At least some things had worked out alright.

Soon everyone had arrived and they were having drinks in the drawing room.

Carl and Gabrielle had called into a delighted Rosalind on the way up and told her the news of the pregnancy, and now they were waiting for an opportune moment to tell everyone else.

"When will we tell your father?" Carl whispered to Gabrielle.

"We could call over to him tomorrow evening and tell him," suggested Gabrielle. She looked at the crackling wood fire, the array of Christmas cards, the many beautifully wrapped presents under the twinkling Christmas tree.

"What's wrong?" asked Carl.

"I feel guilty for not being with Mum tonight," she said.

"Look, we'll see her tomorrow. Anyway she'll be fine – she'll have lots of cake to keep her company!" He smiled at her.

She hit him playfully. "Nasty."

"What about your dad? Where is he tonight?"

"Where he is every Christmas Eve. Down in that Martin's Bar drinking until all hours."

Roger heard the last bit of the conversation and yawned. He looked around and beckoned Louis over to him. He was due to fly to the Bahamas for New Year and he couldn't wait. He could let his hair down there.

"I hope you brought enough with you to get us through the next few days?" he said to Louis.

"Of course . . . when do you want some?"

Roger looked around at everyone playing happy families while 'Winter Wonderland' played on the sound system. "Now's as good a time as any."

He led Louis out through the hall and into the dining room, locking the door behind them. Then he took a mirror off the wall and put it on the dining table. Louis took out a white envelope and poured the cocaine out onto the mirror.

"You first," suggested Roger obligingly.

Louis took out a crisp piece of paper, rolled it up and started to snort.

After a while they heard a lot of commotion in the lounge.

"I wonder what's going on," said Roger.

Quickly replacing the mirror and unlocking the door, they made their way across to the lounge.

Everyone was very excited and fussing around Gabrielle and Carl.

"What's up?" asked Roger.

"Gabrielle's having a baby," said Lauren, wiping away a tear from her eyes.

Roger couldn't hide the look of shock and anger on his face.

"Roger?" Lauren said, looking at him curiously.

He forced himself to look happy. "Great news, brother!" he shouted over.

Blanche was giving Carl a hug. Then she looked at Gabrielle.

"Congratulations, my dear," she said to her with a smile.

Roger sidled over to Blanche. "We'll never get rid of her now," he commented.

"Looks like we're just going to have to accept her," said Blanche, taking a sip of her port.

Roger felt the irritation grow inside him. This baby would make Gabrielle accepted by everyone and put her and Carl at the centre of everything, pushing him out of the way.

Blanche heard her mobile bleep a text on the fireplace. She went over and opened the text.

'Blanche. Wishing you a very happy Christmas. Love from Billy.'

She stared at the text, feeling joyous.

Lauren had gone to bed by midnight and everyone was beginning to slip off to their rooms. Roger's anger had continued to fester inside him all night. Gabrielle was openly hostile to him. This baby gave her all the trump cards. A baby had a way of bringing people together, and he didn't want that with Gabrielle. He remembered hearing Gabrielle saying to Carl about her father being in Martin's Bar. He slipped out of the house, quietly started up his BMW and drove off. He sped down the road into Castleford and made his way over to the old industrial part of the town, pulling up in front of Martin's. He got out of the car and walked over to the entrance. There was much joviality spilling out from inside. The netted windows had fairy-lights flashing on and off over the *Budweiser* neon sign. He opened the front door and walked in. The place was packed and everyone looked drunk as he made his way through the crowd. Christmas songs were blaring from the old juke-box.

He spotted Seán Ford seated at the bar and made his way over to him. Grabbing a barstool, he sat beside him.

"A Heineken, please," Roger said to barmaid. A few seconds later a pint of beer was put in front of him. Roger turned to Seán and smiled at him. It was obvious Seán was drunk.

"Happy Christmas!" said Roger with a smile, raising his beer.

"Same to you!" Seán nodded back with a smile.

"I'm sorry – you're Seán Ford, aren't you?"

"Sure am," said Seán, looking at Roger curiously.

"Seán! We're related! I'm Roger Launcelot. Troy's son!" Roger said with a big smile.

"Well – I'll be – put it there," said Seán, putting out his hand.

Roger shook his hand warmly.

"What has you here?" asked Seán.

"Oh – it's the only place still serving drink in this town. Everywhere else is closed for Christmas."

Seán laughed. "That it is! And they'll be serving until the small hours."

"That's good to hear," said Roger. He made a big show of spotting that Seán's glass was empty.

"Listen, what are you drinking?" asked Roger.

"Oh – em – a Jameson, if you're asking."

"A Jameson, please, double." Roger smiled at the barmaid.

"So you're Blanche's boy," said Seán, scrutinizing Roger.

"Yeah, that's right."

"She was a looker in her day, Blanche. Everyone said it. She's still supposed to be holding up well."

"Yes, she is," agreed Roger. "I just saw your Gabrielle up at the house, in great form."

"Aahh!" said Seán, a look of warmth spreading across his face "She's a great girl."

"That she is," Roger said and held up his glass "And listen – let's have a toast for the good news."

"What good news?"

"Well, you're going to be a grandfather and I'm going to be an uncle!"

Seán's face clouded over. "What do you mean?"

"Gabrielle's pregnant. Did she not tell you?"

Seán stared at Roger in disbelief. "No!"

"Oh – that's funny – she's told everyone else."

Seán took up his drink and downed it in one.

"Another double whiskey, please," ordered Roger.

Nearly two hours had passed in Martin's and Roger kept plying Seán with whiskies.

"I think it's very unfair myself," said Roger. "I mean, Amelia gets married and they give her a royal wedding at the resort and accept her husband with open arms, buying them a stunning house. What does Gabrielle get? Nothing! She had to get married in some low-key ceremony because she had no choice."

"What do you mean she had no choice?" slurred Seán.

"Well, the family said to Gabrielle that they couldn't have you giving her away because you'd show them all up on the day. Get drunk or something. I don't know – it all sounded very snobby to me. The fuss they make about Amelia's husband you would not believe – but then he is some sort of French aristocrat. They never let Gabrielle forget that she is the daughter of their old farmhand."

Seán's face was creased in anger.

"It's shameful if you ask me. She's up there sleeping at

Winterfield House and they're treating her like staff, regardless of the fact that she's going to give birth to their grandchild. My mother hates her, is just rude to her all the time."

"My Gabrielle's too good for them!" shouted Seán.

"Of course she is! But then she's never had anybody to defend her – has she? She's never had anybody fighting for her. Telling them where to go . . . If I was you I would tell them where to go. Right now!" goaded Roger.

"Fucking bastards!" snarled Seán.

"Do you want a lift anywhere?" offered Roger.

CHAPTER 90

Blanche lay in bed beside Troy who was sleeping soundly. She was lying on her back, staring at the ceiling in the darkness. The whole house had a hushed sound to it. She glanced over at her watch and saw it was three in the morning. And all she could do was think about Billy.

There was suddenly a loud crashing sound. Blanche sat bolt upright in the bed.

"What the fuck was that?" said Troy, sitting up as well and turning on the light beside him.

Suddenly there was another crashing sound as the front window of their bedroom shattered.

Blanche screamed in shock. Troy jumped out of the bed and ran to the smashed window. There was suddenly another crashing sound and another. A second window in their bedroom came crashing in as Blanche saw it was a rock that had been hurled through.

"Troy, step back from the window! Somebody is throwing rocks through the windows!" shouted Blanche.

They could hear window after window smash through the house.

"Who the fuck is out there?" Troy shouted out of the window.

Blanche jumped out of bed and put on her dressing gown.

"Come on downstairs," she said and the two of them came out of the bedroom and raced down the corridor to the staircase.

"What's going on?" demanded Amelia as she and Louis came out of their bedroom.

"We don't know!" said Blanche.

They all made their way down the main staircase to the hall below. Carl and Gabrielle were already there.

They could still hear the smashing of windows.

"What is all this racket?" demanded Lauren as she came down the stairs with Roger. A rock was hurled through one of the windows at the side of the hall door, scattering glass across the marble floor and causing a collective scream.

Troy went rushing to the front door and opened it.

As he opened the door a rock came hurling in, just missing him.

"Will you come in, Troy, and close that fucking door!" screamed Blanche rushing to the phone. "I'm calling the police."

"I can hear somebody shouting," said Carl.

"Fucking bastards! Fucking shit-bags. Thinking you're somebody and you're nothing. *Nothing!*" came the shouting as more windows were broken.

"That's Seán Ford," said Lauren in a calm voice.

"*What?*" said Carl.

"I've heard him hollering enough times with drink on him over the years to recognise his voice a mile off."

"Fucking trash! Treating my daughter the way you do! You're not fit enough to lick her shoes clean!" screamed the voice from the front.

"Oh no!" said Gabrielle, burying her face in her hands as they could hear more windows being smashed.

571

"What's he doing?" demanded Blanche, putting down the phone.

"He's mad on drink," said Lauren, unfazed. "It wouldn't be the first time he's turned up here shouting the odds over the years. Though he's never done any harm in the past."

Another window was smashed in the hallway.

"What are we going to do?" demanded Amelia.

Troy walked over to the front door and held it ajar.

"Seán, will you stop throwing fucking rocks at the house!" he yelled.

Another rock came hurtling at the door.

"It's no use. I'm sorry, Gabrielle, but we have to call the police," said Blanche, picking up the phone.

Gabrielle rushed to Blanche and forced the receiver back on the phone. She pleaded, "Oh no, please, don't call the police. I'll go out and talk to him."

"Don't be ridiculous, Gabrielle. You're pregnant. He's throwing things and he's out of his mind," said Blanche.

"She's right. Gabrielle, you aren't going anywhere," said Carl.

Lauren walked over to the front door and opened it slightly. "Seán Ford, it's Lauren Launcelot here. Can you hear me?"

"Yes."

"I'm coming outside, so will you quit throwing them damned stones!" She opened the door and went out onto the steps. Carl and Troy went out behind her.

They saw Seán standing in the forecourt holding two rocks in his hands.

"Put down those rocks now," Lauren demanded.

"I've no argument with you, Lauren – it's the rest of them I hate."

"When you attack this house, you attack me! Now put down them stones!"

Seán thought for a while and then dropped the rocks.

"What the fuck are you doing?" shouted Troy, going over to him.

Gabrielle came rushing out. "Oh, please! He's very drunk!" she begged.

"I'm not going to let them treat you badly, Gabrielle," said Seán.

"What are you talking about, Daddy?"

"I've heard all about it. How they treat you! And you told them all that you were pregnant before you told me. Even strangers."

Gabrielle buried her face in her hands.

A Garda car came up the driveway.

The rest of the family had come out onto the forecourt.

"Who called them?" demanded Gabrielle.

"I did, on my mobile," said Roger.

"I said not to!" shouted Gabrielle.

"Who are you to order what is to be done around here? Look what he's done!" shouted Blanche, pointing up to the house with its smashed windows.

"Causing trouble again, Seán?" asked one of the Guards, getting out of the car.

"You always go off the rails at Christmas, don't you?" said the other.

"There's been a misunderstanding. I'll take him home," said Gabrielle.

"You're not going anywhere with him the way he is," said Carl, holding her arms.

"Let me go, Carl!" shouted Gabrielle.

"Look, we'll take him down the station and let him cool off and bring him home in the morning," said one of the Guards. "That is, unless you want to press charges?"

"Look at the amount of criminal damage he has caused!

He should be locked up and the keys thrown away!" said Blanche.

"I'll pay for the bloody damage!" shouted Gabrielle.

"Big deal! How can we spend the night here in this freezing cold with not a window in the house? And how can we get somebody to fix them all tomorrow on Christmas Day?"

"You own a bloody five-star hotel down the road – why don't you just go and stay there?" shouted Gabrielle.

"It's fully booked!" said Blanche.

"Well, go and stay in Lauren's house or one of the many other houses you own around the globe. It really isn't high on my list of concerns at the moment," shouted Gabrielle.

"Don't you speak to me like that!" shouted Blanche back. "How dare you raise your voice to me!"

One of the Guards coughed loudly. "As I said, I think the best thing is we take Seán away. You can talk to him in the morning, Gabrielle. Come on, Seán." The Guards put him into the car and drove off.

"Well, we sure did act like alley-cats in front of the local constabulary," said Lauren.

Blanche laughed coldly. "Well, after that little demonstration by our new relative Seán Ford, you can forget about this family ever having a good name in this town again. Your father has ruined our Christmas, Gabrielle."

"Well, you know something? I'm delighted you now have a reason so you can display your hatred towards me without having to pretend to like me, which was always done unconvincingly, incidentally."

"I've had my reservations about you from the beginning, I don't deny it," said Blanche. "I think you and your mother couldn't wait to get your hands on our money and our land and our company. You chased Carl for years. You even followed him out to New York and got a quickie marriage before he could realise what he was doing. And now pregnant! You and your mother didn't leave anything to chance. You covered every angle, making sure you were entitled to all your rights."

"Will everyone just shut the fuck up!" shouted Carl.

"You know, if you knew me at all you would know how ridiculous what you're suggesting is. I don't want anything to do with you or your money ever again." Gabrielle stormed into the house with Carl following her.

"Mind the broken glass!" Blanche shouted after them.

Blanche turned and saw that everybody else was staring at her in shock.

Gabrielle grabbed her suitcase and was packing her clothes.

"I'm sorry, Carl. I'm out of here. I'm not spending another minute under the same roof as that woman."

Carl grabbed his suitcase and started to pack as well. "I'm going with you."

She turned and looked at him and fell into his arms sobbing.

"Come on, we'll go and stay at Rosalind's," said Carl, rubbing her back.

CHAPTER 91

Troy managed to get a couple of the farmhands to come in the next morning to assist everyone clean up the mess. Blanche was in the dining room sweeping up glass.

"We can have Christmas dinner in the kitchen – there's no broken windows out the back," she said.

"Not that anybody will be in the mood for much joviality," said Troy.

"I tried phoning Carl but he's not answering his phone," said Blanche.

"Do you blame him after last night?"

Blanche put her hands up. "Oh, don't you dare try and blame me for this, Troy. This is that lunatic's fault."

"You said unforgivable things to Gabrielle last night."

"Tensions were running very high –"

"You have put a wedge in the middle of this family that might never be repaired."

"Oh, screw you, Troy!" She marched off inside.

Lauren called over to Rosalind's the next day. Carl and Gabrielle had gone to the Garda station, collected Seán and brought him back to Rosalind's. He sat in her lounge, staring into the tea in front of him.

"Well, you've really fucked up this time, you gobshite!" said Rosalind, marching up and down furiously.

"What possessed you, Dad?" asked Gabrielle gently, sitting beside him.

"The drink, what else?" he said. "Why didn't you tell me you were pregnant?"

"We were going to tell you today," said Gabrielle.

"Why am I always the last to know?" asked Seán.

"Oh, shut up feeling sorry for yourself, Seán!" snapped Rosalind. "You made a show of your daughter last night."

"How did you find out Gabrielle was pregnant anyway?" asked Carl.

"Your brother told me."

"Roger?" asked Carl, confused.

"He showed up at Martin's last night and bought me a ton of drink. Then he started telling me all about how they've been treating you, Gabrielle. That the sister got a big house and you didn't even get a wedding present from them. That they barely tolerated you and looked down on you. And I just got so mad!"

"I'm going to kill him!" said Gabrielle, her eyes blazing.

"No, because I'm going to kill him first," said Carl, standing up.

"Everyone sit down," demanded Lauren. "There's been enough confrontation and I don't want any more. Is this true, Seán? Did Roger work you up into that state you were in last night?"

"He even gave me a lift out to Winterfield . . . and pointed out the pile of rocks down the garden left over from building that new wall."

"But why would Roger do that?" asked Lauren, bewildered.

"Because he's a bastard!" snapped Gabrielle. "He's

jealous of Carl, he always has been. He's annoyed that Carl is back and outshining him at the company. And he's always had it in for me ever since we were kids."

"I'll deal with Roger – leave him to me," Lauren said, standing up. "Now dinner is being served in the kitchen in Winterfield in half an hour. Are you coming, Carl and Gabrielle?"

"I'm never stepping foot in that house again!" stated Gabrielle.

"Why don't you stay for dinner with us here, Lauren?" suggested Rosalind.

"No, I'll head back to the family."

Rosalind looked down at her husband and raised her eyes to heaven "And I guess we're stuck with you for the day. I'll lay another place at the table."

"It will just be like old times," Seán said, squeezing Gabrielle's hand.

Lauren kept a close eye on Roger over the next few days. She watched his ready smile, his charm, the way he could twist words to get people to think a certain way that he wished them to think. She listened in to his conversations with his mother and to the ones with his father and everybody else, and it was like he played a different role when talking to different people. He was an actor, she thought, a very clever actor. And she realised that she had just been a different audience for him to play to over the years. The way he fed information about people to colour perceptions. All so subtly but effectively done. He had always been her favourite and now she realised she actually didn't know the real Roger. He was only being the person that she wanted him to be. And it broke her heart to realise he was dangerous. That he would manipulate a vulnerable mind like Seán Ford's just to win points against his brother.

He was packing in his room after the Christmas holidays, about to jet off to the Bahamas the next day.

"Hi, Roger," she said, coming in and sitting down on a big couch in the bedroom.

"Oh, hi, Gran," he said.

"Off on your break tomorrow?"

"Yeah, I can't wait. I'm so tired, I really need the break. Been working so hard in the company." Roger continued to pack as he spoke.

"Ah, you shouldn't push yourself so much."

"I have to, Gran. When I'm in there, I just always think of you and about going the extra mile for you. Keeping an eye on things for you. Somebody has to look out for you . . . especially the way Carl has been over the past few months."

"Carl?"

"Listen – forget it."

"No, tell me, Roger – you know you can tell me everything."

"Well, it's no secret in the company. But he's messing up big-time. I don't know where his head is. Dad knows all about it, ask him, he'll tell you. I try to cover for Carl, but it's getting increasingly harder to."

"You're a good boy, Roger."

"I try to be, Gran."

CHAPTER 92

2008

Amelia and Louis walked down the beach on New Years's Day, wrapped up warm in thick coats and scarves to keep out the cold wind. They had their arms around each other as they walked along. They were due to leave Winterfield the next day.

"It's certainly been an interesting family Christmas," commented Louis.

"It's been all a bit eventful all right," agreed Amelia.

"It's like something out of the Jerry Springer show. I fear that I have married into a family of *peasants,* regardless of how much money you have."

"Louis!" Amelia said loudly. "Please don't speak about my family like that."

"This father of Carl's wife is like something from the streets!"

"Well, we can't all have your blue blood, Louis, but we try not to judge. Gabrielle is a very nice and successful person. All the more admirable because she's had a difficult upbringing."

"Oh, spare me your socialism, I'm not in the mood . . .

I had another sleepless night last night thanks to you. You are not sleeping well, Amelia, and it is disrupting my sleep as well."

Blanche was watching the Bloomberg financial channel on the 48-inch wide television mounted on the wall. She made some notes on moving stock and then flicked off the screen with the remote. She took up her mobile and opened the text that Billy had sent to her on Christmas Eve, as she had countless times. She hadn't responded to the text although it was all she had thought about, hoping he'd contact her again. But he hadn't. The thought of Billy distracted her from the cold war that was now rife in the family. Gabrielle and she were no longer on speaking terms after their row at Christmas. Carl and Blanche kept each other at a cool distance, limiting their conversation to work issues. Lauren and Blanche's entente cordiale had simply fallen apart. Amelia seemed pre-occupied. And Blanche and Troy continued to row.

Blanche felt isolated. She felt everyone was ganging up on her. She felt she had no support. Nobody realised the thorn in the flesh Rosalind had been to her over the years, or the abuse she had endured, and it was just continuing through Gabrielle. Well, she was sick of being an outsider. She had her own past too. She picked up the phone and dialled Billy's number.

"Billy . . . hi . . . it's Blanche here."

"Hello, how are you. Great to hear from you!" He sounded excited.

"Did you have a good Christmas and New Year?"

"Very good. You?"

"Yes, it was nice . . . I was just wondering if you had any luck getting a job yet?"

"Do you know, I haven't even tried yet. I've just been taking it easy."

"If you're around some time, I just wanted to have a chat with you. I might be of some help."

"It would be lovely to see you again, Blanche."

Blanche inspected herself in the grand bathroom of The Launcelot Hotel in Ballsbridge. She flicked back her hair and scrutinized herself closely.

She walked through lobby, feeling ever more nervous as she turned into the dining hall. She spotted Billy at a central table.

She had wondered if he would have the same effect on her, seeing him again. Was the first time just a shock effect at seeing him after so long? But as she approached the table she felt the same jolt as before.

"Blanche!" he said, standing up and he kissed her cheek. He pulled out her chair for her and pushed it in as she sat down.

"That's very quaint of you . . . do you open the car doors for your ladies as well?" she asked with a slightly mocking smile.

He laughed and sat down, studying her. "It's good to be home . . . And it's very good to see an old friend again."

She stared at him and smiled and then took up the menu. "I believe we have scallops on today. I insist you try them – the chef here does them to perfection."

The lunch passed by in a flurry of laughter and chat. They talked about old times and what they had been doing in between. Blanche felt liberated. She felt as if she was young again. She felt he looked at her and didn't see the businesswoman, the mother, the wife, the baggage. He looked at her and saw through all that to the real her.

"What happened to your old agency boss? I liked her. There was no bullshit about her."

"Samantha? I'm still friends with her. She's the social queen of the city now. The social editor at the *Review*." Blanche paused and looked down at her cognac. "Billy – I wanted to ask you something. There's a position in my company at the moment that I think you'd be suited to – head of Legal. Would you be interested?"

His face lit up in amazement.

"You look surprised."

"I'm shocked!" He stared to laugh. "Blanche, I'm not a charity case. I'm far from it. I'm very comfortably off."

"Good!" she laughed too. "The truth is, *I'm* a bit of a charity case really. I've had terrible luck really with my legal department. It's a bit of a mess. And I need somebody I can trust. Everyone I've employed seems to think about what's good for them and not what's good for the company . . . I know you'd never be like that. You're the only principled lawyer I've ever met."

"I'm afraid you compliment me too much, Blanche, and insult the profession too much as well."

She sat forward, with a look of pleading on her face. "Oh, will you consider it, Billy?"

"I don't have to – I could never say no to you. Thank you, Blanche, I'd love to work for you."

"That's the best news I've heard for a long time, Billy."

He grinned at her.

"What's funny?" she asked.

"Just you calling me 'Billy'. Nobody's called me Billy for years. It's William now."

"Hmmm . . . don't know if I can get used to that."

Blanche rang a friend of hers who ran one Dublin's biggest law firms after she left Billy – or William as he now called himself.

"I need a favour," Blanche said to him.

"What can I do for you?"

"You know Melissa Canavan who heads my legal department? Could you make her an offer to join your firm that she couldn't refuse? You'll find her brilliant!"

CHAPTER 93

Amelia was at home working on her thesis in the afternoon. The doorbell rang. She walked out into the big hall and opened the door. There was a man in his thirties standing there. He had black hair combed back, a grey suit and was wearing sunglasses.

"Hello," said Amelia.

"Hi – I think I might have the wrong house. Is this where the Murtaghs live?"

"No, I'm sorry, you do have the wrong house," she smiled at him.

"Do you know which is their house on the road?"

"I'm sorry, I've never heard of them before, and although we're new here I would know the names of all the neighbours. Maybe you should try back down the hill?"

"I'll do that – and thanks," he said, nodding at her. He stood there staring at her and she felt a little unnerved.

"Well, goodbye!" she said, smiling and quickly closing the door. She quietly locked it. She listened for the car to start, but she couldn't hear it. She remembered she hadn't seen a car either but he couldn't be up here without a car. He must have parked it up on the road, she reasoned.

"Hi, Carl, how are things? Haven't seen you for a while," said Roger as he caught up with Carl in the corridor.

Carl glanced at Roger and kept walking. "I'm fine."

"Just wondered if you wanted to go to lunch today?" Roger asked, smiling.

"No, thanks – I've something on. And I'm on my way to meet Mum and the new head of Legal so I can't stop to chat – sorry." Carl would have loved to take Roger to task about Seán Ford and last Christmas Eve, but he had promised Lauren not to. And in a way he saw the point; there was enough animosity around at the moment. He steadied himself as he prepared to meet his mother.

Roger watched Carl swan off as if he owned the place. Obviously Gabrielle had turned Carl against him. He felt rage at the thought. He thought about the messing around with Carl's diary he had been doing. That had outlived its usefulness and, besides, he was bored with having to meet Carl's secretary Diana all the time to spy on his diary. The time had come to up the game.

Carl hovered outside Blanche's office door. He could hear talking and much laughter on the other side. He was slightly taken aback. Blanche had been in such bad form for a long time, and she rarely laughed in work anyway . . . unless she was charming a client. He knocked on the door and opened it.

"Ah, Carl, come on in. I want to introduce you to Billy Forrestal, our new head of Legal." She laughed. "Sorry – *William* Forrestal. I will try to remember that!"

William stood up and smiled at Carl, warmly shaking his hand.

"Welcome to the enterprise," said Carl.

"Sit down, Carl," said Blanche. "William, you've heard of the Noble Media Group?"

"Yes, they own one of the newspapers and a few women's magazine?"

"Yes, it was set up in the eighties by Stephen Noble. I knew him and he was a great businessman. He was killed in a yachting accident a couple of years ago. Since then the company has been run by a group of incompetent directors and the company's value has diminished considerably. His daughter, Alessandra, now owns the company and she wants to sell. There are a lot of interested parties, so we have to negotiate hard and keep our cards close to our chest. So, William, can you start to draw up a draft of a contract that we can show to Alessandra's solicitors?"

"Of course I can. Maybe, Carl, we can sit down later and go through the details?"

"Of course. I'm free for the afternoon so just pop up to me any time."

"That's fine, Carl, thank you," said Blanche and he figured he was dismissed.

He nodded, got up and left the office. He hovered outside her door and heard the two of them chatting and laughing merrily again.

Alessandra Noble was twenty-four years old. Her mother was an Italian socialite who had married the charming Irish entrepreneur Stephen Noble in the eighties and had remained married to him for three years – just long enough to produce Alessandra. Alessandra had then been brought up in considerable style in a villa outside Rome by her mother and her next husband, an Italian industrialist. Alessandra hadn't been overly close to her Irish father, but made the trip to

Ireland each summer to spend some time with him. On his death, she had been his sole beneficiary, inheriting his media company. She had no taste for business and even less taste for living in Ireland, the weather strongly disagreeing with her, and had left the company in the hands of directors. She had become very alarmed to discover that the company was losing its value rapidly in their hands. The selling of the company would make her independently wealthy and she decided to sell it as quickly as possible before it lost any more value. She arrived in Dublin in early summer to sell the Media group. A firm offer had been put in by Blanche Launcelot and by another company called Monarch and she was anxious to sell to one of them. As Alessandra descended from the plane, she pulled her cashmere coat close around her as the rain drizzled down. As she looked up at the grey skies she was determined to keep her visit to the country as short as possible. She was met by a car that took her straight to The Four Seasons Hotel as the rain continued to drizzle down.

Roger strode through the lobby of The Launcelot Building and stopped in his tracks as he saw a dark beauty sitting by reception on one of the leather couches, flicking through a fashion magazine. He was over in a second. He ignored the group of suited men also seated around.

"Hello there – I'm Roger Launcelot. Can I help you with anything?"

The girl casually looked up and said, "No."

She had long, very straight black hair, olive skin and dark-brown eyes. Her body was long and lean and dressed in an ice-blue flared trouser suit.

"Are you here for an interview?" he asked.

She looked up again from her magazine and said again, "No."

"Ah, you're not Irish, are you? Where are you from?"

She didn't speak straight away, then answered aloofly, "Rome."

"Alessandra!" said Blanche as she approached them, accompanied by Carl, William and the whole legal team. "Sincere apologies for the delay. This is Carl who you've already been dealing with and William, who heads our Legal. Oh, I see you've met my son Roger."

Alessandra stood up and the group of suited men sitting opposite her also stood up and surrounded her.

"And this is my legal team," said Alessandra.

"Shall we head up the boardroom and get started? Carl will be dealing with you directly on the buy-out but I think it would be nice if we all got to know each other first." Blanche directed Alessandra to the lifts and they were followed by the men, leaving Roger staring after them.

Roger sat swivelling in his chair in his office all afternoon. So that was Alessandra Noble who everyone had been talking about. He was furious that he was just ignored and Carl again was taking centre stage. Roger should have been at that board meeting as well. He kept thinking of Alessandra. He had been quite taken with her. But what he couldn't get out of his head was her indifference to him. He picked up the phone. A couple of calls to Legal and he found out Alessandra was staying at The Four Seasons.

Roger walked into the reception of The Four Seasons that evening and asked reception to call up to Alessandra Nobel's room and tell her Carl Launcelot was waiting for her in the Ice Bar to discuss a business matter.

Fifteen minutes later and Alessandra arrived in, dressed in a flowing white gown, with her olive arms and bosom on view, her long hair flowing, and wearing hooped earrings and bracelets. She looked around the bar for Carl and, on seeing Roger, was confused for a second and then made her way over.

"Is your brother here? He rang up to see me," she said.

"Carl? No, the receptionist must have misunderstood. It's me that rang up to see you."

She viewed him coolly and nodded before sitting down. "I see – you said you had a business matter to discuss with me?"

"Ah – yeah. Drink first? Pleasure before business I always think."

"I'll have a sparkling water, please."

"Nothing stronger?"

"No – I rarely drink."

He ordered a water and another vodka for himself and sat smiling at her.

"Did the meeting go well today?"

"It went okay," she said, taking a sip of her water.

"So what are you going to do with all that money when you've sold your father's company?" asked Roger.

She shrugged. "I haven't given it much thought."

"How long will you be in Dublin?"

"For however long it takes to sell this company."

"What do you work at over in Rome?"

She viewed him in a very bored fashion. "I party a lot, and holiday a lot, and I love fashion . . ." she trailed off.

"You sound like the woman I've been looking for all my life!" he said, smiling broadly.

"What do you want?" she asked bluntly.

He was surprised by her directness. "Just a chance to get to know you. You're going to be in Dublin for a while . . . I know the city . . . maybe I could show you around?"

"I've no need for a tour guide. I don't have a particular interest in seeing anything here anyway. Are you trying to chat me up?" She continued to view him aloofly.

"Eh – yes."

"Well, why didn't you just say so? Come on." She stood up and walked out of the bar without looking back. He followed her and they got into the lift. She pressed a button and they zoomed up to the top floor where she let him into her room.

"Help yourself to a drink if you want," she suggested as she went and sat on a huge armchair.

He went over to the drinks bar and fixed himself a drink, then went and sat opposite her.

He looked at her, smiling and feeling confused. He didn't know how to act with this one. She was giving nothing away. She held herself with such self-assurance. He started to tell stories to amuse her. As she listened, she smiled occasionally.

Then she started tapping her long fingernails on the telephone table beside her in a bored fashion.

"Can we get on with it?" she said.

"Oh – of course!" he said, putting down his drink and walking over to her.

She stood up and pulled him close. "What else is there to do on a rainy night in Dublin?"

The next morning Roger lay in bed, stretched out and relaxed, talking loudly to Alessandra who was in the bathroom, the door open. She hadn't been such a challenge, Alessandra Noble. Behind that beautiful Ice Queen act she put out she was just putty in his hands. She had jumped on him at alarming speed!

She came out of the bathroom fixing her earrings on.

"So next thing he said to her –" Roger was in mid-flow telling a story.

"Okay, I have to go. You can let yourself out," she said, cutting his story off abruptly.

"Oh – right!" he said, sitting up. "I thought we might have breakfast or something."

She viewed herself in the mirror. "No, I don't think there's a need for that level of intimacy – do you?"

"Well – breakfast isn't that intimate – really – well, compared to what we did last night."

"Okay – *ciao*!" she said, heading to the door.

actual fact been dumped by the elusive Alessandra. He initially felt angry, then hurt and finally intrigued.

He did a search on her on Google. It wasn't too hard to find out everything about her. She was one of Rome's most glamorous young socialites and there were lots of photos of her dressed to the nines at different society events. Her stepfather was a wealthy industrialist who had made his money in the not-so-glamorous production of car fan-heaters. There were photos of her mother showing off their villa to some Italian lifestyle magazine. In all her photos, Alessandra had that aloof look that began to irritate him more and more. He never wanted to see her again – that would teach her to dump him. But she was essential in his plan to undermine Carl and so he would have to contact her again.

He phoned her room at The Four Seasons.

"Alessandra, I wonder, could I meet you again?"

"I don't think there's a need – all my dealings are with your brother."

"I think you'll be interested in what I have to say."

Alessandra arrived down half an hour late to The Ice Bar in the hotel, this time dressed in a black flowing dress with a slit up the side.

"Go on," she said, sitting down, bypassing all small talk.

"You are in the middle of tough negotiation with our company and another company Monarch right now."

"Why don't you tell me something I already do not know," she said, her eyes glazing over.

He hid his anger and continued. "What I'm suggesting is that I provide you with all the information you need to give you the upper hand in those negotiations. Our thoughts on all matters, how much we're prepared to spend. Everything you need to know. What we are thinking."

"Betray your own company? And why would you do such a thing?"

"I have my reasons."

"As long as one of those reasons isn't to get back into my bed – that isn't really an experience I feel the need to rush to repeat."

Cheers, he thought, hiding his anger.

"No – it's an internal matter in our company."

She thought for a second and then shrugged. "Sure – why not?" She got up and walked out without saying goodbye.

CHAPTER 95

"I would have preferred to have just gone and seen Gabrielle," said Amelia as they sat in a doctor's surgery.

"Nonsense! I have to work with Carl. Do you want him to think we are having problems at home?"

"Having a problem sleeping is not the same as having problems at home!"

The receptionist called them and they went in. The doctor, Nicholas, was French and an acquaintance of Louis.

"So what appears to be your problem, Amelia?" he asked.

"I'm just having a little bit of a problem falling asleep at night, which is making me tired during the day," she explained.

"A little problem!" said Louis. "She's awake nearly the whole night pacing up and down, keeping me awake! And then she is so tired she is forgetting things all the time."

"Not all the time, Louis!"

"Yes, all the time. I don't even bother telling you any more. You leave the oven on all the time. You leave the freezer door open. I came home and the keys are just sitting there in the ignition in the car and the engine running!"

Amelia sat back, her face creased with worry.

"Often lack of sleep can make us forgetful," said Nicholas. "I'm going to prescribe you a strong sleeping pill that will help you sleep."

She started to rub her forehead. "I so want to sleep properly."

Amelia was meeting Blanche for lunch. A car was pulled in near their entrance and as she drove past she recognised the man sitting in the car as the one who called to her door looking for the Murtagh family. He was wearing the same sunglasses and his car was parked where he could see their entrance.

She picked up speed and continued on her journey.

She met Blanche in The Unicorn and Blanche spent the first half hour giving out about Gabrielle.

"Mother! Please stop!" begged Amelia. "I didn't come to meet you to hear you abuse a perfectly nice girl."

Blanche studied her daughter. She seemed jittery and strained and not her usual confident self. "Are you alright, Amelia? You look very pale."

"I haven't been sleeping too well, but I'm fine now."

"You poor thing!" Blanche reached out and stroked her hair. She was so used to seeing her daughter leading marches and arguments that it was worrying to see her drawn and vulnerable. "Amelia, we're always here for you."

"I know." Amelia suddenly saw the man with the sunglasses sitting at the bar in the restaurant. She watched in confusion as he got up quickly and left.

"Amelia, is everything all right?" asked Blanche, seeing her expression.

"Yes," she shook her head and smiled. "It's nothing."

"As Louis will be in Paris this weekend, why don't you come and stay at Winterfield with us?"

"Actually, that's a great idea. Thanks, Mum."

Blanche was going through some final details with Louis for his trip to Paris.

"Louis, I met Amelia for lunch the other day and she doesn't look very well at all."

"I know – she's finding it very hard to sleep."

"I'm quite concerned about her, Louis, and I want you to be very careful with her."

"I am always."

"Instead of looking like a radiant happily married woman, she's fading away."

"I've been very concerned about her too."

"Well, your priority in life is to make her happy, Louis. I don't want you to forget that."

He contained his anger at her intrusion.

"Mum was suggesting that I go stay with them in Winterfield while you are in Paris," said Amelia that night.

They were in the lounge listening to Bach.

"Oh!" Louis gave a dismissive look of disgust. "And so it starts. I don't know what it is about Irish children, but they can't seem to cut the apron strings with their mothers!"

"What are you talking about?"

"Grown women running back to their mammies at every given opportunity, and the men are even worse!"

"And Frenchwomen have nothing to do with their parents once they get married, do they?" she asked, her face clouded in cynicism.

"They don't go rushing back to Mammy and Daddy at the first problem."

She stared ahead, annoyed.

"Ahhhh!" he said, leaning over to her and kissing her. "I jest. You go home to your mother for the weekend . . . and don't forget to take your laundry for her to do!"

Amelia didn't go to Winterfield at the weekend. She rang up her mother and made an excuse.

Louis was cooking in the kitchen, adding ingredients to a lasagne that he was making. Amelia sat up at the island, a glass of red wine in front of her.

"And to what do I owe this treat tonight? My wonderful husband cooking me dinner?"

"I don't need any excuse to cook my beautiful wife something splendid." He came and kissed her mouth. "Now, go into the lounge and relax and let me cook here in peace," he ordered.

"Spoilsport!" she said, jumping off the stool.

"Well, how did you find it?" asked Louis as they finished the meal.

"Delicious!" she declared, pushing her plate away. "I'm stuffed."

"Good." He reached over and kissed her, then taking the two plates he went over to the dishwasher and began to stack it. "See, I told you that being a vegetarian was all in your mind. You love meat when you don't attach all your guilt to it."

"What do you mean?" she asked, watching him continue to tidy up.

"The lasagne. You loved it."

"Yes, but it was vegetarian lasagne. You used textured vegetable protein – TVP."

"No, I didn't! I used real meat. TVP! How could something that sounds like a high-speed train network taste nice?"

Amelia's eyes opened in horror. "How dare you do that! How dare you give me meat without telling me!"

"But you wouldn't have eaten it if I'd told you."

"That's the whole point, Louis! I am a strict vegetarian and you had no right to do that."

"You loved it – what's the problem?"

She got up abruptly and marched off.

CHAPTER 96

Carl slammed down the phone and cursed loudly.

Fuck that Alessandra Noble! What he had hoped to be a straightforward buy-out of her father's company was turning out to be a nightmare of negotiation. Her demands just got more and more. She refused to sell the company as an entity and wanted to negotiate separate prices for all the different publications in the publishing house. And then she wanted to retain copyrights of interviews and photographs owned by the company. And of course her price for everything just kept going up and up. It was as if she knew how far he was prepared to go, and just stopped short before he would drop out of the deal. As if she could read their minds. And he was sure she was playing them off against their rivals, Monarch.

Gabrielle had now given up work as the baby was due soon and he wanted to spend more time with her at home. Not a chance with all this tough negotiation with Alessandra going on. And of course his mother breathing down his neck all the time.

Alessandra sat in Carl's office with her lawyer. She had the previous week given Carl a fresh list of demands. Roger had informed her that the Launcelots were drawing a line and refusing to accept these last demands. Just when she was about to drop the demands, their rivals Monarch had accepted her list.

Roger's information had been invaluable. She would have been operating in the dark otherwise, prepared to accept anything Carl offered for fear of the deal falling through. But with Roger's inside information, she was always sure of what Carl would accept and at the same time raise her game with their rival Monarch.

"So I'm afraid, Alessandra, I cannot accept your latest list of requests and our final offer is the one we had hammered out previously on the 23rd of last month."

"In that case it is with regret that I must accept the offer that Monarch made for my father's company this morning," said Alessandra. "That, as they say, is that."

Disappointment and frustration clouded Carl's face.

"I won't take up any more of your time," said Alessandra, standing up with her lawyer.

"So when are you going back to Rome?" asked Carl.

"Tomorrow. I can't wait."

"You're going back far wealthier than you arrived. Will you be going into business back home?" He had seldom met such a smooth operator.

"No, this brings my brief flurry into the business world to an end."

"That's a pity, you've a real flair for it," said Carl.

"No, I just got lucky. You need to know when to quit, as I do. Anyway, thank you for everything." She shook his hand and swanned out.

"I can't believe it!" Blanche shouted at Carl in her office. "How could you let the deal for Alessandra's company fall through?"

"She blocked us at every turn. Her demands just kept getting more. She outsmarted us."

"No, Carl, she outsmarted *you*! I wanted that company and you lost it from under my nose! I don't know what's happened to you. The Carl of old wouldn't have let this happen."

"Go on, say it – before I met Gabrielle."

"You said it – not I!"

"You know – I've had enough!" Carl threw his arms in the air. "I don't want to work here any more! I don't have to stay – there's plenty of places I can get a job."

"Don't be ridiculous – as if you'd walk out on all of this."

"Yeah, I would, for a peaceful life – you'd be surprised what I'd walk out on."

"Well, go then – who's stopping you?"

"You're right, nobody. I give you my notice as of today." He turned and strode out.

He went straight home, finding it hard to keep his speed down as he drove.

Carl rushed into their house.

"Gabrielle!"

"In the bedroom!"

He rushed in and found her lying on the bed. She had now finished work and was taking it easy at home until the baby was born.

"I quit! I told her where to go!" he said, pacing up and down.

"You'll be back there tomorrow," she said.

"No, I'm finished with the company. There's loads of other jobs out there where I don't have to deal with a vindictive mother."

Gabrielle sat up. "That's the least of our troubles at the

She chinked her glass against his. "Thank you for all your help – I really couldn't have done it without you."

"My pleasure!" He thought about Carl walking out that day. It had been the talk of the company. He had never expected such an excellent result from his plan. "What time is your flight tomorrow?"

"Midday," answered Alessandra.

"Do you want a lift to the airport?"

She looked slightly surprised. "There's no need. There's an excellent taxi service from the hotel. Anyway, I'd better go to my room . . . Are you coming too?"

Blanche pulled into the driveway of Billy's home at Dartmouth Square, and looked up at the house that used to be her home long ago.

He opened the door.

"Blanche! What are you doing here? It's one in the morning!"

She walked past him and he closed the door.

She walked into the lounge and took off her coat.

"I'm sorry, Billy. I didn't know where else to go. I've had a blazing row with Troy and I wanted to see you."

"You're shaking, Blanche!" He went to her and held her tightly.

She collapsed in his arms, letting him hug her. She looked up at him, their faces inches from each other.

"Blanche . . ."

"I can't help how I feel about you, Billy, I never could. You've always been there, in my mind . . . unfinished business . . . thinking about what might have been." She was suddenly crying, tears falling down her face. "I've never felt what I felt for you with anybody else. And seeing you again has made me realise that."

"Blanche – what about Troy and your family and work?"

"None of it matters. I now know what I've been missing all these years, and it's you. Why should everyone else have love except for me? Hiding myself in work and money, because I was trying to distract myself from the fact that I wasn't in love with the person I was with."

"You don't know what it feels like to hear those words," he said slowly. "You're the reason why all my relationships failed. You're the reason why I could never settle down. Thinking about you . . ."

His hand went to the back of her dress and unzipped it as he held her tight.

Troy sat out in the night air by the swimming pool at Winterfield. The music was playing loudly from the house. David Bowie's 'Wild Is The Wind' flowed smoothly into the night as he rewound the years of his marriage. A decanter of whiskey sat on the table beside him.

Lauren sat up in bed looking through her photo albums. She smiled as she looked at the photos of herself and Niall with the boys when they were younger at Winterfield. She rubbed the photo of Niall.

"I miss you so much," she whispered.

Amelia sat in the lounge in the large empty house and started pacing the floors. She went and looked out at the driveway, hoping that she would see Louis's car lights come up the drive, but knowing they wouldn't. He said he had a very late meeting to go to and not to wait up. She went and tried ringing his mobile again, but it was turned off. She went to her the cabinet quickly, took a jar of tranquilizers and shook a couple of tablets into her hand. Then she swallowed them down with a glass of vodka.

Gabrielle and Carl's son Jude Niall Launcelot was born the next morning.

CHAPTER 97

Roger's mobile bleeped, waking him up. He reached out for it and read the text.

"Hey – I'm an uncle!" he declared, looking around and expecting to see Alessandra lying beside him but the bed was empty.

"Congratulations," said Alessandra as she came out of the dressing room, wearing her coat, bag slung over her shoulder, briefcase in hand.

"I didn't hear you get up," he said.

"I need to go. My taxi is waiting outside and I do not want to miss my plane, believe me. My luggage is already downstairs." She headed to the door.

"Hold on," he said. "Is that it? No goodbyes, no talk?"

She shrugged, said "Goodbye!" and continued to the door.

"Wait, Alessandra!" He sat up and swung his legs over the side of the bed. "I don't want you to just go like this. I think we might have something here."

"We have nothing here, except sex," she said nonchalantly. "You can have my body . . . but not my mind."

"But I think we could turn it into something more," he said urgently.

She stopped and looked at him. "No, Roger. It's impossible. There's nothing to you, so I can't."

"What do you mean – there's nothing to me? I'm intelligent, funny, witty, clever – not to mention good-looking and wealthy!"

"And it's all false, I'm afraid. There's a wall around you and I don't think anybody can get to know the real you, and I'm not so sure it's really worth getting to know anyway. There's no heart to you. You are just a list of things you feel you need to project. An actor."

He snapped, "Why don't you just fuck off then!"

"I'm sorry. I'm not trying to be a bitch, I'm just explaining things. Now I really must go for my plane." She opened the door and looked back at him. "Maybe if there's a real you in there somewhere and he's not *so* bad, then look me up in Rome sometime. *Ciao*!" She closed the door after her.

Blanche walked down the stairs in Billy's house.

"Billy?" she called.

"Hi!" He came rushing out of the lounge, smiling.

She glance at her watch. "It's nearly noon. I can't believe I slept so late."

He came over to her and enveloped her in a hug. "Are you alright?"

She sank into his arms. "More than alright. This feels so good. It feels so right. I feel I've put back the clock years and I'm a young girl again, just starting off in life with you."

He led her into the lounge and sat her down.

"I never dreamt you'd still feel the same way about me as I did for you," he said.

"I'm in love with you, Billy – it's as simple as that. We've wasted so much time and I don't want to waste any more."

Just then Blanche's mobile bleeped and she read the text. It was from Troy and read: *"In case you're interested – you are a grandmother – I'll see you at the hospital."*

Blanche steadied herself as she made her way through the hospital carrying a large bouquet of flowers. She found Gabrielle's room, knocked on the door and walked in. Her face dropped as soon as she entered. Gabrielle was sitting up in the bed holding the baby, Carl beside her, Rosalind on the other side of her. Then there was Troy and Lauren and, to top it all, Seán Ford. Nobody looked happy to see her and you could suddenly cut the atmosphere with a knife.

"Hello," said Blanche, closing the door behind her. She felt a shiver at the coldness of everyone's expression.

"I brought you some flowers," said Blanche.

"You shouldn't have bothered, thank you," said Gabrielle. The room was already full of flowers. Carl took them and put them on a side table.

Whatever conversation had been going on before she entered had dried up.

Blanche ignored them all and made her way to the baby. She smiled broadly as she looked down at him.

"Do you want to hold him, Mum?" asked Carl.

"Of course!" she said.

"His name is Jude," said Gabrielle, handing him over. Blanche took him and cuddled him close to her.

The conversation started up again in a stilted fashion, with Rosalind glaring at her.

"Anyway, I'd better be going. I'll call in later," said Blanche, standing up and giving the baby back to Gabrielle. Hopefully when there isn't this audience, she thought. She looked at Troy and said, "Will we go for a chat?"

He nodded and followed her out. They walked in silence through the hospital and across the road to a small coffee shop where they ordered two coffees and sat down.

"Where did you go last night?" Troy asked eventually.

"Back to Dublin. I needed some space." She studied him before saying, "Troy, we can't go on like this."

He nodded. "I know."

"The rowing, the hostility. We're not making each other happy any more – I want a divorce."

His eyes widened in amazement. "I didn't think you were going to suggest that!"

"What did you think I was going to suggest – marriage counselling? We're gone beyond that. I want out, and I think you do too."

"Divorce never went through my mind."

"Why bother staying together any more when we cause each other such misery? The children are grown up and nearly all married off. There's nothing to stay together for any more, is there? Let's try to get some happiness while there's still some time for us."

"But I don't want to lose you!" He looked desperate.

She reached over and took his hand. "Troy – we've already lost each other. I'm sick of being the outsider. Look at that hospital room up there. They hate me. I want to start anew with somebody who accepts me."

"Somebody new?" His eyes filled with tears.

"I want you to meet somebody too. Somebody who can make you happy, because I can't, Troy. I make you unhappy."

She stood up and bent over to kiss him.

613

"Did you ever love me, Blanche?" he asked, the tears slipping down his cheek.

She was crying too. She nodded and kissed his forehead.

Blanche cried all the way back to Billy's house. He was waiting for her and she fell into his arms.

"Don't cry, baby," he whispered to her.

"Just hold me," she pleaded.

CHAPTER 98

2009

There was a large photograph of Blanche and Troy on the front page of the *Review* under the headline *'Launcelots To Divorce'*.

The article continued:

'In a shock announcement yesterday it was revealed that tycoons Troy and Blanche Launcelot have separated. The couple, who married in 1981, and have recently become grandparents, head one of Ireland's largest companies. The couple were believed to have had one of the strongest marriages in the business community and their split has shocked friends and associates. The business world is now anxiously looking on to see the effect the divorce will have on their business interests.'

Roger looked at his Rolex and saw it was nearly one. He felt he had done enough for the day and would head off. He looked through his mobile, wondering which one of his friends he could go to for an extended lunch. The whole family seemed to have fallen apart. He thought about Alessandra Noble occasionally and was furious at her treatment of him. She had dismissed him like – well, like an inconsequence.

He was still in shock at his parents' separation as was everybody else. They seemed so unbreakable over the years – it was unthinkable that they should divorce. He remembered all their arguments and he had to admit they were never Love's Young Dream, but they just seemed right for each other nonetheless.

Blanche had met all the children, and explained that she was moving in with William Forrestal, who seemingly had a relationship with her in their youth.

Carl was openly hostile to her. He had gone to work at a stockbroker's and his and Gabrielle's contact with Blanche was minimal now.

Amelia, already looking like shit, broke down sobbing.

Roger didn't know how to react, or how to be seen to react, so he just sat saying nothing.

Troy was picking up the pieces of his life, but although heartbroken was coping better than Roger would have imagined.

And yet he had never seen Blanche look happier. She seemed to be on Cloud Nine. That uncompromising determined edge she had seemed to drift away.

In a way Roger had got what he wanted at the company – but he didn't seem to have a family any more. And that was even before the divorce proceedings started.

Blanche and William walked into the large glass building of the Cassidys law firm in the Docklands that overlooked the river. Cassidys were representing Troy during the divorce and they had called a meeting.

Blanche looked at Billy who nodded at her reassuringly as they made their way up to Bob Cassidy's office. He reached over and kissed her. Just one look from him made everything worthwhile. She had the intimacy, the support, the connection with him that she had only dreamed about before. She was deliriously happy with him. He was what she had wanted all her life. Although the backlash felt like a tidal wave. Only Roger seemed to be non-judgemental. Then there were all their friends who were horrified at her treatment of poor Troy. They didn't seem to care that Blanche and Troy were making each other miserable; all they saw was a nasty break up and Blanche with another man. Troy always had an ability to arouse people's sympathy, even when he was as much to blame as the other party.

They were shown into Bob Cassidy's office. And Blanche was shocked to see Lauren there as well as Troy.

"What's she doing here?" she demanded.

"What's *he* doing here?" retorted Lauren, pointing at William.

"William is my counsel," said Blanche.

"Is that what they call them these days?" said Lauren. "If you can bring your lover along then I think it's apt that Troy can at least have his mother here!"

"I think, as Lauren owns fifty per cent of the company, she has a vested interest in how this settlement is worked out," said Bob Cassidy.

William nodded. "That's acceptable to us," he said as he and Blanche sat down.

Lauren looked at William and said, "So you're the home-wrecker, are you? Word to the wise, you don't know what you're letting yourself in for with that one. She's made my son's life a misery. I personally am delighted to see the back of her."

"The feeling is mutual, Lauren," snapped Blanche.

"If we can get on with the matter at hand," suggested Bob. "Blanche, my client is prepared to offer you a five-million-euro settlement on condition that you make no further claim on his business or assets."

"Are you having a laugh?" shrieked Blanche. "I spent my whole life making this family very wealthy. The company wouldn't exist if it weren't for me. I've been absolutely stupid over the years working non-stop for a company that was in my husband's and mother-in-law's name."

"You were well paid," snapped Lauren.

"I'm afraid your proposal is out of the question," said William. "Any court will agree that Blanche's input to the company has been central to its survival and growth."

"My life has been that company and I want fifty per cent of it," said Blanche.

"Forget it!" snapped Troy.

"Blanche wants to split all your assets and shares and buy Troy out of the company," said William.

"No!" said Troy firmly.

"But you'll come out extremely rich and still be the heir to Lauren's half," Blanche pointed out.

"Not a chance," said Troy.

"Then we'll see you in court," said William as he and Blanche got up and walked out of the office.

"Gold-diggers!" Lauren shouted after them.

Blanche sat that night in William's arms on the couch in his home.

"I never wanted it to come to this with Troy," she said. "We've spent a lifetime together, had three children. I genuinely care too much about him."

"Well, why not walk away then?" suggested William. "Walk away from the company and take the money."

Blanche sat up and looked at him. "Billy, I just couldn't walk away from it. It means too much to me. I love it. And I run it. They should keep out of my way as they always have."

"But things have changed, Blanche. You were married to Troy and you headed the family, that's why they didn't interfere. They won't let you run things like you did any more."

And suddenly Blanche felt very much on the outside.

Blanche and William were on all the guest lists in town and were a must-have on the VIP circuit. Troy had never been one for society events and Blanche had shied away from them over the years because of that. But she found that William was her natural social soul mate. He enjoyed parties and balls as much as she did and could go the distance as much as her.

Amelia was on the phone to her mother, studying a photograph of Blanche and William getting into a car in a magazine.

"I think you could be a little more discreet," scolded Amelia. "You're really rubbing Daddy's nose in it being seen out everywhere with this guy."

"I'm just having a little fun, Amelia, what's wrong with that?"

"It's all just so horrible, what's happened."

"I know it's hard for you all to accept. But it's for the best, believe me."

Amelia wiped away her tears. "I just feel everything I held as certain is gone."

Blanche felt guilty over the impact their divorce was having. "It's strange how everyone rounded on me when I

619

didn't approve of Gabrielle and yet everyone thinks it's acceptable not to approve of William."

"It's a totally different situation!"

"Why? Because I'm older? A mother? I'm not supposed to have feelings and desires for happiness?"

"I'll talk to you later." Amelia hung up the phone, sat back and wiped away her tears.

CHAPTER 99

William observed Blanche in her office as she gave a manager a dressing-down.

He watched her tear into him and felt embarrassed for the man.

"We are heading into much tougher financial times and this kind of sloppiness just can't be tolerated any more," snapped Blanche.

"I'll work late tonight to put it right," offered the man.

"Don't bother. I'll do it myself. You can go."

The man got up and hurried out of the office.

"For fuck's sake!" shouted Blanche as she took the paperwork and started delving into it.

He came over to her and started massaging her shoulders.

"Calm down, Blanche. It's not worth you getting this upset over it."

It was dark outside, all the lights of the city stretching into the distance beyond the windows.

"Incompetence just makes me so mad!" she said.

He pushed the file away and kissed her neck. "Come on,

leave that till the morning. We have a booking for dinner tonight at Town and Grill."

"I'm sorry, Billy. There's no way I can leave tonight. I'll be here until after twelve trying to get this sorted."

"Come on – it can't be that urgent?"

"It is, I'm sorry. Look, I need to concentrate on this, so why don't you head home and I'll see you later, alright?"

He looked at her, concerned, and then nodded and smiled. "Alright."

Blanche had hired the best family law firm in the country to fight her corner against Troy and slowly and viciously they hammered a deal out. There were many recriminations, accusations, suggestions, and appeals along the road. There were court appearances in the Four Courts, and the press outside photographing them when they arrived and left. It was billed as the country's most expensive divorce ever.

Troy sat at home in Winterfield House, looking at a photo in the *Herald* of Blanche leaving the court. It was a Friday evening and he was expecting Carl and Gabrielle any minute. It was strange that he was alone in the house. He was so used to it being full all his life. Carl and Gabrielle and Baby Jude came down to Castleford every weekend and stayed with him or with Rosalind, which he loved. It had hit him hard when Blanche left him and filed for divorce. He had loved her so much over the years. But as time had gone on after their separation, he realised how much arguments had been going on between them and the tension that had been in the house all the time. And he felt he was finally ready to let her go and start living his life again. It was almost a relief to be free of the constant trying to get somebody to love you the same as you love them.

He heard the front door opening and Carl shout "Hello?"

"In the drawing room!" called Troy.

Carl and Gabrielle walked in with Baby Jude. Troy reached out immediately and took the baby.

"How's this little fella?" asked Troy.

"He's in great form," said Gabrielle.

She hadn't returned to work and was enjoying being home with Jude. She was also delighted that Carl no longer worked at Launcelots. The pressure of dealing with Blanche all the time was gone and their marriage was all the stronger for it.

"I've reached a decision about the divorce settlement," said Troy. "I'm going to give Blanche what she wants. She wants fifty per cent of the company. She can have what's due to her and buy me out for the remainder. All this hassle and fighting isn't worth it. It's all going to go to you, Roger and Amelia in the end anyway. All we're doing is making lawyers richer squabbling. Besides, she's right. The company probably wouldn't last without her at the helm. I just want to get on with my life now."

Blanche and Troy had a team of accountants and evaluators working round the clock to get the value of assets and the company stock. Blanche sold everything she could get her hands on to get the money to buy Troy out. Troy agreed to sell all joint assets, everything from the Kensington town house, property, stocks and shares, to jewellery and paintings for Blanche to raise the cash to buy him out. Parts of the company were sold off to raise more cash. Winterfield was to be divided. Blanche was getting the main house and Troy the rest of the estate, including the lodge and their first house. Troy wanted to leave the big house anyway. It didn't suit him living there on his own. It had always been filled with his family and it was making him morose. He moved back into the house on the coast road. That house was the only thing he had ever really done on his own.

Whatever Blanche was short to complete the buy-out, she borrowed from the banks. The final result was Blanche owned fifty per cent of the corporation and Lauren still owned the other fifty per cent.

"What strange and unhappy bedfellows we make," Lauren had commented.

And Troy walked away with more money than he knew what to do with and none of the responsibilities of business that he had never wanted in the first place.

"You know, I always said Troy was stupid when it came to business," Blanche said to William. "Now I wonder who the stupid one was. He took none of the responsibility or the stress of the business over the years, but he walks away loaded and his mother will still leave him her share . . . You really don't need to be clever in business – just lucky."

CHAPTER 100

"The recession is beginning to bite hard," Blanche said. "We're going to have to make cutbacks." She was in her office with William.

"How are you going to do that?"

"I guess we'll start with salaries," said Blanche and she picked up the phone and dialled the General Manager of the Heathrow Airport Hotel in London.

"Paul, I'm seriously understaffed in the central London hotel. Give me thirty people you can spare for the next week to go and work in that branch. Fax me through a list of the people in the next hour. It's urgent."

An hour later and a list was faxed through.

Blanche picked up the phone and rang the Manager in the Airport Hotel again.

"Paul, I want you to fire the thirty people whose names you faxed through to me," she informed him.

"*What?*" shouted Paul.

"If you can spare them for a week then they are obviously surplus to requirement. Give them all a week's notice." Blanche hung up the phone.

William looked on in amazement.

"That's a fairly ruthless way of doing it," he remarked.

"It's the easiest and quickest way," said Blanche.

She proceeded to do the same to several hotels in the company over the afternoon.

"I was thinking maybe we could head away for the weekend?" suggested William. "Nothing very exciting – maybe Barcelona for a couple of nights?"

He was in bed with Blanche. She kissed him and pulled him close.

"I'd love to, Billy. But I can't leave Dublin this weekend, I've too much on with the final stages of the buy-out." She saw his disappointment "Maybe the following weekend?"

But there was something on the following weekend as well that stopped them from going.

William watched Blanche talking excitedly on the phone in her office. He was exhausted. It was eleven at night and had been poring over legal documents all day to complete contracts.

"That's wonderful news!" said Blanche, happily hanging up the phone.

"Oh yes?" he asked.

"There's this electronics firm that I've had my eye on for ages and I found out it's about to go into receivership. I made an offer today for it and they jumped at it. I can't believe the knock-down price I got it for!"

William looked at her, the excitement written across her face. She headed over to her drinks cabinet, took a decanter and poured two gins as she continued to excitedly tell him the details. She stopped when she saw he had a glazed look in his eyes.

"What's wrong?" she asked.

"I'm just remembering years ago when you were a young model and Samantha wanted you to take over Darla's contract, remember?"

"Yes," she nodded and shrugged.

"And you refused, because you wouldn't profit from somebody else's misfortune. How you've changed, Blanche! Buying up companies in trouble with relish."

She put his gin down in front of him on the glass desk and went and sat on one of the two leather sofas which faced each other in the office.

"That's the way of the world, Billy. I was incredibly naïve back then."

"Kill or be killed, eh?"

"I'd be mad not to buy that company, Billy. If I don't then somebody else will."

"Oh, Blanche!" He came over and sat beside her, taking her hands in his. "You don't know how I dreamed of being back together with you over the years. It was like I was putting my life on hold, hoping somehow we could get back together. Anyone I met didn't stand a chance compared to the memory of you . . . But you've changed, Blanche . . . you're not the same person you were and I often don't recognise you."

She stared at him. "Of course I've changed. How could I be the same person? I've had to fight and crawl my way up and once I was up I had to do even more to stay on top."

"I know, love. I've been so unfair to expect you to be the same."

She pulled her hands back from him. "I know that look on your face, Billy. I've seen it enough times on Troy's . . . Love turning to disappointment."

"I'm sorry, Blanche . . ."

"Don't, Billy, please! Don't say it!"

"I feel so guilty for causing so much disruption in your life . . ."

"Billy, no, I need you! I'm only feel happy when I'm with you," she begged.

He drew her near and held her tight. "It doesn't feel right for me any more."

She pulled away from him. "I want to be on my own just now," she said.

"Are you sure?" he asked.

She nodded.

"Okay," he nodded and got up and left the room.

She sat there for a long while, staring at the closed door. Hoping it would open and he'd come back in and say he didn't mean it. But she knew he wouldn't. Finally she got up and went to stand by the window, looking at all the lit-up buildings in the dark.

CHAPTER 101

Louis came in with a suitcase. It was Friday evening and he was heading to Paris for the weekend on business.

"Okay, I'm off. See you Monday," he said, reaching down and kissing her.

"Louis, I really wish you weren't going away this weekend. I really want you here."

"Impossible. I've several meetings I can't get out of. Would you have me pull out and anger your mother?"

"It's all about what she wants, isn't it? I don't give a fuck if she's angry about you not going."

"You'll be fine. Besides, aren't you miles behind on your thesis? Spend the time trying to catch up."

Amelia put down the phone after speaking to Louis on the Saturday night.

She got up and walked over to the wall of windows. She turned on the lights outside and the patio and swimming pool lit up. She pressed a button to the right and the wall of windows electronically opened. She walked out and strolled around the patio, taking in the majestic view of the city below.

She looked down at the Jacuzzi at the end of the patio. She went inside, changed into a bikini and, wearing a bathrobe, made her way downstairs and out on to the patio again, collecting an opened bottle of wine and a glass. She pressed a button and the water in the Jacuzzi started to fizz powerfully. She poured a glass of wine and left it on the edge of the Jacuzzi, then slipping out of her bathrobe, stepped into the bubbling water. She lay back and drank her wine while looking out at the city below her. She closed her eyes and put her head back and rested. Her whole body relaxed and she almost felt she could sleep. She dozed off.

"Excuse me," said a voice beside her, jolting her up straight.

The same man who had called to the door that afternoon was standing on the patio.

She jumped up out of the Jacuzzi, her heart beating madly.

"Sorry for disturbing you but I'm looking for the Murtagh family," he said.

She grabbed her bathrobe and tied it tightly around her. She stood frozen, unable to speak. She looked down the fields and could see the lights of her neighbour's house in the distance.

He's still wearing sunglasses, even though it's night, she thought. She quickly raced across the patio and into the house. She felt he was going to grab her and pull her back. She got inside the house and slammed the button that closed the windows and they started closing electronically.

She expected him to come in while they were closing. As they closed firmly, she allowed herself to breathe again. She looked out onto the patio, but there was no sign of him. She quickly pressed the code into the alarm to set it.

Then she ran to the phone and called the Garda.

Louis got as early a flight as he could and arrived back at the house early the next morning to find a police car there and two Gardaí in the living room with his wife.

"Amelia! Are you alright?" asked Louis, rushing to her and putting his arms around her.

"Your wife has had a bit of a scare, Mr Chavannes. A man who had previously called to the house showed up here late last night uninvited."

"My darling! Are you alright?" He held her tightly. "What did he do to you?"

"He asked after this Murtagh family, same as before. I ran into the house and locked the doors and called the police."

"No actual crime was committed, Mr Chavannes. Your wife was out in the Jacuzzi last night and he just showed up asking for a family who as far as we know do not live in the area."

"Out in the Jacuzzi in the night!" He looked at her as if she was mad. He looked out the windows and saw the half-empty bottle of wine out there and nodded, annoyed. "You were out in the night on your own, drinking wine? You know you shouldn't have been drinking when you're taking those sleeping tablets, Amelia!" He turned and looked at the two Guards. "I'm sorry but my wife is on very strong sleeping tablets. She should not be drinking alcohol when she's on them."

"But what's that got to do with anything?" demanded Amelia. "The man still turned up."

"To do what precisely? Ask directions? Amelia, last week when we were out for dinner you drank a few glasses of wine and then you came home and took your sleeping pills before going to bed, remember?"

"Y-yes."

"Well, you woke up screaming at three in the morning insisting Elvis Presley was in the room."

"No, I didn't!"

"Yes, you did, my darling. You were in a trance. The next morning you could not remember a thing."

"But why didn't you tell me?" she demanded.

"I didn't want to stress you." He turned to the Guards again. "My wife has been under a lot of stress. She developed insomnia. And then had to take very strong sleeping tablets, which can be hallucinogenic when mixed with alcohol."

"Louis, I did not imagine that man!"

"Describe him!" insisted Louis.

"He was tall with jet-black hair combed back. He was well dressed in a suit, and wearing sunglasses."

"Wearing sunglasses at night? Maybe you are getting him mixed up with your Elvis Presley fantasy."

"The same man came to the door before during the day, and I've seen him since parked up the road and in a restaurant when I was with my mother!" She was almost shouting.

"Calm down, Amelia. You were drunk and high on sleeping tablets out in the Jacuzzi and you thought you saw him again." He put his arms around her again and held her closely. "I don't know what to say."

"In the meantime, maybe you should increase security

around here," suggested the Guard. "Your wife is very scared, Mr Chavannes. Maybe she needs to see somebody."

"We will go to the doctor tomorrow."

Nicholas examined Amelia.

"Could it be a possibility that you imagined this man?"

"He seemed too real to me – but I don't know any more."

"She is under a lot of pressure as her parents' marriage has broken up as well," explained Louis.

"*Will you stop saying that!*" screamed Amelia. "I did see the man!"

"I'm going to prescribe you some tablets for stress, Amelia," said Nicholas. "I want you to take them during the day and continue taking the sleeping tablets during the night."

CHAPTER 102

The helicopter circled around Monte Carlo as it began its descent. It touched down at the heliport. The back seat door of the helicopter was opened by an attendant and Blanche stepped out into the sunshine. She was wearing sunglasses and was dressed in cream trousers and a black T-shirt, her hair loose down her back. The attendant carried her suitcase. She made her way to a waiting car and got into the back seat as her suitcase was put in the boot.

"Back to the apartment," she said to the driver and the car took off and began to climb the elegant twisty streets. Blanche rested her head back against the seat and thought about the last few days. She had been stationed in Monaco for three months now. Thinking back on it, when Billy had left her she had gone into a kind of depression. The break-up had hit her very hard. And suddenly everything else hit her at the same time. The reality that her long marriage to Troy was over. The ugliness of the divorce. Her estrangement from Carl. The break-up of the family – everyone seemed to have fallen out with somebody. Carl and Roger hardly spoke any more. Amelia wasn't herself and often didn't return anyone's calls.

Then the company was left in a much-weakened position after the divorce settlement, and the economy had changed. When her accountants had jokingly suggested for her to become a resident offshore, saving on taxes which could help put the company back on a sound footing, she had not laughed back. Some time away sounded just what she wanted and needed. Monaco seemed the most attractive choice. Apart from the obvious reasons, weather, social life and beautiful stores and restaurants, she knew people who lived there. Her developer friend Charles Hunt was stationed there, his yacht moored in the harbour. The South of France was a home from home for Samantha. And since Blanche had acquired one of Paris's premier hotels, she was automatically known in France. And, as Blanche soon discovered, money and beauty soon opened any other doors left closed in the principality. She returned to Ireland regularly. William still worked for her. He had given in his notice when they had broken up but she had argued that it was ridiculous. He enjoyed his job, he was very good at his job. Besides, if the truth be known, she wanted him there.

The car pulled up outside the apartment block that was now her home. She stepped out of the car and the concierge opened the door.

"Good afternoon, Madame Launcelot, welcome back," he said.

"Thank you, Michel. I've a case in the boot, you might take it up?"

"Certainly, Madame."

She continued on to the elevator, got in and pressed the top-floor button.

The lift opened and she walked across the hallway and

let herself into the penthouse apartment. Inside the door was an elevated hallway with steps that led down to the huge living area which had a thick white carpet, with white sofas. A wall of floor-to-ceiling windows were at the other end of the room and led on to a balcony which offered magnificent views down across Monaco and to the harbour below and across the clear blue Mediterranean Sea.

Blanche walked through the living room and through the double doors that led to an office. Her PA, Marie, had left some messages on her desk. She picked them up and glanced through them. Nothing urgent.

She checked the time. She had an opening of a gallery to go to that evening and fancied a couple of hours' sleep before.

Blanche took up the phone and strolled into the lounge and out onto the balcony. She dialled a number while she looked out at the breathtaking view.

Charles Hunt answered his mobile.

"Are you in harbour or out at sea?" Blanche asked, squinting in the sunshine.

"Just taking a little cruise, my darling, will be docking this evening. Can I look forward to your company tonight?"

"Yes, dinner would be nice."

"I'll book the Louis XV," he promised.

She hung up the phone. Who would have thought of herself and Charles having a fling after being friends for so many years? But she didn't kid herself that it was anything more than a fling. He didn't want any more and neither did she. In the same way she didn't want any more than a fling with the newspaper editor she'd had dinner with three times in Dublin over the previous week. And she didn't want any more than a fling with the New York restaurateur. Since splitting up with William, she had played the field and she didn't care. She needed it. She needed the company.

She needed the excitement. She remembered the conversation she'd had with her mother.

"I thought you were so together, Blanche, so in charge of your life and then you walk out on Troy and your family," said Harriet who was trying not to look too stern or cry at the same time.

"You always said you feared he might not be enough for me, and in the end you were right," said Blanche.

"And then you move in with this lawyer from all these years ago. Who would believe it! And then you break up with him. And I'm hearing stories back about you, Blanche. That you see these other men all the time."

Blanche cursed the gossip columns. "I'm an independent businesswoman. I call the shots. I decide who I want to see and when."

"You think having all this money has made you in control . . . but I wonder if you really are?"

Blanche popped into the gallery opening she had been invited to on the Avenue de Moulinas and then walked down to the Hotel De Paris. The Place De Casino was full that evening as Blanche walked through it. The streets around the small park were packed with parked Ferraris, Bentleys and Rolls Royces. Glamorously dressed people swanned around the square, drinking and eating in the Café Americano or going up the steps and into the Monte Carlo Casino.

"Good evening, Madame Launcelot," said the doorman at the entrance of the Hotel De Paris.

She walked into the great hall and then into Alain Ducasses' Louis XV restaurant. The restaurant was modelled on Versailles with its high golden ceiling and ornate walls. She spotted Charles at one of the round tables which were impeccably dressed with white linen that fell to the ground.

"How was the opening?" he asked, kissing her.

"Very good. The Prince was there. A lot of people asking for you."

"I missed you when you were away," Charles said as their wine was poured by a waiter and the menus handed to them.

"Did you?" she smiled at him.

"Is it true you were out to dinner with Desmond Brown last week?" He looked at her curiously.

"Yes, quite true." She sipped her drink.

"Do I need to be jealous?"

"No, because you have no hold on me and I have no hold on you. We're just friends who enjoy each other's company." She chinked her glass against his.

She woke up to the sound of a phone.

"What is it? It's three in the morning?" complained Charles, sitting up in the bed.

She reached out for the phone.

"Hello?" she snapped.

"Blanche, it's Troy here . . . Lauren has died."

CHAPTER 103

Lauren Launcelot's funeral was the biggest one Castleford had ever seen. Blanche realised she had to go and made the journey home. As she stood with the family as Lauren's coffin was lowered, she studied them all. Troy looking dignified and sad, but it had to be said looking better than he had in years. Rosalind sobbing her heart out. Carl and Gabrielle holding young baby Jude. Amelia, looking pale and stressed. Louis with big sunglasses on, looking like he should be at a Mafia funeral. And Roger being all things to all people, making sure everyone knew they could rely on him if they needed anything.

And then Blanche saw a figure arrive and discreetly push his way forward.

It was Jack.

He smiled and nodded over to her and she nodded back.

The funeral reception was at the Winterfield Resort Hotel. Blanche remembered the last family do there was Amelia's wedding. How times had changed since then!

"It came suddenly. She was in good health to the end," Troy said to her.

Blanche nodded.

Amelia sat on the couch, knocking back the drink.

"Are you alright, Amelia? You look very pale?" Blanche remarked.

"She's fine. She's just obviously upset about the passing of her grandmother," Louis explained, putting an arm around his wife.

"Amelia, let's go for dinner tomorrow and have a catch-up," urged Blanche.

"I can't. I've too much on."

"Too much on that you can't meet your mother?"

"A mother who lives in Monte Carlo and has a string of boyfriends? And to think you used to give out about my love life!"

"This isn't the time or place, Amelia."

"No, it isn't. So let's just leave it, alright?"

Blanche held Baby Jude in her arms. Gabrielle and Carl were being civil with her and she was being very polite back.

"I don't know who he's like," said Blanche.

"He's like me!" said Rosalind, appearing from nowhere and taking Jude from Blanche's arms. "Yes, come to your grandmother!" cooed Rosalind as she moved off away from them.

Bob Cassidy, the Launcelots' solicitor, approached them.

"Blanche, the reading of Lauren's will is on Tuesday."

"Well, I hadn't planned on going to that."

"Well, it might be an idea that you do. It will obviously affect the company."

"That sounds ominous," said Blanche.

She made her way to the grounds at the back of the hotel and walked through the gardens while smoking a cigarette.

"Blanche!"

She turned around to see Jack. He smiled at her and enveloped her in a hug.

She melted into his arms. It was so good to meet somebody who looked genuinely happy to see her.

"How are you?" he asked.

"Coping," she shrugged.

"There seems to be a bit of an atmosphere in there," he commented as they walked together through the gardens.

"Yeah – you can say that again."

"Rosalind is going around as if she owns the place. Is she still in politics?"

"Oh yes, Ireland's answer to Sarah Palin is alive and kicking. And she's completely outsmarted me. She's going to be the one close to my grandchild, not me. Just because I wasn't flexible enough."

"I was sorry and very surprised to hear about you and Troy," he said.

She sighed. "I guess you were right when you said I shouldn't have married him all those years ago. All I've done is make him unhappy. I've taken over your role of black sheep of the family."

"You're welcome to that role!"

"You were right to get away from this place." She stopped and stared up into his face. "I often wonder – if I was braver when I was younger, what kind of life would I have had?"

"I've a confession to make. Remember when we were in the Caribbean and I said I'd only asked you to run away with me because I was frightened to go on my own?"

"Uh huh." She nodded. eyeing him suspiciously.

"I lied when I said that. I was just trying to save face because you said no. I asked you because I was mad about you."

"Oh, I see!" she smiled.

He smiled flirtatiously at her. "The offer is still on the table. We could still run away."

She burst out laughing. "Jack! You are incorrigible! You never change! I think we both have enough problems without further complications, don't you?" She put her arm around his waist as they turned and began to walk back inside.

The Launcelot family were gathered in Bob Cassidy's Docklands office. Blanche sat in a black suit, her legs crossed, looking around at her family and wishing Bob would get on with it so she could get going. She raised her eyes on seeing Rosalind there again, sitting beside Carl and Gabrielle.

Bob started to speak. "I think that I should point out that Lauren had a new will drawn up in the past couple of months, and she indicated that was because of the circumstances the family were in i.e. the divorce. The crux of the will is outlined in a letter Lauren wrote and, if you permit, I shall read the letter to you now . . .

'My darling family, I've given considerable thought on how to arrange my affairs. I've had a lot to take in, not least the change in circumstances and the new situation my family now finds themselves in with the pending divorce of my son Troy and Blanche. Firstly I would like to give selected pieces of my jewellery collection to my good friend and neighbour Rosalind Ford. To my grandson Roger and granddaughter Amelia I bequeath the funds that have been placed in a bank account for them. To my son Troy I leave the Winterfield estate, all the lands and lodges – but excluding the main house, which I believe will already belong to Blanche after the divorce is finalised. Troy, as my son you are my natural heir, but I hope you understand the reasons why I have done the following. My fifty per cent of the Launcelot Corporation, I leave to my grandson Carl Launcelot. Troy, the reason I bypass you with the company is firstly because if I die during these tense divorce negotiations with Blanche, it could prolong *your divorce with Blanche for years as you battle out the carve-up of the other fifty per cent of the company. And I believe neither the company nor you nor Blanche will survive any further squabbling over the corporation. Secondly, I do not think it will bring you happiness. I now realise the business is not in your blood and it is a chore for you. Also I do not think it would be healthy for you to be tied into the corporation with your ex-wife for the rest of your life. You will be wealthy from the other assets I have left you and from your divorce settlement and I would like you to enjoy life without the shackles of the business. Now you can be free to pursue your life. Most of all I wish you happiness. Carl, you have demonstrated yourself to be dedicated to the business and I believe it will be safe in your hands. I also hope your receiving half the company will bring you back in close contact with your mother Blanche, and that your rift will be healed because of this. Nobody is ever completely happy in these situations, but I hope you all understand my reasoning. In short, I wish you all happiness, and I believe these arrangements offer you all the best chance of this. Lauren.'*

Everyone sat in silence for a while, digesting this.

Then Roger suddenly stood up. "Well, I think that's a bloody disgrace, I do! What the fuck did the old broad think she was doing, leaving everything to Carl?"

Everyone looked at him in astonishment.

"What about me? I fucking worked in that company from the moment I left school! I've given that company blood, sweat and tears!"

"Yes – other people's!" said Gabrielle.

"Shut your mouth! No doubt you are behind this! Twisting a senile old woman around your little finger. *I* was always her favourite!"

"Yes, and she saw through you, Roger," said Gabrielle.

"I think we'd better all shut up," said Blanche.

"Roger, considerable monies have been left for both you and Amelia. I believe Lauren just wanted the company to be left in the safest hands," said Bob.

"Well, you can all fuck off if you think I'm staying in a company that's already half-owned by Carl!" Roger turned and stormed out of the office.

Blanche watched Roger as he furiously threw clothes into a suitcase which was laid out on the bed. She leaned against the wall, legs and arms crossed.

"I can't believe Gran would do that to me! Just hand everything over to Carl!"

"As Bob said, you have been more than adequately looked after financially."

"Yeah, well I'm going to take that money and I'm going to bloody well enjoy myself for a while!" He flung another shirt into the suitcase.

"I'm sure she had her reasons for why she did what she did . . . Look, hopefully it might be years off, but there's still my fifty per cent of the company."

"Forget it. I'm not giving my life over to that company just for Carl to get all your share in the future as well. He takes over when he's there! He took over before, so fuck knows what he'll be like now when he owns fifty per cent! I'm forgotten about when he's around there."

"Why didn't you say how you felt before? We can sit down and work something out."

"I'm not in the mood to work anything out. I'm in the mood to get far away from this dysfunctional family I'm part of."

Blanche studied him. She had never seen Roger like this

before, wearing his heart on his sleeve. He was usually so in control and pleasant.

He sat down on the couch and ran his hands through his hair. "After all my planning."

"Roger," she said, uncrossing her legs and walking over to him. "You're young and when we're young we think everything will just go according to how we want it. But it doesn't, it never does. Take some time off. I think it'll probably do you good. I think for the first time in your life you're being yourself and not caring what anyone thinks or what the consequences are. That's good." She leaned forward and hugged him tightly. "When you feel it's time, come on back and we'll all sit down and come up with a plan that we can all work together so that everyone is happy."

She kissed his cheek, smiled and walked out.

Roger closed over his suitcase, took out his mobile and rang Alessandra's number.

"Hello?" said her familiar accent.

"Alessandra, it's Roger Launcelot here. I'm going to be in Rome for a while."

"And this is of interest to me why?"

He raised his eyes to heaven and shook his head smiling. "You told me to look you up if I was prepared to show you the real me. I'm ready to be very real."

"Interesting . . . And what if I don't like the real you?" she quizzed.

"Well, it might be worth a try to find out."

"Maybe it might."

CHAPTER 104

Louis looked incredibly happy as he and Amelia sat on one of the plush embroidered couches in the Shelbourne bar.

"To your good fortune!" Louis said, raising his glass and chinking it against Amelia's.

"The money is immaterial to me, Louis. I always told her that if I was left money I would give a lot of it away to charity and that's exactly what I plan to do with it."

He looked at her in astonishment and put down his glass. "What nonsense are you spewing now?" His facial expression became very dark. "You are not doing such an imbecile action!"

She looked at him, worried. "But what difference does it make, Louis? We didn't have it before so what we never had we won't miss."

He rubbed his temples. "You are losing your mind! You are quite insane. You are acting so erratically and now you want to give away all our money. You need to be locked up!"

"Louis!" She looked at him in shock. He got up and marched out. "*Louis!*" she shouted after him, but he ignored her.

Blanche looked at the telephone on her desk and finally picked it up and dialled Carl's number.

"Hi, Carl, I think we need to talk, don't you?" she said.

Carl handed Baby Jude over to Gabrielle, and put on his jacket.

"What time are you meeting your mother?" she asked.

"At two."

"Well don't take any crap from her, Carl. You own fifty per cent of the company now and she needs to realise that you are now her equal partner in the business."

"Is anyone ever Mum's equal partner?" he asked with a smile.

He came over and gave her a kiss.

"See you this evening," he said.

"Yeah, I'll have the dinner on," she said and watched him walk to the door.

"Carl!" she said suddenly.

He turned and said, "Yeah?"

She looked at him for a few moments and then walked over to him and hugged him tightly.

There was a new manager at their bank on St Stephen's Green – Kevin Marsh – and Amelia shook his hand as she came into his office.

"So nice to meet you, Mrs Chavannes," he said.

"I hope you're settling into the new job alright?" said Amelia.

"Well, finding my feet." Kevin smiled ruefully.

"I just wanted to lodge this cheque into our account," she said, handing over the cheque from Lauren's estate.

Kevin took the cheque and raised his eyebrows. "That's a big lodgement. I'll lodge it straight away for you."

Amelia nodded and smiled. Kevin started to tap away on his computer and brought up the Chavannes' account.

"Here we are . . . Which account would you like to deposit it in, Mrs Chavannes?" asked Kevin.

"We only have one account in this bank," answered Amelia.

"No – two," said Kevin, realising too late that the second account was only in Louis's name and he had put his foot in it.

Amelia was up and around the desk looking at the computer screen before Kevin could do anything.

Looking at Louis's account containing one million euros.

Amelia was walking in St Stephen's Green, lost in thought. Louis had a secret bank account and a payment of one million euros had been paid in by Blanche Launcelot the day of their wedding. Amelia had forced all the details out of Kevin. Her mind was racing. Why was the money paid? Why did nobody tell her? Suddenly she saw Louis across the street outside the park. It was lunchtime and he must be on lunch. She was about to cross the road and confront him on the secret account when she saw he was with another man. Then she saw that the man Louis was with was the man with the sunglasses who kept calling to the house. The man who had been stalking her.

Carl walked into Blanche's office. They viewed each other as he approached her desk.

"You're looking well, Mum," he said.

This is ridiculous, she thought, you meet hardened businessmen, princes and presidents, and here you are nervous in the presence of your own son. That's because the rest don't matter, she reminded herself.

He sat down opposite her.

"So it looks like we're business partners," she said, sitting back and smiling.

"Yeah. I'm sure I'm not your first choice."

She shook her head. "I always saw you being in charge one day here, so why wouldn't you be my first choice?"

"Because we don't speak any more," he pointed out.

She lit up a cigarette. "Me and Lauren never got on. We were polite to each other at best, hostile at worse. But she made a lot of sense in what she did. And, like her, I do hope your coming back here will open a new beginning for both of us."

"Who said I'm coming back?"

"I had hoped you would . . . Look, Carl, I never wanted things to go the way they did between us. I've been so upset by our falling out."

"You acted very cruelly to Gabrielle. She didn't deserve it."

"It was just very hard for me to accept. There's so much bad feeling between me and Rosalind. She's spent all her life trying to get me out and take over."

"And you've been a complete idiot, Mum. Falling out with Gabrielle like that means that your grandchild hasn't got to know you but knows Rosalind as his only grandmother."

"I know I've been stupid. But I couldn't help myself." Blanche wiped away a tear. "I don't want to fight you any more, Carl. I'm delighted you're back working here. And I want to try to get to know Gabrielle, if she'll meet me. And

I desperately want to meet my grandchild . . . I'm lonely, Carl, can we start again?"

He looked at her, still beautiful, still poised, but he had never seen her vulnerable like this before. He got up and went over to her and hugged her.

"Let me talk to Gabrielle, and we'll meet up and spend the weekend together, how does that sound?"

"Thank you, Carl."

He left Blanche feeling hugely relieved. She had missed Carl so much and now she was being given an opportunity to put things right. The phone rang on her desk and she recognised Amelia's number.

"Amelia?"

"Why did you pay Louis one million euros on the day of our wedding?" demanded Amelia.

"Amelia . . . I-I don't –"

"Don't deny it! I know you did. Did you buy him like you did everything else in your life?"

"It wasn't like that at all, darling. I just wanted to set you up –"

The phone went dead.

Amelia was shaking as she drove all the way back home up in the Dublin Mountains. She ran into her bathroom, grabbed some pills and knocked them back to try and relieve her anxiety. She felt no better and so took another couple. She went into the lounge and tried to think about what was going on. Why was Louis with that man? How did they know each other? Louis' behaviour to her, telling her she was insane. Trying to undermine her. The money in the bank that he never told her about. So, did he never love her? So was their marriage a sham? And then did he want to finish the marriage? But to have her put away so he still could keep his job, his money, his house, his life without Blanche stripping it all away from him? Or better still, just do away with her? Hire this man to kill her and so Louis would get everything. And now with her threatening to give away her grandmother's inheritance, was there a renewed urgency to the situation? Was that what Louis and the man were discussing today? She needed some air and walked out of the house. She began to pace slowly up and down the drive with all these thoughts swarming through her head, wondering what on earth she could do. She paused and rubbed her face and then looked up at the house.

Upstairs in their bedroom window stood the man with the sunglasses, staring down at her waving. She stood transfixed as he continued to stare. Suddenly, he disappeared. Filled with panic, she turned and began to run down the drive as quickly as she could. She could hear the front door open behind her and footsteps behind her. She raced out and began to run down the country road, her turquoise dress flying behind her. She could hear footsteps run behind her and she didn't dare stop or look around, concentrating on the neighbour's roof over the trees. The footsteps behind her seemed to be getting louder as she ran into the big entrance of the neighbour's house. She ran down the drive and up to the front door and started hammering the door, ringing the bell and screaming.

Finally the door opened, and their neighbour Mrs Harris, a middle-aged well-groomed woman stood there in shock looking at her.

Amelia pushed her in the house and slammed the door behind her.

"Mrs Chavannes, what is the matter with you?" demanded Mrs Harris as Amelia raced through the house, locking all the doors and windows.

"There's an intruder in my house and he was running down the road after me!" explained Amelia, at last drawing breath.

"Oh no! I'll ring the police immediately," said Mrs Harris, going to her phone.

"No!" shouted Amelia, slamming down the phone out of Mrs Harris's hand.

"Mrs Chavannes!" said the woman in shock.

"No, if you call the police, they'll just call my husband and he'll say it's all in my mind! Don't you understand?"

"Frankly – no!"

"I can't go back to the house. This might be my one chance to get away."

Mrs Harris looked at the terrified young woman. "Is there anyone we can call?"

Amelia thought for a moment. "Carl, my brother Carl."

CHAPTER 105

Carl was driving back home thinking about his mother when his car mobile rang.

"Carl, it's Amelia," said her panicked voice.

"Oh hi, what's up?"

"Carl, I need you to come and get me. Somebody broke into the house. I need you to come and get me right now! Can I stay with you and Gabrielle for a while?"

"Yes, but what about Louis?"

"I'll explain everything when you get here. I'm in our neighbour's house, the first house down the road."

"On my way." He shook his head in confusion and turned the car towards the Dublin Mountains. He then phoned Gabrielle.

"How did it go with Blanche?" she asked.

"Alright. I'll tell you everything tonight. I'm on my way up to Amelia. She rang me in a complete state. Something about somebody breaking into the house."

"Oh no! She's looking very fragile recently, Carl."

"I don't know what's going on, but she sounded

frightened and asked if she could come and stay with us for a while."

"Of course," said Gabrielle. "Be careful, Carl."

Carl swung the car into the Harris's driveway, jumped out and walked up to their front door. A worried-looking Mrs Harris opened the door.

"Carl!" Amelia rushed out and hugged him.

"She came rushing down in an awful state, and wouldn't let me phone the police even though she said there was an intruder in her house," explained Mrs Harris.

"Thank you for your help, I'll take it from here," said Carl, leading a shaking Amelia over to his car. They both sat in.

"Amelia, what the fuck is going on?" demanded Carl.

"It's Louis, Carl! It's Louis! He's sent someone to make me go mad or kill me, I don't know which, but he's behind it all!"

"*What?*"

"I found it all out today! He has one million sitting in the bank paid by Mum to marry me! He never loved me. And now I know he's been trying to get rid of me! He's trying to make me think I'm losing my mind. He brings me to some doctor friend of his who pumps me up with sleeping tablets and tranquillisers. He tells me that I forget things, that I'm imagining this stalker who keeps showing up – and he was up at the house just now and chased me down here. And today when I was in town I saw the same man walking down the street with Louis. He's going to try and finish me off before I give away Lauren's inheritance. I told him I would! That I would give it to charity and he was furious. I just know it, Carl! I can't spend another night in that house. I won't survive it!"

"Okay, okay, calm down, Amelia. You can come and stay with us. We'd better check the house."

"No, Carl, I don't want to go back there, please!" she pleaded.

"Okay. We'll go straight to ours."

"Thank you, Carl, thank you!" She started to cry but wiped away her tears.

Carl started the car and drove out of the Harris's. He turned right and began to drive down the twisty hilly road.

"I'm just so tired, Carl, I'm so exhausted. I've such bad dreams."

"It's okay. When we get home Gabrielle can look at you and see how you are."

"I wanted to see Gabrielle in the first place, but he said no and insisted I go to this other doctor friend . . . "

"It's alright. Just calm down," he urged as he continued driving.

Amelia took some deep breaths and sat back in her seat trying to relax.

Suddenly she saw the man with the sunglasses standing in the middle of the country road right in front of them.

"Carl!" she screamed. "He's there! That's the stalker there!"

"What? What are you talking about, Amelia?" He glanced at her and then quickly concentrated again on the twisty road.

"There, Carl! In front of us!" she screamed again, as she looked at the man and he started to laugh as he refused to move.

"Amelia! There's nobody there!" shouted Carl as he looked at the empty road.

"You're going to hit him!" she screamed and reached over and grabbed the steering wheel.

The car went out of control and slammed into a tree on Carl's side.

Amelia managed to sit up and looked around, dazed. She wiped away blood from her forehead. She looked at the road where there was no sign of the man. She shook her head and looked to her right and saw Carl slumped over the wheel, the window beside him smashed in by the tree.

PART 7

CHAPTER 106

2010

Blanche sat in a room in The Four Courts on her own. The light shone in from one of the high windows. It was half ten in the morning and the custody case was due to be started at eleven. Thankfully it was to be a closed court, with no spectators or press allowed. There had already been too much press around the family since Carl's death. She remembered the headlines: '*Launcelot Heir Killed in Tragic Accident*'. She remembered the terrible time they had been through, trying to come to terms with Carl being dead.

The door opened and in walked William and Francine.

"How are you today, Mrs Launcelot?" asked Francine.

"Looking forward to getting this case finished once and for all," said Blanche.

"Okay, the sequence of events is you will be interviewed by me first over the circumstances of the custody battle. We have a strong case against the plaintiff, but they have come prepared this time, and Lee Dwyer plays tough, so expect the worse."

William came around the table and squeezed her arm. "I'm here for you, Blanche."

She held his hand and squeezed it.

Blanche walked through the busy court building to an upper-floor courtroom.

She walked in holding her head high. Her heart started to pick up pace as she saw the opposing team were all there already. There were Gabrielle, Rosalind and Amelia. Troy was there as well, sitting away from them towards the back of the otherwise empty courtroom. Lee Dwyer sat in front of them at his bench, going through a stack of paperwork.

She walked to the other side of the courtroom and sat at the front bench across the aisle. William sat beside her and Francine sat at the end of the bench with her file.

"The judge today is Judge Crosby. He's a very fair man who listens to all sides," Francine whispered over to Blanche.

She nodded and looked ahead as the judge came in and everyone rose to their feet. The judge took his seat, looking down on them all, and surveyed the people involved. Blanche's mind drifted back to the day when she heard Carl had been killed as the judge started speaking. The whole day was a blur. And the day after, and the day after. In fact things were a blur for a very long time.

Blanche tried to concentrate on what Lee Dwyer was saying.

"Your honour, Blanche Launcelot has been made temporary guardian of my client Gabrielle Launcelot's son. The courts awarded Mrs Launcelot that custody under strained circumstance which we now will show to have changed. And we also hope to establish beyond any reasonable doubt the unsuitableness of Blanche Launcelot to be a guardian of her grandson, and indeed any child."

They are going for the jugular, thought William, leaving nothing to chance.

CHAPTER 107

2009

Gabrielle had just put Jude down to sleep when the phone call came through. It was Amelia. She was hysterical. She was at the hospital and Carl was badly injured. Being a doctor, Gabrielle was used to accidents, to injuries, to life and death situations. She had almost gone into professional mode as she quickly got Jude up out of his cot and quickly drove to the hospital. When she arrived she found Amelia cut and bruised but not badly injured. She had expected Carl to be in a similar condition, but as the doctors quickly made clear they were fighting to save Carl's life. And it was only then that she slipped out of her doctor mode and started to feel real panic and dread. By the time Rosalind, Blanche and Troy arrived, the doctor had told her to expect the worst. Carl had been on the side of the car that had hit the tree and had received critical injuries.

The news came in the early hours that Carl had passed away.

Gabrielle had sat cradling the baby as everyone went to pieces around her. She had insisted on being left alone and went home with the baby and put him to sleep, then sat just staring into space, trying to understand what had happened. Remembering him leaving a few hours earlier and her getting a strange feeling and giving him a final hug.

Blanche and Troy had just hugged each other in the hospital. Rosalind had been trying to console Gabrielle. While Seán Ford stared at the floor.

Gabrielle remembered there was a lot of fighting and recriminations and accusations. Amelia had been hysterical for a long while. Amelia had caused the accident. She had been hallucinating because of all the tranquillizers she had been on and thought she saw somebody on the road. Then there were some crazy accusations that Blanche had bought Amelia a husband. Finally, Amelia had to be sedated and brought to a clinic.

All Gabrielle could concentrate on was her loss as the funeral came and went.

"Blanche caused his death," Rosalind, who had paid acute attention to the details, had screamed. "She bribed the Frenchman to marry the daughter. And the daughter went nuts when she found out, thought she was seeing things and caused the crash."

There was an inquest into the accident and a verdict of accidental death. Amelia was entered into a treatment programme in the clinic and came off the pills, and a new feud started between her and her mother.

Gabrielle remembered the day she was brought into the solicitor Bob Cassidy's office and it was explained to her that, as Carl's wife, she now had control of half of the Launcelot Corporation.

What use was that to her? She didn't want all that wealth – she just wanted her husband back. Documents were constantly being sent to her from the corporation for her signature and she let them pile up, not being able to motivate herself. On Rosalind and the Corporation's urgings she forced herself to go into the offices a few times, but she couldn't concentrate on what they were saying and went home. She never had any interest in business, and now certainly wasn't the time to learn.

CHAPTER 108

Amelia was given excellent psychiatric treatment in the clinic as she convalesced. She slowly came to understand that she had been suffering from extreme paranoia and hallucinations brought on from the medication, exhaustion and stress.

She refused to see either Louis or Blanche during much of her time in the clinic. Finally, when she felt herself again, she met Louis.

"But how could you think that I would hire somebody to stalk you, or even kill you?" demanded Louis in shock.

"And how could you accept that bribe from my mother?"

"It was a gift."

"I now realise that you were of no danger to me, Louis. But I can't remain with somebody I can't trust."

"But the money was just offered. I would have been a fool to not accept it. It set us up for life."

"I loved you very much, Louis, but I can never trust you again. And deep down, I never trusted you, and that lack of trust spiralled into paranoia."

"But I don't want to lose you," said Louis.

"You'll get over it quick enough, I daresay. The truth is, Louis, you never accepted me for who I am. And I compromised myself so much to be what you wanted. I lost myself trying to be something that I wasn't, relying on pills. And that cost my brother his life."

On the day Amelia was leaving the clinic, she allowed a visit from Blanche. She expected Blanche to come in all glamorous and confident as usual. She got a shock to see Blanche pale and vulnerable.

"I wish you'd let me visit you before, I've been so worried about you," said Blanche.

"Mum, I know everything, I got it out of Louis. How you said he would get that money the day he married me. Did you think I was so unlovable, so awful that nobody would want to marry me without being bought?"

"Of course not! I was just so worried about you, and I wanted to see you settle down with somebody who made you happy."

"Well, he didn't, for the record. And it's now over." Amelia picked up her suitcase and walked to the door.

A tear slipped down Blanche's face. "Where are you going now?"

"I've been offered a voluntary position with a human rights group. I'm starting there tomorrow. I'm staying with some old friends."

"Please come and stay with me, Amelia. I want to look after you. I want to be near you."

"I'm sorry, Mum, I can't." Amelia walked out.

As the weeks went by, Gabrielle found herself feeling increasingly alone and down, as she tried to understand why this had happened to them. One minute they were a young happy family with their whole lives ahead of them and the next their future was over. Rosalind and Seán were completely there for her. But in the evenings when she was alone and the baby was asleep, she took out the bottle of gin and poured herself a couple of stiff drinks. It was only then that she could let herself go and fully grieve. As time went on, she began to drink more. She often thought about both her parents' addictive personalities and realised it must be in her as well, buried away, just waiting for the right situation to bring it out. The drink helped to dull the pain and suddenly she was drinking throughout the day.

Blanche tried so many times to see her grandson, but Gabrielle refused to allow her access. She wouldn't take her calls, she wouldn't return her calls. She called up in person and Gabrielle refused to see her. Blanche realised Gabrielle was very bitter towards her, but she found it torture not to see Carl's son. She found Dublin unbearably lonely. Carl gone, Roger in Rome, Amelia refusing to have anything to do with her. Troy and her having no need to speak to each other any more, even Lauren gone. She continued to see men who asked her out. Often because their company was better than being on her own. She eventually went back to Monaco where she threw herself into the business, flying from Dublin to London to New York and Paris, South Africa and back to Monaco. Her life seemed to be a merry-go-round. An empty merry-go-round. But it stopped her from thinking about the past and her family.

One afternoon she was in her office in her apartment in Monaco. She just put down the phone after talking to her senior manager in London when the phone rang again and she picked it up.

"Blanche, it's Liz Mansfield here," said the concerned voice on the other end of the phone.

Liz was in the legal department in Dublin and she had been assigned to deal directly with Gabrielle after Carl's death. It was Liz's job to try and meet Gabrielle as much as possible and involve her in what was happening and get her to sign the necessary paperwork to keep the business running smoothly. Liz reported back to Blanche regularly and Blanche knew Liz was having a very hard time trying to get Gabrielle involved.

"Is there a problem, Liz?" asked Blanche.

"Blanche, this isn't really in the remit of what my job entails, and you can just tell me to mind my own business, but I'm very concerned about your grandson."

"Jude – why?"

"It's Gabrielle – she's drinking very heavily. I've noticed it for a long while when I've called over with work issues. But the last couple of times she's just been steaming drunk, and she's alone in charge of the baby. Anything could happen."

"I see, thank you, Liz, you did right to tell me."

Blanche was on the next plane to Dublin.

She called over to the red-bricked terrace Gabrielle was still living in. She knocked on the front door. There was no answer. She pushed the door open and found it unlocked. She could hear the baby crying. And on the sofa was Gabrielle asleep, a finished bottle of gin beside her.

Blanche got a fright at the sight and quickly walked into the nursery where she picked up Baby Jude and began to soothe him. She then took out her mobile and rang social services. They were there quickly. Blanche let them in the front door and explained the situation to them. Gabrielle was in a stupor and it took her a couple of hours to come round.

Blanche applied for temporary legal guardianship of Jude and received it. She called Liz Mansfield and the ex-nanny as witnesses. It was the jolt that Gabrielle needed and she quickly stopped drinking. She felt very ashamed to realise that she had allowed alcohol to become such a crutch that she had put her baby in danger. When she had sobered herself up, she rang Blanche and asked for Jude back.

"Not a chance, Gabrielle, I'm sorry. Jude is staying with me where he is safe and can be looked after properly," Blanche had said.

"Blanche, I want my baby back. I'm clean off drink for two weeks, and receiving counselling, so this won't happen again."

"No, Gabrielle. If I hadn't called to the house that night, anything could have happened."

"You can't keep him!" Gabrielle had shouted.

"I can – I'm legal guardian"

"I'll fight you, Blanche. I'll fight you in every court in the country. I'll destroy your business if I have to."

"What will I do?" Gabrielle was pacing up and down at Rosalind's that night.

"Lee Dwyer, he's the best family law solicitor around. Let's put a call in to meet him," said Rosalind. "Why didn't you tell me things were so bad, Gabrielle?"

"It's not easy for me to ask for help, Mum. I'd a lot to contend with growing up with you and Dad, and I always had to cope. In a way, I was the one who held things together for you all. I couldn't admit I was falling apart."

Rosalind and Gabrielle met Lee Dwyer in his plush office in Dublin and went through all the facts.

"To be totally honest, Gabrielle, you've got one attempt at this. Social services have seen you passed out and there are witnesses testifying you are an unfit mother. What might happen is that you get to see Jude as much as possible but Blanche remains legal guardian for now."

"No!" shouted Gabrielle. "Absolutely not! I want to be sole guardian of my child."

"Then we need to establish that Blanche Launcelot is totally unfit to have any guardianship of Jude."

"She's the most heartless nasty woman I've ever met," said Rosalind. "But she's very clever. We need to go after her and leave no stone unturned."

"I'm very thorough, very ruthless and very expensive when I fight a case," warned Lee.

"Good – you might just be a match for Blanche then," said Gabrielle.

PART 8

CHAPTER 109

2010

Lee Dwyer paced the courtroom like a panther stalking its prey.

"As our first witness I would like to call Amelia Launcelot to give evidence."

Amelia strode confidently to the witness box and took her seat.

"Can you explain your relationship to my client and Mrs Launcelot?" requested Lee.

"I am Blanche's daughter and sister-in-law to Gabrielle."

"Can you explain the circumstances surrounding your brother's death?" asked Lee.

"I hold myself fully responsible for Carl's death," said Amelia, speaking slowly and clearly. "We were involved in a car accident together. I had rung him to come to my home in the Dublin mountains as I believed my life was under threat at the time. He came to my aid, and as we drove down the hill I pushed the steering wheel causing the crash."

"May I ask why you thought your life was in danger?"

"I believed my husband had arranged to either have me killed or committed to an asylum so he could get his hands on my inheritance."

"And do you still believe that to be the truth?"

"No – I accept now that he was innocent of these charges. I was very heavily sedated at the time from sleeping pills and tranquillizers and I now realise that I was suffering from severe paranoia and hallucinations."

Lee held up a file. "I have here a report from your doctor and psychiatrist detailing the extent of your ailments. Especially the existence of a stalker. Could you explain about the stalker?"

"I thought there was a man following me. My psychiatrist suggested that the man did turn up to my door initially to ask for directions. That my subconscious found something threatening about him and the situation and I kept thinking I saw him after this, brought on by the heavy sedation I was on at the time. I thought I saw this man standing in the road when I pushed Carl to swerve the car to avoid him. But it was all a hallucination . . . I had discovered that morning that my husband had received a million euros on the day of our wedding. My husband has since admitted my mother bribed him to marry me."

"Is that true?" William whispered to Blanche in shock.

Blanche reached forward and took a sip of her water.

"Thank you," said Lee. "You may step down."

Francine whispered over to Blanche, "Can you deny this accusation if they ask you?"

Blanche shook her head. "No."

Francine sat back, giving William a worried look.

Lee stood behind his bench and said, "I would now like to call Doctor Gabrielle Ford to give evidence."

Gabrielle came forward and took the stand. She looked down at her mother and father who smiled reassuringly at her and then glanced across at Blanche who was viewing her coolly.

Gabrielle steadied herself as her lawyer Lee stood up and approached her.

"Dr Ford, I wonder if you could begin by describing your relationship with your mother-in-law?"

"We were never close. In fact she disliked me from the moment she met me."

"And why was that?" asked Lee.

"She had issues with my family. She and my mother, Rosalind, never got on. Blanche was cold, cutting and finally cruel to me. She never made me welcome. Finally one Christmas Eve things came to a head and we had a full-on row and falling out. After that Carl left working for the family company and we had little or nothing to do with her."

"And what about Blanche's relationship with your baby son during this time?"

"It was non-existent. She came to the hospital when Jude was born, after which he didn't see her. Blanche divorced Carl's father and moved to Monaco which gave us all geographical distance as well as emotional."

As Blanche observed Gabrielle, she wondered why she had never noticed before how articulate and impressive she sounded.

"Thank you, Dr Ford," said Lee and he went and sat down.

Francine stood up and approached the stand.

"Dr Ford. Your husband met Blanche on the day he died, did he not?"

"He did. He had met her on a business matter, having been left half the company by his grandmother."

"Did he not tell you that on that day there had been a reunion and an agreement between Blanche and Carl to start again?"

"I didn't see Carl after that meeting, as he went to get Amelia . . ." Gabrielle broke off and looked at the floor.

"I understand. Dr Ford, after your husband's death, you have inherited his fifty per cent of the Launcelot corporation, is that correct?"

"Yes."

"And what role have you played in the company since?"

"Very little."

"Indeed. Is it true that you have frozen all bank accounts belonging to the company in the past two months? Is it true you have blocked all legal documents that needed signing? Is it true that, due to your lack of co-operation, the once great Launcelot Corporation is now on its knees and will not have enough cash-flow to pay its employees their monthly salaries next week due to your refusing the management access to company funds?"

"Yes, that is completely true."

"And why have you conducted such a negative campaign?"

"Because I want my baby back! I will try anything to get him back. And if that means destroying a company that Blanche loves, then I will."

"Then you admit you were blackmailing Blanche Launcelot? Her company in exchange for your son?"

"Yes. As I said, I will try anything."

"But it didn't work. You tried to interfere in the legal process by forcing Blanche to give you back your son before the legal system could decide if you were a fit mother?"

"I was desperate!" shouted Gabrielle.

"You didn't care about the many hundreds of people

that would be put out of work due to your actions. Still acting on impulse, Dr Ford? Still vulnerable. And still not ready for the responsibility of motherhood."

"I'm completely alright!"

"And how is your drinking problem, Dr Ford?" Francine raised an eyebrow.

"I haven't touched a drop in two months. I admit my drinking problem got out of hand. I now have the problem under control."

"But what evidence is there to suggest your drinking problem is under control?"

Lee stood up. "Your Honour, I have medical reports here to confirm my client has not touched alcohol and is clean from drink."

"Hmmm," said Francine. "As a doctor I'm sure you have many friends in the profession who will say what you want them to say."

"Objection, Your Honour!" shouted Lee.

"Mrs Hammer, please do not call into question the medical evidence involved in this case," the judge warned Francine.

"I apologise," said Francine. "So you think you are now capable of being a good mother?"

"I was always a good mother! Blanche was just lonely and frightened, and decided to take my baby from me to give her another chance because she made such a fuck-up of her relationship with her own children!" Gabrielle almost shouted.

Lee stood up. "I would like to call Mr William Forrestal as a witness, Your Honour."

Blanche and William shot each other shocked looks, then he made his way to the stand.

"Mr Forrestal, you've have been involved in a recent relationship with Mrs Launcelot, correct?"

William looked over at Blanche and then cleared his throat. "Yes, I have been."

"You also had a relationship with Blanche, back in the early eighties. Did you live together?"

"We did for a time, yes."

"Could you tell me why your relationship broke up?"

William looked at Blanche, his eyes concerned. "We just grew apart."

"Hmmm," Lee turned and walked to his bench and picked up a letter. "Is it not true that you were attacked in your home one night and received serious injury?"

It took William a while to answer. "Yes."

"What were the circumstances of your injuries?"

William continued to stare at Blanche.

"Is it not true that Blanche was involved with a terrorist organisation at the time? Is it not true that she was involved in an attempted kidnap of a British diplomat, acting as a 'honey pot', I believe the expression is. Is it not true that your injuries resulted from revenge because Blanche broke rank with this organisation and warned the intended victim."

"It was not like that at all! You make it sound like she was involved in the organisation. She was being duped. She had no idea of what was going on. And when she did finally realise what she was being used for, they threatened her life and mine unless she cooperated."

Blanche sat back in her seat as she felt her family's disbelieving eyes on her.

"Thank you, Mr Forrestal!" said Lee with a smile.

"And now I would like to call Mrs Blanche Fitzclarence Launcelot," said Lee.

Blanche stood up and walked confidently across the court and sat down in the box.

She sat poised and confident, her legs crossed, wearing a beautifully cut black suit. He had spent so much time researching her and talking about her to people who had dealt with her that he felt he knew her intimately.

"Mrs Launcelot, would you care to add further comment to what I was speaking to Mr Forrestal about? About your involvement in a shady militia group and an attempted kidnap."

"I think yourself and Mr Forrestal dealt with everything. I don't think there's a need to add to it."

"But you don't deny what has been said?"

She shook her head. "No. Except to reiterate that I was duped."

"Mrs Launcelot, the press have a bit of a fascination with you, don't they? They like to report on what you wear and your business deals, and your holidays and your . . . men."

She shrugged. "I can't stop them from commenting."

"Let me see, as well as your relationship with the . . ." Lee paused and looked around the courtroom to find that William had left the courtroom ". . . now departed Mr Forrestal – there is your relationship with Mr Charles Hunt. Then the newspaper Baron Harry O'Hagan. There's a rumour of an English Lord?"

"I'm a single woman, Mr Dwyer. I can see whoever I want."

"Hmmm, of course you can. But you weren't always single, were you, Mrs Launcelot?"

"No, I had a long marriage to Troy." She looked down at Troy and smiled sadly.

"But you did have an affair during your marriage, did you not?" Lee asked her loudly.

A murmur started up in the courtroom.

Blanche sat up. "I beg your pardon?"

"Well, maybe it's your ex-husband's pardon you should be begging." Lee walked over to his desk, picked up a slip of paper, strode over to her and put it in front of her. "An affidavit from an ex-business partner of yours, the well-known television personality, Ronnie Richards, outlining the extra-marital activities you had with him."

Blanche took the paper and stared at it.

"Do you deny you had sex with Ronnie Richards halfway through your marriage?" demanded Lee.

Blanche let the paper slip from her hands onto the desk in front of her and shook her head.

"I'm sorry, Mrs Launcelot – I didn't hear you!" said Lee loudly.

"I don't deny it," Blanche whispered, looking down at Troy who was shaking his head in disbelief.

"I put it to you, Mrs Launcelot, that it is *you* who are not fit to have the guardianship of your grandson, with your blatant lack of a moral compass. I put it to you that you cheated on your husband and are still changing boyfriends by the week, providing this little boy with the very worst environment. Incidentally, Ronnie Richards still blames you for his financial ruin in the London property collapse of the early nineties. But I'm not here to expose your business practices, dubious as they may appear. I am here to prove just whether you can provide a moral safe environment for the child that you now have temporary custody of. Would you consider yourself a good mother?"

"I've made mistakes as a mother, I don't deny that. But I always had their best interests at heart – always. I did everything in the hope they would be happy."

"Well, do you think it appropriate to bribe Louis

Chavannes to marry your daughter as she has testified here today."

"I didn't bribe him!" Blanche snapped, sitting forward.

"A payment of one million euro doesn't constitute a bribe in your book?"

Blanche looked at Amelia. "I heard from my son Roger that there seemed to be a spark between Louis and Amelia. I wanted the best for Amelia – a happy home life and financial security – the money was a gift to ensure they had that security."

"Why then didn't you tell your daughter about the gift?"

"Because I knew she wouldn't accept it, with her anti-capitalist ways. If wanting a happy and secure life for my daughter is a crime, then I'm guilty!"

Lee raised his voice to almost a shout. "But why no such gift to your son Carl on his marriage to my client? Why no such open-armed gestures in their case? I put it to you, Mrs Launcelot, that you are a control freak who consistently interfered in the lives of your children and their marriages. I suggest that your years at the top of industry made you a cold and calculating figure who felt you could arrange the lives of your children in the way you arrange a business deal. I suggest you are incapable of showing loyalty, not even to your husband, who you cheated on. And I ask you how you have the audacity to claim that my client is not a fit mother to her own child? And why is Gabrielle not a fit mother? Because she committed the crime of showing weakness? The crime of falling apart because she lost her husband in tragic circumstances. The crime of being human!"

"I'm human!" shouted Blanche. "I feel things too! Don't you dare stand there and say that I don't feel Carl's loss. Ever since he died I've thought of little else. You try and explain to me, Mr Dwyer, how my son could leave my office one minute with an understanding that we would start again, that we would wipe the slate clean, and then a few hours later he is dead. You try and explain to me, Mr Dwyer, how *am* I supposed to feel? Because I don't know. But I know that my whole family blame me for everything going wrong even though I did everything for them. And now you've just given them all a whole heap of other reasons to hate me even more. Gabrielle didn't know that Carl and I made up that day. She wouldn't let me see my grandchild after Carl died, the only connection I had with my son. And then when I found out about her drinking, I wanted to protect Baby Jude. Just like I've always wanted to protect everybody."

"Even from the truth?" asked Lee.

"Especially from the truth!" Blanche's eyes blazed at him.

Francine stood up. "Your Honour, my client has been subjected to very hostile questioning and I request a recess."

The judge took off his glasses. "It's been a very exhausting case for all and so I think we've heard enough for today. We will resume this custody case tomorrow at eleven in the morning."

As Blanche and Francine walked through the court, all eyes were on them.

Lee walked over to Gabrielle and Rosalind.

"Well done!" said Rosalind. "You demolished her! All her nasty dirty tricks and secrets exposed."

Lee looked at Gabrielle. "It's not over yet. Francine Hamer is a talented lawyer who will come back fighting tomorrow. What's more, Blanche Launcelot is a fighter and who knows what she'll come back tomorrow with."

CHAPTER 110

As Francine and Blanche walked quickly through the Four Courts, Francine took out her mobile and rang William.

"William will meet us out front in the car," said Francine.

Outside, William pulled up in the Mercedes.

The press waiting outside spotted them and as Blanche and Francine made their way down the steps, the photographers snapped photos as journalists fired questions. Blanche got into the back of the Mercedes and Francine got into the front beside William. William put down his foot and the car tore off down the street and headed back to Winterfield.

"I'm sorry, Blanche. I never in my wildest dreams thought they would use me to get to you," said William, looking at her through the rear-view mirror.

"Dwyer has done his homework," said Francine. "He has surpassed himself. He has researched every aspect of your life, Blanche. Spoken to so many people."

"I feel completely exposed," she said.

"Gabrielle isn't leaving anything to chance. She told Dwyer to finish you off."

The rest of the afternoon passed with them forensically dissecting the case that day. Looking for arguments, looking for points, looking for anything that could help them win. Blanche looked at her watch and it was seven. She sat back and listened to William and Francine argue over some point.

She put up her hand. "I'm sorry, but I've had enough for one day. If I hear one more legal term I'll scream."

She showed them to the door. William looked at her and smiled as he walked out. She smiled back and closed the door after them, then leaned against it for a while, as all the accusations that had been flung at her that day ran through her head. She went and took Baby Jude from the nursery and held him closely. The doorbell rang and, sighing, she got up and went to answer it.

Troy stood there, looking at her cradling the baby.

He followed her into the lounge. She sat down again.

"How are you?" he asked gently.

"I've had better days . . . Now everyone knows the real me . . . You must hate me."

He shook his head. "Of course I don't. Maybe I would if I was still desperately in love with you and hoping against hope that you felt the same way . . . I accept now you don't."

"Why are you here then?"

"You know why I'm here." Troy went and sat beside her and looked down at the baby. "You have to do what's right now, Blanche. You know that."

She looked at him and nodded.

"Holding on to the baby is never going to bring Carl back," said Troy.

"I know," she said, holding the baby tighter.

"Do you want me to go with you?" he asked.

"Would you? I'd like that." She leaned into him and he put his arm around her.

"Will I wait in the car, or go up with you?" asked Troy.

"Maybe stay here," said Blanche as she took the baby out of the back of the car.

Gabrielle opened the door and got a shock to see Blanche standing there. She got a bigger shock to see she was holding Jude.

"Ohhh!" she sighed as she reached forward and took the baby and walked into the house.

Blanche stood in the doorway for a while and then walked in and closed the door behind her. Walking into the lounge she watched as Gabrielle cradled her baby.

"I've rung my lawyers and cancelled tomorrow," said Blanche.

Gabrielle looked up. "But – why?"

"First of all I'd say I've already lost."

"You deserve to lose. You've caused me a lot of pain, Blanche, keeping him from me," said Gabrielle.

"I'm sorry – but I was very worried. And you wouldn't let me see Jude . . . If you were feeling so down about Carl, why didn't you reach out and ask for help?"

"What – to you? Who slammed every door in my face since you met me? Besides, everything you touch becomes contaminated!"

"Perhaps you're right. After listening to everything said today in court, I'm not feeling very good about myself. I guess there's a reason why I'm alone and my family have all run away from me."

"But don't you understand, Blanche? It's you that has pushed everyone away! You pushed Troy away by not accepting his love. You pushed Amelia away by not accepting who she was. You pushed Roger away because you tolerated his games which backfired. You pushed Carl away because he stood up to you. You could be the centre of a loving and caring family instead of in a lonely Monte Carlo penthouse."

Blanche studied her. "Where did such wisdom come from? Not either of your parents anyway!"

"Blanche!" snapped Gabrielle.

"Joke!" Blanche held her hands up in the air and smiled.

"Carl used to say that you were very witty and clever and loving, but you just let your demons get the better of you."

"Did he say that?" Blanche asked.

"Blanche, I'll inform my lawyers to release all the frozen bank accounts first thing in the morning, to allow the company to start working again. And I want you to play a role in the baby's life."

"Thank you, Gabrielle, that's all I wanted. Can we make this work? Running the company together and trying to be a family?"

"We can try."

Blanche stood up. "I'd better leave you two to get reacquainted." She walked to the door and then turned. "Gabrielle, I'm so sorry that I caused you pain and hurt in the past."

Gabrielle nodded and hugged her baby.

Blanche walked out of the house and sat into the car beside Troy.

She sighed loudly and turned to him. "Oh Troy. Where did it all go wrong?"

He smiled at her and gently took her hand. "But don't you realise yet, Blanche? It was never really right in the first place."

683

CHAPTER 111

The company had been saved in the nick of time by Gabrielle releasing funds and things were beginning to move smoothly again. Gabrielle had even taken a small role in the business and it seemed to do her the world of good. And Blanche liked having her there. It was like having Carl there. And she found she had a lot in common with her. Gabrielle was a no-nonsense hard worker, and Blanche admired that. Having Gabrielle in the company also gave Blanche the ability to see Baby Jude at all times as Gabrielle insisted on bringing him into the office with her. And outside the office, true to Gabrielle's word, Blanche was allowed to see Jude whenever she wanted for however long she wanted. Having said that, a competition was already developing between her and Rosalind as to who could spoil him the most.

Amelia had thrown herself fully into the human rights role she had been handed. She had made a full recovery from her breakdown and was also now campaigning vigorously against the dangers of prescription drugs. Blanche had never stopped trying to make amends to Amelia, and constantly called her and bombarded her with emails and letters. Amelia had begun to slowly respond. Finally she agreed to meet Blanche and spent the whole dinner lecturing her on the sins of being a tax exile. Blanche accepted the criticism, agreed with most points Amelia made, and made a donation to Amelia's human rights organisation at the end of the meal. They met again soon after, and a more relaxed and less militant Amelia showed up, full of questions about the revelations of the custody case.

"You were involved in an illegal military group! I can't believe it!" Amelia had declared incredulously. She listened intrigued as Blanche slowly opened up and gave the details. And as Blanche revealed more things about her past, Amelia became more fascinated. She started to see her mother in a new light. She saw the young poor girl traipsing the streets of London ready to be exploited rather than the tough model turned businesswoman.

"I was thinking," said Amelia. "I know Gran didn't want me to give away the money that she left me, and I don't want to keep it. I'd like to set up a charitable foundation in Lauren's name. What do you think?"

"I think Lauren would like that very much," said Blanche.

"I wouldn't know how to run a foundation like that or ensure the income and turnover was managed correctly. Would you help me with it?"

"I'd love to," said Blanche.

Roger had seemingly found love and his match with the indomitable Alessandra Noble in Rome. Blanche guessed Roger was always meant to be a playboy and now he had found the right companion to enjoy such a life with. He kept promising that they would return to Dublin one day soon and he would start working in the company again –

he was just trying to get Alessandra to make the move. Alessandra remained reluctant.

And Troy. Word filtered back to Blanche from all their friends that Troy was doing just great. He was enjoying his life immensely. He had all the money he wanted and none of the responsibility of the company. He enjoyed a close relationship with the rest of the family and took life easy, the way he always wanted to.

Blanche was heading out to Monaco for a long rest and, as she walked through the quietness of Winterfield House, she remembered how Lauren had said years ago that she could almost feel the presence of Niall's first wife in the house. Blanche had looked at her as if she was mad at the time. But now as she stood at the top of the landing in the stillness of the night, she understood what she was saying. She could almost hear Lauren and Niall having one of their passionate arguments that raged into the night. As she walked down the stairs she could almost see a young Jack standing looking up at her like the first night they met, smiling flirtatiously at her. As she reached the bottom of the stairs, she could almost see the front door open and slam and a petulant, young and beautiful Rosalind come gliding through the lobby. As she looked to the left, she could almost see their three children Amelia, Roger and Carl squabble at the dinner table. And as she walked into the lounge it was as if Troy was standing at the drinks cabinet pouring himself a whiskey. She turned and walked through the lobby to the front door, turned around and took a final look around and then closed the door after her.

CHAPTER 112

Blanche's penthouse in Monaco was full of friends and she circled around talking to them. She was having a belated fiftieth birthday party.

"Hello, Blanche!" came a cry across the room and Blanche saw Samantha moving towards her.

"I'm so glad you made it," said Blanche. "How was Cannes?"

"Brilliant. Had a great time. You should have joined us. In fact, I met an old friend of yours there."

"Really – who?"

"I hope you don't mind, but I invited him along tonight," said Samantha. "Well, actually – he invited himself along."

Blanche looked around the room and saw Jack smiling at her.

She raised her wineglass to him and nodded. He walked over.

"What are you doing here? I thought you were in LA?" she said.

"I've temporarily relocated to the Riviera. I'm staying in

Cannes. I came for the film festival and decided to stay on."

"Oh – why?"

"Well, it has the sun, and sea, and the casino up the road here – I still like to gamble, you know . . . and a few other attractions."

"I'll leave you two to catch up," said Samantha knowingly and she walked off.

"And have you got your usual accompaniment of a stunning high-achieving girlfriend in tow?" asked Blanche.

"No – I'm single this time."

"Unusual for you."

"More unusual for *you*."

"Who said I am?"

"I enquired." He smiled flirtatiously at her.

"I see!" she laughed.

She put down her glass, and they walked out onto the empty balcony.

"You look as lovely as the first day you arrived at Winterfield," he said.

"You weren't there that day. It took you a few days to turn up as I remember."

"You've got a good memory."

"I've an excellent memory."

"I've often wondered what kind of life we would have had if you accepted my offer and ran away with me back then."

"I think we both know what would have happened. You would have dumped me at the sight of the first leggy blonde!" she laughed.

He moved closer to her. "We could have ruled the world together."

"Or destroyed it! And killed each other along the way!"

"But what a journey it would have been." He was trying to be serious but started laughing.

"I guess we'll never know now," said Blanche. "How long are you going to stay down here?"

"Not sure . . . I just have a little bit of unfinished business to attend to . . ." He moved closer to her, lightly putting his arm around her waist.

"I hate having unfinished business," she said, looking up at him.

"I'm delighted to hear it . . . Thirty years is a long time to leave business unfinished between us . . . You know, Blanche, I've spent my life looking for a woman just like you."

"And I've spent my life running away from men just like *you*!"

She moved closer to him as his arm around her waist tightened.

"I suppose when you think about it, we've no ties any more – no responsibilities to other people," said Blanche.

"We're free agents."

"People would talk," she warned.

"Good! Let them talk. We're both very used to that by now."

The waiter came out on the balcony and seeing they had no drinks said, "Excuse me, can I get you a drink now . . . or would you like more time to decide?"

Blanche looked at Jack and smiled as she said, "No, we don't need any more time . . . I think we've waited long enough."

THE END

AMBITION

BY

A. O'CONNOR

Franklyns – London's high-end store for the rich and famous – is being run into the ground by its egocentric owner Karl Furstin, who uses the store's bank account as his own personal trust fund.

In steps retail legend Stephanie Holden, a single mum with a real rags-to-riches story, to try and bring Franklyns back from the brink.

But not everyone is happy with the new management. HR director Nicola Newman, who's used to getting her own way, is determined that Stephanie will fail and sets out to sabotage her every move, while making a few moves herself on the man of her dreams.

Franklyns' general manager and the store's ladies' man, Paul Stewart, owes his success to Furstin, but will he play along with the new management or double-cross them on his way up the ladder?

As she tries to rebuild her fragile relationship with her wayward son Leo, will Stephanie be able to add Franklyns to her list of success stories? Just how far will the cold and calculating Nicola go to hold on to the control, and the man, she yearns for? Blinded by success, will Paul finally see the happiness that's standing right in front of him?

ISBN 978-1-84223-396-2

PROPERTY

BY

A. O'CONNOR

The boom has been good to the Cunninghams. Property baron Cormac has taken the family business to new heights, building luxury homes for Ireland's élite. And always by his side, and on the cover of the property supplements, is his beautiful wife Denise.

Lisa, Cormac's sister, enjoys the good life as one of Dublin's high-flying estate agents – working for the dynamic and handsome Michael Farrell. And Michael is enjoying himself too, working on bigger and more outrageous stunts to promote the Cunninghams' developments.

But when award-winning journalist Ali O'Mara storms into this glitzy world she raises awkward questions. What lies at the heart of Denise and Cormac's unconventional marriage? What lengths will Lisa go to, to get the man she craves? And when Ali and Michael's romance threatens the Cunningham empire, can they survive the backlash together?

ISBN 978-1-84223-277-4

POOLBEG WISHES TO
THANK YOU

for buying a Poolbeg book.
As a loyal customer we will give you
10% OFF (and free postage*)
on any book bought on our website
www.poolbeg.com

Select the book(s) you wish to buy
and click to checkout.

Then click on the 'Add a Coupon' button
(located under 'Checkout') and enter
this coupon code

 USMWR15173

POOLBEG (Not valid with any other offer!) POOLBEG

WHY NOT JOIN OUR MAILING LIST
@ www.poolbeg.com and get some
fantastic offers on Poolbeg books